PRAISE FOR AVA MILES

NORA ROBERTS LAND
Selected as one of the Best Books of 2013 alongside Nora
Roberts' DARK WITCH and Julia Quinn's SUM OF ALL
KISSES. USA Today Contributor, Becky Lower, Happily Ever
After

"Ava's story is witty and charming." Barbara Freethy #1 NYT
bestselling author

FRENCH ROAST
"An entertaining ride...{and) a full-bodied romance." Readers'
Favorite

THE GRAND OPENING
"Ava Miles is fast becoming one of my favorite light
contemporary romance writers." Tome Tender

THE HOLIDAY SERENADE
"This story is all romance, steam, and humor with a touch of
the holiday spirit..." The Book Nympho

THE TOWN SQUARE
"Ms. Miles' words melted into each page until the world
receded around me..." Tome Tender

COUNTRY HEAVEN
"If ever there was a contemporary romance that rated a 10 on
a scale of 1 to 5 for me, this one is it!" The Romance Reviews

THE PARK OF SUNSET DREAMS
"Ava has done it again. I love the whole community of Dare
Valley..." Travel Through The Pages Blog

THE CHOCOLATE GARDEN
"On par with Nicholas Sparks' love stories." Jennifer's Corner
Blog

THE
DARE VALLEY SERIES

THE
BRIDGE
TO A
BETTER

USA TODAY BESTSELLING AUTHOR
AVA MILES

ISBN-13: 978-1-940565-27-9
www.avamiles.com
Ava Miles

I've never seen an author dedicate a book to herself, but after writing this book it seemed appropriate. Once you read it, you will understand why. So, here's to me and all my facets: the beautiful, the wild, the vulnerable, the trusting, the doubting, the scared, the brave, the hidden, the exposed, the funny, the sad, and the spiritual and very human.

To A—for meeting me on the other side of the bridge.

And to my divine entourage, who helped me build the bridge to my better life.

Acknowledgements

My Fairy Godmother gratitude to Team Ava for all they bring to my better life. To Sienna, for always being there and branching out in new ways to support me; to Angela, for totally getting my stories and messages and being the best editor in the world; to Louisa, for the creative alchemy she brought to this cover; to Em, for breathing life into my characters in audio and conveying my heart; to Hilary, for handling all things audio with incredible ease and efficiency; to Leigh and Beth for their eagle eyes on my manuscripts; and for my Angels, who support me in the best way an author could ever hope for.

To Tabitha King and Dr. Katie DeFore for giving me insights on the medical challenges for people with intellectual disabilities.

T.F. You are one of the most magical elements to my better life, and I believe in you.

And finally, to all my readers: to the ones who simply read; to the ones who contact me; to the ones who connect on social media; to the ones who tell me their own stories and how my books made a difference in their lives. Thank you for reading and may you be blessed by the time you spend in Dare Valley.

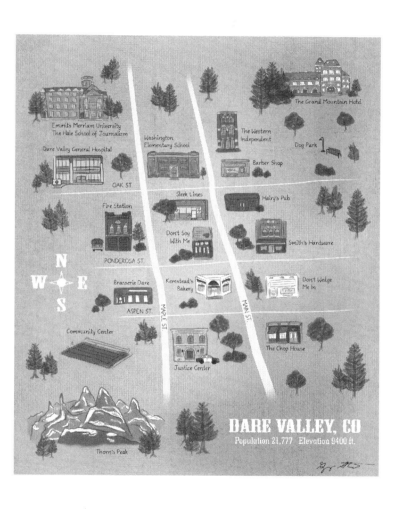

PROLOGUE

Over Two Years Ago...

Natalie Hale had never been colder. The blanket of snow she could see through the window seemed to stretch on forever, like the world's longest wedding train. Given that she'd been at her best friend's funeral only minutes before, the comparison seemed crazy. A wedding was all about celebration and joy, neither of which could be found in a field of frozen gravestones.

Her husband continued to speak, a muffled litany of white noise, and she curled deeper into her seat in his SUV. His hand touched her thigh, and she heard him calling her name off in the distance. Then he jostled her.

"Natalie!" she heard him say louder, this time through the fog.

The effort to turn her head zapped all her energy. Blake Cunningham's sandy brown hair was dotted with sweat at the temples, which was strange when everything was so cold.

"Honey, you're still freezing," he said in a strange voice.

It took her a moment to realize it was hoarse.

"Hold on. We're almost home."

There was a burning under her bottom, and it took

her a moment to remember he'd turned the butt warmers on high. The temperature inside the car read eighty-seven degrees. That must be why Blake was sweating. Why wasn't she? Then she remembered. Death's cold fingers had touched her, turning her to solid ice.

She buried herself deeper inside her wool coat and shut her eyes. Time passed—an unknowable quantity— and then a car door slammed and strong, familiar hands drew her out into the cold air. Her husband's muscular arms wrapped around her as he led her up the garage steps.

Touchdown greeted her when they reached the kitchen, winding excitedly around her legs. Her body felt like an ancient glacier as she bent down to pet the beagle. Even the dog's smiling face couldn't melt her. She straightened with effort to see Blake filling the red tea kettle and putting it on the Viking stove.

"How about a grilled cheese?" he asked, his brow knit as he loosened the navy tie around his neck and undid the button to his gray suit jacket. "You didn't eat anything today."

Food? She'd once loved it, but her taste buds had joined the rest of her in this wasteland of winter. She hadn't been able to taste anything for days, which scared her to bits since she ran her own catering business. But even when she tried to figure out what to do about it, she couldn't. Her mind couldn't process anything right now. Even choosing an outfit for the funeral had been hard, which was crazy since all she'd needed to do was wear black.

"I'm not hungry."

Blake helped her out of her coat, gloves, and scarf, and then wrapped his arms around her. "I know you're not," he whispered into her ear, "but you've lost fifteen pounds, honey. You need to keep up your strength."

She laughed hysterically, and he snapped back to

look at her, his eyes wrinkling with concern.

"Fifteen pounds won't kill me. Now, forty? That's another story." Kim had been eighty-four measly pounds when the cancer took her. She had only been thirty, the same age as Natalie.

His throat moved like he was searching for a response, but had none. He smoothed the hair back from her face with exquisite gentleness. "I'm calling Coach to tell him I won't be able to play Monday night."

A jolt of something other than cold spurted through her system. "But you've never missed a game. Not once in your whole career."

His thumbs caressed her face. "You need me more than my team right now. Everyone will understand."

But weren't the Denver Raiders playing the New England Loyalists, their rival for the division? How was Denver supposed to win without their star quarterback? "But it's Monday Night Football."

"It doesn't matter. Come on. I'll pour you your favorite tea, and we can cuddle on the couch."

He wanted to cuddle? She couldn't bear it. There was a white-out blizzard swirling inside her. Cuddling wouldn't keep it away. She knew only one sure way to battle its frigid temperatures.

Keep busy. Don't touch anyone. Block everything out.

"Go to the game, Blake. I'll be fine."

"You're not fine, honey. Your best friend and sister-in-law just died. No one would be fine after that."

He'd only started calling her honey since Kim had been diagnosed. She hated it. Before, she'd always been babe, carefree babe.

"I don't want to talk about it."

He was going to press her to talk about how she felt like he was some sports psychiatrist, and the energy it took to fight him off was draining. Why wouldn't he just leave her alone? Stepping away, she turned to leave the kitchen. The bathroom seemed the best choice. He wouldn't follow her in there.

"Natalie," he called. "Honey, where are you going?"

Away from you, she wanted to answer, but her mouth was too dry from the cold to muster the response. She heard his footsteps behind her, and another jolt went through her. He *wasn't* going to leave her alone this time.

"Natalie, you can't keep running from how you feel. Honey, I know it hurts, but you need to talk about it and have a good cry. Please just let me hold you."

A good cry? What in the hell was he talking about? There was nothing good about crying. She never cried.

"Leave me alone, Blake," she ground out, biting her tongue. The pain barely computed.

"I can't. You keep asking me not to hold you or touch you, but the more I do as you ask, the more you slip away from me. Natalie, honey, *please* let me help you."

She turned around as an arctic blast of cold shot through her internal landscape, punctuated by thunder. Thunder snow was the worst kind of storm. "I don't want your help. I'm handling it. Just leave me alone."

He ran his hands through his sandy blond hair, that hair she loved raking her own hands through, and planted them on his hips. "I can't do that. Honey, you're hurting. I love you. Let me help you. We'll get through this together."

"There's nothing to get through. Kim is dead, and nothing will bring her back." Some remote part of herself started screaming at the injustice, but she retreated from the sound, running through the cold drifts of snow in her mind to a sanctuary of numbness. She couldn't let the emotion come back. It would destroy her.

"Natalie," Blake called out, and this time he increased his pace.

He was going to catch her, she realized. The rest of her flight to the bathroom was more of a mad dash, and out of instinct, she locked the door behind her.

The knob rattled. "Natalie! Dammit, don't lock me out."

She'd never done anything like this before, and her eyes were glued to the doorknob. Off in the distance she could hear him pounding on it, pleading with her to let him in. Touchdown was barking like background music to Blake's pleas.

The freedom of doing something so bold rolled through her. She *could* lock him out. She could lock everything out.

Opening up the cabinet under the sink, she dug out the tile cleaner and a sponge. The etched panels of their Italian marble shower suite sparkled from the cleaning she'd given them yesterday, but she shook the tile powder on them anyway and scrubbed until her hands burned. Her body warmed from the brutal cleaning, and it felt good. Cleaning was the only thing that made her feel warm *and* numb—a combination she loved. It was her new favorite home.

The powder from the can sprinkled over her black dress as she shook it wildly over the mosaic tiles that had been inset in the center of the shower to showcase the cozy shower bench Blake had designed with his architect. Her mind flashed to all the times she and her husband had made love on that bench, and some of the numbness started to fade away, replaced by a sense of loss so poignant, she sank to her knees in the shower, indifferent to the fate of her black designer dress, shoes, and hose.

No, she could not remember those times.

She was not allowed happiness. Not now that Kim was dead.

Blake's voice had finally disappeared in the background. All around her was a blissful quiet.

Her hands burned from the abrasive cleaning product, and her knuckles leaked blood, but she continued to scrub. Harder. Faster. Panting, she felt her black hose tear as she inched across the tile floor. She looked down to see the run had wrapped around her right knee and darted to her ankle. Even her black shoes were spotted with white, but she didn't care. She would throw this whole outfit away when she was finished cleaning. It was a horrible reminder of all she had lost.

An unusual rattling interrupted her reverie. She turned her head to see what the metallic jingle was and watched as the doorknob dropped to the floor. Blake entered the bathroom, Touchdown barking in distress by his side.

His face rippled with shock and horror as he looked at her. *"Oh, honey."*

She wanted to cower in shame like a leper who was caught bathing by a stranger. She had to hide her sores. She had to make him go away. Sinking back onto her knees, she pushed a strand of hair out of her eyes.

"I told you to leave me alone. I'm cleaning."

"You cleaned the shower yesterday, honey."

Damn that word again.

He approached her slowly and crouched down on the floor of the shower beside her. His body was so large and bulky, she felt caged in.

"Come on, honey. Let me help you clean up and change clothes. Then you can have your tea. Oh, Natalie. Your hands...."

Another destructive wave of icy snow was approaching again, like Blake's very appearance had shifted the wind. No, he'd brought the wind. It was his fault.

"I don't want tea. I don't want anything."

"Honey, your hands are bleeding." He covered them with his own and pressed them to his chest in a tender caress. "Natalie, you can't keep doing this. Promise me you'll *never* lock me out again. You scared the hell out of me. I was afraid..."

It took her a moment to understand what he meant. He'd thought she was going to hurt herself? No, she couldn't do something like that even though she could now understand why people did. This cold, this pain...you had to do whatever it took to escape it.

"Blake, let me deal with this my own way."

"Not like this," he said, lifting her up bodily and carrying her out of the shower. "Not anymore."

Her muscles wouldn't work to fight him, almost as if they were paralyzed by frostbite. Touchdown barked his distress as Blake removed the tile cleaner and sponge she was still clutching from her claw-like grip. He was gentle as he washed the caked white powder and blood off her hands, applied salve, and bandaged them.

She caught sight of herself in the mirror and stumbled back. White powder was streaked in her wild, curly hair, and it made a violent slash across her dress. Dear God. She looked like a crazy woman, someone left out in the woods for weeks, all civilization stripped from her.

How could he love her like this?

She *hated* herself like this.

But he didn't leave her alone. He undressed her slowly, his hands gentle as he bathed her in their Jacuzzi tub like she was a child. She endured it because she wasn't really present—inside, she was running from the love and worry in his eyes, running from his touch. Then he toweled her off and brushed her hair out, making her bite her lip to fight the pain his tenderness caused her. After dressing her, he kissed her forehead.

"There. That's better. Now come have some tea."

When his strong, determined arms led her to the bathroom door, she eyed the doorknob lying on the ground.

She couldn't lock him out. Blake would always find a

way to get to her. But would that change the longer the ice stayed inside her? She wasn't his sassy, sexy wife right now. She was cracking, splintering, going crazy. She could see it now. The media paid attention to Blake, and she would probably end up losing it in the public eye, which would embarrass them both and probably harm her catering business. He would stop remembering her as the woman she'd been, and then he would stop loving her too.

Who could love this weak, pathetic, wild woman ravaged by the wilderness of grief? She didn't want to become this...thing.

His arms were wrapped tight around her, but she still stumbled as he led her back to the blazing fire he'd made in the den. The blaze hurt, her whole body burning and tingling to adjust to the heat. She didn't want to hurt like this. She *refused* to hurt like this. She had to remain numb somehow, living somewhere between the cold wasteland inside her and the welcoming bonfire of her family, her husband, her life. If she stayed numb, she wouldn't go crazy. But Blake would never let her shut down on him. No, he'd press her and love her until she succumbed to the pain. She was *going* to go crazy. Mad-dog crazy.

She was going to have to leave him.

CHAPTER 1

The incessant pounding of hammers woke Natalie. She rolled onto her back and tucked the pillow around her ears to muffle the sound, but the racket didn't subside. She let the pillow flop back into place and glanced over at the clock. Nine thirteen. And on a Saturday to boot. Darn it all to heck.

Sleeping in on the weekend was a luxury she'd started allowing herself to make up for all the sweets she'd given up eating, treats like salted caramels and dark chocolate gelato. Her intake hadn't been healthy, and she'd finally succumbed to better nutrition.

Her ex-husband, Blake Cunningham, would be delighted if he knew. He'd always tried to entice her to drink some of his green grass, mineral-loaded, mumbo-jumbo smoothies. Cripes, he'd made her feel like a slob on movie night when she ate buttered popcorn while he savored kale chips. Kale chips!

If he hadn't been one of the NFL's top quarterbacks, she might have teased him about eating like a hippie to get his goat. But Blake was no hippie.

He'd been on her mind way too much lately, and no wonder. Over a month ago, she'd told him she was leaving Denver to take a fantastic job as the head of catering at Dare Valley's famous The Grand Mountain Hotel, part of a chain of upscale boutique hotels stretching across the west. Blake had freaked out and promptly retired from the NFL. Moments after his press conference, he'd texted her to say they weren't finished. Even if they *were* legally divorced.

No word had come from him since that monumental day, but the press had dug deep for a reason for his retirement and found it. His brother had died shortly before Blake's announcement. Adam had been ill for the better part of a year, afflicted with the cardiac issues so common in people with intellectual disabilities. And she hadn't even known he was sick.

She'd reached out to Blake—his last text message be damned—but he hadn't called back or even texted. Worried, she'd called his parents to give her condolences and had learned Blake was taking some time off to deal with his grief. They hadn't mentioned what he had planned for *her,* and she hadn't asked.

He *was* going to make another play for her, and she knew it. Despite herself, her heart shook like the pom-poms the cheerleaders for his old Denver Raiders squad used. She had enormous compassion for his loss, and an undeniable desire to see him, but she kept reminding herself that they were done and their relationship was in the past.

Perhaps she could figure out what to do if it didn't sound like a flock of giant woodpeckers was hammering on her head. She rolled out of bed and dug her arms into her rose silk robe. Time to find out what her neighbor was doing.

She stepped out into the warm June morning. The sun was beaming golden shafts of light through the towering pines overhead, the ones that crawled up the mountains all around her. Dew teased her bare feet, and she wiggled her toes in the grass to savor the sensation.

Though her family was from Dare Valley, they'd relocated to over-crowded Denver when she was in high school. Being back home felt liberating, and she couldn't stop marveling over how it felt to have Mother Nature right outside her door.

When she spied the reason for the racket, she skidded to a halt. There was a new bridge across the creek that marked her property line! A bridge that hadn't been there yesterday.

Eight men with orange hard hats were hard at work. What. The. Hell.

Her neighbors hadn't consulted her about this. Her brother, Matt, had told her they were nice people, and he had reason to know. She'd bought this house from him so he could move in with his fiancée.

Undeterred by the fact that she was wearing a flimsy robe, she strode across her yard toward the bridge. Oh, she was going to give them a piece of her mind.

"Hey!" she shouted at the construction workers who were securing the final beam to the posts anchored to *her* side of the creek. "Stop that! Stop that right now. You're trespassing. All of you."

The men cursed under their breath, but the warm breeze carried the words to her. She frowned as she stalked closer, not caring if she was giving them a show in her robe.

"We're under orders to finish this," one of the men called out, pushing back his orange helmet. "Any issues you have, you can take up with the owner."

Her gasp of outrage made them all duck their heads, but they immediately started pounding long nails into the wooden beam, hammering at an almost frantic pace now.

"Ohhhh," she screamed in silent rage, skidding to a halt a good distance away from them.

Take it up with the owner? She didn't care what Matt had said about her neighbors being a nice, laid-back family of four. If they didn't take this bridge down, she'd take them to court over it. She liked her privacy, and the only possible use for such a bridge was to access her property.

She stayed where she was, plotting her next move. The men finished up, and then scurried like cockroaches back across the bridge to her neighbor's land. Running over there half-cocked wasn't going to get her anywhere, so she took a few cleansing breaths and studied the bridge. Nearly twenty feet long and eight feet wide, the bridge was already stained and varnished. Something was carved into the posts, but she couldn't make it out. She scratched her head. How had they built such an elaborate bridge *overnight* without her knowing?

Something wasn't right.

Then she heard the joyful bark of a dog.

And she knew.

Her heart broke open in her chest before she even saw him. Touchdown! Then the little six-year old beagle came barreling across the bridge toward her.

Blake.

Even though the hair on her neck prickled with anticipation, she squatted in the grass and opened her arms to the dog she loved. Touchdown yipped as he streaked across the bridge and jumped into her embrace. She hugged him close and let him lap at her face, not caring that his body was streaked with sweat and dirt from playing in the surrounding woods. God, she had missed this dog.

Heavy footsteps sounded on the bridge, and she looked up. The birds started chirping melodiously. Even the squirrels seemed to pause in their play. Blake walked toward her with purpose, dressed in a simple white T-shirt and khaki shorts, his shoulders as broad as the posts the construction crew had used, his legs still so muscular her mouth went dry. Damn it all to hell. His effect on her hadn't diminished one bit.

When he reached the end of the bridge, he stopped and smiled at her. Simply smiled. The marks of grief were visible in the new grooves around his mouth. Her heart melted like wax.

Oh, Blake.

"I told you I wanted to share Touchdown with you." His deep voice sent a crackle of electricity through her as it spanned the distance between them.

He *had* told her. Repeatedly. Even though it had killed her, she'd refused. The temptation of allowing him back into her life had been too strong.

She stood, still holding a squirming Touchdown in her arms. "I tried to contact you. Blake, I'm so sorry about Adam. More than I can say."

His eyes filled, and he knuckled away the tears he wasn't scared to show anyone. They used to joke about him being the one who cried. After a loss. While watching a teammate be carried off the field on a stretcher. After winning a Super Bowl. He had always worn his heart on his sleeve. Most of the time his intense emotions scared her.

She took a half step toward him, desperate to comfort him, and then realized she was naked under her robe. Bad idea.

"I went off the grid for a while. Mom told me you called her," he said in a hoarse voice. "It meant a lot to her. Despite how things ended between us, they still really love you."

Hurt and regret washed over her, and she clutched the dog to her chest, trying to pull the pieces of herself back together. "When I heard, I...didn't know what to think...and when you didn't call me back..." She couldn't tell him how much that had worried her. How the thought of his suffering had kept her awake those first two nights.

"I picked up the phone at least a hundred times to call you after he died, but I stopped myself." He swiped at his nose. "Please understand. I didn't want you to come to the funeral to try and comfort me—something I knew you would do. It's who you are, babe."

Yeah, she'd always been able to give comfort. Her problem was the inability to accept it.

"So now I know a little of how you felt when Kim died," he said.

The eyes that met hers now were filled with love and hurt and empathy. And there it was again—that softening inside her she'd so feared. She fought to steady herself against it.

"I'm here to help you through it," he said, his voice deeper now. "Maybe it will bring us back together. God, I hope it does. I hope it can at least give us the closure we need to live our own lives. I couldn't get over you, Nat, despite everything."

In a moment of pure honesty, she could admit to herself that she hadn't gotten over him either—far from it.

Her knees were shaking now. "So this bridge...you're what?" It took a moment for her mind to wrap around it. "You're the owner of this bridge?"

"Yes. And the new owner of the house next door." He traced the bridge's post absently. "I told you I wasn't letting you leave me. Not after the progress we made a few months ago at the Spring Practice Dinner."

Off balance, she set Touchdown on the ground. He'd bought the house next door?

"Blake. That was nothing." The words came automatically. Even after the divorce, she'd continued to cater the Raiders' events. This year's dinner had been a monumental disaster.

He tucked his hands in his pockets and strolled toward her. "You kissed me, Nat."

"I was—"

"You can't blame it on being drunk," he said, pointing his finger at her. "You were working."

So, she got a little carried away when she drank. As in, she didn't always remember what he called The Natalie Show. "My future boss was there, so I was...preoccupied," she said lamely.

"Bull. You were preoccupied because of me. If I didn't matter, I wouldn't be able to get to you. And you wouldn't have kissed me. You certainly wouldn't have cried for the first time since I've known you."

That lone tear had betrayed her. He knew she never cried. Not even after Kim died. She wouldn't allow the weakness. Couldn't bear it.

"You're making too much of that," she said, throwing her arms open in exasperation, only then realizing her robe was practically gaping open. She immediately brought the edges together.

"Some would say I am," he said with a new shadow in his brown eyes.

"Please tell me you didn't retire because of me." Surely Adam passing away had to be the reason. She couldn't handle the guilt otherwise.

He exhaled sharply. "You're hoping it's because Adam passed away. Sorry, Nat. Adam had been ill most of the year, and while I took his death hard, it wasn't the reason I left football. It only showed me the truth. It's why I decided to take action to make things right between us."

Rooted to the ground, she could only gape at him. So, he really *had* retired because of her. "Blake! Football is everything to you."

"I know what I need," he continued. "I need you. So does Touchdown. That's why I moved next door."

"But how could this happen without me knowing?" she sputtered.

"I paid the past owners enough to send all their kids to Harvard, and they agreed to move out in secret once they found a new place. I knew you'd book it the minute you found out I was next door. That's why I gave you some time to get settled. Of course, you left most of your stuff in our house in Denver, so there couldn't have been too much to unpack."

"I can still move," she told him even though it would be financially challenging. Matt's house was large, and on the far end of what she could afford. But she loved it. After leaving Blake, she'd rented a two-bedroom townhouse in a not-so-great neighborhood in Denver. At the time, she hadn't cared where she lived—hadn't cared about much of anything. Leaving the house she and Blake had lovingly created together without anything but an overnight bag had almost destroyed her.

"Running away won't solve anything."

Her heart beat in painful bursts. "You have to stop this, Blake. I didn't want you to give up football for me."

He looked down at his hiking boots and kicked at the turf. "I know you didn't, but I couldn't win you back from Dare Valley with my schedule. This was the only way I knew to show you how much you mean to me. How much I still love you. Nothing else has worked."

And there it was. That vulnerability. In a man so big and strong, it seemed almost impossible. It was the very trait that had made her fall for him in the first place.

"But you can't do this. You love football!"

"It's done," he said in that same dismissive tone he used when pushy reporters asked him why he'd thrown three interceptions. "Touchdown can come across the bridge and visit you now. I figured we can split custody."

Like she didn't know where that was leading. "I don't think that's such a good idea."

Touchdown whined, and she leaned down to give his soft ears a rub, mindful of her robe.

"He's yours for the next few days," Blake said, ignoring her and walking back toward the bridge. "I'll bring his stuff around, but I know you'll want to buy your own set when you get around to it. No one is more independent than you."

"Blake!" she called out, trying to remember he'd just suffered a monumental loss. "This can't continue."

At the bridge, he turned. "Babe, it's only beginning. This bridge is my ticket to a better life. It's my bridge back to you."

His bridge to a better life? She almost dropped to her knees in shock, her heart pounding even faster in her chest.

When he was out of sight, she scooped up Touchdown and approached the bridge on trembling legs. Her mind told her she had to look at the symbols carved into the wooden post. Infinity symbols were etched everywhere in the wood, and the sight of them made her clutch the beagle tighter to her chest.

They'd had an infinity symbol engraved in their wedding bands.

This time she did sink to the ground.

CHAPTER 2

Blake strode into the house to dig out his smartphone. He'd purposely turned it off right after the press conference, not wanting to deal with the media blitz that had surrounded his shocking early retirement. He'd called his parents from a friend's phone to tell them he was okay and that he needed to take some time to himself. Since they understood him, they hadn't tried to convince him to come home or to relinquish his quest for Natalie. They'd only said they would be praying for him and he should call if he needed anything. He'd touched base with them from the cabin's landline two weeks later to tell them about his plans, which was when he had learned Natalie had reached out to them, to him.

It had been a struggle not to listen to her message and call her back, but he'd wanted to talk to her in person once his plans were in place. He hadn't wanted her compassion to be the only emotion between them.

Besides his parents, the only people he'd talked to were his lawyer and assistant. They'd arranged the purchase of this house. Thank God money had prompted the former owners to vacate it so quickly.

He'd gotten restless hiding out in the cabin he kept in Vail—the place he'd always used for escape when the media was hunting him.

Turning on the phone again after all this time took more courage than he'd expected. But it had been good for him too, allowing him to grieve in peace. He'd taken long walks in the mountains to help clear his mind. And he'd poured his energy into staging this move to Dare Valley, trying not think about what he'd left behind. Football. God, his heart burned as the text messages started to flood onto his display.

A recent one from his buddy Jordan Dean, quarterback for the Atlanta Rebels, made his gut churn.

I feel like a freaking male stalker. Where in the hell are you? Your mom says you're okay, but you just up and quit football without a word? How can you be OKAY? CALL ME!

His parents had mentioned Jordan and a few of his best buddies had called the house. His closest friends knew their number, and he'd figured a few might try and reach him at their house, which is why he hadn't stayed with them.

He scanned a few more of the texts. Most of them were from the media, no shock. Cripes, he had over a thousand text messages and was maxed out with forty voicemails. Wonderful. It was going to take some time to dig his way through them. Well, Kelly could do it for him when she drove up. His assistant would spend Monday through Wednesday working in Dare Valley; he'd secured a standing reservation for her at The Grand Mountain Hotel because of the commute. He didn't need her full-time anymore, and one of his former teammates had been delighted to hire her for her remaining time.

Kelly was an organizational genius and had handled his move with her usual efficiency. He didn't want to touch anything in the Denver house until he knew how things turned out with Natalie, so Kelly and a load of interior decorators had outfitted this new place to his tastes. He'd brought some clothes and toiletries with him, but little else—not even his Super Bowl ring.

He scrolled through his voicemails and located Natalie's.

Blake. I've just heard about Adam. I am so sorry. Why didn't you say anything? I know things have been...well, weird, but..."

She trailed off, and he waited to hear the rest of the message, his heart pounding hard.

"Well, I just wanted you to know how sorry I am. Adam was a beautiful man. I can't imagine how much you and your parents are going to miss him. I'll...goodbye, Blake."

Her hesitation was enough to put a knot of emotion in his throat. He'd known she would feel sympathy for his loss, and while he appreciated that, he wanted a whole lot more from her.

He dialed up one of his best football buddies, who would undoubtedly be worried about him. Sam Garretty played for the Washington Warriors, but they'd met years ago at the famous football camp Sam's dad ran in Ohio, which they all called the Once Upon A Dare Camp in honor of Coach Garretty's annual speech at the camp opener. Blake had made seven friends for life at that camp, including Jordan, but he'd avoided calling them over the past weeks. He was afraid of how they'd react to his monumental decision to leave behind the sport they all loved.

"Hey, Sam," he said when his friend answered.

"Glad you finally checked in," Sam replied in the steady voice for which he was known. He never lost his cool—not even if his team was down three points with twenty seconds left. "Some of the guys were ready to hire a private investigator to hunt you down."

"I'm not surprised. Jordan's latest text said he felt

like a stalker." The way his mouth curved felt good. "Jordan always was a worry wart."

"I won't ask why you did it."

"It wasn't only because Adam died," he felt inspired to say.

"I know it wasn't. We all know it wasn't."

Because they all already knew how much he loved Natalie and wanted her back. They'd flown in to see him after the breakup, and they'd kept up a steady flow of visits to show their support. He wouldn't have survived without them. And after it had become clear that Adam wasn't going to pull through, they'd been there for him again. He rubbed the bridge of his nose as emotion rolled through his chest.

"You don't have to spill your guts, but I have to ask: how are you really doing?"

The breath he blew out would have been enough of an answer for Sam, but he owed him more than that. "I don't know yet. We knew we were going to lose Adam— heck, we've known all year—but it still hurts like hell. And I've just seen Natalie. I bought the house next door to her."

"You're in Dare Valley then? How'd she react to seeing you?"

He thought back to her flushed face, the worry in her beautiful blue eyes. Since Kim's death, the color of her eyes had reminded him more of the blue ice of glaciers than the blue tongues of firelight. It had been good to see that warm blue color again today.

"She's not overjoyed, but she didn't lambast me like she probably would have done if I weren't grieving. I connected our properties with a bridge. We can share Touchdown now."

And other things, he hoped.

He was convinced the bridge was the key to a better life—just like he'd told her.

"Jordan said he wanted all of us to drop everything

and fly out to see you when you resurfaced. Zack said he'd order us a case of bourbon. No one mentioned strippers, thank God."

No, their group of guys wasn't into that part of the life. When they got together, they acted like boys again, pulling more practical jokes than should be legal.

"Bourbon sounds good," he said. "I guess I don't need to worry about my alcohol consumption anymore."

"Like you'd ever get drunk."

He'd learned to stick to his limit the hard way—by puking on the high school football field the morning after a night of carousing. But losing Natalie had made him take leave of his senses for a time. He'd fought the divorce like crazy before admitting to himself that she wasn't coming back. Then he'd chosen to numb himself with alcohol on a few desperate nights, even if it meant being sick later.

"Beyond getting Natalie back, what else are you planning to do?" Sam asked. "You always have a plan. You'll go bonkers if you don't have something to do."

Most of them thought about what life would look like after football. Sure age was a factor, but every player knew injury could come out of nowhere and end a promising career. Frank Garretty had drilled that into their heads each summer. Blake could still hear his gravelly voice shouting across the freshly mowed football field in his annual speech, the one they referred to as Once Upon A Dare.

Playing professional football is not some fairy tale, boys. It's hard, exhausting work. You'll be tested in every way a man can be. There are no daisies and buttercups in this game. If you want everything handed to you like some princess, get off my field right now. If you're going to play football for me or any coach worth his salt, you're going to have to dare it all. So, here's my challenge to you punks. I dare you to be more than you ever imagined...

If one of the campers wimped out during speed drills and made the other kids run an extra five miles after practice, that person had been dubbed Cinderella for the whole week. Jordan had even fashioned a crown once out of shoelaces and paperclips, which Coach hadn't liked—not one bit.

"I've been thinking about it a lot, actually," Blake said, "and I'm going to start a football camp for kids with intellectual disabilities. Boys only at first. I figure with what I've learned from your dad and my brother..." He broke off, choking on his grief for Adam.

"Adam would be proud of you. My dad too. I know I am. How can I help?"

That was Sam—always practical, always willing to lend a hand. "I don't want to take you away from your dad's camp."

"Who says I can't be involved with more than one camp?" his friend fired back. "Assuming you're going to limit it to a week like Coach does."

He was, but even so, he'd been reluctant to ask the guys for help. First, it was flag football. And second, working with healthy kids at football camp was challenging enough, what with the punk attitudes, horsing around, and off-the-field issues. But they hadn't spent much time around kids with intellectual disabilities, except, of course, for Adam. And they certainly hadn't coached them. Even he wasn't sure how it would go.

"Thanks, man," he said and coughed to cover the emotion clogging his throat. "Yes, it's going to be a week. I've already rented a dorm at the local university here after they agreed to let me use their field."

Okay, so it wasn't just a vague plan. He'd drafted the whole thing while he was in Vail and then made a handful of calls with the strict understanding the discussions were confidential. The athletic director of Emmits Merriam University, Tom Hudson, was a big

Raiders fan, and the prospect of helping Blake host his first football camp had thrilled him. From there, it had been relatively easy.

He and Kelly were working their way through the list of things they would need, anything from a call for volunteers to supplies. And he had a lead on some medical staff that could help out whenever a physical issue came up for one of the kids. Now that the bridge had been built, the announcement would go out today. He had made his personal plans known to Natalie. Now, he would make his next steps known to the world.

"Sounds like you're moving forward, all right," Sam mused. "Not that I'm surprised. You never were one to sit around. What's your end game, Blake?"

Nothing got past Sam Garretty. "I want to get more involved with the Special Olympics." But it wouldn't take up all his time, and that terrified him. Natalie had a full-time job. He would need something else. "Beyond that, I don't know yet."

"You'll figure it out," Sam said. "And you know all of us will do whatever we can to help out with the camp and anything else you need."

While Blake had played with many different guys and teams in his career, his football camp family had been a constant in his life. "Thanks, man."

"Now, when can we come visit? I promised to call the others as soon as I heard from you."

It didn't surprise him to hear the other guys had guessed he'd call Sam first. Everyone knew he was the best listener of the group. "Whenever your schedule allows. I'm free."

"Fine. We'll come this weekend. Hope you have enough room for all of us. I am not bunking with Jordan again. That guy has more hair products than the last woman I dated."

Jordan's impeccable grooming was an ongoing joke in their group.

"Fine. So long as you understand that I'm going to abandon you all in a heartbeat—for a few hours at least—if Natalie agrees to go out with me this weekend."

A rude snort echoed over the line. "She won't. One thing I love about that woman is that she won't let anyone rush her. She always takes her sweet time to make a decision."

And wasn't that ever true? Natalie hadn't agreed to date him right away, though he'd wanted to—badly—ever since he first caught sight of her talking with one of the Raiders' admin staff at an event she'd catered. It was the way she laughed—with such gusto that her entire body shook and her glossy dark curls bobbed up and down—that had drawn him to her. He had wanted to make her laugh that way. It had taken a while for him to win her over and convince her he wasn't some bad boy QB who would break her heart. But even then, she'd kept part of herself closed off, distant. She'd poured so much love into him and their relationship, he'd learned to be okay with that...until Kim had died and Natalie had locked herself inside that guarded place and thrown away the key.

He'd given up for a time, but after Adam got really sick, he realized something: while all the bargaining and begging in the world wouldn't keep Adam on this earth, he still had a chance to be with the woman he loved. And that tear at the Raiders' dinner... Well, it had been enough to tell him what he already knew—she missed him too, and she was close to relenting.

"She's pretty upset, huh?" his friend asked.

"Not as much as she will be when she stops mollycoddling me because of Adam." As much as she might want to be sweet, she had plenty of piss and vinegar in her. It was something he loved about her.

Sam paused. "You know we're here for you, right? All the way. Not just for the whole retirement thing and Adam, but for your Natalie campaign too."

"I know."

"I'll call the guys then. We'll see you this weekend. And promise me you won't put me in a room with Jordan just because I bitched about it."

He laughed, and it felt good. Having a guys' weekend was just what he needed. "What did Coach always say? Never show your Achilles."

"If you do it, there will be retribution."

How many practical jokes had they played on each other over the years? Everything from pouring honey into cleats when they were kids to driving off with someone's new ride at a party they were all attending. But they drew the line at tampering with a man's jock strap. Some things were sacrosanct.

"You're on my turf, Garretty."

"Oh, I'm shaking, man."

He hadn't realized how much he missed his friends' banter after his self-imposed seclusion. "Thanks for not trying to talk me out of any of this or telling me I'm crazy."

"I hope you know I never would. Put on your dancing shoes, Ace. You're going to be boogying to Natalie's tune for the foreseeable."

He couldn't wait to match her moves.

CHAPTER 3

Natalie had one mission in her head when she walked back into her house. Find the salted chocolate caramels she'd hidden from herself in the laundry room. Stat.

"Your daddy...has simply lost his mind," she told Touchdown, who trotted joyfully beside her.

Then she realized she was falling back into old patterns. Talking to their dog when she was upset with Blake, referring to him as Touchdown's daddy. Of course, Blake had called her Mommy. This had to stop.

"Touchdown." The dog only wagged his tail. "Get used to me calling him Blake." She moved the liquid detergent aside and rose onto her tippy tiptoes to grab the box.

Hiding food from herself had been pathetic enough. Shoving three chocolates into her mouth at one time was a whole new level. But the chocolate tickled the back of her throat and the caramel coated her tongue, and for those few precious moments, she was lost in the thrall of the chocolate O. Blake didn't exist. Her past with him didn't exist.

And then it was over, and her stomach turned

queasy. He was back. He was living right next door. He'd built a freaking bridge to connect them and bared his soul. Again. And he was sharing Touchdown with her.

This had to be some kneejerk reaction to grief, right?

The dog nuzzled her calf. Sliding onto the floor, the candy box still clutched in her hand, she pulled the beagle's little body onto her lap. She petted him with one hand while using the other to deliver more chocolates into her mouth.

"What in the world am I supposed to do with him, Touchdown?" she asked, her stomach growing queasier with each chocolate.

Disgusted, she set the box aside. He was *not* getting to her—even though he already had. She closed her eyes and leaned her head back against the washing machine. Then she started chuckling to herself. What a greeting card she was: woman slumped on the floor of the laundry room with a dog, her mouth and hands stained with chocolate.

Over Your Ex Yet? It Doesn't Get Any Better Than This.

And the girls were falling out of her robe! Again. She wondered if Blake had noticed her accidental peek-show. Then her chuckle turned into a full-on laugh. He was a guy. Of course, he'd noticed.

Pushing off the floor, she headed into the kitchen. She needed to talk this out with her two sisters. Moira and Caroline were driving up from Denver today for their standard Saturday lunch with her mom, her Hale cousins, and some additions by marriage.

Drive faster and come to my house first. I need to talk.

Moira responded.

Caroline is pressing the metal.

Pressing the metal? Colloquialisms had never been

Moira's thing.

Well, she needed to get dressed. But first she could at least get Touchdown some water. And give him a tour of the house. By the time her sisters arrived, her features were more composed. Sure, her stomach was still churning from her unplanned chocolate splurge, but she was dressed. Presentable.

The minute they walked through the door Touchdown scurried over to them, yipping with joy, and she knew the cat was out of the bag.

"Oh, you sweet boy," Moira cooed, falling to her knees on the floor to receive kisses.

Caroline glanced around the room. "Blake's here?"

"He paid the family next door to leave. We're neighbors now."

"Holy shit," Caroline said, giving her a brief hug. "That poor guy. When I think about him losing Adam... What did he say?"

"Yeah. What did he say?" Moira said, standing with the beagle curled up in her arms.

She threw her hands out. "What do you think? He left football to win me back, and he's sharing Touchdown with me until that happens."

"It's kinda romantic," Moira murmured. "And sad. He must miss his brother terribly."

"I know that...but even so, he can't just move in next door. We're *divorced!*" she said, hating the way her voice was rising in spite of her. Panic laced with a healthy dose of confusion.

Caroline walked over to Moira to pet Touchdown, and her sisters shared a look. *Uh-oh.*

"Natalie," Moira said, putting Touchdown on the ground, "I'm sorry you're so upset, and I wish I could say something to change that. But maybe you being upset is what this is all about. Perhaps this is a blessing in disguise. You need some kind of closure with him, and he obviously needs the same from you if you're not going to be together anymore. Losing his brother probably made that clear to him."

Her sister might as well have struck her with a baseball bat. "Look, I left Blake because he wouldn't give me a baby. End of story. What happened with Adam doesn't change that."

Caroline worried her lip. "Blake came and talked to Mo and me a while ago...after you left him. He told us about the baby discussion."

She put her hand back, felt empty space, and stepped back until she found something to hold onto. Anything. Her heart pounded in her chest, her ears. So, the ugliest lie she'd ever told had been revealed.

After Kim's death, it had hurt too much to be around Blake, so she'd invented a plausible excuse to leave him—one she'd thought he would never be able to forgive, not in a million years. Otherwise he never would have let her leave to stew in her numbness alone. She'd picked a stupid fight about wanting a baby immediately, which he'd dismissed—as expected. As far as her family knew, it was the reason she'd left.

His words still echoed in her mind:

You're damn right I won't give you a baby right now. Not when you're hurting over Kim and barely functioning. When we make a baby, it will be because we're so excited we can't see straight. Not out of grief.

She'd walked out on him the very next day, the horror of what she'd done burning in her belly. And it had all back-fired on her. Blake *was* able to forgive her anything, it seemed. It only made her feel more like the pond scum she was.

"You never said a word to me," she choked out, her cheeks red with shame.

"You weren't in much of a listening mood," Moira said softly. "You were hurting. We all were. We didn't...know how to help you and Blake."

But she remembered her sisters asking if she was

sure she wanted to divorce Blake. They'd even suggested marital counseling, which she'd refused out of hand.

"You're on his side," she said with a gasp of shock.

Caroline gently took Natalie's hands. "No, we're on yours. Always. But if we're being honest, we both like Blake. He loves you, and deep down, we know you still love him too."

"Don't tell me what I feel," she said, her hackles rising, almost like her skin had popped out barbed wire to protect herself.

"Maybe you should listen to what he has to say," Moira said, coming to stand beside Caroline. "He left football for you, after all."

She shoved away from them, feeling ganged up on, and almost stepped on Touchdown in the process. "I cannot believe this! Tell me the truth. Have you been in touch with Blake since I left him, or did you just talk to him that once?"

When they both looked down rather than meeting her eyes, she wrapped her arms around herself, hoping to ward off the pain spreading through her gut.

"He was worried about you after Kim," Caroline said. "We all were. So, yes, he would touch base every now and then to make sure you were okay."

"You betrayed me."

"No," Moira said in an even voice. "We never once tried to interfere with you two."

"But you just told me this is a blessing in disguise," she said, acid coating the words. "Was anyone else in touch with Blake?"

Her sisters shared a glance.

"Tell me."

"I know he talked to Mom and Dad and Matt after you left," Caroline said. "It hurt him to learn what you'd told us about your split...that it was over him not wanting a baby."

What was wrong with him? How could he still want

her back? He had to be off kilter somehow.
This...couldn't be love. "Great. So everyone knows *I'm* in
the wrong."

"Natalie," Moira said, taking a deep breath. "No
one's saying that. But Blake was a part of our family for
a long time, and we all lost him when you left him. You
never understood that."

"Because he was my husband, and it was my right to
leave." Why couldn't they understand that she'd had to?

"But he was my friend, and I had a right to talk to
him after you dropped him," Moira said. "He was
grieving over Kim too."

Her cheeks burned now. She knew he had been
devastated over losing Kim. But she hadn't been able to
deal with her own feelings, let alone his. "Dropped him?
Is that what you think I did?"

Caroline bustled in between them like a referee
between two boxing opponents who'd just crossed the
line.

"Yes!" Moira answered. "He's a wonderful guy, and
as far as he's concerned, you hang the moon. Look at
everything he's done to get you back! Look at everything
he's done for you. There aren't many guys like that. Tell
me you're happier without him, Nat, because I sure as
hell haven't seen evidence of it."

"Enough!" Caroline shouted, causing Touchdown to
whine in the corner. "That's enough. Everyone obviously
has strong feelings about this, so I suggest we take a
time-out."

Her skin felt raw and uncomfortable, as if it had
been stripped bare by the ugliness of the past. Inside
she was shaking, as much from seeing Blake as from
hearing her sisters tell her what they really thought of
the situation. "Tell Mom and the others I'm not feeling
well today."

"Natalie—"

"No, Caroline. I need some time to myself after

hearing all this. Please go."

They reached for each other's hands as they turned to walk toward the door. That small sisterly touch made her chest hurt, and she had to fight the urge to rush over, embrace them, and tell them all was forgiven. That she was a horrible person for what she'd done. To them. To herself. But most of all, to Blake.

But she couldn't.

If she did, they'd be right, and Blake would have succeeded in scaling her fortress again. She wasn't about to allow that, whatever his reasons for coming back.

They said goodbye to Touchdown and gave her one last look before they left. Once again, she was alone and numb, unwilling to feel anything. Just like after Kim died.

It was no more than she deserved.

CHAPTER 4

Andy Hale didn't always have Saturdays off from rounds at Dare Valley General Hospital, so he made the most of them when he did. Usually he would go on a hike or a bike ride up the canyon with his son, but today Danny was playing with his best friend, Martin, a couple of houses down.

The house wasn't in the best condition, but then again it never was. Between his long hours as a doctor and his role as a single dad, he didn't have much time to clean. Hanging out with Danny would always be his priority, and if his kid wanted to play a few video games or read four stories instead of the usual two, well, then that was what they did. Dishes and laundry eventually got done. The lady he'd hired to clean the house once a week kept it from becoming a total pigsty. Sure, he asked Danny to try and clean up after himself, but the kid was only five.

And he dirtied more shirts and pants than Andy could comprehend. How had his mother managed to do the laundry for all five of them when they were kids?

His stomach growled, and he rubbed it. The Hale clan was getting together later for a BBQ at his brother's house. He'd purposely eaten light since two local chefs would be bringing food to the potluck.

He was picking up Danny's train set lying in front of the TV, making a cursory attempt at tidying, when the doorbell rang. He stashed the toy in the blue plastic chest in the corner of the family room and jogged over to answer it. He opened the door to find his brother standing on the threshold, looking pissed.

"What's wrong?" he asked as Matt walked inside. "Your grill out of propane?"

"No," he responded, tossing his car keys in his hand. "Blake is here."

His head jerked back. "Huh? What do you mean *here?*"

"He's Natalie's new next-door neighbor. He paid the Howards some obscene amount of money to secretly move. And he built a freaking bridge over the creek of my old place to connect their two properties. He plans to share Touchdown with her."

Everyone had wondered where Blake had gone after shocking the world with his retirement. Then the press had reported the news of his brother's death, and Andy had taken a moment of silence to grieve with his old friend. Blake and Adam had been as close as he and Matt were.

The whole family knew he wanted Natalie back, and had for some time, although they'd agreed not to interfere. Andy had always liked Blake and had considered him a brother until Natalie bushwhacked them all by leaving him. It seemed death's call had given Blake a renewed fire, and part of Andy admired it.

"How's Nat handling it?" he asked neutrally.

"How do you think? She asked me to look into the legality of the bridge. I asked her what difference it would make. I mean, if she makes a big deal of this, it will only become the talk of the town. Adam just died, for heaven's sake. I don't want to kick a man while he's down, but he has to back off. Natalie is freaking out."

"If she's freaking out, it probably means she still cares for him." Something he'd always suspected.

"I think we should go see him," Matt said. "Get your shoes on. I assume Danny's at Martin's since he didn't jump me the second I rang the bell. We can stop by to tell them we'll be back in a bit."

Andy shifted his weight. "I don't know, Matt. What about our family pact to stay out of it? I think Natalie and Blake need to work this out on their own."

Matt punched the air. "Look, I used to love the guy. He was part of our family, and it tore me up when he and Natalie split, but we can't let this drag on—no matter what he's going through. Nat made her decision, and it's time for him to accept that. She's already fought with Caroline and Moira about it."

That didn't sound good. "What happened?"

"Well, they broke the pact. They said she should give Blake another chance. They might also have mentioned that they've always liked him, and they admire him for giving up football for her."

Well, it was something worth considering, wasn't it? Blake lived and breathed football like Andy lived and breathed medicine. But his former brother-in-law had always carved time for Natalie and his family—his own and theirs—into his hectic football schedule. Andy was the same way, so he and Blake had shared a certain understanding because of that similarity.

"All right, I'll go with you, but I don't like it." He tugged on his shoes. "I also want you to promise me two things."

Matt leveled him a glance. "And what would that be, Andy Cakes?"

Jeez, how he hated that nickname. "That you won't be mean to him. He just lost his brother."

"Give me some credit."

"They don't call you Matty Ice for nothing."

"I'll ignore that. What's the second thing?"

"We hear his side of things."

His eyes narrowed like he was about to play hardball. "I've already heard his side of things, and I'm not saying he's wrong, but it doesn't matter. Natalie is our sister."

Being a lawyer, Matt saw the world more black and white than he did. Andy opened the door, grateful he didn't need a jacket. Summer was finally approaching, thank God. Late snowfall a couple of weeks ago had made him want to pound his head into the ground. *Die, winter, die,* he'd chanted as he shoveled the drive for the umpteenth time.

"Well, *I* haven't heard his side of things," he told Matt as they walked over to Martin's house.

"That's because you were dealing with your own stuff then, and Blake knew not to bother you."

He halted in front of Martin's front door. "That's because he's a good guy."

Matt shook his head stubbornly as he rang the doorbell. "Doesn't matter. Natalie wants him gone, so he's gone."

After seeing how closed off his sister had become since Kim's death, Andy wasn't so sure he agreed.

CHAPTER 5

When Blake opened the door to see his two former brothers-in-law, he had to fight the urge to pull them into a hug. He hadn't seen them in almost two years. He and the Hale brothers had been close, and losing Natalie had also meant losing her family.

"Here to break my legs?" he asked instead. After all, Matt probably wouldn't respond too well to a hug right now. He looked like a pissed off defensive linebacker eager to flatten him to the ground.

"No," Andy replied as Matt opened his mouth— probably to say something very different. "We're just here to talk. Blake, I'm so sorry about Adam. More than I can say."

"Yes, you have our deepest condolences," Matt said, dialing back the PO factor.

There was a flare of grief in his chest. "Thanks. I appreciate that. He had a tough year before he passed. In the end, I think he was ready." The day before he'd died, his brother had confessed how much pain he was in and how tired he was of fighting. Blake had told him it was okay to go, and Adam had given him one last smile before slipping into unconsciousness.

When he held out his hand for a shake, Andy bypassed it and pulled him into a hug. "It's really good to see you, man."

He clapped him on the back before releasing him and had to wipe away some tears when he pulled away. He held out his hand to Matt, waiting to see if he would shake it. "I don't expect a hug."

Matt snorted, but he shook his hand willingly enough. "Funny. I'm not much of a hugger."

It was a start.

He'd made this move to Dare Valley knowing he would have to win over Natalie's family as much as he would Natalie. The Hales were a unit, and he knew he had allies among them. The question was, would that influence Natalie? She had a head like a rock when it came to listening to anyone.

"Come on in," he said, heading to the kitchen. "I know it's early, but would you like a beer?"

"I'm fine," Matt replied, now sounding every inch of his nickname, Matty Ice.

"Sounds great," Andy added, and Blake didn't miss the elbow he landed in his brother's ribs. "This is a big change from your place in Denver."

Blake opened a beer for himself, then slid an IPA and a bottle opener to Andy across the navy granite island in the center of the kitchen.

"Sure you don't want one?" he asked Matt, who shook his head.

"Let's head outside. Nice to have warm weather finally. Winter was a bitch this year."

"Blake," Matt said in a cool tone, "this isn't a social visit. Natalie informed me this morning that you up and bought my neighbor's house and built a bridge connecting your properties."

Rather than answer right away, he led them out to the back patio. Sure, the deck was smaller than the one he had in Denver—heck the whole house was smaller by two thousand square feet—but it had a killer view of the mountains. Settling back into a deck chair, he kicked his feet out in front of him. This conversation was going to take a while—or so he hoped—and he wanted to get comfortable.

Andy sat in an adjoining chair and pushed another toward his brother. "Come on, Matty Ice. Take a load off."

When Matt dropped down into the chair, Blake settled the bottle on his knee and looked from one of the Hale brothers to the other, staring each of them straight in the eye like he'd do with his teammates in the middle of a losing game.

"Two months ago at the Denver Raiders' annual spring dinner, your sister kissed me. Even more telling, she actually cried. I *know* she still loves me, and God knows I love her. I left football to show her she's everything to me in the hopes she would finally let me back into her life. After Kim died, she totally shut down."

Andy flinched, and though he hated to bring up memories that were painful for all of them, Blake pressed on.

"She wouldn't talk about it. She wouldn't grieve. And then a few days after the funeral, she picked a fight with me about having a baby and left. I tried to...dammit...reach out to her, but she wouldn't even talk to me, let alone agree to marriage counseling. She sure as hell wouldn't go to the therapist I recommended so she could talk about Kim."

This time Matt looked away, his jaw locked. Blake took a sip of his beer to wet his dry throat.

"You both know her. She hasn't been herself. I'm not saying I expected her to do jumping jacks after Kim died. But Natalie shut out the world around her. I know what it's like to grieve for a brother, and your sister hasn't let herself mourn Kim."

"How do you know she hasn't worked through her emotions since she left you?" Matt asked.

"She was living in a crappy place in Denver. You both know it. She didn't paint any walls or put up any pictures. She refused to take the majority of her stuff from our house. That's not Natalie."

"How do you know that?" Matt asked, leaning forward in his chair. "Were you spying on my sister?"

"No! I would never do that. A couple times in the beginning, I dropped by with Touchdown. She closed out that poor little guy too, and you know how much she loves him."

"Maybe she was just ready to be done with you," Matt said, rising from his chair. "Maybe there was other stuff going on between you two."

Anger spurted hot and fierce through him. "What are you talking about? Do you think I messed around with other women while we were married?" He rose and got in Matt's face. "You damn well know I love your sister. I would *never* have cheated on her."

"Enough!" Andy shouted, yanking on his brother's shirt. "Sit down. Both of you."

Blake sat down and took some deep breaths to regain control of himself. Spouting off at Matty Ice wasn't going to help anything. Matt resumed his seat.

"Matt, I agree with Blake here."

"Grief takes time—"

"No one knows that better than I do," Andy said. "But Natalie changed after Kim was diagnosed, and she hasn't come back."

"Neither have you," Matt said in a hoarse voice.

Blake's throat thickened, hearing that. Andy ran his hand through his hair and took a drink of his beer.

"Yeah, not the whole way, but I'm making progress. Shit, God knows I've cried, and I don't say that to sound like a baby, but I'm a doctor. Crying is the body's way of coping with grief, and if grief isn't processed, disease, depression, and a whole list of other stuff can lie in wait for a person."

"Natalie never cries," Matt said. "Some people—"

"Then it's all the more significant Natalie cried in front of Blake at the dinner," Andy interrupted. "I'm not saying I'm pushing for them to get back together. It's her choice. But I think we need to be honest about how she's doing and help her."

"I'm here because I want to help her too," Blake interjected. "Look, I want her back. I won't lie. But if she really doesn't love me, doesn't want to be with me, then I'll let her go. But we both need closure. I..."

He broke off, feeling the rawness of the emotion, the pressure of the odds against him.

"I want her to be happy again, and if I can help with that...well, then leaving football was worth it. If we can't be together, then at least we can help each other heal. She can move on, and so can I. But after that kiss and her reaction to it...well, I know in my gut she still loves me. Just like I knew we could run a quarterback draw in the Super Bowl and score."

Matt and Andy were big enough Raiders fans to understand what he was saying. That play was considered one of the all-time greatest, and he'd called it on a hunch. All of them went quiet, and for a long moment, the only sound was a woodpecker doing damage to the mighty oak thirty yards off. Blake fell deeper into that place inside himself where everything was calm, the one he'd learned to seek out at life's toughest moments. It took a while, but he got there.

"So, how's Danny?" he asked, wanting to steer the conversation to happier trails.

A smile softened the tense line of Andy's mouth. "Growing up fast. He loves living in Dare Valley. He'll be happy to see you...when and if the time comes."

That was fair. No need to confuse him. "I've missed that kid." God, he was getting choked up here. "Losing

Natalie was hard enough, but...I've missed the rest of you too, dammit."

"Ditto, man," Andy said and took a swig of his beer. "What are your plans beyond winning my sister back?"

He told them. It would be public knowledge today, anyway.

"That's great, Blake," Andy said. "Adam would be really happy about your camp. It's a wonderful tribute. He always loved to throw the ball around."

So many memories flashed through his mind that he had to clear his throat. "Yeah, he did."

"Anything you need on that score," Matt finally said, "you let me know. It looks like I'll be mayor come November since no one's stepped forward to challenge me after the primary."

His offer indicated he was softening. "Thanks. Congrats, by the way, on your engagement and your foray into politics." Matt had always been a natural leader, so it hadn't surprised Blake to learn he was about to become Dare Valley's new mayor. "I always said you would have made a great quarterback if you could throw a decent spiral."

"Suck it, Cunningham," he shot back, a phrase they'd bandied about years ago.

His chest lightened. "Now that I'm retired, I'll have more time to teach you how the big boys do it."

Matt snorted. "You're delusional."

He laughed, and the sound was rich and deep enough to scare off three squirrels that had been lurking on the deck.

"I'll talk to Natalie," Andy said casually, and Blake's heart rate spiked.

"Thank you."

"It's still up to her," Andy added, finishing off his beer and setting it down on the ground.

"Like she'd ever make a decision based on someone else's opinion," Blake said dryly. He ran a hand through his hair. "You need to know, I don't want to hurt her, but this thing between us...and Kim...it's going to hurt. It'll be like putting a shoulder back in the socket." Having dislocated his shoulder before, he knew just how acute that pain could be.

"I know it," Andy said. "Good thing you have people around who know how to bandage things up."

"Just don't be too hard on her," Matt added with a small smile. "She needs to know she's tough. It's who she is."

Her attachment to that identity—her belief that being tough meant standing firm against normal human emotions—was what was hurting her, but then he couldn't say too much to her brother about that. In many ways, Matty Ice and Natalie were cut from the same cloth.

"I'll be as gentle as I can be," he promised.

"Good. Now, why don't you grab me a beer? Seems I'm behind you guys."

He rose with a smile on his face. "Have it in a jiffy."

As soon as he was in the house and out of their sight, he did a victory dance. He felt like a champion right now.

After all, every football player knew a Super Bowl was won one victory at a time.

CHAPTER 6

Natalie decided the kitchen sink needed a good scrubbing, hoping it would keep her cold hands occupied and keep her mind from betraying her with thoughts of Blake. Touchdown sat on the floor, grinning at her like a goofus, and darn it all if she didn't find herself smiling too—when she wasn't frowning, of course.

She hadn't heard from her mother yet, but she'd heard from the rest of her Hale lunch crew, who had offered their support. Moira and Caroline had spilled the beans. Not that Blake's presence in town would stay secret for long anyway. Once Mr. Football Fancy Pants strutted his fine butt down Dare Valley's Main Street, everyone in town would know he was here...heck, everyone in the country.

The very thought of the press descending on the small town and bothering her again gave her a headache. After Blake went "missing," various reporters had contacted her, hoping for the story behind the story. She'd taken the Fifth. The calls had stopped after the news about Adam's passing was published. But now everyone would suspect that Blake hadn't left football only because of Adam. He'd left it because of *her*. Why the heck else would he be living next door?

The town gossip was going to drive her crazy. It was one part of small town life she hadn't missed. She'd have to shut it down as soon as possible.

Someone rapped on her back door, and she let out a loud grumble. Only Blake would use that door. Touchdown was already letting loose a volley of happy barks by the time she opened it. Blake's hands were full of Touchdown's stuff. He stepped inside so quickly she had to take a step back. After setting Touchdown's things down on the nearby kitchen table, he reached a hand out to her face.

"You have hair in your eyes."

Her belly quivered with lust as his fingers caressed her cheek, pushing the lock behind her ear. In that one simple touch, she could feel all the pent-up longing inside him.

His brown eyes held steady on her face. "I know what you're thinking. I'm thinking the same thing." Then his nose scrunched up like he'd detected an unpleasant smell, and he flinched. "Were you cleaning?" he asked, his eyes darting around the kitchen.

It was impossible to mistake the fear lacing his voice. She flashed to the time she'd cleaned the shower after Kim's funeral. Something popped inside her heart, and *oh,* how it hurt.

"You only clean when you're upset, babe. I'm sorry for that."

How could she hope to fight with someone who knew her so well? After being married for three years, he knew every intimate detail about her.

"Do you have any idea how complicated you're going to make my life once the press hears you've moved in next door? Blake, I just moved back to my hometown and started a respectable job. I don't need or want that kind of attention."

"Your new boss doesn't give a flying F what anyone thinks or says."

"Still jealous of Terrance?" she quipped. Blake and her celebrity chef boss had sized each other up like mad dogs at the Raiders' dinner. Even though Terrance was over the moon about someone else, he'd helped out Natalie by intimating he was her new love interest.

"No, but I was sure as hell jealous at the Raiders' dinner. It would have been nice if you'd told me he was interviewing you."

She crossed her arms. "I wasn't feeling particularly nice that day." And she now felt more guilt than she could run up a flag pole. At the time, she'd had no idea about Adam's declining health.

"You made that clear," he said, scooping Touchdown up. "Hey, boy. How's Mommy treating you so far? Did you get paw prints on the kitchen floor?"

Her insides pinged when she heard him call her "Mommy." Hadn't she just been thinking about that? "We have to call each other by our real names now, Blake. You're not his daddy, and I'm not his mommy."

"Come on, Nat," Blake said, nudging her playfully in the ribs. "It will only confuse him. Plus, you *are* his mommy. He was barely a week old when you met him, and he can't get to sleep without your yellow shirt. Doesn't that prove something?"

He gestured to Touchdown's gear, and sure enough, there was her old shirt—the one Blake had admitted to taking on the road with him so he could always have her smell nearby. Gestures like that had always turned her to mush. Her knees quivered. All her emotions were rising to the surface again, and she wasn't sure she had the power to hold them back anymore.

"They're only names, Blake. Please do this *one* thing for me since I know you won't take the bridge down."

He lifted his left shoulder in a slight shrug. "I can't take the bridge down. It's my road back to you."

"Blake!"

"Okay! I'll stop. I've pressed you enough for one day." He glanced around the room. "You haven't hung anything on the walls yet."

The knowing look in his eyes had her fiddling with the hem of her shirt. "No."

All the art they'd chosen on fun shopping outings had remained on the walls of their Denver home. Correction, *his* home.

"If you want some of the paintings from the house, let me know."

He'd made that offer—and so many more—after she left him.

"I'm fine. Thanks."

His jaw locked, and he gave Touchdown a sweet hug before setting him down. "In the interest of full disclosure, you have the right to know your brothers visited me earlier."

Part of her wasn't surprised. Matt had been fighting mad when she'd called him about the bridge. "I don't see a black eye," she said even though she knew neither one of them would be that cruel.

His mouth tipped up at the corner. "Matty Ice started off pretty cool, but he mellowed. I told your brothers why I'm here...that you haven't grieved over Kim yet and we haven't...dealt with whatever this is between us."

She fisted her hands in the hem of her shirt, feeling exposed and more than ganged up on. "You had no right to talk about me—about us—behind my back. But then again, you already did. Moira and Caroline told me earlier you'd been in touch with everyone but Andy."

His jaw turned hard. "I had every right to talk to them! You lied to your family about me and tried to make me into someone I'm not. A guy who doesn't want kids with his wife. You didn't play fair."

It was true, and the shame of that knowledge stung

her cheeks, but she hadn't wanted to risk losing their support. Her family was everything to her, the one thing she could fall back on when the world went crazy. "I know I didn't play fair." It was as much as she could admit to him right then.

He huffed out a sigh. "I cared about them, Nat. I still do. They had a right to know my side. I didn't want them thinking I was some insensitive prick who would say something that awful right after his wife's best friend and sister-in-law had died."

He was like a harsh light, and since she was someone who wanted to stay in the dark, she strode away from him on impulse. Then she stopped in her tracks, realizing she was bringing him further into the house—not a wise plan. "So we're choosing sides then? You're trying to get my family to gang up on me."

His face fell. "No one wants to gang on you, babe. We love you. You're not *you,* and you haven't been for a while now. I'm only drawing attention to what everyone else in your family has already noticed."

Yeah, and how had she reacted when Moira and Caroline finally mentioned it? She'd pushed them away.

Just like you did with Blake, she heard a voice say gently in her head.

She ignored it. "Why does everyone keep harping on this? I just want to be left alone."

He had his arms wrapped around her before she could blink.

"No, you don't. Babe, you're not a loner. As someone who just lost his brother, I know there's a balance between dealing with your grief in private and surrounding yourself with people who love you. You pushed the rest of us away completely."

He was getting way too close to the truth, and it made her quake inside. Her face was scrunched against his chest, and though she wanted so badly to let herself be comforted by him, she locked her muscles against the feel of his hard body pressed against hers. Finally she did push him away. Hard. He loosened his grip, giving her more room, but he didn't totally drop those sinewy arms of his.

"Let me go, Blake."

"Just let me hold you for a minute. Is that going to kill you? Don't you remember how much you loved for me to hold you, simply hold you, when one of us came home after a crappy day at work?"

Oh, how she remembered. She had grown to crave his strong arms around her. They always provided whatever she needed—comfort, security, strength. And she'd provided that same simple comfort for him after each devastating loss, on and off the field. At times it had terrified her how much she needed him.

But even the comfort of his arms hadn't taken away the pain of Kim being diagnosed with cancer, and so she'd avoided his touch, anyone's touch, fearing she'd shatter into a million pieces and go mad.

"God, you still smell the same," he whispered. "I could never forget that smell."

His warm breath against her ear made the hairs on the back of her neck raise. Being this close, she could feel his heart pounding like he'd run a sprint—the rapid beat matching her own. Something liquid rolled through her belly, cradled against his hips as she was.

It had been *so* long.

Her body's longing for him shot across her pores, so strong she wanted to soak him up like parched earth to rainwater.

When he pressed a soft kiss to her head, an alarm chimed inside her head. Everything inside her was weakening, wanting to lean into him, wanting to open herself once more. She shoved again, fighting him in earnest now.

He reluctantly released her and walked to the back door. "I'm sorry I pushed you. I'm trying to be patient,

Nat."

His words stole any response from her, and she stood there, rubbing her arms to ward off the lingering scent and feel of him on her skin. The *temptation* of him.

"The guys are coming this weekend. I don't suppose I can talk you into making your cheese dip for us."

The abrupt change in subject jarred her. He didn't need to tell her who was coming. His football buddies were always there for him, and for that, she was glad. "You expect me to make you guys food? You have to be kidding."

"Then can I have the recipe? I'll need to cram something in Jordan's mouth to stop him from freaking out about me retiring."

His friends had always been so much fun to be around. None of them were married except for Blake, but they'd always made her feel welcome, and she'd enjoyed making them drool over her cooking. They'd reached out to her after the divorce, but she hadn't replied. Now it was all coming back to her very doorstep.

"I can give you the recipe," she said, "but I can't imagine you being able to make a white sauce."

"Well, if I can't pull it off, I can call you."

His strategy was becoming all too clear. "Blake, this whole thing is crazy," she said, throwing out her hands in frustration. "You simply cannot stay here forever and live next door to me."

"No, I'm hoping this two-house arrangement will be short-lived, and you'll let me sweep you off your feet again."

God, could her heart hammer any harder in her chest? "You never swept me off my feet."

"Sure I did, babe, and you delivered the greatest sack of my life, the moment I saw you."

Her fingers itched to touch the sandy blond hair at

his temples, so she clenched her hands into fists. "What are you going to do here, anyway?"

He gave a lop-sided smile. "Oh, I didn't tell you earlier, did I?"

And as he laid out his plan for her, she felt her heart squeeze in her chest—an almost painful sensation. So, he wasn't taking some cushy job as a sports commentator. God knew there were standing offers. But this...it was all so dear. How many times had she watched him throw the football around with Adam in the backyard and "pretend" tackle him?

Adam had been a shining light—a wonderful soul who saw the world differently from everyone else. Her last conversation with him had been an ugly argument. He'd come by her place to talk with her after her breakup with Blake. He'd been so angry with her—an unusual emotion for him—and deeply hurt. He'd begged her to talk to Blake, going on and on about how much Blake loved her. How destroyed he was by the way she'd up and left.

She'd never spoken to him after that day. And now he was gone too. She had to breathe through the wild emotions coursing through her veins like quicksilver.

"I mean it when I say that I am sorry about Adam. I am." She stomped her foot to punctuate her statement. "But you make me feel like I'm kicking a puppy when you come over here and talk about us getting back together. You're putting...too much pressure on me. I don't want to hurt you...more than you're already hurting." She could see the evidence of sleepless nights in the shadows under his eyes.

"I know you're sorry about Adam, babe, and I know you're upset about me moving here. So, why don't we just try and be friends again? That's how we started our relationship, and I think it would be good for us. Will you be my friend again, Natalie Hale?"

His guarded expression told her that he was

expecting rejection. That look on his face was enough to crack the ice at the core of her. "Okay. We can be *friends.*"

He released a long breath. "Good. Good." He leaned down to give Touchdown a swift rub and then opened the back door.

"Blake," she called out as he was leaving.

Turning, he gave her a sad smile. "What?"

"How about you hire The Grand Mountain Hotel to cater any food you want for when the guys show up? That way..." Oh, this was so awkward, she couldn't meet his eyes. "That way, I can make the cheese dip and anything else you might want with my staff...in a more official capacity." As a peace offering, it was the best she could do.

"That's a mighty nice offer," he said hoarsely, clearing his throat. "Thank you."

Her heart was beating so fast she could barely catch her breath. "I'll...draw up a contract once you make up a list of what you want."

"That sounds great. I'll sketch something out. You two have fun. I'll see you soon."

His broad back faded through the glass door, and she sank onto a nearby chair, awash in messy emotions threatening her control. She could feel the madness breathing down her neck.

You have to stay numb, you have to stay numb, she repeated over and over as she lowered herself to the kitchen floor and started to scrub.

CHAPTER 7

Facing down the Hale clan and all its adopted members took guts. Natalie arrived at Matt's house late to ensure everyone else was already there. As she'd expected, conversations started to lag the instant she closed the door behind her. Whether she was ready or not, it was time to face them.

Moira and Caroline reached for each other's hands, and when her nephew, Danny, made a move toward her, her brother, Andy, put a hand on his chest and kept him in place. Their eyes met, and she knew he was going to speak his mind to her—and she also knew she wouldn't want to hear it. Her mom came out of the kitchen with Matt, who clapped his hand on her shoulder in solidarity.

They were all on Blake's side. She could feel it. Even Matt now. Well, the speech she'd rehearsed while cleaning every tile of every floor in her house would hopefully put a stop to any future meddling.

"Can I have your attention, please?" she called out to the people in the den.

Others strolled in from the kitchen to see what was going on. She watched as Terrance emerged in the doorway, wiping his hands on his black apron, and gave her a nod.

"As I am sure you've all heard by now, my ex-husband, Blake Cunningham, has moved to Dare Valley. Next door to me, actually. We've agreed to be friends. As for his other thoughts about us, well, that's Blake. Some of you know him. Others don't. He's a great guy, who just suffered a huge loss, and I don't want things to be awkward. I don't want you to take my side; I don't want there to be *any* sides, although there usually are in divorce. I just want you to give us our space. It's...cleaner that way."

There was a burn under her ribs as she said those words. What she really wanted to say was that she didn't want them to try and influence her when she already felt like she was bobbing along on a raft in the middle of the ocean. She caught sight of her mom's frowning face and forced herself to continue.

"This whole situation is unusual, I'll admit. There may be press arriving in town since Blake's retirement was such a big deal, and you might be contacted due to your relationship with me. I wanted to warn you about that so you can refrain from commenting."

"Are you warning us about *pesky* journalists?" her Uncle Arthur barked out, leaning on his cane. "Does that include me?"

The relief she felt that someone had finally broken the silence allowed her to release the breath she'd been holding. "Yes. You most of all, you stinker. Don't expect me to give you an exclusive for *The Western Independent*. I love you, Uncle Arthur, but not that much."

"Well, shoot. You've crushed an old man."

She wanted to kiss him right then and there for lightening the mood. Danny looked confused, and no one else had cracked a smile, but at least some of the crushing pressure in the atmosphere had eased up.

"Blake is here to run a football camp for kids with intellectual disabilities as a tribute to his brother," she told them, having decided to share all the information she had in one fell swoop in the hopes of staving off more questions later. "It's a wonderful thing he's doing, and I'm happy he's doing it."

Suddenly a memory of Adam laughing flashed through her mind, and she felt a sharp pang of grief, which only saddened her more. Blake had always said that she and Adam laughed the same way—with their whole hearts and bodies.

Something cracked in the silence, making everyone turn their heads away from her. Natalie's cousin, Jill, darted over to pick up the rattle her daughter, Mia, had tossed onto the hardwood floor. Hitching the baby up on her hip, she patted her on the back.

Natalie cleared her throat and stood there awkwardly. The whole room was back to staring at her. "That's...ah...all."

Hell. That had felt worse than reciting the Declaration of Independence in a school talent competition in the third grade.

"Okay, people," Jill called out. "Natalie's said her piece. Let's get back to the feast."

The relief made her sway a little. Jill wove through the crowd and pulled her into a hug with the drooling Mia.

"Thanks, Jill," she whispered.

"Hey! It's okay. I remember how weird it felt when Brian came back from the Big Apple. And we didn't even have a marriage behind us. If you need anything, I've got you."

"You're a life saver," she said. Jill was quickly becoming her favorite family member. Why couldn't everyone else be this supportive, this understanding?

"Can I be a green one?" her cousin quipped.

Though Natalie rolled her eyes, she couldn't hold

back a smile. Mia grabbed a hunk of her hair and shoved it in her mouth, which only made her smile grow broader. The baby was super sweet—all chubby cheeks and sparkling eyes. "Can I hold her?" she asked. If she was holding a baby, no one could talk serious to her, right?

"Sure," Jill said immediately, transferring her into Natalie's arms. "Brian has her twin in the kitchen. He and Terrance were running Jane through another blind wine tasting. I swear, that girl needs to be on a wine game show or something. She could win millions."

Of course, Natalie's future sister-in-law already had millions, and her ability to discern the winemaker and year of a French vintage by simply drinking a sip was a hobby. Or a skill. Natalie still wasn't sure which.

"Hey, Sis," Matt said as Jill wandered off. He kissed her cheek and squeezed her arm. "Ah...Andy and I went to see Blake."

"Blake told me. Let's not talk about it now." Or ever. She'd rather talk about the new bumper sticker she'd slapped on his car, directly over the last one, in their ongoing Bumper Sticker War. This one said: *I Pick My Nose, and I Like It.* It seemed suitably unprofessional for the next mayor of Dare Valley.

He nodded. "I can respect that." And then, with a smile, "I'm going to go have a good pick."

Jane stepped forward and pulled her into a hug, baby and all. "We missed you at the lunch, but I totally understand why you weren't there. What a shock it must have been to have Blake move in next door."

"Blake always was full of surprises."

"Well, if you need to talk to anyone, you can count on me."

"Thanks, Jane." Her future sister-in-law was a peach.

Danny finally ran over to her, and she awkwardly leaned down to hug him with her left arm, keeping Mia snuggled in her right. "Hey, kiddo."

"Is Uncle Blake really back?" he asked with wide eyes. "And Touchdown too?"

By rights, five-year-old Danny shouldn't even remember Blake, but his love for that sweet dog, along with the fact that Blake had been the quarterback of his favorite team, had stuck with him. Danny was a huge football fan, following in her family's footsteps.

"It's Mr. Cunningham now, Danny," she said gently. "He's not your uncle anymore."

His mouth scrunched up like he was trying to remember why that was. "Oh, that's right. Because you don't live with him anymore."

Simple logic, thanks to Andy. "Right."

"Okay. Can you put Mia down so I can play with her? She likes my trucks."

Her human shield gurgled as Danny tickled the exposed section of her tummy. How was she supposed to refuse such a request? She set Mia down, and the little girl immediately crawled to Danny.

"She's trying to stand," Danny said, putting his little arms around her to support her as she grabbed his legs.

Mia stood, sure enough, clutching Danny's shirt, and wove in place in her pink ballerina slippers. Her grin was contagious.

"Hang onto her tight, Danny," Andy said from behind her. "Little kids sometimes let go because they're still learning."

"I've got her, Dad," Danny said, his arms gripping her now like he was holding a human hot potato.

"Hey, Sis," Andy said in an easy tone, hugging her and kissing her on top of her head. "You've had quite a day."

She could tell he wanted her to give Blake another chance, so she hadn't known what to expect from him. His relaxed demeanor was enough to tumble at least one of her walls. "Yes," she only replied.

"Come on, let's grab you a drink, which you could probably use. Then we'll make the rest of the rounds so you can eat."

Like she could force any food into her churning stomach. But a drink sounded good. She looked around for her mother, but April Hale was nowhere in sight. Her mother loved Blake—always had. She'd even caught her wearing Blake's Raiders jersey on a few game days. Her mom was probably biding her time, waiting to express her disapproval in private.

Terrance met them halfway to the kitchen, as if he'd been waiting for her and Andy to stop talking. Even though he was technically her boss, they were also good friends. At work she called him Chef T like everyone else, but outside of it, he was simply Terrance.

"Hey," he said, bussing her cheek. "Sounds like you went nine rounds today. How about I make you a Manhattan? I brought my Luxardo cherries."

All cherries were relatively equal, she'd once thought. Then Terrance had introduced her to Luxardo cherries. Like the name, they were exotic and magical and oh so good. She might have eaten half a jar one night—all by itself. "Andy was just talking about finding me a drink. Make it strong."

He winked. "You got it."

"I'm going to learn how the master makes a Manhattan," her brother said, and the two headed into the kitchen together.

With no excuse to follow them, she made the rounds alone, hugging her increasingly pregnant cousin, Meredith, and kissing her hubby, Tanner, on the cheek. Terrance's fiancé, Elizabeth, squeezed her hand and offered her a sweet consolation about men moving to Dare Valley with ideas. Hadn't Terrance done the same with her?

Rhett, their crazy Southern transplant, lifted her off the ground, making her almost squeal like a little girl.

"Sugar, you just say the word. I've heard tell that I'm the only one bigger and taller than your ex in this crowd. If I can't bleed him dry at the poker table, I'll call him out if he so much as makes a wrong move."

"And I'll hold his jacket," his wife, Abbie, said, patting her small baby bump.

"Well, *I'll* bring my shotgun," Deputy Sheriff Peggy McBride said.

"And *I'll* hold her jacket," her husband, Mac Maven, said, giving her a wink. "My wife doesn't mess around."

She hugged all of them, even Mac, who was her big boss. As owner of The Grand Mountain Hotel and a number of other hotels, she worked technically for him even though Terrance was her daily supervisor and partner in crime, as he liked to call himself. When she went to work on Monday, she'd talk to Terrance and Mac about her agreement to cater Blake's little party. It was something she wanted to do, even if her motivations made her a bit queasy. She knew they'd be fine with it, and she didn't plan to say much more than that she was helping out a friend.

Moira and Caroline kept their distance, lingering across the room from her, and for that reason alone she could barely take a swallow of the Manhattan Terrance brought to her, Andy by his side, gushing about how ridiculously good the cherries were. It was funny to hear two grown men act so excited about cherries—as delicious as they were—but Natalie didn't feel much like laughing when she saw her mother frowning at her from across the room.

"Drink up and go talk to her," her brother said. "You'll feel better."

She wasn't sure about that. The Manhattan wasn't as delicious as usual since her taste buds seemed to have dried up, but it was strong. Fortifying. Deciding it was finally time to take her medicine, she left the guys and headed over to where her mom was standing beside

Uncle Arthur, who was sitting in one of Matt's recliners.

He smacked his knee. "Save the best for last?" he quipped with an endearing grin.

Close to eighty, her great uncle was still witty and fun, not to mention one of her favorite people in the world. "Of course." She leaned down to kiss his wrinkly cheek. "Even if you are a pesky journalist."

"Just tell those national reporters 'no comment,' and if they press you, hang up on them. It's their job to be pushy and nosy. I should know. That's how I've trained my staff to be." He laughed.

"Hi, Mom," Natalie said awkwardly, daring a glance at her.

"Hey, honey," she said and rose to hug her. "I'm glad you came. Why don't we step outside for a breath of air?"

Her mom had never needed to step outside for air before, but the grip she gave Natalie's hand warned her not to refuse. Torches flickered in the backyard around the patio. The ring of fire felt appropriate. She was the poor, sap of a lion about to be whipped by a lion tamer.

April Hale didn't smile as she closed the door—she only gazed at Natalie gently, the soft wind blowing the gray hair she wore cut to her chin. "I heard what happened. Come here, honey."

"I'm fine, Mom, really," she said, patting her back, wanting to push away.

Her mom squeezed her. "No, you're not, and it's time we stop dancing around this. Blake might have brought things to a head by moving here, but it's been a long time coming."

Now she did push away and had to squint as the western sun came out from a cloud in all its piercing glory. "Mom, please don't do this. I'm handling it."

"Are you?"

The gates to her inner fortress lifted as she felt the siege begin. She crossed her arms over her chest, ready to do battle. "Mom, I didn't say a word when you left Dad, but have you *handled* things with him?"

"Since I know you only become mean and vindictive when you're upset, I'll ignore that." She put her hands on her hips. "If you must know, I pretty much did exactly what Blake did with you. I asked your father to talk to me. When that didn't work, I suggested marital counseling. After receiving the cold shoulder for three months, I told him I was leaving if he wasn't willing to work on our marriage."

Her hand gripped the doorway as she reeled in shock. It was the most detail she'd heard about her parents' split. "Mom, I'm sorry."

She shook her head. "When he went to the hospital and stayed there for three days, only coming home to change clothes, I made good on my promise. I hate saying this Natalie, but I love you too much not to speak up. You're more like your father than you want to admit. When you're hurting, you go off in your separate corner and become...unreachable. And you have no idea how hurtful that can be."

Her harsh intake of breath came from the part of her heart that had been wounded by her mother's words. "I'm sorry you think that, Mom," she made herself say. "I'm sorry you're disappointed."

This time when her mom wrapped her arms around her, she couldn't make herself return the embrace. Her arms hung by her sides like they didn't know what to do.

She was like her father? It couldn't be true!

"I'm not disappointed in you, and you don't have to apologize to me, honey. But you're not happy. You've put on a brave face for the past couple of years, but you're not over Kim's death, and the way you left things with Blake...well, it needs resolution. For both of you. I'm glad he's here, even if losing Adam—God rest that poor boy's soul—was part of the reason. Besides, he's given up a lot to come to Dare Valley."

Everyone *was* on Blake's side and not hers. It wasn't fair! She stared unblinking over her mom's shoulder. Usually Dare Valley's natural beauty delighted her, but all she wanted to do was pack her things and move back to Denver. Today. The urge to run was like a desperate hand pushing on her back.

"I know what I'm saying is hard for you, but honey, I only want you to be happy."

Why was everyone talking about being happy all of a sudden? Life wasn't happy all the time. Good people got sick and died for no reason. Like Kim. Like Adam. None of it made any sense.

"Please say something, Natalie," her mom whispered.

"I don't know what to do," she finally admitted. "I don't know what to say to any of you right now. All I feel is wrong and confused and upset, and I hate that. I hate that you're all making me feel that way."

Her mom put her hand on her arm in that Mom Touch no one else in the world could duplicate. It was like liquid sunshine pouring into her veins. Her eyes burned as a pocket of jagged emotion rose up inside her, melting away the icicles in her wasteland. She wanted to shy away from it out of instinct, but she needed it. A few seconds of warmth wouldn't kill her, would it?

"We're not trying to make you feel like you're in the wrong."

"Why didn't any of you talk to me about this before?" she asked, her voice rising.

Her mom gave a loud sigh. "We tried. Don't you remember? But you told us to leave you alone. You didn't talk to me for three days. Honey, we saw how you pushed Blake away. I was scared to lose you. We all were."

She loved her family. This conflict was killing her. Without them, she didn't know where she belonged in the world.

"Blake and I agreed to be friends," she said as a point of consolation. "I...know he's hurting from losing Adam." And she wanted to be there for him even if it was like walking a tightrope without a net below.

"That's a good start," her mom told her with a smile. "He'll need people around him to help him get through this. I called his parents when I heard about Adam. I wanted you to know that. And I want you to know I'm going to go say hi to him after Caro and Mo head back to Denver."

"I'm sure he'll appreciate that," she responded, and even she heard the coolness in her voice.

"Natalie, I love Blake and think he's a great guy, but you're still my daughter. I love you no matter what."

But was that really true? After all, her mom had just told her she was a lot like her father, and no one in the family was too fond of him at the moment.

"Thanks, Mom," she said, speaking over the part of her that was screaming: *Thanks? Seriously? She just took you to the woodshed, you idiot.*

"Make peace with your sisters. They only want what's best for you."

"I will." She had to. They were her best friends.

"Good." Her mom kissed her on the cheek, but there was something hesitant about the gesture. They'd lost the precious ability to be natural with each other, and Natalie's heart broke a little more.

As soon as they went inside, she sought out her sisters. They partially turned away, like they were expecting her to walk past them. Heart rapping hard in her chest, she bore her shoulders back and faced them down.

"I'm sorry," she whispered. "For what I said earlier. Please forgive me."

Caroline sighed and reached for her. She squeezed her eyes tight, letting herself enjoy the sensation of her sister hugging her tight. They were going to be okay.

"I'm sorry too. You're our sister and best friend. You have our support, whatever you choose."

She pressed her face into the curve of her neck. When she turned to face Moira, she immediately knew her younger sister wasn't going to be as forgiving.

"I really am sorry."

"I am too," Moira said, "but I hope you can understand where we were coming from."

So, Mo was going to hold her ground. Why wasn't she surprised? "I heard you. We'll just have to agree to disagree on it. I don't want it to hurt our relationship."

"It won't," Caroline said, sensing the fragile truth was being threatened.

Moira had a stubborn Irish streak a mile wide, and being in human resources, she knew how to speak her mind and handle conflict. Caroline, on the other hand, wined and dined nervous artists and prospective sellers at the art gallery where she worked in Denver. She was a pro at telling people what they wanted to hear to get her way, not that she was ever mean or under-handed about it.

"Can I simply ask that we not talk about Blake?" That was the only way she saw this working.

They exchanged a look.

"We won't ask if you won't tell," Moira said.

"What are you drinking?" Caroline asked to smooth over the increasing tension between them. "I saw Terrance bring you something special."

Now she could finally take a real sip of her drink, and she did. A healthy one. "It's a Manhattan with the most divine cherries in the world."

"I hate maraschino cherries," Moira said, and Caroline nudged her.

"Maraschino cherries give all cherries a bad name." Because they were her sisters, she fished out one cherry apiece for them. "Give these a try."

Caroline made a moaning sound. Moira's eyes

widened, probably at the bourbon, which wasn't her favorite, but then a pleasurable sound popped out of her mouth.

"What are you moaning over?" Jill asked, rushing forward. "Please, tell me. It's been a while."

"Red," her husband called out in an aggrieved voice. "Please don't make me come over there and give you something to moan about."

Jill blew him a kiss. "I love teasing him," she said conspiratorially. "It only makes him work harder when we get home."

Natalie snorted out a laugh. Her cousin had an uncanny ability to cut tension.

"Maybe you can steal Terrance's cherries and take them home with you," Natalie said, giving Jill a sly wink.

She linked their arms together. "I love where you're going with this. Come on. I can distract Terrance with my Latin moves, and you can steal his cherries. He slaps his hand over his eyes every time I do the salsa. The poor man can't stand me talking about the Latin dance lessons I gave him in his quest to win Elizabeth back."

"Probably because he felt humiliated," Natalie said, even though she'd been a happy spectator at the dance class where Terrance had strutted his stuff.

"It worked though, didn't it?"

As they walked to the kitchen, Natalie glanced back at her sisters, who had hung back. Moira was talking with her hands, and Caroline was nodding.

Sure, they were talking again, but all was not well. Not one bit.

CHAPTER 8

Blake was humming when he got home from a thirty mile bike ride up Sardine Canyon that had made his legs shake toward the end. Touchdown greeted him with happy barks. A sense of loss—heavy and deep—suddenly rolled through him when he realized what tune he was humming: the Raiders' fight song.

The sight of the pine trees crawling up the stone of the mountain, swaying in the gentle summer breeze, was beautiful, but paired with the stark quiet inside him, it reminded him of how drastically his life had changed.

There would be no more running out onto the field with his teammates to do battle as nearly 40,000 people cheered. There would be no more team practices, no more joking around with the guys between plays to keep things light. There would be no more two-minute drills, preparing the team to surge forth to victory when they were losing. The glory was behind him.

He looked at his hands, his best friends for most of his life. They weren't going to ache or cramp anymore from too many passing drills. They weren't going to feel electric as he palmed the ball before he launched a fifty-yard pass. God, what was he going to do with himself all day?

His football camp was only going to be one week in July. Sure, there were plenty of preparations to make, but his people would be doing much of the work under his guidance. What else could he do in Dare Valley? He'd risen at six o'clock to start his day for over thirty years. Now, he was up at the crack of dawn with nothing more to do than run ten miles, bike in the mountains, lift weights, and do some yoga. It wasn't enough. It wasn't going to be enough.

Even if Natalie... Correction. *When* Natalie came back to him, he would need to have more of a purpose.

Time.

He'd struggled against the clock for his entire professional career. He knew how long a minute or a second could be. How the action in that tiny speck of time could change an outcome.

He had too much time on his hands in Dare Valley and that had to change. Kelly had sorted through the offers that had come pouring in while he was in Vail, and new proposals continued to arrive by the hour. ESPN, Fox, and CBS had all wanted to meet with him to discuss a future as one of their NFL commentators. He'd turned them down nicely. He knew one thing for sure. He didn't want to *comment* on football.

Of course, there had been tons of endorsement offers, some of which he could do without too much hassle. And then there had been the offers to coach. His old high school in Ohio had said they'd love to have him as their head football coach, and while he appreciated that—and the twelve other high school offers—it would mean living somewhere other than Dare Valley.

He'd received offers to serve as an assistant offensive coach in both the college and professional leagues, but again, he'd have to leave Natalie to do it.

Part of him still wasn't sure he could make it as a

coach. He wanted to see how well the camp suited him first—whether the role fit his skin, so to speak. Once he knew, he could face the geography issues.

The most interesting job offer had come in from the Special Olympics. He'd been a long-time contributor, so they already knew a great deal about Adam. After hearing about his camp, they'd asked if he would consider becoming the lead athletic director for flag football for North America, working with the various state chapters. But again, the job was at their headquarters in Raleigh, North Carolina, and it would involve a fair amount of travel.

The truth was, he needed more time to see how things would shape out with Natalie. Right now, he wanted, *needed* to be close to her.

Once camp ended, he would allow himself to look toward the future. Or—and his heart sunk to the floor at the very thought—once it became clear he and Natalie weren't going to get back together.

He'd told Special Olympics that while he appreciated their offer, he was still trying to settle into his new life. They'd agreed to keep the door open for him and had offered their assistance with his football camp. Their support had meant the world, and he'd agreed to help them out with any smaller projects pro bono, so long as it didn't involve travel. They'd asked for his feedback on their new flag football manuals, and he was stoked. It was a start.

"All right, Touchdown. I'm finished moping." He smiled at his dog, who was busy chasing off a few squirrels. "Are you as thirsty as I am?"

The dog barked and scampered back to him. They were about to head inside when a blue Subaru pulled into his driveway. April Hale emerged from the vehicle with a soft smile on her face. Her salt-and-pepper hair was shorter than he remembered it, chopped to her chin, but it looked good on her. She wasn't wearing her ring, he noticed, and he supposed it was something they had in common now. His own ring sat on the table by his bed, waiting for the moment when Natalie would slide it on his finger once again. He was a firm believer in the power of positive thinking. Most days.

"Hi Blake," she said as she came across the gravel drive. "And hello Touchdown. Hope it's okay I came by." The dog rolled onto his belly immediately, and she gave him a few strokes before standing again.

"Of course, April. It's always good to see you."

He'd hoped she would come see him, but he'd realized it might be a pipe dream. April loved her kids first, last, and always, but she'd made room in her heart for Blake as another son.

"Blake, I was so sorry to hear about Adam. There are no words to say how much. He was such a dear man. I've been thinking about you and your parents a lot."

"Thanks," he said, feeling his throat grow thick. "That means a lot. Mom said you'd called. She and Dad were grateful to hear from you."

"No parent should have to bury a child. Come here, honey," she said and hugged him.

She was at least four inches shorter than Natalie, so he had to lean way down to hug her. Touchdown nestled against his leg, sensing he needed the comfort. He wiped away a few tears and sniffed when he shifted away from her.

"Well, now... You're still looking fit as a fiddle, I see," she said, playfully pinching his bicep like she'd often done in the past, trying to bring some humor into the tense moment.

He shrugged his shoulder, playing along. When Kim had been in the hospital, there had been a steady stream of joking or teasing to lighten the mood. He and his family had done the same with Adam. Otherwise, the atmosphere would have been too oppressive to bear.

"My friends are wondering how soon I'll start to get

fat now that I'm not playing." Even he knew retirees lost some of their muscle mass, so he was trying to make peace with the change. No one could maintain the bulk of a professional athlete without *being* a professional athlete.

"I can't imagine you ever getting fat. Not that you wouldn't still be cute as a button with a few extra pounds around the middle like the rest of us." She patted the small rise of her belly.

"Come on, April. You've had five kids, and you still look fabulous. Will you come inside for a drink?"

"I'd love to," she said and followed him into the house. "How do you like it here? I imagine it's a big change from the Denver house."

Yeah, and he loved that place almost as much as he'd prized his first football. He planned to keep the house until he knew what his future held, but he would have to make a decision about it at some point. Without Natalie in it, it was like a faded old door, stripped of its original glory.

"This is fine."

In truth, none of this new house felt like him. It was almost like he was living in a hotel suite with four acres. He planned to build a new place once he and Natalie reconciled, or at least that's what he dreamed of doing. Sunlight streamed in through the skylights in the vaulted ceiling, and the mahogany wooden beams crossing the ceiling gleamed in various shades of brown and red. The architect of this two-story craftsman had favored an open-rustic floor plan. There were worse places to live.

"What can I get you? I have water, juice, beer."

"How about a beer?" she said and laughed when she saw his expression. "Just kidding. Water is fine."

He added a lemon to it to be fancier and grabbed one for himself too. Drinks in hand, they headed out to the open flagstone deck in the back, where they settled onto the comfy tan patio furniture arranged in a square near the grill station and fire pit. The hot tub gurgled softly off to the right.

"It's funny how different things are out here," she said "I don't know if I'd like the quiet. Or not being able to see another house. I'm a fraidy cat about remote places."

"But you grew up in Dare Valley."

"In town. Big difference." She took a half sip of her water, bobbled the glass, and rose out of her chair as it splattered on her cream capri pants. "Oh, I'm so clumsy."

She wasn't usually. Which meant she was nervous. "Let me grab a towel."

When he returned, she dabbed at the spot as best she could and finally laid the towel aside. "Well, you're here."

Only three little words, but they summed up his whole life right now. "Yes."

"I'm glad actually. I've been worried about Natalie for some time...ever since Kim was first diagnosed. She hasn't dealt with that—or leaving you. I can't say I'm not worried about how she's going to react to having you around, but I don't think the status quo is good enough for her."

No, it hadn't been for him either. Even football couldn't put a dent in the subterranean loss he'd felt when Natalie walked out of his life. The failure of Adam's health, and his eventual death, had only made it worse.

"There's already been some conflict in the family over your return. She fought with Moira and Caroline about you."

He held his tongue, not wanting to get into the internal Hale family dynamics. He'd known his return would put pressure on her relationships, but he hadn't seen another way.

"I talked to Andy and Matt."

"Yes, they told me." She reached for his hand. "I'm really happy to hear about your plans for this camp. Adam would be so proud. I bet your parents are too. It's already the talk of the town."

It surprised him more than it should have. The statement they'd released to the press had been picked up by national outlets. He'd wondered how the locals might react.

"I don't know if I can help in any way, but I'd like to do something," she told him, letting go of his hand with a gentle pat. "Maybe I can be a water girl."

He had to bite the inside of his cheek to keep from laughing, though it felt good to find humor in something. April Hale, a water girl? Now, that would be the day. But then he stopped to consider how his players would respond to a sweet, older lady. They might like it. "We're still outlining our needs, but I'll let you know."

"Good. I'm here on another errand as well. I was a bit surprised to be called, but since you were my son-in-law once..."

Now, she'd piqued his curiosity. God, he hoped it wasn't some fundraiser. He loved to support good causes, but he wanted to stay out of the public eye as much as possible at the moment, especially given how much Natalie seemed to dread gossip about their relationship.

"The head of the local school board called me to ask about your plans. I went to school with Cormack Daly way back, and he was always a big thinker, if you know what I mean."

He didn't, so he took a drink of his water and waited for her to continue.

"Cormack reminded me that the high school was looking for a new coach; he's head of the selection committee. They let the last guy go because the administration wasn't happy with the past couple of football seasons." She shook her head. "This is so silly. I can't even believe I'm asking you this."

Now he saw where this was going, and his heart started to race.

"He wanted to know if you might consider coaching the high school team. They were about to make an offer to someone else, but then you showed up, and they decided to hold off. I told him I didn't know your plans, but Cormack can be very bull-headed, and he insisted I ask you. If it's crazy, I can tell him that without blinking an eye."

A high school football coach *in Dare Valley?* He could stay close to Natalie. Then his belly knotted. "I don't have any coaching experience."

"Cormack didn't care about that. He said, and I quote, 'Quarterbacks lead men into battle, and if Blake Cunningham can lead the Raiders to the Super Bowl, he can lead a bunch of snot-nosed kids to the state championship.'"

"That was a pretty good imitation," he said even though he had no idea if Cormack sounded like he had a deviated septum.

"So what do you think?" she asked.

"Did he mention when they'd want the new coach to start?"

She shook her head. "No, but if they were already that far along in the hiring process, they probably want someone soon."

He frowned. His upcoming camp and Natalie were his two biggest priorities. And then there was the big question: did he want to coach? Could he be good enough at it to win? "Let me mull it over. My life...is still shaping up. I'm open to new possibilities."

"And Natalie will be here for the foreseeable future," she added with a twinkle in her eye.

"Yes, I know."

"So you're planning to stay?"

It was a question that kept him awake at night. How long *was* he willing to stay in Dare Valley if Natalie and he weren't together? Would there come a day when he was forced to accept there was no hope? He stopped those negative thoughts right in their tracks. He needed to stay positive. Like he had always been about his career, about a game, about...winning Natalie after that first night he met her.

"I plan on staying as long as it takes and giving it my all," he replied, his heart hammering in his chest.

She patted his leg and stood. "I figured as much."

He rose as well.

"You always did cast a long shadow, Blake," she commented, pointing to the Herculean one filling up most of the patio, beside which her own shadow seemed diminutive.

"Shadows are only illusions, April. It's a person's actual presence that counts."

"Hmm. You always were a wise boy."

Boy? He hadn't been called that in a while, but to her, he supposed it was true.

"April, do you have any advice for me? About Natalie?" He wasn't above asking for help, and her mother knew her in a way even he didn't.

"Don't back down. Natalie is so much like her father sometimes. I told her so the other day when we fought about you."

She'd fought with her mom too? She never fought with her mom—or her sisters. Poor babe had to be shaking like a leaf inside for this to happen.

"I don't envy you, Blake. She's a tough nut to crack. Out of all my children, she's the toughest, the most self-contained. You're going to have to get her to crack about Kim's death and her feelings for you if you want to give things another go. Neither will be easy."

Tension coiled in his chest like a snake waiting to strike. "I know. That's why I'm afraid I might fail."

Okay, he could confess that to her even if he didn't like to admit it to himself.

"Fail? I've never once heard you talk like that, even when you were playing ball. If you lost a game, you always chose your words so carefully. You would say the other team played better, but you never referred to yourself or the team as losers or failures." She kissed his cheek. "Remember that. I need to get back. I'm meeting some friends for a tennis game. Come by anytime you're in town. I live at 22 Aspen Street near the Community Center right off Main Street."

"I'm glad you came for a visit, April." He walked out with her. "I missed you. All of you."

As she opened her car door, she gave him a playful wink. "We missed you too, Mr. Fancy Pants."

He laughed as she closed the door and drove off. Natalie had started calling him Mr. Fancy Pants years ago. She'd made sure he knew how unimpressed she was with his status as an NFL quarterback, and to prove it, she'd boldly dubbed him Mr. Fancy Pants. The first time she'd brought him home to meet her Raiders-loving family, she'd broken the tension by using that nickname in her introductions to everyone. From that point on, he'd felt like an adopted Hale and not some star quarterback they cheered for every Sunday.

As he went inside, he found himself whistling. Mr. Fancy Pants needed to come up with some meal suggestions for his party this weekend so he could share the list with his sexy caterer.

Could he entice Natalie to do something friend-like when he swung by to drop off the list and pick up Touchdown? As he entered the den, he caught sight of the red plaid throw on the Italian leather couch, one of the few things he'd brought from Denver as a reminder of better times. An idea formed.

She couldn't refuse a trip down memory lane with her favorite book characters, and if it happened to remind her of the passionate sex life they used to have, what could it hurt?

Mr. Fancy Pants was on the case.

CHAPTER 9

One of the new nurses, fresh out of school, gave Andy a smile as he scrawled his name on the last chart on his rotation. She was interested in him and had made no bones about it. And she wasn't alone. Being a widower and single dad apparently only made him dreamier to his female co-workers at Dare Valley General Hospital. He'd overhead a few nurses say as much in the break room. Some people had watched too many episodes of *Grey's Anatomy*, if you asked him.

He'd never thought it was a good idea for doctors to date staff. When things went south, and often they did, simple interactions with patients could turn awkward, not to mention that a simple request for a scalpel during a surgery might be met with a frozen silence. None of that was fair to the patients who'd placed themselves in their hands.

Now that he was single—something of which he still needed to remind himself—he still didn't think it was smart to date anyone at the hospital. Not that he'd found anyone who tempted him. Sure, some of the female staff were funny and beautiful—or as beautiful as anyone could look in scrubs—but so far he hadn't felt any attraction.

He changed out of his scrubs into tan shorts, a green T-shirt, and an old pair of Birkenstocks. As he walked out of the hospital into the warm afternoon sunshine, he took a moment to breathe in the air and scan the mountains still dotted with patches of snow at the peaks. Summer hadn't completely melted away the cold vestiges of winter, but he understood that. Appreciated it. Time hadn't fully eased the pain of Kim's passing, and he expected it never would.

Some things weren't meant to fade. Certainly not the love of a lifetime.

But he knew that was his excuse for not trying to "get out there." He didn't expect to find someone he loved or was as attracted to as Kim. But recently, he'd been feeling the internal pressure to try a little harder to move on, to engage with life. He'd been doing his best to ignore it, but today, he was about ready to blast those doors open to help Natalie, and in doing so, himself.

His regular babysitter had agreed to stay a little longer with Danny so he could talk to his sister. His Lexus SUV climbed the road to the foothills where she lived with a purr. When he knocked on her door, he rubbed his stomach, hoping to ease the unsettled feeling in his gut.

Her normal smile of greeting didn't flash across her face when she opened the door. No, she had a guarded expression he understood all too well.

"I thought I'd give you a few days to settle," he said, not beating around the bush as Touchdown launched himself at him with a volley of wild barks. "Will you take a drive with me?"

He leaned down to give the Beagle a rubdown, wondering again if he should get Danny a dog. He'd been begging for one since Matt had gotten Henry. Keeping up with his son was a full-time job already.

A frown crested across her mouth. "Are we talking

about Blake?" She'd already changed out of her work clothes, into cutoff jeans and a white T-shirt, but she didn't look relaxed. No, not one bit.

"Yeah. And Kim."

Something flashed in her eyes. For a moment, he thought she'd refuse.

"Then I'll take my car."

Right. This way she could leave if she didn't like what he had to say. But at least she was coming. She gave Touchdown a pat and closed the door on him. He barked for a moment, but he quieted down quickly. When she didn't lock her house, he smiled. He'd stopped locking his doors too. Danny thought it was cool.

"I'll follow you," she said and headed to her car.

He'd chosen one of Kim's favorite places in the area for good luck: Black Lake. It was easily accessible by car, so they wouldn't have to hike a ways to it. Few people if any would be there since it wasn't accessible by one of the main trails. Kim hadn't been a hiker so much as a rabid picnicker. Sure, she'd hike, but she enjoyed being in nature too much to pass it all doing a power walk.

When they arrived at Black Lake, he took a waterproof blanket out of his rig and spread it out by the water's edge.

"I haven't been here in a while," she murmured, kicking off her shoes and sitting on the blanket.

He carefully retrieved the letter from his pocket and sat down beside her. Handing it to her was tough, so tough the sudden pressure in his chest made him feel like he was about to explode. She eyed it with curiosity, but when she opened it, her whole face fell.

"I want you to read it," he said in a hoarse voice and made himself lean back on his elbows in a pose of relaxation, something he definitely wasn't feeling right now.

He closed his eyes and recited the words to himself.

He'd read it so many times, he knew it by heart. Kim had asked him to open the letter on the first-year anniversary of her death, and it had broken him then. A year later, its effect hadn't lessened.

Dear Andy,

I asked you to open this letter today because it's now been a year since my death. I can't imagine what you've been through. After I learned I was sick, I would lie in our bed at night listening to you breathe and try and imagine how I would feel if you were the one who had cancer and died, leaving me alone with Danny. Even though imagining it created the most incredible agony inside me, the reality is probably much worse.

I knew it would hurt you too much if I tried to talk to you about finding someone else to love after losing me, so that's why I wrote this letter. A part of you probably still feels bound by the vows we made even though I'm not there anymore. While you may not want to hear it, and honestly I don't want to say it, I want you to find someone else to love.

You won't rush. That much I know. Heck, you didn't even rush when we first started dating and were so hot for each other. You always take your time. That's why you were meant to be a doctor. With every relationship, it's like you are always monitoring the vitals, the progress, looking for a change in the status.

I won't tell you to choose a good mother for Danny because I know you will. I won't even tell you to choose someone who makes you laugh because you'll find the right person for you. And why do I believe that? Because I believe in angels, and when I get to heaven and it's the right time, I'm going to ask God to let me come back and help you find the next woman of your heart.

I only ask that you let me.

This is hard to write, and I'm crying, partly because I know you're probably crying as you read this. But you'll know when you're ready to start being open again, putting yourself out there. As someone who had the privilege of being loved by you, no one knows better how much love you have to give.

Give it, my love, when the time comes.

I'll be there, rooting you on, wishing you every happiness always.

I love you,

Kim

When Natalie set the letter between them on the blanket, she turned her face away, but he saw her throat ripple as she stared up at the massive blue sky. She was fighting tears again. She always fought them, and today he didn't make any comments about the effect it had on the physical body, about how good it was to sometimes let go and give in to grief. Instead, he gave them both a moment to settle and waited for her to break the ice.

"When you brought me out here...that's not what I expected," she told him, still not looking at him.

"I've never shared that letter with anyone," he said, falling back onto the blanket and looking at the puffy clouds overhead.

Kim, if you can hear me, help me with Natalie right now. I need you.

The winds shifted the clouds, and he caught sight of a fleeting shape of an angel with wings before it disappeared. He was able to smile over the twinge in his heart. He didn't care if he'd imagined it.

"When you left Blake, I was so mad at you," he told her.

Now she gave him her complete attention, turning to stare at him with narrowed eyes. *"What?"*

"Until you told me about the whole baby thing, I thought, how in the world could you leave a man who loved you like that? How could you throw away all those years together after we'd all just learned how precious every moment is with the people we love? I was mad because you still had Blake, and I didn't have Kim anymore."

She drew her knees to her chest and rested her chin on them, staring straight ahead now.

"Before Kim died, she told me to watch out for you. It scared her to see the way you were locking everything up inside you. I wasn't...in a much better place...and when you left Blake...well, I couldn't focus on it. I believed he'd turned into some big douche bag after the story you told us. But that wasn't true, was it?"

Her head fell forward. "No, it wasn't. I'm a horrible liar, a terrible person. Are you happy now?"

Her hackles were spiking up more every minute, but instead of backing off, he scooted closer until their shoulders touched. "Blake still loves you, and he's worried about you. Can you really tell me, being completely honest now, that you don't fully understand what it meant for him to retire from football?"

"Of course, I know! I saw his elation after every day of a good practice. Saw him do a victory lap around our living room after a win. Watched him shut down for a day after a horrible loss, barely speaking."

He drew his knees up too. "You're not over Kim. I might not be either, but at least I've grieved her."

"Grieving her won't bring her back. You have your way of handling things, and I have mine. I...it's best not to dwell on the past."

"Dad always used to say that," he said, seeing her face flinch.

"Dammit, why is everyone comparing me to Dad all the sudden?" she spat out. "I'm nothing like him."

He wondered who else had made that comment, but decided not to ask. It wouldn't help.

"You know, when you met Blake, Kim told me he

was the best match in the world for you. He was still tough, which you'd respect, but he also ran on emotion, which you needed to balance things out in your relationship. My suspicion is Blake is the only one who truly knows how to unlock all the grief you feel for Kim, so you pushed him away out of self-preservation."

"Don't," she said softly. He could tell he was actually getting to her from the ragged sound of her voice.

"I showed you that letter from Kim because I'm willing to make you a deal. I'll start being open to finding someone new if you give Blake another chance."

"You're joking."

The crushing pressure was back in his chest, squeezing out all his breath. "No. I'm serious."

Her shoulder nudged him sharply. "Did you and Blake make some sort of pact?"

"No," he said immediately. "I only want to honor Kim. If she thought Blake was the best match for you, I'm going to do my part to help you reclaim that relationship. I didn't...before. I was going through my own crap and trying to be both father and mother to Danny."

His throat thickened. Most days, he didn't think he was doing very well with the mother part. How could a man hope to assume that role too? But Danny seemed to be thriving, thank God, and he knew Kim was being their son's angel in her own way.

He thanked God for that too.

"So, you think I should just up and take Blake back?" she said with steel in her voice.

Choosing his words carefully, he put his arm tentatively around her shoulder. "No, I think you need to give him a chance to remind you why you fell in love with him in the first place."

"And talk about what happened," she added, not leaning her head against his shoulder like she normally would.

"The talking part will happen, but first you need to let him back in. You said you've agreed to be friends again. God knows, he needs one after losing Adam and leaving football. Why not start there?"

"And you'll go on a date if I do this?" she asked, and he could hear the challenge in her voice.

"I agree to be open to finding a woman I *want* to date. When I find her, I'll ask her." He knew he had to be clear about his intentions. Just going out with someone wasn't what he wanted. Okay, he really didn't want to find anyone, if he were being honest, but reading Kim's letter again had helped confirm what he already knew somewhere inside. It was time to push his boundaries and try to be open to new experiences.

"Blake won't be content to be only my friend," she said. "He never was."

"That part is up to you," he told her, dropping his arm from her shoulder. "All we want is for you to be happy."

"Then why won't you guys leave me alone?"

"Because you're not really happy. You're letting life pass you by."

"You're not happy either."

He felt the punch of that truth in his solar plexus. "True, but I'm happier than you."

"You have Danny."

Now he saw the whole baby drama with Blake in a new light. Perhaps there had been a seed of truth in it after all. "You think having Danny made Kim's death hurt less for me?"

The quiet stole around them when she fell silent. He let it lengthen, unsure if she would answer him.

"I thought it might have helped," she whispered. "At least you have a piece of her in him."

He swiped at the tears in his eyes, thinking about how his heart stopped every time Danny smiled like his mother or made a gesture with his hands that reminded him of Kim. "We all have a piece of her in Danny, Nat."

This time she remained silent, and he knew she wasn't going to say anything else.

"Well, I should get back so I can give Danny a bath." His watch told him it was nearing six-thirty. The babysitter would have fed him by now.

He rose and offered her a hand, which she took. He didn't release it once they were both standing. "I love you, Nat."

She bit her lip and pulled away. "I love you too. Just...please give me some space about this."

She was already heading to her car as he folded up the blanket. "You've had too much space, Nat. Two whole years of it."

Her response was to slam the car door. He took a moment to enjoy the quiet. Between the hospital and Danny, he didn't have a lot of silence except in the darkness of the night. Silence during the day was spectacular, filled with the vibrant colors of blue, green, and brown. He didn't feel as alone in this silence.

Keep helping her, Kim. We have a long way to go.

As he left, he patted the letter he'd tucked back into his pocket. Natalie wasn't the only one feeling trepidation over the future. He'd never wanted to imagine a future without Kim, but it appeared he would have to start.

He always kept his promises, even when they broke his heart.

CHAPTER 10

When Natalie heard someone rapping their knuckles in a peppy tune on her back door, she knew it was Blake. She took a moment to compose herself.

She'd spent an hour rearranging the items in her kitchen pantry after her chat with Andy, but it hadn't done much to shove Andy's concerns to the back of her mind. In fact, she was having a tough time receding to the quiet, numb place she ran to whenever she became too frazzled, too charged with emotion.

The sweet dog was already at the door, barking with animation, pawing excitedly at the frame. Blake smiled at her when she opened the door. The alluring scent of truffle fries hit her nose, followed by the char of hamburger, and she looked down at the picnic basket he was carrying.

"Did you eat at Ajax earlier?" she asked.

"Without you?" He shook his head. "No, I haven't been back there since we went together. But Aspen is only forty minutes away, so I thought I'd bring you something special as a way of saying thanks for agreeing to do the catering this weekend."

He opened the picnic basket—she recognized it as

the one she'd bought for them when they were dating. She tried not to think of how thoughtful it was that he'd brought one of her favorite possessions from their home. Inside lay her favorites: the tavern's signature cheeseburger and truffle fries.

"The chef said you could broil the fries to make them crispy again," he told her.

A flash of pain tore through her chest. "Thank you."

He dug into the basket for a stainless steel frozen container—something else she'd bought for them—and thrust it out to her. "Open it."

When she did, her knees went weak. "You brought me their salted caramel and banana milkshake?" Hadn't she just eaten a few of her secret stash of caramels in the laundry room after coming home from Black Lake?

His smile was lop-sided. "It *is* your favorite. And I stopped at the Rocky Mountain Chocolate Factory and bought you an English toffee apple."

Now she was deeply suspicious. "But you never approved of me eating that much sugar…" She bit off the words *when we were together*.

He barked out a laugh. "I was full of myself. I just want you to be happy, and little makes you happier than food."

Andy's words came back to her like a wave, powerful and impossible to fight. Blake *did* want her to be happy. Maybe it was time to stop fighting that quite so hard. "Thank you," she repeated, her throat clogged with emotion.

The smile turned into a besotted grin, the one she remembered from their courtship. He was embarrassed, but happy to have pleased her.

"And I brought *Outlander* on Blu-Ray. I was hoping we could have dinner and watch a few episodes together." He bounced on the heels of his feet as he awaited her decision.

Outlander? Memories swirled around her like a

powerful hurricane. She'd read the bestseller in high school and had immediately fallen for Jamie, the sexy, soulful Highlander hero…just like her mother, who'd passed the book along to her, and the rest of the global population who'd read it. The book was one she turned to whenever she needed a quick fix after a crappy day. She remembered the day Blake had finally asked her about it in bed.

She'd shared the whole story with him, and then, without intending to, she poured out her fantasies about Jamie. Always keen on pleasing her, Blake jumped out of bed to claim the red plaid throw she'd bought for the downstairs couch. When he returned, it was tied around his corded waist.

They weren't the Fraser colors, but it didn't matter. And she didn't even laugh when Blake uttered the worst Scottish accent imaginable. Later her laughter died completely when he kissed his way down her body and made love to her with the kind of intensity she'd always imagined between Jamie and Claire.

Jerking herself out of her reverie took effort. Her heart was drumming in her chest now, and there was a pool of lust in her belly. Blake's gaze was hot, and she knew he was remembering it too.

"I'm only suggesting we watch the show, Nat," he said quietly, but his body language told her a different story.

No, he wanted her to remember. His nostrils were slightly flared, and the pulse in his neck was beating strong. Despite working for Mac Maven, she wasn't a gambling woman, but if she took the picnic basket away from his waist, she was sure she'd see evidence of his arousal.

Her breath stopped in her lungs.

"It's a start," he said in a gentle voice, one that told her he wouldn't ask for more unless she wanted it.

He'd never pushed for more while he was marooned

in her friend zone all those years ago. Sure, he'd looked at her with longing and lust plenty of times, but he'd always honored her wishes. She was the one who'd finally leaned in to kiss him one night as the credits to *The Mirror Has Two Faces* scrolled down his big-screen TV. He'd watched one of her favorite chick flicks without protest—like it was the biggest prize in the world. And that was it for her. Her control fell away, and she'd poured all the yearning and desire she'd repressed into their first kiss.

"Okay, you can stay. We can watch the first couple episodes." She'd already watched them all, of course. And it would be safe. Jamie and Claire didn't kiss until much later in the series, when they were married. Now that was one episode she could not watch with Blake. She'd go up in flames if she sat there watching it with him, remembering how much joy she'd always found making love with him.

At least until Kim's diagnosis. Then, she hadn't wanted anyone to touch her, least of all Blake, and sex had become awkward and strange between them until he'd stopped trying to comfort and reach her that way.

"Did you already eat?" she asked, not seeing his favorites in the basket.

He set it down on the kitchen island. "I got myself a Cuban sandwich and some veggies while I was there. I...ah...left them at the house. I'll just run and get them, if that's okay."

So, he hadn't assumed she'd succumb to his invitation. She felt her lips curve into a smile before she made her mouth go flat again. "I'll grab some plates and warm up my fries."

"Good. Great." His head bobbed like he realized he was overdoing it. "Be right back."

He ran off, so eager he left the back door open. Touchdown raced after him. She watched Blake through the windows. Good God, he was moving so fast he looked like he was running the option to score a touchdown.

Her heart careened in her chest, and she spun into action, crossing to the stove to flick on the broiler and set the table. No, she decided, setting the table would be too weird and date-like. Better to eat on the couch and start the show right away. That way there'd be less talking.

She wasn't sure she could handle more talking.

When Blake returned, he wasn't even breathing hard. Poor Touchdown headed for his water bowl and slurped greedily. Blake stood in her kitchen with his take-out bag in his hands, shifting his feet like he was unsure of himself.

Well, join the club, she wanted to say, but she ignored her own unease by checking on her sizzling French fries.

"What would you like to drink?" she asked.

"I'm good with water."

She shut the oven and opened the cabinet to the right of the sink, but he stepped in and took the glass before she could grab it.

"You don't need to wait on me. Keep your eyes on the fries."

Picking up a spatula, she opened the oven again to turn them. "Yeah, I'd be heart-broken if they burned."

"I'd drive up there to get you some more," he said, filling his glass with water from the tap.

Her throat closed, and she stirred the fries quickly, trying not to analyze the funny feeling in her heart. When the fries were done, she grabbed a potholder and took them out and set them on the granite countertop. Blake reached a hand out playfully, watching her face, waiting to see if she would slap it away—an old game they played. He would order a salad or veggies and steal some of her French fries. She let him have a couple, and his grin spread as he popped them into his mouth.

"Never imagined anything could taste so good."

Hmm...that was a euphemism if she'd ever heard one. "Are you planning to succumb to the food dark side now that you've left football?" she asked before she thought better of it.

His grin faded, and she could tell he had to force a smile to return to his face. "Some would say I have to be even more careful now that I'm not burning five to six thousand calories a day."

That number had always boggled her mind. She was lucky to burn two thousand in her most strenuous workouts.

"Like you'd ever get fat," she said.

"Your mom said the same thing." He finally set his take-out bag on the counter, like he'd only just decided she would let him stay. "She visited me today. I wanted you to know."

She ate a French fry, hoping it would counterbalance the bitterness in her mouth. It didn't completely. She scooped the fries onto a plate and claimed her burger from the insulated compartment in the basket.

"I had them keep the bun separate so it wouldn't get soggy on the bottom. I know how you hate that."

That familiar intimacy with him was weaving itself around her. Dangerous and yet tantalizing. "Thanks."

She handed him a plate, and he unwrapped his Cuban. Sure enough, he had paired it with the spinach and pear salad, which *was* delicious, and their roasted beets with pistachios.

"I thought we could watch the first episode while we eat," she said as she finished assembling the burger on her plate.

"Sure. Is the silverware where you always kept it?"

She paused for a moment, feeling tension settle between her shoulder blades. "Yes."

He pulled open the cabinet to the right of the sink and procured two sets for them. "Can I grab anything else for you?" he asked, picking up her plate and his own, balancing his water in the crook of his massive arm.

God, the bulge of muscle there made her want to trace the angles and curves all the way to his shoulder.

"No. I'll just...put the milkshake in the freezer." *Put myself in the freezer.* "I'll probably only drink half of it anyway. Since you brought the caramel apple." God, she was going to be sick after all this sugar.

"I'd be impressed if you could manage both. Can Touchdown sit on your couch while we eat?"

The dog barked, hearing his name. They'd had a power pull over that in the early days of their marriage. She hated having dog hair on their expensive cream-upholstered sofa, but Blake loved to watch game tape with Touchdown on his lap. Ultimately, she was the one who'd caved, though she'd insisted he take over vacuuming the couch, which he'd done. Sometimes. Unless he let the cleaning lady do it.

"Ah...he can sit on it."

So far she'd kept him off the couch, but tonight was different. If Touchdown sat next to Blake, she wouldn't have to sit next to him. It was going to be hard enough to keep her eyes off his freaking gorgeous legs. No one had better legs than Blake, not even Beyonce. His massive thighs were thick with muscle, making his legs a portrait of angles and ridges designed to inflame the senses. His legs had been her downfall, and the khaki shorts he was wearing did nothing to hide their masculine beauty.

She followed them into the den after grabbing a glass of red wine and some water. When she reached the couch, she discovered Blake had already outfoxed her. Touchdown sat on his right, leaving the middle seat for her. She set her glasses down on the teak coffee table and laid out the red napkins she'd tucked under her arm.

"I wasn't sure how to run your entertainment center."

She turned everything on, then put the disc in and hit play for the first episode. After settling back onto the couch, she picked up her hamburger and bit in, unable to contain a moan.

"Glad you like it," he said, laughter in his voice. "I always loved how much you enjoy food."

More dangerous territory. She didn't need him telling her all the things he used to love about her. "How's the sandwich?"

"As good as I remembered. Feel free to have some salad or beets."

"You're only saying that so you can steal more French fries."

He plucked one off her plate with a grin. "Only a few."

She made herself turn her attention from his sparkling brown eyes to the television and prayed the show could distract her from the surrealness and sweetness of eating a meal with Blake again, vegging out in front of the TV. Just the three of them like old times.

They watched in silence, munching on their food. Her hand stole onto his plate to grab the beet and pear slices he'd saved for her. When he didn't reach for the fries she'd left him, she placed them on his plate. He muttered his thanks and kicked back with his feet propped on the coffee table, giving her a way-too-tantalizing view of his legs. Of course, he knew how she felt about his legs, so she wondered if he'd done it on purpose. But when she looked at him from the corner of her eye, he seemed engrossed in the show. He was idly stroking Touchdown, she noticed, who lay on his right leg, a content expression on his furry face.

Jerking her attention back to the show, she watched the first meeting between Jamie and Claire. Blake winced when the nurse set the Highlander's dislocated shoulder. She watched as he rubbed his left shoulder, the one he'd dislocated in a game against the Washington Warriors. He'd taken a deadly sack after airing the ball out forty yards for a touchdown that led to a last-minute win. She had to fist her hands in her lap to keep from rubbing that shoulder in comfort like she'd done so many times in the past.

"You'd better grab your shake," he said, noticing she'd finished her food.

Pausing the show, she rose and poured half the shake into a glass, leaving the other half for tomorrow. She'd already overeaten, but she didn't care. And she wasn't going to feel bad about enjoying two desserts. She was so not including her earlier candy binge in her count.

When the first episode finished, she hit play for the next one—afraid to disturb the peaceful silence between them. Even though her bladder was screaming, she didn't move to relieve it. Touchdown was snoring softly by the end of the second episode, and when the credits rolled, she reached for the remote.

"Maybe we can watch the next one some other time," Blake said before she could decide whether to stop or hit play. "You have to go to work in the morning."

He'd always been good about that. He had never asked her to wait for him to shower and dress and talk to the press after his late evening games. Sometimes she'd be asleep when he finally did get home, but he wouldn't wake her up to talk about the game. He'd save everything he wanted to discuss for when they were both home the next day—even if it was only for a few hours because of his hectic schedule.

Without asking, Blake stacked their plates and glasses and rose, leaving her with nothing to sweep up except a few stray bread crumbs.

He drew a folded piece of paper from the pocket of

his shorts as they walked back into the kitchen together. "Some ideas for your menu and times for our meals."

Their truce was so delicate she could only nod and watch him set it on the kitchen island.

"They stuck pretty well to the book, don't you think?" he asked, loading the dishes into the dishwasher.

The paper towel she'd grabbed to wipe down the counters fluttered to the floor. "How would you know that?"

He lurched forward to pick it up and handed it to her. "I...ah...read the series."

Her hand curled around the paper towel. "You did? When?"

Okay, that was a stupid question. She watched with some helplessness as red stained his ears.

"After you left. I...ah...was trying to see if Jamie could give me any ideas about winning you back."

The paper she was holding crumbled in her fist. *Oh, Blake.* She thought back to what Andy had said...how Kim had believed Blake was the best possible match for her. What other man would read his ex-wife's favorite romance novel to look for relationship clues?

"And Jamie did," he added in a voice rough with emotion. "He came back to Claire and laid his heart at her feet even after she made it clear she didn't want him anymore. He bared his soul to her and asked her to forgive him."

The vibration of her rapidly beating heart shattered every wall of numbness she'd enclosed herself in, and raw, oozing hurt poured out.

His brown eyes were both hopeful and wary when they met hers. "I hope some day you'll forgive me too. I'd better be going."

As he walked to the door to open it, he whistled for Touchdown, who awoke with a snort and leaped off the couch to join him. "Do you want Touchdown to stay for another day or two? You haven't had him for so long…"

No, and she hadn't had Blake in her life for so long either. This one night had been a stark reminder of all those lonely and awful evenings she'd spent alone in front of the television, trying to forget a past she could never completely erase.

"No, we had a deal." A pressure was rising in her chest. She couldn't let him leave like this. Not after tonight. "Blake, there's nothing to forgive."

A harsh sigh crested out from him, and his hand clenched on the door he was about to close. "There has to be something. Otherwise, you wouldn't have left like that."

Before she could muster a thought—even process what he'd said—he was striding across the yard in the moonlight to that bridge he'd built, the one he hoped would bring them back together. Their sweet little dog pranced behind him.

She sank down into the middle of the kitchen, the smell of truffle fries still strong and sweet in the air. He thought he'd done something wrong?
Of all the hurts she'd borne, that one she could not abide.

CHAPTER 11

Sam Garretty had a knack for knowing what Blake needed, so it didn't surprise him when his friend arrived two hours ahead of the rest of the guys on Saturday morning. He bear-hugged him at the door and clapped him on the back. Emotion squeezed his throat as he realized he'd never again play against Sam on the football field or hug him after a cutthroat game, regardless of which team won. God, he was going to miss that.

"Are you here to mother me?" he asked when they broke apart.

"Heck, I only mother my rookies. You're way too old for that." When Touchdown barked, Sam reached down to pet the dog. Though it was technically Natalie's turn to watch him again, she was busy seeing to the lunch she would be serving them later.

When his friend straightened, they stood there smiling at each other like idiots for a moment.

"It's good to see you, man."

Sam gave his shoulder a slight shove. "You too." He picked up his leather satchel and strolled inside after Blake and Touchdown. "Well, at least you're not living in a hovel."

"This house might be smaller than the one in Denver, but it's still nice. Come on. I'll show you where you can put your stuff."

He led him upstairs and down the hallway to one of the three guest bedrooms. A few of the guys had said they didn't mind sleeping on king blow-up beds in the basement. Grant had made him laugh by offering to sleep with him in his massive California King since he must be lonely out in the big bad woods.

"Jordan was upset to hear you won't be bunking together," he told Sam.

"Good. I hope you stuck him with Zack. That guy's hair has gotten downright raggedy. I'm sure Mr. Dean can help him on that score." He laughed and threw his satchel on the bed. "By the way, Jordan says he's found the best Smuck award ever."

Every time they got together, the last "winner" chose the next competition and the outfit for the new one. One time the game had involved how many marbles they could pick up in sixty seconds with their toes. Logan had "won" that one since he had the smallest feet. The "winner" had the honor of wearing knee-socks with fur on them. Hunter had picked them out, and everyone joked they must have belonged to one of his many exes. Another time, Zack had found some hideous hat with its own black light with the words *Alien Abduction Imminent* printed across the front.

The Smuck had to wear the piece-de-resistance in question for the duration of their time together, including whenever they went out in public. So far Blake hadn't "won," but they ganged up on him every time, hoping to make him a full member of the Smuck Club. And with Jordan as the most recent "winner," he knew the QB was going to come at him hard.

"I've never 'won' the Smuck award," he said, preening like a peacock, "so I'm not concerned."

"You might be off your game this time," Sam said,

following Blake back to the kitchen as Touchdown raced ahead to his water bowl.

"How about I whip us up a Blake juice special, and we can chill on the deck?"

"Sounds good," Sam said, resting his hip against the island. "So, how are things going?"

Blake opened the refrigerator and took out some organic apples, carrots, and pears. His mega-juicer would make short work of them. He dug into a cabinet and pulled out some chia seeds and maca powder to add to the drinks when he finished juicing.

"A local school board member asked Natalie's mom to see if I'd be their new football coach," he said in a neutral tone. It was the only offer that interested him right now, so it was the only one worth mentioning.

Sam scratched his cheek. "I can see their logic. Everyone outside the league thinks that if you played, you could probably coach."

"We both know that's not true. A football camp isn't coaching." And wasn't that what concerned him? If he took this on, he didn't want to let those kids down. They would want to win. Heck, he would want to win. It's what he did.

"Doesn't mean it's a bad idea though."

"I called the board member off the record." He ran Sam through the conversation.

Cormack Daly *did* have big ideas, just like April had warned him, and Blake wouldn't have been surprised if someone told him the guy collected sharks as a hobby. Blake had dealt with his kind before. He wasn't sure he could be trusted, and the last thing he wanted was for word of their conversation to leak out. Natalie would be upset if she heard he was thinking about staying in town permanently. They were not in a place where he could even bring it up yet.

"I told him I didn't have my long-term plans set, that I was just getting settled in Dare Valley and focusing on my upcoming football camp." Of course, Cormack hadn't liked the delay and had proceeded to sell him harder.

"Just because the guy's a prick doesn't mean the offer's no good," Sam told him.

"I know. They'll need to hire a new coach soon though. They've already put one candidate on the back burner because of me."

Sam sat on a bar stool as Blake juiced the fruit. He poured the juice into two glasses when he was finished and dug out spoons. They both dished some maca powder and chia seeds into their drinks, stirring in the companionable quiet.

"Do you want to do it?" Sam finally asked, standing up to put his spoon in the dishwasher. "I'm sure you've gotten plenty of other offers." One thing he didn't worry about with Sam was cleanliness. Now with some of the other guys...

"I'm still not sure I'm coaching material. And I...want a better idea of where things are going with Natalie before I make a commitment like that."

"That's understandable," Sam told him as they headed out onto the deck.

Touchdown followed them, and then ran off to chase a couple squirrels leaping from tree to tree.

"I'm not sure when I'll know...about Natalie. As for the coaching thing...I feel like I'll have the answer after camp."

Sam rested his hand on his shoulder when they both sat down. "It's okay to spin your wheels for a bit and see where it takes you. What did Coach always say about plans?"

Leave it to Sam to be level-headed. "You'll have to help me. Coach said a lot of things."

"Never react to life. Be the determiner of your own fate. If Cormack presses you again, tell him you can't make a decision yet. If he decides to wait, and you decide you want it, then it's meant to be. If not, something else will come along to make you happy. Or you can fashion your own opportunity, just like you've done with the camp."

His mouth tipped up in a smile. "I could pretty much kiss you right now."

"Good Lord! You have gone crackers out here in the woods." He jostled Blake's shoulder playfully. "Drink your juice."

The temperature was in the mid-eighties, and there were no clouds to mar the beautiful sunshine streaming down on the deck. He'd taken to spending most of his days out back, either reading up on coaching kids with intellectual disabilities or running through the progress on the camp with his assistant. And he'd been poring over the materials Special Olympics had sent him, making notations in the margins.

"How's the camp shaping up?" Sam asked. "I told Coach I'd be helping you this year."

"I called him to talk about the camp." Coach had told Blake that he had a lot to offer the world and that he had every faith he'd figure out the next step, even suggesting he'd be a great coach if he decided to go that route. "He was supportive, but I could tell he wasn't exactly thrilled I'd be stealing some of you guys. He told me you'd bowed out of Once Upon A Dare this year."

Sam shrugged. "I found a replacement—like all of the other guys did. We weren't about to leave Coach in a lurch. He needs to get over it."

But Coach didn't like last-minute changes. "You don't have to help," Blake made himself say.

"Like hell I don't." Sam kicked off his shoes and wiggled his toes in the sun. "Besides, I can help him next year—and you. Just couldn't manage both this summer."

"Thanks, man," he said, kicking his shoes off too as he sipped his drink. Whoever said fruit juice was for sissies had never enjoyed the real thing.

"You know we have your back. So, how many applications have you received for the camp so far?"

"In less than a day, we received more than four hundred."

Sam tilted his head to the side. "But I thought you were going to limit it to forty."

"Exactly. I knew the need was great, but I wasn't expecting *this*." And he was still a bit shocked. He'd thought about trying to expand the camp, but this was the first one. It was on a tight timeline and he wanted to get it right. Next year, he could look at expanding.

"All right, we've waited long enough. Tell me how things are with Natalie," Sam said, draining his juice and setting his glass on the small table between their chairs.

How to answer? Natalie talked with him whenever they swapped Touchdown, but he hadn't been invited over for another meal. Likely because she didn't want to raise his hopes too much. Of course, their *Outlander* watch party had pretty much shot his hopes to the moon. He'd gone around like a love-sick schoolboy for the past few days.

"Good, I think. She and the hotel are catering a few of our meals this weekend, except for Saturday night when we'll go into town. I rented part of the Irish bar for us."

There was an indelicate snort from his friend. "Catering, huh? That's mighty nice of her."

"Yes, it is." He then told Sam the story about their friends-only meal the other night. "I think...she feels guilty about me leaving football and...hell, I'll put it out there...I think she's a little sorry for me because of Adam."

"She probably feels guilty for leaving you like she did, especially now that you've forgiven her. And as far as her feeling sorry for you...you just lost your brother, man. There's nothing wrong with a little compassion."

But he wanted more than that from her. Isn't that why he hadn't said anything to her about Adam until coming to Dare Valley? His mind started spinning to a weird place, and since he wanted to retain his positivity about Natalie—about his hopes for a future with her—he changed the topic to his other favorite subject.

"Why don't you tell me a bit about your upcoming season?" he asked. "Since we aren't going to be playing against each other, you can spill the beans." And it would give him a taste of what he'd been missing.

"Sure. And hey, that means I can call you and ask for advice now and again."

"Yeah, you can." Even he heard the glee in his voice.

Sam began walking him through the Washington Warriors' offense and then moved onto their defense. By the time he rolled around to outlining their opponents for the coming season, there was a solid banging on the front door. Touchdown barked and darted to the front of the house.

"Guess our one-on-one is up," Blake said, rising.

He jogged to the front door, fearing the guys would knock it off the hinges, and swung it open to reveal six hulking figures grinning back at him.

"Well, at least you don't look like an ancient retiree," Atlanta Rebels' Jordan Dean barked out as he rushed him.

"I could still kick your ass," he said, slapping him on the back as they hugged.

Then he went from one guy to the next, man-hugging each of them with all his strength. His football brothers were in the house. All was well in his world at this moment.

"I think I see more gray in your hair," the Boston Stars' prize wide receiver Logan Eastwood said when they broke apart. "Good thing Jordan brought his special hair dye."

He cringed. He was going to have to lock his door at night.

"I'll keep your hair safe, Blake," New York Tigers' QB Hunter Cahill told him as he stooped to pick up Touchdown.

"My hair is just fine," he told them, hoping he was right. God, he wasn't going gray, was he? Shit, he was way too young for that. He'd have to drink more smoothies or something.

"Your hair doesn't hold a candle to mine," San Francisco Stingrays' defensive lineman Grant Thornton said, ruffling his messy page-boy brown locks that were the subject of many a fan tweet.

"Not even Jordan can compete with your do," Sam said as he made his own round of greetings. "No one can."

"Hey, I resent that," Jordan said, tilting his head back like he was a male model awaiting admiration.

"You would," Blake called out. He'd been good-naturedly ragging other players ever since he first started playing team sports at the age of five. He realized he'd been missing this...a lot.

Brody Keller, the Chicago Titans' wide receiver, gave him a playful shove. "I can't believe you up and retired on me. I was going to kick your ass when we played this year."

"You're only sore because I retired before you could beat me."

"He sure is," Zack Durant, quarterback of the New Orleans Akkadians, said. "I'm pissed too. We were even at two wins apiece. Guess we'll have to figure out some other way to break that tie."

Everyone fell silent for a minute, and Jordan locked eyes with him.

"How are you really doing?" the QB asked.

His chest squeezed tight, but he lifted his shoulder. "About how you'd expect. I still miss Adam like crazy and find myself grieving at the oddest times when something triggers it." Last night, it had been Adam's favorite song coming on the radio as he'd driven back from his run. "And then there's Natalie..."

"Ah...that girl," Hunter said quietly.

Even though they all knew his reasons for retiring, he still said, "I want her back in my life. Right now, we've started as friends. It's...I'm hopeful. She even agreed to cater our meals this weekend."

"Good," Logan said, clapping him on the back. "Now, how about you show us inside this place?"

When Grant bent down to pick up his black leather duffle, Blake saw the stretch Hummer parked catawampus in his driveway. His buddy was so big he'd almost blocked the view.

"Which one of you yahoos drove that monstrosity?" he asked.

"That would be me," Jordan said. "Grant and I flipped for it, but he chose tails."

"Everyone knows you always lose when you choose tails," Zack said.

They'd argued over the science of the coin toss for years since it was one of the most important factors in a football game. Most of them were team captains who had been in charge of the coin toss. Some of them favored heads while a couple outliers were rabid about always calling tails.

"Don't make me punch you this soon in the weekend," Hunter said, and he and Zack got into each other's faces and started playfully shoving each other, causing Touchdown to bark and leap at their ankles.

"Come on, girls, you can continue the pillow fight inside," Blake said, herding them into the house.

After storing their gear, they piled into the kitchen. Suddenly the wide open space felt like a closet with all the giants hulking about. Sam dispensed beers to the ones who wanted a brew and made some juice for

Hunter and Zack. Grabbing his own beer, Blake followed the guys out onto the deck where they all dragged a few more deck chairs around his patio table until they were seated in a lop-sided circle.

"God, smell that mountain air," Hunter said and then promptly started to cough.

Grant reached over and pounded him on the back. "Guess he can't handle the purity after all those New York fumes he inhales daily."

"No," Hunter said in a raspy voice between coughs, "I think I swallowed a bug."

Everyone started laughing at that, and when Jordan rose to give Hunter the Heimlich, their hilarity spiraled out of control. Touchdown barked and then raced off, as if deciding he'd had enough. He caught Sam's look and grinned. Yeah, they were thinking the same thing. These guys might be yahoos...but they were their yahoos.

The rattle of metal sounded behind them, and Blake craned his neck to see what it was. Natalie was standing at the side of the house, fingering a trio of gold bracelets, an annoyed expression on her face. He glanced at his watch and winced. He'd forgotten to put a note on the front door to tell her to come in and set up lunch. Instead she'd had to come around the back to look for him.

Hunter rose from his chair first. "Hey, babe. Good to see you. We were all worried about putting Blake in charge of feeding us, but it looks like he ordered up the best like usual. How have you been?"

"Fine, Hunter Punter. How about you?"

The grin she gave his friends made his breath catch in his throat. It was a bit like old times again...except *not*.

"You guys were braying like hyenas," she continued "No wonder you didn't hear me knocking on the front door."

"What can we say, Nat?" Jordan called out. "We like

to walk on the wild side."

The other guys rose as Blake did. He watched her walk across the rest of the yard, taking in the sight of her white capri pants, black T-shirt, and sexy gladiator sandals. The Celtic knot tattoo on the inside of her ankle had his mouth watering. He'd seen it before, sure, but he'd never had the guts to ask her when she'd gotten it or why. He only knew it had appeared after their divorce—and he found it incredibly hot.

The guys all kissed her, hugged her, and lifted her off the ground. "Okay, enough of all that," she said, giving Grant a playful wink. "I need to let my people in."

"I'll do it," Blake said, hoping to catch a look from her—anything that would tell him how they were doing today. They both knew it was weird, her being back with this group as the caterer, not as Blake's wife.

"I'll help you," Sam said, slapping him on the back as if sensing his unease.

His status with Natalie was as changeable as the weather right now, and he knew it.

She *finally* looked at him as he slipped inside the kitchen with Sam. He lifted his hand in greeting, waiting for her to smile. When she didn't, he felt more than a little unsettled. Having her with the guys brought back so many good memories for him, and he'd hoped she would feel the same. Then he opened the door and let two strangers into his house to set up the chafing pans and unpack the food. Now he understood why she hadn't smiled. Things might be familiar, but they were also horribly different.

He wondered if that would ever change as far as Natalie was concerned.

CHAPTER 12

Though she was loathe to admit it, Natalie had missed this motley crew of giants. Sure, they'd always been easy on the eyes and charming beyond measure, in the way most superstar athletes were, but they also genuinely cared about her.

Always had.

Even if she'd up and left their best friend for no reason.

They were loyal to Blake, so she'd felt self-conscious and awkward about seeing them today. But it had quickly become clear that they were doing their best to be nice to her. She could almost hear their pact. If Blake wanted her back, they were going to support him one hundred percent. Even if she'd been a bitch.

Grant picked her up from behind, making her scream. "I'm going to toss you over to Zack."

They'd played this game with her many times. And yes, sometimes it was fun, but she was supposed to be working. She tickled his ribs, and he immediately let her go and released a high-pitched giggle.

"Hey, now, no need to be mean," he said, putting plenty of space between them.

"I swear, if the guys in the league knew you were this ticklish, they wouldn't have to tackle you."

Brody advanced on him, and Natalie knew to get out

of the way. A tickle fight was about to commence. She felt a strange sort of pride for having started it.

"Don't you dare touch me!" Grant raved, but Brody, Logan, and Jordan rushed him, and soon the defensive lineman was running for his life across the yard with the others in hot pursuit. Touchdown raced after them, barking in short bursts.

Zack and Hunter exchanged looks.

"Guess we should probably follow them," Hunter said. "They might run into a bear and get mauled."

Zack snorted. "I'd love to see that."

Natalie put her hands on her hips. "It's time for lunch, so you'd best bring them back while the food is hot."

Not that the chafing dishes wouldn't do their job, but she knew these guys. Once they started horsing around, it was hard to get their attention until hunger descended. Then they turned into a pack of starving wolves. She didn't plan on letting things unravel to that state of affairs.

"Yes, ma'am," Zack said with a salute. "We'll bring them back. And your little dog too. Assuming Grant still has his pants on."

She shook her head. "Like I haven't seen his ass before. How many times do you think you've pulled this sort of random crap around me?"

Hunter burst out laughing. "A lot. Not that we've ever pantsed Sam."

No, no one would dare strip Sam's pants off. "How many times have you gotten Blake?" She'd seen it happen at least twice. Both times had made her hot. And that was so not something she needed to be thinking about right now.

Zack scratched his goatee. "Probably a half dozen. He's not the fastest, but he has pretty impressive evasion tactics."

"And he's mean," Hunter added.

Yeah, Blake didn't go down without a fight.

"All right," she said. "Go get those morons and tell them it's time to eat."

She hated to sound like their mom, but this had always been her role with them, and it felt natural. At least she wouldn't have to clean up after them this weekend. A few of them could be downright pigs.

Blake stuck his head through the open door as Zack and Hunter jogged off in the direction of Grant's high-pitched giggles.

"Who are they pantsing?" he asked with a grin.

"Grant. He was going to toss me around, so I tickled him. It devolved from there."

He strode forward, his sandy brown hair gleaming in the afternoon sunshine. Sometimes looking at Blake was blinding. It wasn't just the mega-watt power of his grin. No, it was the easy power that radiated through his whole body, as natural as the electricity that ran through a house.

"So, you're the instigator, huh?" he asked, standing beside her. "It's good to have the guys here. I really appreciate you taking care of the food, Nat."

She could feel the pull of other memories—various weekends when they'd hosted the guys together, as a unit. Her walls rose a few inches as an unwanted sense of yearning rolled through her.

"The Grand Mountain Hotel took care of the food," she heard herself saying. "I was only the executor."

When he didn't say anything, she stole a glance at him. He was frowning.

"I thought we were friends again," he said in a soft voice, one she had to strain to hear over the racket from Grant and the guys.

A pressure rose in her chest. "We are." But how exactly could she backtrack to being friends with her ex-husband, particularly when she knew he wanted more?

He turned his head and stared into her eyes. She

met his gaze and didn't blink since he didn't. There was hurt there, yes, but determination too.

"Guess who's got Grant's pants?" Jordan called out, emerging into view with a pair of tan shorts held high in his hands. "Too bad I can't tweet this out."

She drew her gaze away from Blake to watch Jordan catapult over one of the deck chairs like he was jumping into the end zone on a quarterback sneak. Everyone had agreed their gatherings were to take place in a cone of silence. If other people saw them out and about and tweeted about it, well, that was another thing.

"Do you want to hide Grant's pants or should I?" Jordan asked them, shaking the article in his hand.

Like she'd touch them. "If you're going to hide them, you'd better do it quick," Natalie said. "They're coming back."

Sure enough, Grant was running toward the porch in nothing but his form-fitting black athletic shirt and a pair of navy underwear, his massive legs as big as tree trunks. The other guys were jogging behind him, laughing so hard they could barely keep up. Touchdown was now doing mad circles around his buddies. He was as out of control as the rest of them.

"I'm going to cut you, Jordan!" Grant called out as Jordan darted into the house. "Sorry about my appearance, Natalie."

He didn't blush—after all, these men were accustomed to using locker rooms—but he did cross his hands over his crotch. At least they'd only taken his pants. Sometimes the guys went a bit further.

"Grant!" Blake shouted. "Go put on another pair of pants. We have women around."

"Shit. Right. Sorry again, Nat."

"I'll...ah...finish setting up if you can referee these guys into shape," she told Blake, heading inside. "Good luck with that."

It was hard not to admire the sheer perfection of

Grant's butt as he jogged into the house. Sure enough, her two female assistants stared at him as he came inside. Who could blame them? Grant was all muscle—every woman's dream.

As she'd expected, her staff already had the food laid out buffet style in the kitchen, just like the guys usually preferred. Thick cuts of ham and prime rib filled the room with a delicious savory scent, which mingled pleasantly with the aroma of her famous dill-infused sour cream potato salad. A mountain of cheese and fruit lay on the four platters her staff had brought in. And of course, her special cheese dip was showcased in the center of a chip bowl.

Sam cocked his head at her as he grabbed a cube of Swiss cheese. "You've outdone yourself as usual."

She patted one of her assistants on the back. "Thanks for setting this up. Everything looks great. You guys can head out."

That earned her a forlorn look, but her helpers traipsed out the front, which was probably for the best. Through the windows, she could see Brody and Logan bent over at the waist, guffawing with abandon. And this was only the beginning. By Sunday night, everyone would be completely out of control in the best way possible. When they got together, they tended to devolve into the little boys they used to be at football camp.

"Do you know what the Smuck award is on this trip?" she asked Sam.

"No, but Jordan was in charge of it, and he says it's a doozy." He shook his head. "They're already losing it."

"And you love every minute of it," she said, tempted to grab a piece of smoked mozzarella from the platter. Smoked gouda was yummy, but smoked mozzarella was something else altogether.

"Usually," Sam said, coming to stand beside her. "Not when they stick lizards in my bed."

Yeah, she remembered that weekend at Logan's cabin in Nevada. It was the reason she'd imposed the no-live-animals-or-insects-in-the-house rule for when she and Blake hosted.

"How's your mom?" she asked, thinking of how interconnected her life had been with Blake's. She hadn't just known these guys; she'd known their families. And Jordan's girlfriend, Grace, had become a real friend. That had all disappeared, and she suddenly felt that loss keenly.

"Mom's great. Said to say hello if I saw you." He paused. "Honestly, I wasn't sure if I would see you."

Since she hadn't planned to visit with them until Blake had asked her to help with the food, she only nodded. "I'm glad it worked out."

"Me too." He popped another piece of cheese in his mouth.

"So, what do you think about Blake retiring?" she ventured to ask, trying to appear casual by straightening one of the chafing pans.

"I don't think that's the right question."

Busted. Leave it to Sam to cut to the chase. "Okay, why don't you tell me what you think about what he's done?"

"You know as well as I do that he didn't retire from football simply because Adam died." Resting with his back against the kitchen island, he gave her his complete attention. "Natalie, you cut him open with a chainsaw when you left, and he's never gotten over you."

She couldn't repress a gasp. "Well...don't mince words, Sam."

"You asked. After seeing *everything* he's gone through lately, I'm going to give it to you straight." His eyes locked with hers. "He would do anything for you—even give up football. If you don't see that, and if you don't value it, then you're not as smart as I always thought you were."

His opinion had always meant a lot, but this level of honesty made her legs tremble. "So you think I should take him back?"

He let out a long sigh. "Only if you love him like he loves you. Otherwise, give him the closure he needs to move on with his life. He's a good man. Don't muzzle him, Natalie, just because you're scared."

"Scared? I don't know what you're talking about." Even to her ears, it sounded like pure bravado.

"After years of playing ball, I know when someone's scared, and that's what I see when I look at you." He put his hand on her shoulder. "I know you suffered a great loss when your friend died, but that wasn't Blake's fault. He only wanted to help you, and you were too scared to let him."

Her mouth parted at his insight. How much had Blake told him? "You don't know anything."

"He grieved for Kim too, you know, and now with Adam…he needs our support, and he hasn't been afraid to ask for it. The minute he asked for help with his football camp, we all rearranged our schedules to be there. And we're here this weekend, just like we've been there a dozen other weekends since you left him."

She felt like slime, and it was becoming so normal, you'd think she'd be used to it by now. "I'm glad you guys have been there for him."

"Why haven't you been?" His brow cocked in pure challenge. "You're like one of the players on the team who distances himself from everyone else when he's going through a tough time—on or off the field. I know those guys. You have the same desperate look in your eyes. There's nothing wrong with needing someone when you've hit bottom, Natalie. The people who know when to ask for help are stronger than the ones who insist on standing alone. Does Blake look weak to you?"

No, but he looked lonely and unsure and vulnerable, and seeing him like that sometimes scared her. She didn't want anyone to think those things of her. Ever.

"Your eyesight must be getting poor if you see anything desperate about me." She rubbed the tightness around her diaphragm, scarcely able to breathe. "I'm not a football player, Sam. You're comparing apples and oranges here."

"No, I'm not. I've learned a football team is a microcosm of society, and I've pretty much seen it all after playing the sport for nearly thirty years."

"A microcosm of society? What have you been reading?"

"The classics." His hand squeezed her shoulder. "Natalie, I've always liked you. For a long time, I thought you were the best woman in the world for Blake. But I love him, and you've put him through hell. Don't expect to erase all of that by showing up here with smiles and your cheese dip. The only thing that will do that is your honesty. I hope you'll find the courage inside you to make the right choice."

Then he kissed her cheek and walked over to the patio door. "Hey! Enough caterwauling," he called. "Let's chow."

As the men hustled inside, Touchdown trailing behind them, she cleared her throat and tried to compose herself. The guys grabbed plates and started loading up on the food, and Grant reappeared fully clothed. He'd found a permanent marker somewhere and written on his shirt: *No Pants=War.*

She stepped back and bumped into a tall, hard body. Even though all of these men had hard bodies, honed by their sport, she knew instantly it was Blake. Her bottom had always fit perfectly into the curve of his pelvis. Then there was his smell: man, leather, and spice.

Feeling off balance, and not just from Sam's comments, she turned around. His brown eyes searched her face.

"Everything okay?"

She forced a smile. "Why wouldn't it be?"

"I saw you talking to Sam. You looked upset."

Upset was too tame a word. "I'm fine. I'll leave you all to it. We'll bring over brunch tomorrow, like we arranged."

He laid his hand on her forearm, and her skin puckered at that one simple touch. "Don't let him bother you. He's...loyal to me, that's all."

All the guys were, but she respected Sam's opinion the most. He had always been the voice of wisdom for their group. So his words had cut her down to size, and it had hurt, even if she'd deserved it.

"Have fun." She tried to walk by him, but he grabbed her hand.

"Thanks, Nat." The light in his eyes suggested he was talking about more than her role in preparing the food. Right now, she couldn't deal with that. She could barely deal with her own pain and confusion. His overwhelmed her.

"See you guys tomorrow." She gave a lackluster wave as she backed up to the door. "If one of you lands in jail, do not *call* me."

They laughed as she let herself out. Touchdown didn't follow her, which wasn't a surprise. He adored Blake's friends. Walking across the bridge back to her place in the silence, tracing the infinity symbols engraved in the wood, she remembered how Blake had described this construction.

The bridge to a better life.

As she reached her own house, part of her felt like she'd left her one and only chance behind her.

CHAPTER 13

All the guys stuffed their faces except for Blake. It was all too familiar. The taste of her cheese dip made him think of happier times, like her feeding it to him on a chip at one of their picnics or them serving it for their annual Fourth of July party. It was enough to make him lose his appetite.

After they finished eating, he ran them through his thoughts about the camp. "Okay, let's put it out there," he said, standing in front of everyone in his den. "Besides meeting my brother, who has interacted with people with intellectual disabilities?"

Only two people didn't raise their hands: Brody and Logan. It was more than he'd thought. Good.

"Zack," he said, "why don't you tell us about your experience?"

His buddy sat up straighter on the couch. "The Make-A-Wish Foundation contacted me about Emily wanting to meet me. She was a huge New Orleans fan, and she'd just had a severe cardiac incident and wasn't expected to make it. They asked if I could visit her at the hospital." He looked down at the hands he'd joined prayer-like. "When I showed up, she looked so sick, but the smile she gave me...man, it chokes me up, thinking about it. She couldn't talk a lot without tiring herself. Her breathing..."

Yeah, Blake remembered how laborious Adam's breathing had become after his first cardiac incident over a year ago. He'd even struggled to smile, and Adam had *always* found a reason to smile.

"She complimented me on having a great arm and being a good team leader, and then she told me I was going to win a Super Bowl someday. She said she wished she could see it. I gave her one of my game balls and signed a few things. You know. Then I sat with her until she fell asleep. She died two days later."

Some of the guys had to clear the emotion out of their throats. All of them believed in giving back to their communities, and most of them had visited sick kids in the hospital at some point. A few also played pick-up games at the local community centers with kids from rough neighborhoods. Once they'd all recovered a bit, a couple of the other guys shared their stories, and any final concerns Blake had about stealing his guys away from Coach for the summer faded. He needed them, and not only because they were great camp leaders. They had heart.

After everyone finished sharing, Blake ran them through the specifics of the arrangements for the camp. "We'll be split up into different age groups. The first will be composed of kids ten to thirteen and the second fourteen to eighteen. You can sign up for whichever age group you'd rather coach. From there, we'll slot the kids into various teams."

"Jordan should sign up to work with the youngsters since he'll fit right in," Grant said, tugging on his replacement pair of pants.

Jordan still hadn't coughed up the lineman's shorts, and Blake suspected he would probably come across them in some wild location after all of them had left— like the freezer.

"Har-de-har-har," Jordan said. "But yes, I'll happily take the youngsters. I'm not super fond of high schoolers. Talk about attitude."

"Then Brody should volunteer for that group," Logan said. "He's got plenty of attitude."

Blake knew the bantering would continue if he didn't put a stop to it. He simply gave them *the look*. They shut up.

"Breakfast will be served from seven fifteen until seven fifty-five. We'll start warm-ups at eight and then go into drills a half hour later. I want to run drills for a few hours a day, before and after lunch. Then we'll break into smaller groups. Defense and offense. Run some more drills, some specific plays. Then we'll scrimmage until four when camp ends. After that, the kids will have some time to themselves before the evening activities start."

"Man, I miss those days," Logan said, kicking out his feet. "Jordan and I used to row out onto the lake after practice and see who could stand in the canoe the longest while the other one rocked the boat."

"Of course I always won," Jordan said, buffing his nails against his shirt like an idiot.

"As I was saying," Blake interrupted. "I want everyone to have fun. We'll have campfires, movie nights, and a dance party since some of you like to strut your stuff."

Zack rose and gave them a preview of his moves, earning some obscene comments and the suggestion that he should join the Chippendales after retiring.

"Let's talk about the sport specifically," Blake said when they died down. "It's going to be a bit strange for us, since it's flag football, so I want everyone to practice pulling the flag. It's harder than you might think."

"Only for you primadonna QBs who don't use your precious hands for anything other than throwing the pigskin." Grant cracked his knuckles. "Some of us are used to using our hands to bring you pretty boys down."

Blake rolled his eyes. The non-QBs in the group always said the QBs weren't as tough as they were. Well, they'd see about that once the Smuck competition rolled around.

"To practice flag pulling, you can have someone play with you or you can even pull it from something stationary," he said, continuing.

"Or put it on your dog," Hunter commented. "Zack's St. Bernard would be perfect."

"Like hell. I'll be playing with my girlfriend," Zack said.

"Is that what you call her?" Hunter shot back.

"Guys."

That shut them up again, but they didn't look the least bit sheepish. Not that he'd expected them to. "I also don't want any swearing. Coach Garretty taught all of us you don't need to use bad language with kids to be effective."

Everyone nodded. Coach had the oratory skills of a fire-and-brimstone preacher. His pulpit was one hundred yards of green grass. Coach could chew your butt like none other.

"While I respect Coach, some of his other tactics may not be right for my camp." My, he liked the sound of that. His camp.

"Adam taught me there's a fine line between encouraging someone with intellectual disabilities and letting them motivate themselves to greatness. I don't want anyone pushing too hard or singling a kid out. This first camp is going to involve a lot of firsts for us. I'd rather err on the side of encouragement this time."

"I couldn't agree more," Sam said, and the others nodded their agreement.

"But don't pity them or mollycoddle them either. Adam always hated that." He handed out two manuals to everyone. "What you have before you are the coach's flag football manual for kids with intellectual abilities and the official rule book. Read them. Study them. *Brody.*"

"Hey, just because I barely made it through school doesn't mean I don't read," he protested.

"Man, you never read the game plan when we were at camp," Zack said, giving him a look. "I had to cover your ass with Coach Garretty more times than I can count."

"I'm a professional athlete now, and I do my homework. *Blake.*"

"Just saying." He held up his hands. "That's a pretty good overview for now. I'm working on a solid meal plan with a nutritionist who specializes in food for athletes with intellectual disabilities."

"It had better involve some junk food, Blake," Logan said. "That was the best part of camp. Chewing potato chips and shooting the breeze."

He'd forgotten about that. Yeah, junk food had been an important part of bonding. "I'll keep that in mind. I also will have some medical volunteers on hand. We'll have some training on special medical issues to be aware of the day before camp starts. All the kids will have had physicals clearing them to play, but muscular, breathing, and cardiac issues can appear out of the blue."

That's always the way it had happened with Adam. He'd be fine one day, and the next...

"We'll be vigilant, Blake," Sam said, knowing better than anyone the ups and downs they'd experienced with Adam's health.

"Thanks. Okay. Any questions?"

He answered a few questions, which included a liberal amount of playful banter. Finally Jordan stood and put his hands on his hips.

"Who's ready for the Smuck competition?" he boomed out in his best TV announcer's voice. "I think our surprise guest is waiting outside."

Blake groaned out loud. God only knew what his buddy had in mind for the competition. Some of the guys followed Jordan out. Sitting down in the chair Logan had vacated, Blake kicked out his feet.

"Twenty bucks he rented some clowns," Sam said.

"Perish the thought!" Blake exclaimed. "What does he expect us to do? Juggle?"

The guys were hooting in the hallway. Then Grant let out a high-pitched girl scream.

"It's not clowns," Sam said.

The guys danced into the room, wiggling like nervous dipshits. After a few seconds, Jordan strutted after them, a boa constrictor wrapped around his waist.

Blake's whole body shivered. Shit. He hated snakes, and Jordan damn well knew it. Their eyes locked, and he saw the same fierce competitiveness he was used to seeing in the mirror before a game gazing back at him. Jordan wanted him to go down and bad.

"Okay, who's going to be the biggest Smuck this time?" Jordan asked as the snake's— What in the hell should he call the fifty-year-old woman in the khaki uniform who had followed Jordan into the room and was standing in a military stance beside him? Its babysitter?

"Guys, this is Zeus. He's a thirteen-foot boa constrictor from Brazil." Jordan grabbed the back of the snake's head like he was shaking it in greeting.

Blake could only stare in horror as the army-green body colored with brown and cream spots clenched and rippled around Jordan's waist.

"*Shit, man,*" Zack said with a wheeze. "I know you have it in for Blake, but do you have to make the rest of us suffer?"

Grant launched into some colorful *Snakes on a Plane* quotes in the worst Samuel L. Jackson impression known to mankind. All of the guys laughed—except for

Blake.

"I'm going to kill you, Jordan," Blake ground out.

"So, you want to go first?" Jordan replied with a grin. "Great! Guys, this is Alice. She's a...herpetologist from the Denver Zoo."

"Say that three times fast," Logan called out. "Hi, Alice."

The woman didn't crack a smile. Snake Woman was serious, and who could blame her? She hung out with giant snakes that could crush a man's larynx in ten seconds. The Raiders should draft her.

"How many pounds did you say Zeus was again?" Jordan asked.

"Fifty-eight," Alice informed them in what had to be her best lecture voice. "And here's a little known fact about the difference between males and females. Females are larger in length and girth than males."

Hunter snorted beer out of his nose. Brody barked out a laugh. Even Sam's mouth twitched.

Okay, so Snake Woman had a sense of humor.

Jordan pretty much laughed like a loon. "Alice, you naughty, naughty girl, you."

"Let's take the snake out back," Blake suggested.

There was no way in hell he was letting Jordan accidentally let that snake loose in his house. He didn't wait for the guys to follow him. He felt something on the back of his neck and freaked, thinking it was the snake. It was only Grant, tickling his neck, a stupid grin on his face.

"You all planned this together," he accused.

"Not everyone was in on it, but yes, we had to get creative. You're pretty much indestructible when it comes to the Smuck competition. We had to take you down, Blake."

Hunter walked by with a bounce in his step. "By any means necessary. Oh, this is going to be so good."

"Just remember," he warned, pointed his finger at

them one by one. "You have to hold that bastard too."

"Please, Blake," Jordan crooned. "You'll hurt Zeus' feelings."

He shot him a gaze that would have made most men tremble. Jordan only lifted the snake higher around his waist.

"Hey, Brody, if this snake wasn't male, it would remind me of that yoga teacher you dated in college. You remember the one I mean? She was like some freaking contortionist."

The wide receiver gave a deep sigh. "How could I forget? She could actually touch the top of her head with the soles of her feet while blowing bubble gum. I wonder what ever happened to her."

Jordan cleared his throat, which doubled as a way to mask his laughter. "Okay, who wants to go first? I obviously have the record so far. What has it been? Like eight minutes so far."

"Yep," Logan said, holding out his smartphone. "We started the count the minute Zeus wrapped himself around Jordan."

Convenient. Blake crossed his arms across his chest. No way he was going first.

"Okay, Blake can go last since he's never been the Smuck."

Alice looked a bit amused as she helped Jordan unwrap Zeus from his body. The snake's tongue slithered out and touched the woman's face. He flinched, and some of the guys jumped back.

"No f-ing way that snake is kissing me," Zack said.

"Oh, don't be a baby," Hunter said, stepping forward to take the snake. "Don't you have big snakes and shit down in Louisiana?"

"Do I look like I hang out in the bayou, Hunter Punter?" Zack replied, using their friend's nickname from camp. Before his skills as a quarterback had become apparent, Hunter had been the punter. And he'd sucked. Bad.

"Call me Hunter Punter again, Zack Sprat, and we'll see who gets kissed by the snake."

Great. The childhood nicknames were coming out early this weekend.

"Just take the damn snake, Hunter," Blake said, "or this is going to last all day. We have somewhere to be tonight."

"Where are we going, Ace?" Logan asked.

Okay, so Blake had a cooler nickname than some of the other guys. "I rented out part of the local Irish bar in town called Hairy's."

"Awesome," Brody said. "I'm assuming they have beer, pool, darts, and Irish music."

"Take it easy, Riverdance," Blake replied. "They have that and more."

Hunter lasted a minute with Zeus. Zack clocked in at thirty-three seconds before yelping. And so it continued until they got to him.

Jordan was still in the lead with eight minutes plus, but then again, he'd always had a reptilian brain. Mr. Cool, Sam, had managed to come close at six minutes and fifty-eight seconds. The snake had stared him down and started to curl around his neck, thereby ending the standoff.

"He's a smart one," Sam muttered as Alice helped him resituate the snake on Blake.

Breathing deeply, trying to clear his mind like he would before a high-pressure game, Blake tried to stay calm. But he nearly freaked when he felt the snake's scales against the bare skin of his arm. Soon Zeus' muscles were clenching around him, making every hair on his body stand up in high alert. Then there were the snake's eyes as its head lifted to peer at him. They really were beady. A cold sweat broke out across his back, where he could feel the snake's powerful muscles shift and clench around his body.

"Snakes are ectothermic," Alice informed them all in that instructor voice of hers, "so they really love being warmed up by the human body, especially the waist, which carries so much body heat."

Thank you for that PSA, Snake Woman, he wanted to say.

But then Zeus darted up his chest, heading straight for his face. He started shrieking even before he felt the slithery tongue on his neck.

"Okay, I'm the Smuck, I'm the Smuck!" he shouted. "Just get this thing off me!"

The guys started howling, and Snake Woman stepped in and untangled Zeus from him.

"Does anyone want to try and lift Zeus over their heads?" she asked.

Grant shivered. "Ma'am, I can dead lift that snake four times over, but there is no way in hell I'm touching that sucker again. I'm going to have nightmares."

He wasn't the only one. Someone tickled Blake's back again, and he swung around to find Jordan smirking at him.

"Twenty-three seconds, Ace. You lose...or should I say you 'win'?"

"You don't have to be such a poor sport about it," he muttered.

"Oh, yes I do. I'll be back with your award, sunshine."

Blake steeled himself for the worst humiliation possible.

"This moment has been coming for years," Sam said with a grin that did little to appease him.

Judging from the grin on Jordan's face as he sauntered back onto the deck, holding a white box, he knew he was going to pay and pay bad.

"Thank you, Alice. We really appreciated having you here." Jordan stuck something in her free hand.

"Bye, fellas," she said with a smile. "I have to say I

was a little concerned when I got this request. Usually I visit children's birthday parties, but I have to admit, you guys are a lot more fun than you look on TV."

Snake Woman left them without a backward glance, but Zeus watched Blake over her shoulder until she disappeared from view.

As soon as she was gone, Jordan shoved the box at him. "It is my honor as the winner of the last Smuck award to hereby present this one to Blake Cunningham. May you enjoy your weekend in Smuckville."

He opened the box and cursed as he drew out a black T-shirt with pink letters on it that said *Call Me Maybe,* a pair of black 1980s Don Johnson *Miami Vice* sunglasses, hair mousse, and a hideous pair of acid-washed cut-off jeans.

"You've *got* to be kidding me," he said with a groan.

"The mousse is inspired," Logan said, leaning in for a closer look and elbowing Blake in the gut.

He was supposed to stick that shit in his hair? "That's one word for it."

"I'll even help you style," Jordan said, running his hands through his own perfect locks.

According to the gossip and fashion blogs, no one in the whole NFL had better hair than Jordan Dean, and didn't he know it. He was like James Dean's hair twin, and they sometimes called him James instead of Jordan. Okay, and Jimmy Dean too, when they stooped for a little sausage humor.

"No way you're touching my hair, Dean," Blake said even though he had no idea what to do with that gunk. And they were going out tonight. In public. Usually he wasn't vain, but wearing this? People were going to think he'd experienced a nervous breakdown and was now living out some 1980s Don Johnson fantasy.

"Oh, stop your bitching," Jordan said, reaching out to tug his T-shirt. "You knew there was going to be payback."

He gave him a playful shove. "I can undress myself, thank you."

"Then hop to it, Ace," Logan called out. "We don't have all day."

He stripped in his backyard, making the guys cat-call and whistle like they were all twelve. As he changed into the outfit Jordan had chosen, he tried not to wince at the tight fit of the T-shirt. If he made any sudden moves, he was going to rip it at the shoulder seams and no way was he turning this monstrosity into a wife beater.

"Too bad you couldn't find a fake mullet for him," Zack commented, stroking his chin as he circled Blake. "You could have doubled for Billy Ray Cyrus back in the day."

Don Johnson was bad enough. "You guys are dead meat," he ground out.

"Ohhh," they all cried out, clutching themselves in fake fear.

He was going to unleash practical jokes on the lot of them the likes of which they'd never seen. And lock himself in his bedroom before they could strike back.

"When are we heading to the Irish place?" Sam asked with a way too cheerful smile.

The plan was for them to eat at the bar, but now he was desperate to talk them out of going into town. Like that would work. The mob was hungry for his public humiliation.

"Seven," he told them.

He glanced over at the bridge, wondering what Natalie was up to tonight. If she saw him like this or heard about the snake, she'd likely fall over laughing. Well, he had to wear the stupid costume all weekend, so she'd see him like this soon enough. Suddenly, the prospect of wearing this Don Johnson throwback outfit in public wasn't so bad.

Not when it was sure to make her laugh.

CHAPTER 14

Natalie found herself twiddling her thumbs at home on Saturday night. Her sisters were busy this weekend. Moira was at a wedding, and Caroline was hosting an art opening. While they weren't back to being easy with each other yet, they'd checked in with her a couple of times during the week, which had made her feel better. Though it was awkward not to talk about the giant pink elephant of their argument, both of them had respected her privacy so far, and she appreciated that.

Matt and Jane were out of town at a poker tournament where, according to Matt's ongoing text updates to the family, she was kicking butt. Her mom was having a girls' night with her own friends, many of whom she'd reconnected with after moving back into the area. And Andy...well, they hadn't spoken since their talk at Black Lake.

Around eight o'clock her phone buzzed. Seeing it was Andy, she had the horrible impulse to ignore his call. Which was exactly why she forced herself to answer it.

"Hey, Andy Cakes," she said, hoping to keep it light.

"Hey. What are you doing right now?"

She glanced at the TV program she'd paused before answering. "Watching an old episode of *Friends.*"

"Oh brother. I'm saving you from Ross and Rachel drama. I decided to be spontaneous and see if the neighbor girl would come over and watch Danny. He's asleep, so she was happy to agree to take my money to hang out at my place and watch cable. You and I are going out to play some pool or darts. Your choice."

"Are you hoping I'll be your wing woman tonight?" she asked, trying to feel out his intentions for this brother-sister outing.

"I *said* I would give it a try, and trying means getting out of the house on the weekends. Are you game?"

"Sure. Why not?" What else was she going to do? Keep listening for more hilarity from next door through the open windows? The screams she'd heard this afternoon had made her very curious.

"Meet me at Hairy's," he said. "We'll see if you've lost your magic at the pool table."

"You wish." Few could beat her at her favorite game. "See you in twenty?"

That would give her time to put on something more suitable than her blue cotton jammies. If they were playing pool, she didn't want to wear anything too dressy, maybe just jeans and a simple white T-shirt. She didn't want to look like she was trying to pick anyone up.

"Perfect. Don't be late. I hate drinking alone in a bar."

Walking into a bar alone on a Saturday night could be awkward for anyone, even if you were meeting friends. How much worse would it be for a widower trying to return to the dating scene?

"I'll swing by and pick you up."

Was that a relieved sigh she heard? "Thanks, Nat."

After changing her clothes and refreshing her makeup, she headed out. There was a new bumper sticker on the back of her car, courtesy of her brother, Matt.

Worms Make Me Horny.

Good Lord. Where did he find them? Probably the same place she did. On the Internet. She'd wondered if their ongoing bumper sticker war would continue with all this Blake drama. Apparently their teasing hadn't changed, and she was glad. She'd have to retaliate tomorrow, and she had the perfect one in reserve: *I Dig Poker Chicks.* She knew Jane would love that one.

The warm glow of the town's lights made her smile as she made her way down the foothills to the valley. It only took her five minutes to arrive at Andy's house, which was one of the things she loved about small towns. Andy was already letting himself out of the house and jogging to her car. When he got in, he turned in his seat to face her.

"I'll only ask this because...well, hell. Am I dressed okay?"

Ah, his vulnerability was touching. She patted his knee. "Jeans and a navy T-shirt look great on you."

He eyed her. "Good thing I didn't wear white. We'd be twins."

She sped off. "Like we haven't had people wonder about the whole twins thing before."

"I thought about asking our cousins to come, but I knew Jill couldn't since Mia has an ear infection. She and Brian showed up with her at the ER yesterday because she wouldn't stop screaming."

"Oh, no," she said. "Poor baby."

"And Meredith's getting way too pregnant to want to hang out in a bar on a Saturday night."

"Yeah, it would be pretty hard to tote that watermelon she's carrying through the crush." Besides, she had sexy Tanner to see to her needs. Why wouldn't she stay home? "We'll be fine on our own." *Don't be so nervous,* she wanted to tell him.

Finding a parking spot on Main Street proved more difficult than she'd expected, and she had to settle for a spot on Aspen Street near the Justice Center. The night air was cool, and she was glad for her jeans. As soon as they showed their IDs and walked into the pub, she realized her open-toed sandals were less of a good idea.

She'd been to Hairy's Irish Pub hundreds of times. Tonight it was packed to the gills like she'd never seen it before. It wasn't surprising that the booths were filled with people eating dinner, but even the bar area and the aisles were jammed with guests. Someone was going to step on her toes. It was a given. She stood on her tippy toes to see what was going on, but all she could see were camera flashes.

A couple of the new Irish sayings above the bar caught her eye as more people pressed in behind her.

Kilt. It's what happened to the last guy who called it a skirt.

I'm Irish. We Don't Keep Calm and Carry On.

And another kilt joke. *Balls like this don't fit well in trousers.*

She was laughing now despite the crush. "The Rockies aren't playing, are they?" She couldn't make out what was on the TVs situated around the bar.

"No." Andy put his hand on her arm. "Ah...Blake and his friends are here. In the back room. Playing pool and darts. It's cordoned off, but they're visible."

That explained the camera flashes. Great. Blake and his boys were tonight's spectacle. She hadn't asked him about their plans. She only knew they hadn't needed her to cater their dinner.

"Do you want to go?" her brother asked.

The thought crossed her mind, but then she realized it was ridiculous. He and the guys were doing their own thing, and she and Andy could do theirs. If they ever managed to get to the bar.

"No," she responded. "Let's see if your people skills can get us some beer."

Someone put a hand on her shoulder, and she

turned her head to see an older man in his sixties grinning at her. Seriously?

"Natalie," the man said, leaning way too close to her face to be ignored. "I'm Cormack Daly, the head of the school board for Dare Valley."

"Oh, hi," she said, edging her head back, waiting for the punch line. "This is my brother, Andy Hale."

"Yes, I know. I went to school with your mother. She was kind enough to talk with your ex-husband for me about taking over as the new head football coach."

She had? How could she have interfered like that? Feeling thrown off, she took an unintentional step back and bumped into someone. "Sorry," she murmured. She'd wondered about Blake's plans long-term, but so far, he hadn't mentioned it, and she sure as heck wasn't going to ask.

"We're so happy he's considering it," Cormack said, sounding like something was stuck in his nose. "He said he needed some more time to decide, and while we understand that, we really need to line up a replacement. You understand. I was hoping you could use your influence over him to nudge him in our direction. I'd planned to talk to him tonight, but they aren't letting anyone join his private party."

Andy met her eyes and then looked heavenward. She wasn't sure if he was praying or feeling as incredibly uncomfortable as she was.

"Cormack, in case you didn't know, Blake and I are divorced. He makes his own decisions now."

He sputtered. "But he's living next door to you."

"Exactly," she said. "Excuse us."

There really wasn't anywhere to go in the crowd, but she pushed her way through a few feet to be away from that horrible man. Her insides were shaking. If Blake took the coaching job, that meant he'd be here for... She did the calculations. He'd never quit a team after only one season. My God, he could be living next door to her for years.

"Breathe," Andy said, cupping her elbow. "Don't let that man get to you."

How could she not? She wanted Blake to do something that made him happy, but taking a permanent job here? In Dare Valley?

Suddenly, the crowd rippled, and the people in front of them pushed them backward. Andy's hand clenched on her arm, but they both fell back a few steps, bumping into the people behind them. Sure enough, someone stepped hard on her toes.

"Hey," she yelled at the people in front of her.

No one cared. Camera flashes blinded her.

Someone called out her name. "Natalie!"

She couldn't see who it was at first, but then Jordan was coming her way, parting the crowd like Moses through the Red Sea, a giant bouncer of a man beside him fending off requests for selfies and autographs. When he finally reached her, the bouncer stared down his would-be fanatics. More cameras flashed, blinding her.

"Nat! I'm so glad you're here. You've gotta see Blake. He finally won the Smuck Award."

Her mouth parted in shock. "You're kidding!" This was monumental enough to make her mind stop turning cartwheels at the thought of Blake's job offer.

"And *I* dressed him," he proudly said, pointing to his chest. "Hey, aren't you Nat's bro?"

Andy smiled and stuck out his hand. More cameras flashed, and people started whispering and pointing at her.

"She's Blake's ex-wife," a dishwater blond woman whispered, taking a not-so-subtle picture with her smartphone.

Then a tall guy behind Jordan, who looked like he was barely out of college, said, "She's the reason he left football. I don't care what the press said about his brother. Why else would Blake move to Dare Valley right after she did?"

Her head started to pound. It took a moment for her to return her focus to her friend and her brother.

"Yes, Andy," her brother was saying.

"The doctor or the lawyer?" Jordan asked, not caring that everyone around them was listening with prurient interest and snapping pics. God, she'd never been able to tune out this sort of thing.

"Good memory. The doctor."

"Awesome. Come join us. It's going to be impossible to get to the bar in this crowd." He leaned close to her ear. "We have our own waitress."

"Sure you do," she said, "but I don't think..."

Jordan wasn't even listening anymore. He put a hand on her back to lead her through the crowd with the bouncer. More whispers followed her. She even heard someone boo her. Jordan's jaw tightened, and she knew he must have heard it too. Andy craned his neck to see who it was, his mouth pressed into a flat line, but it was impossible to tell in such a close crowd.

Maybe this isn't such a good idea, she thought. When they reached the closed-off area, another bouncer nodded at Jordan and let them all through. The guys were clustered around the pool table as Logan and Zack squared off. In the corner, trying to be inconspicuous, sat Blake. But there was no way someone in that get-up could avoid attention. She started laughing, all the earlier whispers and boos and worries erased by pure hilarity.

"Guess who I found?" Jordan called out.

Some of the guys tossed out greetings while others nodded to her. Logan winked, that little rascal.

"I had to invite her and her brother, Andy, to join us. I mean, who better to see Blake the Smuck than Nat?"

Blake pushed off the wall and took off the horrible black sunglasses. When he reached them, Jordan clucked his tongue.

"You have to wear the shades, Blake," the quarterback said. "It's part of the look."

"Didn't you have to use the *ladies'* room, Jordan?" Blake asked, meeting her gaze.

The look in his brown eyes was intense, and it shot a bolt of heat down to her very toes. Blake was studying her like he was trying to figure her out after their earlier interaction. Unable to sustain eye contact, she looked down, her heart pounding. Even dressed like an idiot with some hair product spiking up his curls, he fired up all her engines.

"I ran into Nat on the way and couldn't pass this up," Jordan said. "So, what do you think of Ace's walk of shame?"

Her eyes ran down his outfit as he and Andy exchanged greetings. The *Call Me Maybe* logo in pink was enough to set her lips to twitching, but the acid-washed jean cutoffs showing off his incredibly fine legs made her laugh. Loud and hard. Sexy and funny. It was impossible to resist.

"Go ahead," Blake said, putting his hands on his hips. "Have your fill. These guys still haven't."

"Not even close." Jordan kissed her cheek. "What do you want to drink?"

"How about a Guinness?"

"Great. Andy?"

Her brother was trying to keep a straight face and failing. "Same. Ah, Blake, what in the hell do you have in your hair?"

He dug his fingers through the spiky curls. "Mousse. James Dean over there plans to be a stylist when he retires from football."

"That's a good one, Blake," a couple of the guys called out.

Everyone knew about Jordan's flair for hair products. Even ESPN's commentators had joked he had the best helmet head in the NFL.

"I don't know why you haven't gone with that style before," she said, sputtering.

His lips twitched. "I knew this would make you laugh."

The intimacy in his voice made her stop guffawing mid-laugh. Andy coughed and shifted on his feet.

"We don't want to barge in on your party," she said, trying to recover from the shift in her awareness of him, from the sudden desire to run her hand down the hard line of his jaw. "We'll just..."

He took her arm and led her to the pool table. "I heard someone out there booing you. If you don't want me and the guys to beat the hell out of the haters, you're staying here until you leave. No one's touching you. Do you hear me?"

The hard line of his jaw told her he meant it. He was pissed, but he was doing his best to keep his cool. She nodded.

"I take it you and Andy came here to play pool," he said, turning his back on the crowd taking pictures of them.

"And maybe find Andy a date," she told him in lowered tones so her brother couldn't hear.

His brows rose, and they shared a look. "I'll help him out, Nat. You don't need to worry about him."

The air in her lungs froze. Even though he hated crowds and was pissed off about some bystander booing her, he was willing to do this for her. She almost hugged him on the spot.

He gave her arm a gentle squeeze and then turned away from her. "Andy, my man," he said. "Let's see if we can scare up some more of Hairy's delicious potato skins."

Andy blinked, but Blake was already putting a hand on his shoulder and leading him back out into the crowd.

"Take care of my girl," Blake called out over his shoulder.

His girl. She looked down at her shoes, feeling off center.

"Old habits are hard to break," Sam said, appearing by her side. "Come on. You and me can play some darts while Blake runs whatever errand is needed with your brother."

"Andy's agreed to start dating again," she found herself telling him as they walked over to the dart boards on the wall.

"That's brave of him. I hope he finds the most amazing woman ever."

More amazing than Kim? The feeling of being off-kilter changed to one of sharp grief. How was Andy supposed to do that?

"Come on," Sam said, thrusting a set of darts into her suddenly cold hands. "Let's play."

She focused on her target and drilled the first dart in the center.

"Bulls-eye," someone crooned in a booming voice from behind her.

Looking over her shoulder, she saw Grant sauntering over to them.

"She's one hot mama tonight. You'd better watch yourself, Sam. She might beat you."

Suddenly, Natalie *wanted* to beat him. She wanted to rub his nose in defeat after what he'd said to her earlier. She threw her second dart.

"Bulls-eye," Grant crooned out again.

Logan came over and slung an arm around Sam's shoulders. "She's killing you man."

Sam shoved him. "I haven't even had a turn yet."

Her third dart missed the center by a millimeter, but it still gave her twenty points.

"Ohhhh," someone called out, and she turned to see Jordan heading toward them, her beer in one hand.

"Mr. Cool is going down." He gave her a high-five and handed her the drink. "Blake is getting your brother a beer, and he'll make sure he drinks responsibly."

She snorted with laughter and watched Sam hit one bulls-eye, an eighteen, and a sixteen. Her innate competiveness pushed all thought from her mind as she sipped her beer. In the end, she beat Sam by thirteen points.

He inclined his head toward her like the good sport he was. "Good game, Natalie."

Schadenfreude must be real because she felt better for having beaten him.

"Anyone else want to play?" she asked, twirling a dart around in one hand as she reached for her Guinness with the other.

Professional athletes couldn't ignore an outright challenge. Grant cozied up to her. She beat him flat. Jordan stepped forward with that cocky grin of his. She knocked him on his ass. Hunter came forward next with narrowed eyes, falling into game mode, she could tell. He was the best challenger, but she still beat him by three points.

"Boys, we have got to find Natalie another challenger," Jordan said. "She's the Queen of Darts tonight."

So, they thought she was good at darts? Time to show them what she could do at pool. Feeling a bit cocky, she strode up to Logan and pulled his pool stick away from him. She held it out horizontally like it was a samurai sword and wielded it at them.

"Who's going to play pool with little ol' me?" she asked with a purr.

The guys all hooted and shouted. Zack twisted his stick until it crossed with hers, the Obi-Wan Kenobi to her Vader.

"Think you can play with the big boys?" the quarterback drawled out.

She shoved their sticks against his chest—or he let her. "I know I can."

He waggled his brows. "Then let's do this."

After racking the balls, she broke at an angle and pocketed two solid balls in one shot. She made two more shots before missing one. Zack took over, and she discovered he wasn't kidding about his skills.

"Someone *is* a big boy when it comes to pool," she commented as he bent over at the waist and sunk a red-striped ball into the right corner pocket.

His mischievous grin had her tapping her finger against her pool stick. She was going to have to play dirty. Which meant lots of bending over. It had always worked on Blake.

Sure enough. It worked on Zack too. Men were so easy.

When she leaned back against the table in victory like a satisfied cat, he gave her a once-over. "If you weren't Blake's..."

Grant looped an arm around his neck. "She cheated you, Zack Sprat. No man can beat a woman when she uses her wiles like that."

"No man minds getting beaten when he gets to watch," the flirty quarterback fired back.

Rubbing her hands together, she turned to face the rest of the guys. "Who's up next?"

Jordan strode forward. "Since I'm the only one in a committed relationship, I'll play. I'm immune to the charms of other women."

Now that made her smile. Jordan was a flirt, but he was faithful. "How is Grace?"

His smile said it all. "Great. She finally managed to pry out the chicken fricassee recipe from that fancy chef you two enjoyed in New York City. I gave it to Blake for you."

She and Blake had met them for New Year's in New York three years ago. She was touched Grace had remembered. Suddenly she felt a pang of loss for her old friend, for all these old friends.

Pasting a smile on her face, she said, "I can't wait to try it. Please thank her for me."

He winked. "Will do. Now, Nat. Are you ready to go down?"

These guys were all swagger, but she could trash talk with the best of them. Blake had refined her craft there.

"I don't know, Jordan. Aren't you afraid all that gel in your hair will throw you off balance and make you miss your shot?"

"Ooohhh," the guys hooted.

"She's got your number, Jordan. Good thing Blake isn't playing. He'd scratch with all that mousse in his hair."

She glanced over at the crowd, hoping for a glimpse of Blake and Andy. They hadn't come back, which either meant Blake was still searching for someone, or they'd found a likely candidate and he was hanging around to help Andy get his game back. The breath in her chest evaporated, and she had to cough to reinflate her lungs. Dammit. Why did he have to be so sweet and supportive?

Turning her focus back to the game, she found she needed it. Jordan was a solid player and had a few trick shots up his sleeve.

"Someone knows how to work his stick," Logan called out.

God, these guys acted like a bunch of teenagers. She rolled her eyes. She beat Jordan in the end, and then Hunter too. A round of drinks arrived, and she was handed a shot of tequila.

"Bottoms up," Jordan said as all the guys clicked their shot glasses together.

All except Sam. He didn't do shots.

Jordan poured everyone another shot from the *Patron* bottle. Natalie looked at the shot glass for a moment, knowing a second shot wouldn't be the wisest decision. But for some reason she didn't care. Nothing leveled a person out like tequila, and tonight she just wanted to forget everything. She downed the next one. Jordan poured another, and she went for her third. By the time she found her pool stick, her hands were tingling. Her body was floating a couple inches off the floor. She felt fabulous. If she closed her eyes, she could even pretend that the clock had re-wound to happier days and she and Blake were married again and out having fun with his friends.

Grant volunteered to play her, and when it was all over, she didn't care he'd beaten her. The pool stick kept slipping from her hands.

Jordan brought more shots around on a tray, swishing his hips like a Vegas waitress.

She was reaching for another when Sam said, "I think you've had enough."

The harmonious float she was lying on suddenly lurched. In slow motion, she turned to face him and stuck her finger at his chest. Or at least she thought it was his chest. Her finger only met air, and she stumbled into him.

"Don't tell me what to do!" she told him and realized her words were floating too, like seeds from a dandelion she'd used to make a wish.

Cool, her fun drunk self said. She felt like the rock star, Pink, right now. Having fun on a Saturday night. Playing with the boys. Drinking too much. There was *nothing* wrong with that.

Jordan stood like a statue with the tray in his hands, unsure who to defy, her or Mr. Grumpy Face Sam. She took the decision away from him and picked up a shot. After tossing it back, she flicked her hair over her shoulder and looked at Sam.

"You were out of line earlier," she told him, feeling a sweet buzz in her head.

"I'm sorry I hurt your feelings, Natalie," he told her, and Jordan peeled away like a fast car.

She pressed her hand to her chest. "My *feelings*?"

She didn't have feelings. Something wove, and she realized it was her when Sam put out an arm to hold her in place. A woodpecker tapped on her shoulder, and she tilted her head to the side to tell it to buzz off. But it wasn't a bird—it was a massive finger. She followed the digit up to the arm and then up to the face.

Blake was staring at her with narrowed eyes. "Have enough to drink, babe?"

Andy leaned into her face, and she wove backward when she saw two of him.

"Jeez, Nat, how much did you drink?"

Sam shook his head. "Jordan brought around tequila shots."

"Great," Blake said. "She goes crazy when she has tequila."

"I do not," she said like a little kid and then giggled. "If you're talking about that one time when we went to Mexico and—"

Blake put his hand over her mouth. "That story isn't for public consumption. Andy, why don't you head out so your babysitter can go home? I'll see that Nat gets home safely."

"I can get back home fine," she told them, leaning against Blake's solid chest.

"Did you drive here?" he asked her.

"Oh, crap." There were two of him, and both faces were so pretty she reached up and pinched his cheeks.

"That's what I thought," Blake said with a grumble.

"She picked me up," Andy said.

"Then take her car. We can figure the rest out tomorrow when she's sober."

Blake signaled for something with his fingers, but Natalie couldn't make it out. Moments later, Jordan appeared with a grin and a glass of water. He thrust it out and bent at the waist.

"My lady," he said in a British accent, making her giggle.

"Jordan, you have lost your mind." Blake ran his hand through his hair and cursed. "Damn mousse. Is everyone like this?"

"Pretty much," Sam said. "I'm glad you and I refused to drive into town in that monstrosity Jordan rented. You take care of Nat, and I'll herd the rest of the cats into the Hummer. Grant's cuing up to sing the Notre Dame fight song."

"Gee, that sounds like fun," she said, looking for her singing buddy.

"If he gets going, we're doomed," Blake said. "You'd better stop him, Sam."

With that, the man walked off. He was so serious all the time.

"Are you sure you have her?" Andy asked with a dark frown.

She patted his chest in her best imitation of patty-cake. "Don't you know anything, Andy Cakes? Blake has always *had* me."

The men shared a glance.

Her laughter snorted out. "He had me at hello. Get it."

"Oh, brother. Take two aspirin and call me in the morning," her brother said, kissing her cheek.

"Wait," she cried out, grabbing a hunk of his shirt. "Did you find anyone to talk to tonight?"

He glanced upward. "Yes. Blake was most helpful. Her name is Valerie. I'll tell you more later when you're guaranteed to remember."

"Blake is the best friend ever," she said in all seriousness and then gave a gigantic hiccup.

"Yes, he is," Andy said agreeably. "Hiccups signal—"

"I know," Blake said. "We're out of here. Catch you later, Andy Cakes."

Her brother shot him a look. "If you hadn't been such a good wingman..."

As Andy walked off, she snuggled closer to Blake. He was warm. "Have they turned on the air conditioner or something? It's freezing in here."

Blake swore softly. "First hiccups and now the chills. I know what comes next. We need to go, babe."

She pressed her hand to her skull, which was starting to hurt. "What comes next, Blake? I can't remember."

He hustled her out of there with the help of that giant bouncer man, the other guys trailing after them. The camera flashes made her eyes turn to dry balls in their sockets, she blinked so much. Her stomach started to churn. When Blake buckled her into the passenger seat of his SUV, she moaned.

"Hang on, babe."

The sound of the car door slamming made her wince. Her head rolled over on the seat as she turned her head to look at him. He was so darn pretty. Tonight all she wanted to do was fall back into the world they had once shared. The one where they'd always been there to take care of each other, to love each other. She was such a sap.

"I love it when you call me, babe," she said after he was settled in the driver's seat.

The sigh he released was harsh in the quiet of the car. "Now you tell me? Your timing sucks." He turned the key in the ignition and started to drive.

She closed her eyes. "You said it wrong."

"Huh?" The car was picking up speed, and her skin started to turn to fire.

Then she realized Blake was the fire. He'd always blazed larger than life. Why else had she been so attracted to him? He helped keep the cold inside her at bay.

"Your timing sucks, *babe.*"

He didn't respond, and she cracked her eyes open to look at him. There were still two of him, and each one looked bigger than Hercules.

"Ah," he finally said. "How could I forget?"

"Don't know," she mumbled. "You never forget. Not even things like my birthday or our anniversary like some other guys. Are we almost home?"

"Yes, babe. We're almost home. Go to sleep."

"I'm not tired," she said, feeling like she was sitting around a big, happy bonfire on a quiet stretch of beach. "Let's sing a song."

He groaned. "Please, babe. *Go to sleep.*"

"No. How about 'You Are My Sunshine'?" It seemed appropriate. Hadn't she just been thinking about firelight? Wasn't the sun the biggest, baddest ball of fire in the universe?

She launched into the song, but he didn't join her.

"Why aren't you singing?" she asked, pausing. "Come on. One, two—"

"*Natalie.* Please just close your eyes and go to sleep."

"Oh, you're such a fuss budget sometimes," she said. "Let's have some fun. I feel great."

"That's what I'm afraid of," he muttered.

The lassitude coursing through her only grew more powerful. She placed her hand on his knee and stroked the hard muscles there. Blake would come around.

He loved her. He'd do anything for her—even if it meant singing her silly song.

CHAPTER 15

Blake's worst nightmare was happening. When Natalie drank too much, she either passed out or starred in The Natalie Show. It was famous among her siblings and friends. She became a flirty entertainer, completely uninhibited. Tonight he was going to get a show, it seemed. How could Jordan have forgotten that? His friend was dead meat.

She continued to belt out "You Are My Sunshine," giving him a pounding headache. Braving the crowded bar to help Andy find a date had been bad enough. But he'd seen the plea in Natalie's gaze, not to mention the fear in Andy's, and it had felt natural to help. While he wasn't a widower, he remembered the first night he'd tried to move on with his life after Natalie left. It had been a catastrophic failure, the kind he still dreamed about, and not in a good way.

He'd hoped to soften Andy's experience. The woman Blake had spotted from across the room hadn't wanted to *be* at the bar with her two girl friends, and since Andy wasn't a bar kind of guy either, he figured they might be a good match. The two of them had hit it off after some initial awkwardness, and Valerie had agreed to meet him for coffee. Score one for Hale. He hoped it went well.

When he reached Natalie's house, he cut the engine. Her piercing alto rendition faded.

"Where are we?" she asked. "Are we on vacation?"

Terrific. She was already showing signs of confusion. "We're at your place, babe."

He lurched out of the car, wanting to run for it. If she didn't even remember where she lived, he was really in for it.

One of Natalie's favorite classic movies was *The Philadelphia Story,* so he'd watched it with her one movie night. Near the end of the film, he'd realized something—Natalie turned into the character played by Katharine Hepburn when she drank. Tracy Lord might not climb up on a restaurant bar and conduct her own *Coyote Ugly* number like he'd seen Natalie do, but she did act outside the norm and fail to remember everything when she woke up the next morning. Exactly like Natalie.

"What do you mean *my place?*" she asked in a slurred yet sassy voice when he opened her door.

He braced himself and helped her out of her seatbelt. Touchdown appeared beside the car with a happy bark. "You live here now."

Her hands pressed to his shoulders. "You're playing a practical joke on me, aren't you? Why would I live *here?* I love our home."

He knew that, and it was the only reason he'd stayed there, contending with the daily torture of living in a place stacked ceiling-high with memories of her. He reached out to help her down from the car, and it was a good thing he did. She was unsteady on her feet.

"You're going to have to carry me," she told him, batting her eyelashes at him in the moonlight. "Like Prince Charming."

While Natalie could be unnervingly practical in day-do-day life, her romantic side opened up when she drank. It didn't happen often, so each memory was treasured. He remembered the vacation they'd gone on after his one and only Super Bowl win. She'd jumped into his arms and asked him to sweep her off her feet.

He'd always loved that side of her, so seeing it now hurt. Bad.

He grabbed her purse, picked her up, and carried her to the house. She toyed with the ends of his hair, running her fingernails down the back of his neck from time to time, knowing it drove him wild. Somehow wearing a football helmet for so many hours had made his neck more sensitive to touch.

At the door, he tried the doorknob, and was relieved to find it unlocked. Managing her and unlocking the door was more than he could juggle. Touchdown led the way inside, his tail wagging like he was delighted to see Blake carrying Mommy again. At least someone was happy.

The pounding in his head worsened as he set her down. "Come on, Nat. Let's get you into bed."

She wove a bit and faced him. "I'll get ready, if you get ready."

Her hands moved to the waistband of his jeans. Pure torture. He stopped them from touching him. He was going to be either canonized or knighted after tonight. He decided to try a different strategy. Maybe if she expended enough energy she'd fall asleep. It worked with Touchdown.

"How about some music?" he asked, digging into her purse for her smartphone.

Pulling up her playlist, he walked over to the docking station he'd seen in the kitchen and plugged in the phone. Pink's edgy music poured out, and Natalie's body immediately started to dance.

"Good choice," she crooned. "Come dance with me and Touchdown."

How many times had they danced like this? Usually, he could unwind enough to join her. Tonight, his muscles were tight and uncoordinated. As soon as he came over to her, she placed her hands on his chest, her touch driving him wild.

"What's the matter, honey? Tough day?"

Her concern was a harbinger of old times. Oh, how he wanted things to be like this again. But not when she wasn't herself.

"Yeah, it's been a tough week, and I'm tired. How about you dance? I'll make you something to eat."

It wouldn't be too long before she got the munchies anyway. God knew she'd need something to soak up all that tequila. He dug into her refrigerator, going with a grilled cheese with an over-easy egg in the middle—one of her favorite hangover cures. After pulling the ingredients out and walking over to the counter, he glanced over at her.

All the air arrested in his lungs, and his whole body locked in place.

Somewhere in the middle of the kitchen she'd lost her T-shirt and jeans and was now dancing in her bra and panties to Pink's "So What?" Her taste in lingerie had never sucked, and his mouth went dry at the sight of her white bra wrapped in black lace. Touchdown was doing circles around her, and it would have been funny, if he hadn't turned hard as hell in three seconds.

Her body was the same breathtaking combination of strength and sexiness it had always been. Smooth lithe skin flowed under the lights in the den. Her hips shimmied in a way that had his own pelvis twitching. And her arms... Well they wove through the air with all the erotic, fluid appeal of a belly dancer.

He dropped the ingredients on the counter with a thud as his pulse hammered in his neck. The egg cracked, the liquid leaking across the counter. He was so enthralled by the sight of her dancing, he didn't even reach to clean it up.

She was so in her own thrall, her eyes were closed.

The tequila was taking her to a new dimension, he knew. She was humming along with the music.

God, he'd missed her. Missed her like this.

Tearing his gaze away from her body was harder than facing down the player who'd delivered a dirty hit on him and popped his shoulder out of the socket. He started breathing deep, hoping to corral his thoughts. But his normal ability to focus was limited around her.

Forcing himself to clean up the mess from the cracked egg, he then moved on to make the grilled cheese. When it was piping hot, he scooped it onto a plate. He couldn't take seeing all her tantalizing flesh, so he detoured through the house to her bedroom to locate her favorite nightshirt. She usually slept nude—like he did—but they'd always kept PJs for visits to family. Her cedar chest lay at the foot of her bed, just like it had during their marriage. He'd sent it to her because he hadn't felt right about keeping her hope chest.

If he were honest, he'd also hoped returning a few keepsakes to her would help remind her of all they'd had. He opened it with shaking hands. The nightshirt was folded on top, but sitting just under it was something he hadn't expected.

Her wedding dress was still wrapped in the plastic sleeve at the bottom. He fell to his knees. God, he'd assumed she would have gotten rid of it. She'd been so insistent about wanting nothing from their home, their marriage. Nothing that would remind her of him.

Unable to control himself this time, he lifted the dress out. It smelled like the perfume she'd worn that day. The hints of jasmine and vanilla brought back memories of the secret smile she'd given him as she walked down the aisle. Oh, God.

He held the dress against his chest, his eyes burning now. At the bottom of the chest was their favorite wedding picture, the one he'd added to the chest before sending it over.

Then he spotted the black box and knew it held her engagement ring, the one he'd given to her on bent knee on a warm Saturday afternoon in June after he'd taken her on a picnic in the mountains. Her wedding ring was probably nestled in beside it. He couldn't touch that little box right now. He knew it would break him completely to see the infinity symbol engraved in the bands, just like the ones he'd had engraved on the bridge. He set her dress on top of it, hiding it from view.

But he couldn't stop himself from reaching for the photo. He drew it out, trembling everywhere now, and traced the outline of her face. Like usual, she'd eschewed fashion trends. She'd left her hair down and curly like he preferred, and instead of going with a sleeveless wedding dress like most brides, she'd chosen one covered in Spanish lace. They were standing in front of the ocean, on the beach outside of Santa Cruz where they'd exchanged vows. In the picture, she had her hand on his cheek, her long lacy sleeves blowing in the breeze. He was gazing into her eyes, his eyes full of love, and his hands gripped her hips to him.

"I love that picture," she said brightly from behind him, wrapping her arms around his neck. "Take me to bed like you did on our wedding night."

Her easy touch broke his heart once again. He made himself replace the wedding mementos and reach for the nightshirt he'd dropped to the floor. Thrusting it at her, he rose to his feet.

"Put that on, and then come and eat."

He had to get out of her room, away from her touch, or he was going to do something he regretted. Like kiss her. Hold her. His willpower was rapidly approaching zero.

As he strode out of the bedroom, he leaned down to pick up Touchdown. If he had something occupying his hands, surely he couldn't put them on her.

She came out, holding the nightshirt under her eyes

like it was some veil and she was the exotic dancer sent to seduce him, which only made Touchdown bark. Pink was singing about the walk of shame now, which seemed appropriate. If he acted on his feelings, he was going to feel a whole heap of shame tomorrow.

"Why are you acting so weird?" she asked, dancing closer to him. "I've never seen you this uptight. Why don't you let me loosen you up?"

He ran to the kitchen and gave Touchdown a treat. When she found him, she was dancing and...yes, weaving more than just a little. He knew he'd have to leave her and hope she'd eventually pass out on her own.

He slid the sandwich toward her. "Eat. Take two aspirin. Drink a glass of water. And go to bed. I'll check on you tomorrow."

Her face looked as though he'd slapped her, and he cursed. To his shock, tears formed in her eyes.

"What's wrong with you?" she asked, all the teasing and seduction stripped from her voice. "You're scaring me."

Having experienced his fair share of pain and confusion over the past two years, he understood the emotions shaking her.

"You're not yourself right now."

She clutched the nightshirt to her body. "Don't you want me anymore?"

Not want her? How could she accuse him of that after everything? He crossed over to her and took the nightshirt from her hands. "Raise your arms."

She did so meekly now, and when it fell over her body, she raised her troubled eyes to meet his. "I'm sorry for whatever I did to make you this mad."

A sigh gusted out of him as his heart burst. "I'm not mad." He headed to the door.

"Where are you going?" she asked when he opened it.

Touchdown gave a happy bark and whined and pawed at Blake's leg like he wanted to go out. "Stay, boy." At least one of them could watch over her. "I'm going next door. I'll see you in the morning."

"Dammit, tell me you love me. Right now."

He squeezed his eyes shut. Even if he said the words, she wouldn't remember. What would it hurt? "I love you. Now eat your sandwich."

"Uh," he heard her rasp out and looked over immediately.

Her body was sliding across the kitchen island in a ladylike slump. Should he help her or leave?

"I don't feel well," she whispered.

Finally. She was crashing. And right after she'd broken his heart to smithereens again. Touchdown barked as if to remind him of his duty to take care of her, of the vows he'd made to stand with her in sickness and in health. Like he could have forgotten them. He strode back into the house as she started to fall. After catching her in his arms, he lifted her like a small child and carried her to her room.

"I'm going to be sick," she said, slapping a hand over her mouth.

He made it to her bathroom in time and held her hair as she vomited. He rubbed her back throughout, and when she was finally spent, he rose to fetch a glass of water so she could rinse her mouth out. Her hands were shaking so badly he had to help her hold the glass. He didn't even bother to hand her a warm cloth—he simply washed her face, trying to be gentle and yet mechanical.

"You poor baby. You really did a number on yourself, didn't you?" he asked when she rested her forehead on the toilet seat.

In all the time he'd known her, she'd only been this sick twice before. Once, after celebrating his Super Bowl win. The other time had been on a different vacation.

She'd blamed tainted sushi, but he was reasonably sure it had had more to do with the sake she'd drunk with it.

When enough time had passed after her final bout of sickness, he tenderly scooped her up, breaking open more doorways in his heart, and carried her to her bed, where he tucked the covers over her. She immediately crawled over to the right side of the bed.

His heart received the final knock-out punch of the night. She still slept on *her* side of the bed. He'd tried sleeping in the middle after she left, but he'd soon reverted to sleeping on the left. It was the only way he could fall asleep.

"Blake," she called gruffly.

"I'm right here," he rasped out. It was where he felt he belonged.

Her eyes opened, and even though they were bloodshot and filled with pain now, they gazed at him with renewed focus. "Hold me."

His plans to flee turned to dust. He couldn't ignore her quiet request. He tucked her in and settled down on top of the covers, making sure to keep enough distance between them. When she cuddled close, he gritted his teeth and locked all his muscles into place so he wouldn't soften against her.

Then she murmured, "I love you," and he felt the first tears fall from his eyes.

CHAPTER 16

Natalie awoke to a pounding headache and a mouth as dry as the desert. When she tried to turn over so she could die, she couldn't. She cracked one eye open and groaned.

Blake.

He was on top of the covers dressed in the most hideous outfit she'd ever seen him wear. Her mind started to turn like a rusty old wagon wheel, sending images from the night before flashing through her mind.

She and Andy going to Hairy's Irish Pub. Playing darts and pool. Downing shots with the guys.

Oh, God. Tequila was the devil.

And that was all she remembered. Great, another Natalie Show had premiered.

Peeking under the covers to see what she was wearing, if anything, she was somewhat relieved to discover she had on her underwear and a nightshirt. Not surprising really. Blake had never crossed that line before, even though last night must have been hard for him. *Hard.* If she hadn't been in agony, she might have laughed.

She let her lone eye close. It hurt too much to keep it open. Blake must have taken her home. Had Andy helped? The strong frame next to her stirred, and the bed dipped, making her clutch her stomach.

"Don't do that," she hissed.

"Sorry," he whispered. "I'll go get you some aspirin and water."

"And tomato juice," she reminded him.

"Do you want me to add the egg?"

She almost up-chucked right there. "No."

Even though she suspected he was taking care to inch off the bed, the movement felt as profound as the trembling of the earth under a herd of dashing buffalo. She moaned long and deep as he left the room.

Moments—or an eternity—later, he returned to the room. "Okay, let's do this," he said. "You'll feel better once you get this stuff down."

He put his hand under her back and neck to raise her, and she bit her lip to still the cartwheels flipping in her stomach. "I hate this part."

"I know." His touch was gentle as he settled the rim of the glass against her lips.

She managed the pills and a few sips of both the water and the tomato juice. He helped her lay back down, but she found herself missing his warmth and the sweet touch of his hands, which had helped dispel the dizziness.

"I don't feel as dizzy when you hold me," she admitted. At this point, she had no pride.

A hefty sigh gusted out, and then he lay back down beside her. His warmth drew her. His strength anchored her. She nodded off, and when she surfaced, the dizziness was gone. She rolled onto her side and put her hand on his chest, the only place it seemed to fit when they were squashed together this way.

"I must have done a doozy last night," she murmured, wanting more water to counter the dryness in her mouth, but not daring to move. Her tomato juice might decide to dance an Ole.

"Yes. Jordan is going to have to answer to me later. I

can only hope he got as sick as you did."

Unlikely. He outweighed her by nearly a hundred pounds. "Not my best moment." Well, she'd wanted to forget, and she'd certainly managed to meet that goal.

He grunted in acknowledgment.

"Did I do anything I should regret?" she asked.

"Other than dance around in your underwear to Pink? Nah."

She almost dove under the covers then and there. "So, I didn't throw myself at you?"

The muscles in his chest clenched where her hand lay. "I managed to talk you down. You weren't in your right mind."

A powerful wave of grief rose up in her. So, she'd managed to hurt him again, using his desire for her against him. She should hide under the covers in shame, after all.

"I'm sorry," she whispered.

Something patted her hand. "It's okay."

But it wasn't. She could hear the edge in his voice. He'd thrown her nightshirt over her and stayed with her, sleeping on top of the covers like they were teenagers dating, too scared to have sex, but too attracted to stay apart. She suspected there was more to it, but she was too afraid to ask him *how* she'd thrown herself at him.

"I'll make it up to you." Her mind couldn't think beyond the present moment, but she'd think of something when she felt better.

"You don't have to balance the scales, Nat."

No, he'd never kept score. Not once during their time together. She'd always loved that about him.

"Are you feeling better now?" he asked. "I need to head home to let the caterers in and deal with the guys."

"Oh, God, I forgot. Brunch. I am the worst professional on the face of the planet."

"I...ah...wasn't sure what to do when your assistant

called, so I texted her back and told her to show up without...well...you. I knew you'd be embarrassed if I answered your phone."

This further evidence of his consideration sent a sweet pang through her chest. She turned her head and forced eyes open. Ten eighteen. They would be arriving at eleven. "I can help."

He gently pressed her back down when she tried to rise. "Don't bother. It's not like they don't know what to do. Everything's ready, right?"

When she nodded, a bolt of pain shot across her temple. She clutched it.

"I'll check on you later."

Could he be any sweeter? She felt the urge to curl up into a ball.

"Thanks," she rasped out instead.

A soft kiss landed on her brow, and his hand stroked the hair from her forehead. "Get some rest."

The movement in the bed when he left was more akin to a flock of pigeons landing, and sure there was a jolt in her stomach, but not the roll she'd experienced earlier. She nodded off again. By the time she finally managed to crawl out of bed and into the shower, she'd downed the tomato juice and more water. She'd be drinking buckets today. The steam and water helped, and after she dried herself and wrapped herself in a towel, she forced herself to deal with the one thought that now wouldn't leave her consciousness.

If he'd found her nightshirt, he must have found her secret too.

She walked to her cedar chest and opened the lid. The wedding picture she'd placed inside with her dress was lying at an angle, but the black box holding her rings lay undisturbed.

He had seen these precious mementos and touched them. She sank to a knee and wondered what he'd felt. He'd sent these items over in her hope chest with the note *No one should be without their hope,* but try as she might, she couldn't force herself to get rid of them.

Picking up the frame, she stared at the picture inside. She radiated all the good things about life in that one snapshot: life, love, joy, and hope. Looking at it, she could finally admit she wasn't happy, not like she'd been before Kim's death. She'd given up believing that she could be, that she deserved to be. How had it ever come to this? Blake living next door and taking care of her when she was drunk, even though they were divorced.

Her eyes tracked to the imprint of his body on the covers and the pillow.

Her stomach rolled, but this time, it wasn't from excess.

It was from grief.

CHAPTER 17

Sam was reading the Sunday paper at the kitchen table when Blake let himself in through the garage. He and Andy had orchestrated the return of Natalie's car—Andy had dropped it off, and then Blake had dropped Andy off. They hadn't really talked about last night, thank God. All he really wanted to do now was take a long shower before the caterers arrived.

"Everyone still asleep?"

"I think a few are showering. We might need to wake the others up with ice water after last night's antics."

He wasn't even going to ask what they'd gotten up to after he left. "I'd be particularly happy to wake up Jordan that way."

"Sounds like fun. How is Natalie?" Sam asked, folding *The Western Independent* and settling it in his lap.

"Hung over. Shock." He made jazz hands, which normally would have made Sam laugh. But his friend didn't play along.

"How are you after playing husband last night?"

The bold question would have gone unanswered had anyone else asked it. "Shitty. She pulled one of her Natalie Shows and danced in her underwear."

His memory couldn't seem to stop replaying that scene, and the mere memory was enough to arouse him. It was embarrassing. And heartbreaking.

"I'm sorry," Sam said quietly and rose from the kitchen table. He poured a cup of coffee and slid it to Blake.

The coffee burned his lips, but he kept gulping, needing the pain as much as the caffeine. He'd barely slept. Being next to her again, feeling her warm, soft body so close, hearing her breathe...even those cute little snores she made when she was conked out had been like finding a trove of long-awaited treasure. And it had made him cry, dammit.

Sam's hand rested on his shoulder, and he welcomed the show of support.

"She threw herself at me and was shocked when I turned her away. She said...she loved me." The knife slid under his ribs again, tearing open his flesh.

"Then you were right to come here," Sam said. "She might have been drunk, but you know what they say—in vino veritas. Everything will work out. Somehow."

He couldn't think about that right now. When the guys left later, he would take a long hike in the mountains and try to clear his mind.

"I'm going to take a quick shower."

"Don't be surprised if you don't find any clean underwear," Sam told him when he was halfway across the room.

He did a double take. "What did they do?"

Sam grimaced. "I tried to put a stop to it after the first few, but...I gave up under duress. Some of the guys—not saying who—climbed one of your trees and stuck all your briefs on the branches. In hindsight, it's not as bad as the time we put all of Jordan's briefs in the freezer."

He glanced out the window, but couldn't see anything from his vantage point, so he walked out the back door. "You're shitting me."

"Wish I was, although I did think it was pretty creative in the beginning."

He watched a squirrel carry one of his navy briefs in its mouth and run up a tree. Were they using his underwear for blankets or something? He could see the ad now.

Ride the Squirrel Craze. Discover men's underwear for blankets. Keep your nuts warm.

His eyes tracked to the right, and sure enough, his underwear were flapping in the breeze on the highest branches possible, like a men's-only May Pole. The sheer number of them and the amount of colors he wore made his face flush.

"Whose brilliant idea was this?" he asked.

"Jordan and Grant's. Who else?"

He growled in his throat. Normally he would laugh something like this off, but he'd slept two hours tops and had woken up with blue balls.

"You're telling me they used all my briefs?"

"Cleared out your drawer," Sam said with barely disguised glee.

Blake turned at the sound of heavy footfalls in the hallway. When no one emerged, he strode over and discovered Grant hiding behind the wall like a little kid.

When the lineman saw him, he held up his hands. "Don't kill me. It was Jordan's idea."

"Right." He rubbed the stubble on his face. "I'm showering now, and I want all my underwear down by the time I finish."

Grant shook his head. "No way, Ace. We...ah...made a brother's pact. The only person who can get them down is you."

He and Sam had started the brother's pact at camp to make sure no one welshed on a dare or a bet or a practical joke. Now he was eating his own words.

"Terrific. Let the caterers in if I'm not out yet."

He headed straight to the shower. It was intolerably brief and cold, and he elected not to shave as he tugged on yesterday's underwear and Don Johnson getup. No way was he going commando in tight acid-washed jeans. He didn't need anything rubbing or chafing down south. When he returned to the kitchen, the caterers were already setting up. He started when he saw Natalie slowly peeling saran wrap off a bowl of fruit, wincing with every inch uncovered.

Of course she'd come. She prided herself on her professionalism—always had. The smell of food had to be pure torture for her, not to mention the noise from the five guys who had emerged from back rooms with wet hair and clean-shaven jaws. Jordan wasn't among them and neither was Zack.

Sam waggled his brow as if he knew what he was thinking. He nodded.

As he passed Natalie on the way to the cabinet, he rested his hand briefly on her shoulder. She looked back at him. Her skin had a gray pallor, and her hair was still wet from her own shower. But she stole his breath away.

"I told you that you didn't have to come," he said. What he really wanted to tell her was that she looked beautiful, even hung over.

"I know you did. Thanks for helping Andy this morning."

"You're welcome."

He moved to the cabinet and pulled out two pitchers. Sam grabbed one, and they filled them first with ice and then with water before tiptoeing into the room where Zack and Jordan were bunking. Once they were inside enemy territory, Blake crooked his finger for Sam to take Zack while he positioned himself over Jordan.

Pretty boy Jordan was sleeping in the nude on his stomach, tangled in the covers with one butt cheek sticking out. Zack was sleeping on a blowup bed in the corner by the closet. He must have lost the coin toss.

Blake raised one finger at a time, counting to three, and then he and Sam simultaneously upended the pitcher all over the guys. Atlanta's marquee quarterback screeched, lashing out with his hands as the water soaked his bed. Zack squealed bloody murder and rolled off onto the floor.

Shoulders shaking with laughter, Blake watched as Jordan rose onto his haunches and glared at him.

"Payback's a bitch," he said, letting one eyebrow rise.

"You guys so suck," Zack shouted, tossing water-soaked pillows and sheets in their direction.

"How does it feel to be wearing the same underwear, Ace?" Jordan fired back.

The man never cried uncle. It was what made him a great player. Sack him, and he sneered.

"About as great as an ice bath to the privates. Brunch is ready." With that, Blake left the room, Sam chuckling as he followed him out.

The guys were stuffing their faces when they came back into the room. He spotted Natalie in the corner of the kitchen, fiddling with a container of something. All of her assistants were gone. She must have sent them home since everything was laid out. He wondered why she was lingering. Did she want to talk to him? His heart clutched with hope.

Logan set aside his bagel with a grin. "How badly did you get Jordan?"

"Pretty bad, from the sound of it," Grant said. "Zack could have doubled for some exotic bird."

"Must be all those Vegas entertainers he's been dating." Blake affected a hard gleam in his eyes as he scanned the group. "Let that be a warning. Next time you want to decorate my tree with my briefs do me a favor and leave one clean pair for me to wear. These jeans chafe like hell."

The guys all laughed, and Natalie looked over, her eyes wide. Then she stepped over to the window and looked out, likely to see the spectacle. She was biting her lip when she turned around. When she waggled her finger at him, he walked over without hesitation, as if she were a magnet.

"I'll go get you some new briefs," she whispered when he lowered his head to hear her.

His mouth parted in surprise. "You don't have to do that."

"What are you going to do? Climb the tree and wash them? I know you. The guys touched your briefs, and I think I saw a few robins perching on a red pair."

Ugh. He hadn't thought about the birds. Or the guys' hands.

"I can have my assistant get some tomorrow," he told her. "Be faster than the mail." The tips of his ears burned as he considered what it would be like to ask her. Usually he ordered them online himself, which Natalie had reason to know.

Three years ago someone had taken a picture of him buying his briefs at Cherry Creek Mall and tweeted it. The picture had instantly gone viral. His fans had started tweeting about switching to his brand for good luck on game day, and several had shared pics. If there was one thing he didn't need to see in a pic, it was a hairy man with a big belly pointing at the waistband of his briefs.

"I know...what you like." Her cheeks flushed, putting a dent in her gray pallor. "And I owe you. After last night."

"I told you, you don't owe me," he said as Jordan walked into the kitchen and glared at him. He shot him a wide-toothed smile.

"I know, but I want to do this, Blake. I'll send Touchdown over when I leave for the store. He was taking a nap."

The dog probably hadn't slept much better than Blake. Maybe he was as confused as Blake was about this whole situation. Still, after last night, Blake could feel the simple bonds of intimacy wrapping around them once more. Here he was, talking with her in the kitchen about buying his briefs. He had to remind himself she was his *ex*-wife, but in truth, he didn't think of her that way. Never had.

His gaze dropped to her mouth, and he wanted so badly to kiss her, just a simple husband-and-wife thank-you kiss, for being in the kitchen while he hosted his friends, for running personal errands for him. For being his partner. Her lashes lowered, and he knew she was aware of him. Then she licked her lips. Lightning struck. She always licked her lips when she was thinking about kissing him in public.

Stepping back was a challenge, but if he planned to win her back—and he did—he had to give her the space to realize *she* wanted him back. All the way.

"Thanks, Nat. Just text me when you return, and I'll jog over to get them. I don't want the guys commandeering them and adding them to that poor tree out back. Do you think it's embarrassed?"

A puzzled crease appeared between her brows. "Who?"

"The tree."

A shy smile played up those gorgeous lips of hers. "Maybe. I'll just...head out."

He clenched his hands to stop them from reaching for her. She moved by him so slowly, he felt her body heat penetrate his sensitized skin.

"I'll see you guys later," she said at the door. "Jordan, the next time you come around with tequila, I'm going to kill you."

The quarterback blew her a kiss. "The next time I have tequila, you can make us some of your famous margaritas."

"Deal."

The other guys waved and said their goodbyes. He watched her walk off in the sunshine, the light picking up the red and gold highlights in her hair. He slumped against the counter.

The next time...

She was including him in her future again, even if she didn't fully realize it yet. He dished himself a plate of food and came over to the table, checking to make sure the lone chair wasn't oozing with honey or some other disgusting substance. He'd bet money the practical jokes weren't over for the weekend, and time was running out.

"*So...*" Jordan said as he bit into blueberry multi-grain French Toast. "Looks like tequila wasn't such a bad idea after all."

"Shut it," Blake said as he chewed. Good manners flew out the window when they were together. Then his neck prickled. "Wait. Did you get Natalie drunk on purpose?"

"Who could forget The Natalie Show?" His friend lifted a shoulder. "You ended up staying over, didn't you? And she just agreed to buy you new briefs, right?"

Of course. Everyone knew about the Twitter incident. "What are you? A lip reader?" The question was rhetorical. They all read lips pretty well after spending most of their adult lives playing in ear-splitting crowd noise.

"Had to help a friend out," his buddy said.

The guys were all looking at him now, and he shifted in his seat.

"You were all in on it." He could read it in their faces now—all the careful planning that had gone into their game. Renting the snake so he'd lose. Making sure he was the Smuck so he could make Natalie laugh. Getting her drunk so he could take care of her. And his briefs...

"You are so diabolical." Then he got choked up.

"Man, I love you guys."

They all had a moment of back slaps, fist bumps, and man-hugs.

"I'm sorry about the ice water," Blake mumbled after their moment of bonding.

Jordan lifted his hand to his ear. "What did you say?"

Sam elbowed him in the ribs. "Know when to cut the cute factor, Jordan. It can get annoying."

Blake found himself smiling throughout the rest of the meal, even if he was wearing day-old briefs and the ugliest 1980s outfit of all time as his underwear swung in the breeze in the tree outside.

When Natalie texted him later to say she had his briefs, he jogged over with a newfound bounce in his step, Touchdown running at his side. She was waiting for him in the middle of the bridge. Somehow it felt like a sign that she'd met him halfway. The package was warm from her hands when she handed it to him awkwardly, their fingers grazing each other. It did crazy things to him, thinking of her hands on his briefs, even wrapped like they were in plastic.

"Well...I'll see you later." She had taken a few steps away from him before he found his voice.

"Would you like to go running with me tomorrow after work?" During the offseason, they'd run together a few times a week.

"I...ah...sure." Her mouth tipped up. A half smile.

His heart burst in his chest. "Great. I'll come by and get you."

She nodded and scampered across the rest of the bridge, Touchdown prancing behind her.

He clutched the briefs to his chest. Something had changed last night. She still loved him.

More than anything he wished she could remember the words she'd told him last night.

CHAPTER 18

Andy took a minute out of his jam-packed Monday to check his emails as he chomped on a sandwich. He'd seen fifteen patients so far today and expected he'd see at least that again before he headed home. There were a couple emails from the hospital administrator with hospital policy reminders about MRSA. A patient had contracted the staph infection after having open heart surgery, and everyone was in a panic from the hospital board down to the cleaning staff. He'd taken to showering and changing at the hospital before he went home.

He texted Natalie again. She'd told him she was mostly recovered from her hangover, but hadn't said much else beyond thanking him for returning her car. He wondered how she was digesting the news that Dare Valley High had offered Blake the head coaching position, but that was a topic he knew not to raise. Sometime this week he'd have to thank Blake for acting as his wingman and looking after his sister. The way Natalie had acted with Blake under the influence gave him hope. She still loved him. It had been all over her face.

A Skype chat box appeared in the right-hand corner

of his screen, and he grinned. Lucy O'Brien was typing.

Hey Andy Cakes. How's it hanging?

Only his best friend going back to kindergarten could ask him that. Not even his sisters could get away with it. He set his turkey on whole wheat back on the thin cafeteria napkin and rubbed his hands on his blue scrubs.

Hanging a little longer now that it's summer. Winter's a bitch on male pride.

He was already grinning. They hadn't seen each other much in the last few years. She'd come to Kim's funeral, of course, and they'd met up for lunch when she flew into Denver International Airport on her trip home for Christmas last year. Other than that, she spent most of her time overseas, taking heart-breaking and inspiring photos in developing countries. Magazines like *National Geographic* and non-profit organizations like CARE International loved her work, making her successful at what she did. She'd always had sass as a kid, but as an adult she seemed fearless and unshakeable. Lucy O'Brien was a force of nature.

LOL. Male pride indeed. Didn't know you had a complex. Hah. How's all your saving the world stuff going?

Some people thought doctors were gods—lower capital g. He didn't. His father had shown him that they were all too human. And after Kim's diagnosis, he'd been forced to face the depths of his helplessness. He'd been trained to heal, and he'd failed his partner. But Lucy understood his calling. It was something they shared. She traveled the world to tell stories through pictures. He stayed in a building with over three hundred hospital beds and took care of those who needed him. Even when he couldn't make them all better.

Hospital stuff is fine.

How's Danny? she typed.

Wonderful. He's playing T-ball, and he scrunches up his face when he's trying to hit the ball.

So far his son tended to hit the ball more than he missed it, which was earning him some special attention from his coach. Andy only wanted him to have fun. Competition would inevitably come later. Danny had faced enough adult emotions and situations in his life. Andy wanted to preserve his child's precious innocence for as long as he could.

He must have gotten that from Kim. As I remember, you sucked at baseball.

Everyone else—even his family—tiptoed around talking about all the things Danny had inherited from Kim. Not Lucy. It was one of the many things he appreciated about her.

Thank God for that, huh? Do you remember when I hit my own face with the bat? Shudder. I still have nightmares. So, what part of this awesome world are you in?

He braced himself. When she wasn't in touch with him, he knew she most likely didn't have access to email. Many of the places she visited didn't even have electricity or running water, least of all Internet. Sure, some of the hotels she stayed in did, but when she drove into the bush, as she liked to call it, she was far from modern conveniences. And he couldn't help but worry.

I'm in Congo. You should see it. It's one of the most beautiful and terrifying places I've ever visited.

Congo? His respiration altered. His heart rate picked up a few beats per minute. Stress. Anxiety. He knew the symptoms.

Aren't they having a war over there, Luce?

He hoped using her nickname would soften the question.

I'll have you know I take some of my best pictures in a war. Don't worry. I know how to take care of myself.

She always said that, but it didn't make him less afraid when he found out she was in a place where she could easily be killed. He'd lost Kim. He didn't want to lose his old friend too.

Be careful. Please. This is the daddy in me talking.

You sound like Harry. He wants me to come home and take over Hairy's. Like that would work. I'm not hairy enough.

Her dad had started Hairy's Irish Pub before she was born. He'd been drinking to celebrate opening his business while he wrote up the paperwork, hence his infamous mistake of calling the bar Hairy's and not Harry's. While Andy loved the place, he had trouble imagining Lucy being confined by that one space. The world was Lucy's oyster.

I was there the other night with Natalie. It never changes in the best way possible.

The best brews always flowed from the tap. The peppy Irish music always played in the background. And the crowd...well, there were always people to meet.

I met someone there as part of my foray back into dating. Kim wanted it.

Sure, he broke out into a sweat every time he thought about going out with Valerie. They had texted, but he'd put off setting up a time and date for their get-together, blaming his schedule at the hospital. His chest grew tight as he thought about doing things like holding the door open for her or putting his hand on the small of her back as they walked to their table.

Do YOU want to start dating again? Lucy typed after a short delay.

He studied the screen, his throat in a choke-hold now. It was a question he was trying to avoid, so leave it to Lucy to ask what needed to be asked. Only to her and Natalie could he confess the truth.

Not really. I could probably die a widower, but is that me cutting myself off from human contact and hiding or...shit...is that me worrying I'll never find someone nearly as wonderful as Kim?

Few women are as wonderful as Kim. Make sure you hold out. You have to WANT this, Andy, or you'll be miserable. The woman too. Don't listen to all that cultural bullshit about moving on from the death of a spouse after one to two years. Listen to your heart. It's always your best guide.

This is why he looked forward to her emails and their chat sessions. Sometimes she knew him better than he knew himself. No one besides Kim had ever known him that way.

You're a prophet. A goddess. People should worship the ground you walk on.

I was in a polygamist village last week. Don't think it didn't happen. I still have my crown.

If it had been anyone else, he'd have sworn she was joking. *When you come home, you'll have to show me that. When ARE you coming BTW?*

The cursor flashed as he waited for her to type. Glancing at the clock, he realized he needed to get back to work.

Not sure. I'll be out on location for a while this time. We have to zigzag around a bit.

What she meant was there was a freaking war underway, so she had to travel around the battles. Sweat beaded his brow as he thought of the danger. He wanted to write: *Come home. Please. Stop making us so worried. Why can't you settle for a calm, normal life?*

But he knew her answer. He knew her. She'd never be happy tied to one place.

Instead he wrote: *Take care of yourself. Shoot those fabulous pics of yours and send me some so I can see where you are. Danny loves them.*

She was always sending him shots of the places she traveled and all the people she encountered. When Danny was old enough, she'd started taking pics of animals too—something new for her. His son still kept the photo of the baby camel she'd shot in Egypt in his room. The funny, fuzzy face always elicited a smile. Lucy had liked the little fella because he was unabashedly goofy, like her.

Get back to sticking people with needles and stuff, you medical cretin. The generator will be going out soon, which means lights out for me. I feel like a kid again, going to sleep at nine o'clock.

No lights after nine. She'd mentioned that rule before on other trips to equally remote locations. He wondered how she bathed. Some places didn't even have water, he knew, and even the ones that did might not have clean water. He made himself stop obsessing over her living conditions, not to mention all the diseases, worms, and viruses he'd heard horror stories about.

Speaking of sticking people. Please tell me your shots are up to date.

Yes, Dad. Now go back to work. I'll write when I'm back. Big hug. Luce.

Be waiting to hear from you. Keeping you in my thoughts. Hugging you back. Andy.

She signed off, and he wanted to click her back. The worry still lingered, as it did every time he knew his fearless friend was somewhere particularly dangerous. As he finished his sandwich, he took a moment to call in some help.

Watch out for her, Kim. I'm counting on you.

He went back to work feeling a little more at peace.

The best angel in the universe was looking out for his best friend halfway around the world.

CHAPTER 19

Monday started as a real bitch of a day. She'd dreamed about Kim. While she couldn't remember what she and her best friend had talked about, it didn't matter. In the dream, they were together again, laughing, Blake's hand rested in quiet connection around her shoulders, and Touchdown was splayed at their feet—just like it used to be. She was sweating and panting when she awoke, and so cold she had to spend over thirty minutes in the shower to get warm again.

After finally falling into the numb place inside her, she made her way to work. Jill popped her head in as she was drinking her first cup of Italian espresso made from Terrance's incredible machine in the High Stakes' kitchen. Her cousin danced a salsa all the way to her desk.

"Sooo," she drew out, waggling her rusty-colored eyebrows. "Someone hung out with her ex and scads of gorgeous football players on Saturday night."

Not that she could recall much of it. "Yes. Andy and I ran into them."

"I heard you beat them at darts and pool from Hairy's bouncer. He's a regular at Don't Soy With Me."

Of course he was. The giant of a man probably liked

hazelnut soy lattes.

"Can we not do this?" she pleaded, a headache starting at her temples. "I have work to do, and this whole...thing...makes me uncomfortable."

Jill slouched her frame and walked to the door like a chagrined child. "Okay."

Her voice was downright pathetic, which made Natalie feel instantly guilty. "Hey. I'm sorry."

Her cousin spun around. "I'm sorry too. I keep forgetting how hard this must be for you. It's just I saw the pics on Twitter and Facebook. You looked so happy again. Some people were hinting...well..."

Oh no. She knew what was coming, but she asked anyway, "What?"

"Ah..." Her cousin studied her shoes like they held the keys to making millions. "They were hinting...that is...implying—"

Dear God, when Jill stuttered like a nervous school girl, the earth tilted on its axis. "What, for heaven's sake?"

"That you and Blake have reconciled." Bright spots of red on her cheeks. "They even said he was helping Andy work the crowd and find a woman."

Oh, crap. She'd never thought the town gossips would interpret it that way. "He was simply..." What could she say? "Being kind. It's hard for Andy to get back out there."

"Of course it is. I can't imagine what it's like. If I lost Brian...and only had our girls." She sniffed.

Natalie's throat closed. This was not what she needed right now. Jill was supposed to be all piss and vinegar. Not maudlin sentiment. "If you hear anything else, please don't tell me."

"You can trust me, Natalie." She made a zipping motion over her lips. "Okay, back to work."

After her cousin left, Natalie met with the catering staff. While everyone kept the discussion professional, she could all but hear the questions bouncing around inside their heads. Thank God her two assistants yesterday hadn't mentioned her epic hangover. As they were leaving, she decided to draw a line in the sand.

"If you hear any of the rumors floating around town about...well, Blake and me, I'd ask you not to mention The Grand Mountain Hotel's catering contract with him. People might misunderstand further."

The only response she received was a quick shake of their heads, and then they were heading out the door. How much more awkward could things get?

When Terrance knocked on her door, her guard instantly went up. "What is this? The Gossip Deli? Do you want to take a number?"

The scar near his mouth shifted with his wince as he strutted in and closed the door. "I take it you've heard the rumors."

"Yes," she said. "I would have heard them yesterday, but..."

"You were hung over," he finished, shrugging at her gasp. "There was a pic on Twitter that had you pretty well plastered against Blake as he led you out of Hairy's. There's one of you getting into his SUV and another of your brother taking your car home."

Why did people like social media again? She wanted to curse. A big, fat doozy of a curse. "Do people not have anything better to do with their lives?"

"It's a small town," he said. "And Blake's famous. More famous than I am. Do you remember the kind of shit I had to put up with on Twitter a few months ago?"

The footage of him punching the man who'd harassed his fiancée had gone viral. None of it had been pleasant. Then again, none of it ever was.

"I don't miss that part of our life," she told him. "Everywhere we went, people were watching, taking pictures. Heck, it's so bad Blake can't even buy his own underwear anymore."

Terrance's brows rose. "I...ah...remember that. Not a boxer man, is he?"

She shut her mouth. There was no way she was mentioning she'd bought Blake new underwear yesterday.

"I came up here to see how you were doing," Terrance said, "and now I have my answer. You're strung up pretty tight." He came around her desk and sat down on the edge, not bothering to move the caterer's budget for their upcoming corporate event with a major automobile manufacturer.

"It'll be fine," she said, even though she wasn't so sure. Somehow, she couldn't block out the thought of Blake looking at their wedding picture in her cedar chest. Had he opened the cover to her wedding gown? Then there was the memory of him sleeping on top of the covers, holding her tight, after she'd done God knows what to entice him to make love to her.

"It's okay to be uncertain, Natalie," Terrance said softly. "I know you have a history with most people in this town. You don't have to pretend with me. I'm here if you want to talk."

From day one, she and Terrance had been friends, nothing more. Maybe she needed one now, one who had no memories of her and Blake together.

"I'm...scared of him being here. He's...so damn sweet and thoughtful. It makes me mad, but mostly...it breaks my heart again. We were so happy until Kim was..." She turned her hand over, eyeing her bare wedding ring finger. "Kim was my best friend, and when she got sick, I couldn't think or see straight. I didn't want to. Have you ever had something hurt so bad you'd do anything to stop it?"

"Yes," he murmured, taking her hand in a gentle clasp. "What do you want to do with Blake?"

After this weekend, she didn't know. When she was with him, it was so easy to fall back into old comfortable patterns, ones she'd loved, ones she'd missed. But where would that lead? Hanging out, watching TV, and taking a run...all those things felt good; they felt right. But her wounds were still oozing underneath. She feared the underneath. Feared it so much she'd barely slept last night, imagining their after-work run and what it might turn into.

They were heading somewhere. Even she could no longer deny it.

"I don't want to hurt him," she said, which was the truth. But she was already failing at that. "He's been through so much lately. And *I* don't want to be hurt anymore."

He didn't say anything. Simply reached out and took her hand. The silence made her edgy. Why wasn't he saying some empty platitude or trying to give her advice? Because he was one smart cookie. He knew there was no good advice in this situation. What had Andy said? She and Blake would have to find the way together.

"If you need to get out of the house—or cook up a feast—you're always welcome at our place. You know that, right?"

She squeezed his hand and released it. "Yeah. Thanks, Terrance."

"Are you still okay to go to Denver tomorrow for the client meeting? I can take it if you'd rather stay closer to home."

Getting out of town sounded like a good idea. She might have to force herself to return. "I still want to take it. In fact, I'm going to text my sisters to see if they'll meet me for lunch." They'd be upset if they found out she'd come to town without calling. Besides, if she met them on their own turf, it might help them all get beyond the unease Blake's return had caused.

"Sounds like a good plan." His wink was mischievous, the kind Chef T gave the cameras during the filming of his TV show. "Catch you later, Hale."

When he left, she texted her sisters immediately about meeting her at TAG, one of their favorite restaurants. They both instantly responded in the affirmative. She was glad. This at least was something she could control.

After making the reservation, she just sat there staring at her ceiling, thinking about Blake, about his body, about the way his eyes seemed to light up whenever she came into the room. She kicked her shoes off under her desk and vowed to do some work. Of course, she fired up social media instead and clenched her mouse as she clicked on pictures of her plastered against Blake at Hairy's, of her gazing up at him with adoration as he bundled her into his car.

By the time she headed home at the end of the day, she realized she was feeling like one of her favorite soufflés: airy with anticipation, but liable to fall flat if she wasn't handled carefully. Blake texted her shortly after she walked in the door.

Holler when you're ready. Your carriage awaits.

He was being sweet again. She changed into her workout clothes and yanked on the laces of her running shoes, her mind trying to summon up all the reasons this was a bad idea. When she was ready, she pulled her hair back into a ponytail. Thought about adding a colored lip gloss. Great. She was thinking about putting on makeup to work out.

Ready on this end, she texted back.

His text was instantaneous. She could almost see him holding his phone, waiting for her cue.

See you in a sec.

When he pulled into her driveway, he didn't wait for her to get in the car. No, he put it in gear and hopped out. Touchdown ran over to him and was immediately swept into a hug before being set back down. Then Blake turned to face her.

The afternoon sunlight reflected off his sandy brown hair, spinning it to gold. Her breath caught in her chest. His powerful biceps strained under his bright blue workout shirt. The wind blew down the canyon and pressed that shirt to his abs, giving her a view of the ridges there. Her eyes lowered—she couldn't help it. His legs bulged with power as he strode with purpose toward her, that damned light in his eyes shining bright from seeing her. Like it always did.

He stopped in front of her and gave her a killer grin, the kind that made her go weak in the knees. "Hey! How was your day?"

How many times had he asked her that very question? Thousands? And he didn't say it in that throwaway manner people did—he *meant* it. He wanted to know all the details—the highs, the lows, the in betweens.

He shifted on his feet when she didn't reply, and she saw him gulp, like he suspected she was retreating from him again. His hand reached out into the space between them. She jolted and took a step back. The light in his eyes faded, his smile dimming like a cloud had covered the sun.

"It's only a run, Natalie."

She knew he had intentionally chosen not to use her nickname.

"People are talking about us all over town," she said, even though that wasn't why she was pulling away again. "And on social media too." She wished she had the courage to mention his high school coaching offer, but she wasn't that brave.

His face hardened. "Let them talk. It's none of their damn business."

His hard tone shook loose some of the tension in her belly. When it came to the media and "talk," Blake had never cared what was said. Sure, he'd gotten smarter about not feeding the fire by allowing public speculation of things he'd rather keep private, like which brand of underwear he favored, but he never let it stop him from doing what he wanted.

And that same old question popped up in her head: What did she want? Her mind returned to her conversation with Terrance. She didn't want to hurt Blake. But she didn't want to be hurt either. She looked down at the shadow he cast, always larger than life, and noticed the way it intermingled with hers. Though she'd never told him, the reason she'd turned down his advances when they first met was because she'd sensed—even then—that if she allowed herself to fall in love with him, to need him, she'd never stop. That had scared the shit out of her.

It still did. But if she didn't go with him today, it would hurt her as much as it would hurt him. And the part of her that feared letting down her guard and falling for him again was currently weaker than the part that couldn't stand to see him walk away dejected.

"Okay. Let's go."

His chest rose as air filled his lungs again. He'd been holding his breath, she realized, with a sharp pinch to her heart.

"Okay," he said easily. Too easily.

They walked to the car. His steps faltered, so unlike him. She looked over to see him correct his balance as he moved around the hood of the car. He had decided against opening the door for her at the last moment.

Something inside her howled as she watched him lower Touchdown into the passenger seat.

Touchdown licked her face when she got in the car, and once she was situated and buckled in, she forced herself to say the words she needed to say. "Can we please use one of the off-beat trails?"

His hand froze on the gearshift. She watched it clench around the handle.

"Of course," he said, and this time there was an edge

in his voice. "I've been going up to Killer Pass for that reason. Is that suitable?"

That reason. Suitable. Oh, how she could hear the accusation in his voice.

"That's fine," she answered and stroked Touchdown to cover the tremble in her hands.

When she glanced at him out of the corner of her eye, she saw the tight lines around his mouth. Something like a heavy hand pressed on her chest. She hadn't wanted to hurt him.

But how could he not be hurt? She'd basically said *I don't want to be seen with you*, though it wasn't what she'd meant. They just needed some space to figure this out without everyone watching. Isn't that why she'd asked her family not to interfere?

And yet, regardless of how hard she tried to fight it, some stubborn part of her seemed intent on killing almost every good thing between them—almost every good thing in her life—and it wasn't finished yet.

CHAPTER 20

The worst field Blake had ever played on had been at home against the Charlotte Falcons. Before the game, ice had rained down with punishing intensity, coating the hard ground. By kickoff, the sheets of sleet had turned into heavy snow. He'd spent the entire game slipping and sliding in the pocket, digging his toes into his cleats to gain purchase to step back for a pass. Right now, he felt like he was on that same field with Natalie. Every time he thought he'd found a few feet of solid ground, he'd discover it was coated in ice.

She seemed to be pushing him away again, and his heart lay swollen in his chest. Still, he struggled not to raise his walls, not to fight with her. He'd focused on his running as soon as they hit the trail, and she seemed to be content with the silence.

They couldn't fight if they didn't talk.

They couldn't get back together if they didn't talk.

He wanted to hit something.

Touchdown ran between them, almost like a peace mediator, panting away. All his buddies joked that the beagle was in better shape than all of them. Blake held back, letting Natalie set the pace like he'd always done. She worried her lip as she ran, making him all too aware of her breasts bouncing just a tad under her red sleeveless sports tank. Her slender arms had the curve of muscle and were dotted with freckles. Her legs were a flash of smooth white as she kept pace with him.

Thorn's Peak pierced the ocean-blue sky ahead, and lemony rays of the afternoon sun touched the rugged landscape. The rock face of the awe-inspiring Great Wall curved along the pass. Bats and birds flew out of the tiny holes in the rock. He caught sight of a moose and her calf on the humpback-shaped ridge dotted with pines and conifers. The pass was fairly flat, but the incline was deceiving. By mile three, Natalie was puffing, her face tomato red. Her chin was set with pure determination now.

"You don't have to grit it out, babe," he said, throttling back even more.

Her eyes were cold and hard when she glanced over. "I can do it."

His stomach burned. He knew that look. She was angry, most likely with herself. He settled back into her pace. By mile four, he wasn't breathing hard, but she was nearly gasping. He slowed again.

"Shit. Fine." She waved her hand. "Go do your thing. I don't want to hold you back."

Her words held an ominous ring. Some things never changed. Usually he'd run ahead. She'd walk. Then he'd angle back once he was ready, and they'd run home together. But this wasn't about that.

"Let's walk a bit," he said, dropping his pace to a simple stretch of the legs.

She stumbled and went down on one knee. Hard. Touchdown barked in response to her pained cry.

He was kneeling beside her in seconds. "Here. Let me see."

She sat down and grimaced at the blood seeping out of the wounds. Brushing at the gravel and dust, she bit her lip.

"Go ahead and shout. I know it has to hurt."

She swatted his hands aside, which only pissed him off. He ripped off the hem of his shorts and dabbed at the wound.

"Stop coddling me!" she yelled. "I'm fine. Now, go ahead and finish your run. I'll follow you at a walk."

His jaw popped. "I'm not fucking running ahead."

She put her hand on her knee, almost protectively, still gasping for air. "But you always run ahead!"

"I don't have a quota anymore." *I'm not in the NFL anymore.*

"Keep going, dammit! Don't stop for me. It's only a little scrape."

Anger shot up from his liver to his throat. "I'll damn well stop for you if I want to. Spending time with you is more important than ticking off miles—even if you're pissed off, even if you don't want to be here. And I'm certainly not leaving you when you're bleeding on the trail."

Her lip wobbled before she bit it again. In those seconds, something horrible and ugly shimmered between them, something that reminded him of those last days they'd lived together.

He sat on the ground next to her. Dared to lower his hand to her calf to create one tenuous connection between them, a few scant inches from the Celtic knot tattoo on the inside of her ankle, the one he still hadn't asked her about.

"How is it we're farther apart today than we were yesterday? What happened?"

"I don't know," she said with an edge to her voice.

Her breathing was stabilizing. Touchdown was nuzzling her torso, giving her comfort, something Blake wished he could do.

"Yes, you do know," he pressed, prepared to hear the truth at last. "Tell me why."

Her gaze flew to his. "Because everybody thinks I'm crazy for ever leaving you! You're the best guy on the planet. Everyone thinks so." The hand she was using to prop herself up grabbed a fistful of soil. "You take your drunken ex-wife home when she drinks too much. You don't screw her when she throws herself at you even though you probably wanted to."

He felt sick. "I'd never *screw* you."

"And to make it worse, you hold my head when I puke, put me in a nightshirt, and sleep in your clothes on top of the covers because I asked you to stay." Her ice-blue eyes narrowed. "I asked you, didn't I?"

His throat closed. "Yes."

Her breath gusted out. "Oh, Blake."

Touchdown lay down on the ground between them, adding to their fragile connection. Blake's free hand stroked the dog's belly. He couldn't bear to mention he'd seen the black box holding her rings in the hope chest.

He made himself look into her eyes. Hers were wary and filled with pain. "You said you loved me."

She hung her head. "I cut you like that, and yet you stayed?"

"You asked me to." His heartbeat pulsed in the hand on her calf, as if coming alive through the sheer act of sustained touch.

"Sam pretty much called me a bitch for leaving you," she whispered.

"He'd never do that." His friend was brutally honest, but he wasn't cruel.

"Don't be so sure. And coming from him...well, it hurt. Even if it was true. I never expected him..."

"I've told you before, and I'll say it again. No one's opinion matters to me—not my friends or your family or the press. The only one that matters is yours." *And you told me you loved me the other night.*

"I'm so confused," she admitted softly, so softly he had to strain to hear it.

He wasn't confused. He knew what he wanted. But

he could admit to his own weakness. "Well, I'm afraid. Being near you again, even sitting in this dirt beside you while your knee bleeds, makes me want to wrap you up and never let you go. I'm afraid you won't let me." *Again.* He left the words unsaid.

She scooted closer, her bottom spreading dirt out like a fan behind her. Touchdown ambled to the side as she set the side of her body flush against his. His hand curved around her calf, and when she didn't protest, he kept it there, his fingertips tingling now.

Dropping the rag he'd given her for her knee, she laid a tentative hand on his chest. His breath seized in his lungs. She faced north, and he faced south, and even though they were positioned in opposite directions, they seemed closer than ever before.

Her trembling hand wasn't its usual icy cold as it trailed up his neck, but each time those wary blue eyes met his, they would flicker away. When she cupped his jaw, he let his eyes close. She was touching him again, and her caress was this side of heaven.

Her fingertips traced his mouth next. He felt her scoot even closer, and then the briefest touch of her mouth slid across his lips.

He knew that mouth. He'd kissed it in the light. He'd kissed it in the dark. For years, it had been the first thing he'd sought in the morning, and the first thing he'd craved when he arrived home at night. His pulse thundered as he waited for more than a mere brush. Seconds ticked by. The wind ruffled his hair, making all the hairs on his neck prickle with awareness. She conducted another pass of his lips, but nothing more. His hand fisted in the dirt, like hers had earlier. He fought the urge to grip her calf.

God, he thought, *oh God. More. Touch me more.*

The pressure increased until she was sipping at his upper lip, the corner of his mouth, the fullness of his bottom lip. He locked his muscles, afraid to move, to startle her from this precious reunion.

"Why aren't you kissing me back?" she asked with a catch in her throat.

A strangled noise rose from his chest. "I'm afraid to."

"But why?" she whispered, her breath warm and fragrant on his skin. "I thought this was what you wanted."

"It is...but I want it to mean something." He squeezed his eyes shut tighter. "I don't want this to be about me taking care of you."

Her hand curled around his neck in benediction as her mouth kissed his chin so damn sweetly he felt tears pop into his eyes.

"Blake. It's not because you took care of me." She stopped herself from saying more, but he heard the words left unsaid: *It means something.*

It was the permission he'd been seeking, the opening he'd prayed she would give him. He opened his eyes.

With her face just inches away, he could make out the fine, pale hairs on her soft cheek. His hand lifted. He watched it travel with the uncertain speed of a balloon in the air, unsure of where it was going. His fingertips finally reached for her face. He traced the curve of her delicate jaw, the line of her soft cheekbone. They traveled up, smoothing her brow.

This time, she let *her* eyes close, and a sigh gusted out of her, hanging in the air between them. His exploration continued. He reacquainted himself with the beauty of her face. His thumb traced the curve of her upper lip and then the bottom. Her mouth parted, and the knowledge that she was fighting the urge to suck his finger into her mouth like she'd always enjoyed doing turned him rock hard in an instant. That would be too intimate. Some touches were tipping points to new plateaus, and right now, they needed to keep to the flats.

Cresting to a higher level would be too taxing, too stressful to this new connection between them.

His mouth settled onto hers with more pressure, and then they were kissing for real. Even though he'd kissed her thousands of times, this kiss felt like their first kiss. Filled with hesitation. Laden with unfulfilled promises. Heavy with questions. Burgeoning with hope.

Then her mouth opened under his, and she answered one of his questions. She wanted to take things deeper. He fell under her spell. His tongue slid into her mouth slowly, another question. *How far?* She answered by rubbing her tongue against his. They circled and danced, and he didn't care that his lungs were screaming for air. He never wanted this kiss to end.

She inhaled sharply through her nose some moments later, struggling for breath, but still she didn't pull away from their connection. Her hands cupped his face now, tracing his jaw with sweetness. The fingers he had around her calf slid up ever so slowly until he could grip her thigh.

Her moan crossed the short distance from her mouth to his, and he felt the vibration ripple through his body, down to the very nuclei of his cells. She slanted her head to the right, and he answered her silent request. The kiss turned wetter, the passes of their tongues swifter—until this time he was the one who groaned.

Time faded away. He lost sight of where they were, of the hard ground beneath them. All he felt was the rapid rise of her chest as she breathed into his mouth as they kissed. All he felt was the warmth of her skin, the curve of her breast against his chest.

They kissed and they kissed and they kissed until the light behind his eyelids darkened and the mountain air cooled. Somewhere in the back of his mind, he realized the sun was setting. The practical side of him said they were four miles from the car, and she was hurt. Darkness would soon descend, making the dirt trail more difficult to follow.

Another part of him wanted to gather sticks for her like the men of old used to do for their partners and build a fire for them. He could hunt down an animal to spit so they wouldn't go hungry. And when their bellies were full, he'd make love to her by the light of the fire as the stars bore witness to their love.

She broke the kiss first but followed up with little pecks at his mouth, all the sweeter because he could feel her pulse against him, thrumming with desire.

"It's getting dark," she murmured, her voice all sensuality now.

He hadn't heard that voice in so long, and he had the urge to find his phone and record it so he could play it later when they returned to their separate homes, separate beds.

He sighed and rested his forehead against hers. "I know, but I don't want to leave." *I don't want to lose what we just found again.*

"Neither do I, but even as tough and manly as you are, you're no match for wolves and coyotes and everything else that goes bump in the night."

For her, he would have pitted himself against all of that and more. His hand stroked her thigh one last time and gave it a gentle squeeze. Her muscles twitched in response, and her legs shifted restlessly.

"Wolves and coyotes are misunderstood. They're not that bad." What was he saying?

"Well, if we had camping gear, I'd feel differently, but we need to go." She leaned away and pushed off the ground.

His arms came around her as he helped her stand. "How's the knee?"

"Fine," she said like he expected. She always said something was fine when he knew it hurt.

Still neither of them moved. Thorn's Peak was a black spear in the sky now. Streaks of violet and turquoise covered the ridge. The sky above them was turning into a blanket of stars, shining like brilliant diamonds.

Tell me this means something, he wanted to say again. *Tell me you won't step back.*

They started down the trail again. Her gait wasn't natural, so he knew her knee was hurting. Touchdown trotted along the pass ahead of them—their little sentry. Blake's eyes adjusted to the change in the light so he could make out the edges of the trail where sage and brush began.

As they walked, all his old fears resurfaced, and with each step, he grew more and more uncertain.

And then he felt her fingertips brush his hand. He looked over. Even in the descending darkness, there was starlight in her eyes, the kind he used to see when they would wake at the same time in the middle of the night, as if designed, and make love.

She suddenly tripped on the path. He grabbed ahold of her hand to keep her from falling again. When she straightened, a second passed, and then another. She didn't let go.

They walked through the darkness together.

Chapter 21

The meeting in Denver had only served to show Natalie how much her life had changed, both personally and professionally, since making the move to Dare Valley. As Natalie parked on 14th Street in Denver's Larimar Square, she realized she hadn't missed the city as much as she'd expected.

Too many people lined the sidewalks, walking briskly to restaurants or coffee shops or offices. And the traffic she'd suffered through to get there in the morning...well, it had given her way too much time to obsess over the monumental shift between her and Blake last night. That kiss had been like an earthquake, breaking apart the landscape inside her, which she'd grown accustomed to seeing as smooth and flat. Now all her feelings, all her hurts seemed to be exposed to the harsh light for him to see.

The meeting had gone well—a former client had agreed to let The Grand Mountain Hotel serve its catering needs—but her stomach had roiled the entire time. In truth, she was a little nervous about meeting her sisters for lunch. She wasn't sure what, if anything, to tell them about Blake, but she wanted things between them to be back to normal. Lately, their interactions had been more shallow than usual, which she knew to be her fault. After all, she'd asked them not to push or press or ask questions. That wasn't how they were with one another.

She was heading down the sidewalk to the restaurant she'd chosen for lunch when a bulky man in a cheap gray business suit stopped in front of her and stared at her with narrowed eyes. When she tried to move past him, he snagged her arm.

"Hey, aren't you Blake Cunningham's ex-wife?" he asked, his tone hostile.

She yanked her arm away, but he stepped in front of her, forcing her to either stop or walk into him.

"I saw you with him on Twitter this weekend," he spat. "You cost us this coming season, bitch. I hope you're happy."

Her heart pounded in her ears as other people stopped to stare.

The man who'd hurled insults pointed at her and announced in a louder voice, "She's the bitch who made Blake Cunningham retire."

A few boos echoed in her ears. She stood frozen in place—unable to respond to the onslaught with any of the witty comebacks she'd normally hurl in the face of rudeness. His insults had picked at her raw place.

A comforting hand curled around her shoulder. "Hey, numb nuts!" Moira said to the man. "Why don't you grow a pair and stop blaming someone for our QB retiring? I can tell you that Blake Cunningham has a big enough pair to make his own decisions, so I'll ask you to shut your mouth, or I'll call a police offer and have you charged for accosting a woman on the street."

His eyebrows rose so high they reached his receding hairline.

"Now how about an apology?" Moira said, staring down the crowd.

"In your dreams, bitch," the man snarled and

walked off, giving them the bird over his shoulder.

She was embarrassed to realize she was shaking. Yes, the guy was clearly a jerk—the type she'd normally turn into mincemeat—but he'd made her realize something anew. The whole Raiders nation was suffering because of Blake's retirement...and it was her fault.

"Are you all right?" Moira asked, shaking her slightly to help her snap out of it.

"What happened?" Caroline asked, breathing hard, as she rushed up the sidewalk toward them. "I heard you yelling at that nasty man, Moira, so I sprinted in my heels. Are you guys okay?"

Her sister tossed her head back so her hair could settle down her back. "We just faced down a rabid Raiders fan, no big deal. Natalie! Are you okay?"

"I'm fine," she said, adrenaline pouring through her system. People had stopped walking on the sidewalk and were staring at them, and she couldn't shake the fear that everyone in the vicinity was talking about them—about *her*.

"Let's get to the restaurant," Caroline said, flanking her other side.

With her two sisters guarding her from further harm, they walked into TAG. With its unique continental flavor, anchored in the head chef's Hawaiian roots, it was one of her favorite restaurants, but she could barely focus as her sisters led her to one of the smaller red booths nestled against a brick wall.

"Can I get you something to drink?" their female server said.

"Whisky," Moira told the woman, who was eying them with concern. "Neat. For all of us."

"I have to drive home," Natalie said, trying to lock her muscles so she would stop shaking.

"One won't hurt you," Caroline said, "and if you need to stay over tonight, you can crash at one of our places."

All the tense weeks since their fight seemed to slip away. They'd defended her so naturally—without even thinking about it. "Oh, God. I'm so sorry for what I said to you both, for how I've acted. That guy was right. I'm a bitch."

Moira grabbed her hand. "No, that guy was totally out of line."

The server came back with their drinks, and they all picked them up.

"To sisters," Caroline said.

"To sisters," she and Moira added, although hers was more of a mumble.

She only sipped the liquor, but it did the job. The fire raced down her throat and cut through the remaining haze in her brain. "I can't believe that guy," she said aloud. Sure, people had booed her before— recently, even—but for a stranger to call her a bitch on the street? Blake would lose it if he heard. All the more reason not to tell him.

"Have there been other incidents like this?" Caroline asked.

She told them about Hairy's, which caused them both to frown.

"Yeah, we saw the pictures of you and Blake on social media. We—"

"It looked like you had a lovely time," Caroline said, giving a pointed glance at their sister, as if to remind her the subject was forbidden. She handed out the menus the server had set on the table.

They both picked them up, studying them a lot more intently than needed.

"How about we share the taco sushi to start?" Caroline suggested. "It's ridiculous. Where else can you have ahi tuna with sushi rice served with mango salsa and guacamole?"

"Sounds great," Moira said, still not looking away

from her menu.

Natalie pressed her hand to her aching stomach, realizing she wasn't hungry. No, this was hurt, the kind of belly hurt that came when a person was at odds with the people closest to them.

The server came and took their orders. Moira chose the fish tacos, Caroline the chicken ones, while she selected the hanger steak, hoping a little protein might settle her stomach.

Except she knew it wouldn't. The only thing that would do that was making it right with her sisters.

"I don't know how to fix things between us," she told them as they both traced the rims of the water glasses their server had brought them. "I mean, we talk, but we don't talk."

Moira raised her brow in challenge, and she could almost hear what she was thinking. *This is how you wanted it, Nat.*

But she didn't want it that way anymore, so even though it was hard, she started to tell them about everything between her and Blake. How sad and lonely he sometimes seemed and how much guilt and pressure she felt. Caroline reached for her hand when she told them about offering to cater his Once Upon A Dare guys' weekend. Moira finally reached for her other hand when she told them about getting drunk at Hairy's and how Blake had stayed with her after she'd put on a particularly epic Natalie Show. Her chest felt like it was enclosed by manacles by the time she reached the part about kissing him last night—and how it had made her more scared and confused than ever.

Everyone fell silent, and the server brought their food. She could tell her sisters were scared to say anything given the way she'd shut them down before.

"I know what I said," she said in a low voice, mostly because her throat was as tight as her chest now. "But...well...shit...just tell me what you're thinking."

Caroline nestled closer. "I would say you two are in a good place. It's only natural to be confused, but it sounds like some things are becoming clearer."

Moira met her eyes. "You still want him, and you're both taking care of each other again. You helped him with his guys' weekend, and he helped you when you were drunk. I'd say that's progress."

"That guy—the one on the street—is my worst nightmare," she said, pushing the greens of her salad around on her plate. "I'm afraid everything he said is true. You can't imagine how guilty I feel about him giving up football. I know this camp he's doing is going to be incredible, but I worry about the after part." It felt unburdening to share the thoughts she had barely even expressed to herself.

She proceeded to tell him about her run-in with Cormack Daly at Hairy's.

"Wow. I don't know what surprises me more." Caroline popped a leftover piece of the taco sushi into her mouth. "That mom would talk to Blake for this guy or that Blake might become a high school football coach."

"You have to admit," Moira said with a grin. "He'd look good on the sidelines."

Natalie snorted out a laugh. "Yeah, but the outfit wouldn't entail nearly enough spandex." Personally, she'd enjoyed seeing his legs encased in football pants.

"But his handsome face would be," Moira teased.

"Stop it!" she said, and this time she could tell they were okay with one another because there wasn't any heat to it. She would have said it the same way if they'd been sharing a room and her sister had thrown a pillow at her.

"Just saying," Moira responded with that same silly grin on her face.

"I'm not going to talk to Mom about her role in all this."

Caroline nodded her head slowly. "Good idea."

"I concur with Caro here," Moira said. "Mom doesn't like being called on the carpet."

Who did?

"I haven't said anything to Blake about the job either," she said, even though her mind kept spinning circles around it. What would it mean if he took the job and stayed? What would it mean if he rejected it? "We don't discuss the future."

"Probably wise," Moira said. "You need to discuss the past first."

Yeah, and if they survived that…maybe, then maybe they could talk about the future. "I don't know where any of this is leading," she whispered, feeling that familiar squeeze in her heart. Even after kissing him— which had been at once hot and heartbreaking—she felt more at sea than ever.

Of course, she wanted to kiss him again. Couldn't wait to kiss him again. Couldn't wait to see him smile in that earnest way of his. She turned to sap just at the thought of it.

"Give yourself plenty of time to see where things go," Caroline offered, taking another sip of her whisky. "You don't need to rush things."

She needed to tell her body that. Kissing was one thing, but sex was another. It would be a huge step, and while her body was raring to go, she didn't think she was emotionally prepared for what it would do to her.

"It's okay to be scared," Moira said, cutting a piece of her fish taco and putting it on Natalie's plate. "We're here for you. For whenever you want to talk. And I'm sorry…for what I said earlier. I can be a bitch sometimes too."

"Friends?" Natalie asked them.

Caroline bumped her side. "Silly, don't you know sisters are forever friends?"

They finished their meals, and she took care of the

check as an extra way of saying thank you.

But as she drove out of Denver, the pressure rose inside her again, increasing the closer she came to Dare Valley. Caroline said to give herself time to figure out what she wanted with Blake.

What was the old saying about time marching on?

She just hoped it wouldn't march all over them.

Chapter 22

Blake marked his time by his progress with Natalie in the coming weeks.

Two days after their first kiss, she kissed him again while they were watching their next *Outlander* episode. Three days after that, he initiated a kiss after they went for another run in Killer Pass. Four days after that, he cupped her hips to his and kissed her and kissed her after a quiet evening of steaks and baked potatoes and playing Frisbee with Touchdown.

Her cues became his compass. So far, she hadn't invited much more than kissing and light touching—completely clothed. Certainly nothing south of the waist, which seemed forbidden territory. He stayed in well-traveled areas: her mouth, her jaw, her cheeks, even the lobes of her ears. Sometimes he journeyed east to her right shoulder, rubbing it to ease the tension she carried there. Other times, he journeyed west to the curve of her neck to remind himself of the taste of her skin.

They were dating again, and even though they'd been married, there was a newness to spending time with her. Some of her likes and dislikes had changed. She wasn't eating as much ice cream, and she was over her reality TV craze. And she was quieter, sometimes so quiet he had to force himself to inhabit her silence with her. At those times, he knew she was floundering, not knowing what to say, not knowing where they were going. Often, he would simply hold her hand until the moment passed.

They didn't go out in public together, sensing it would put too much pressure on their new bond. And he didn't amp up the romance by bringing her flowers or other gifts—at least not yet.

Touchdown journeyed back and forth between their separate kingdoms. The bridge was the connection point between them, and more often than not, he and Natalie met in the middle. When he knew she was coming over, he would wait for her in the center of the bridge, listening to the burbling water of the creek underneath. If she'd invited him, he would find her tracing one of the infinity symbols carved onto the rail of the bridge, staring off into the sky, Touchdown at her side. She never mentioned the symbol they'd had engraved on their wedding bands, so he didn't either.

They spoke less, but connected more. And Blake told himself he was satisfied. Sure, he wanted more, but the simple joy of being with her again was enough.

Or it was enough until they returned to their separate kingdoms.

She was sharing the details of her days with him, and he was keeping her abreast of the preparations for the camp. But that was it.

They didn't talk about her family, and he made himself be all right with that. He went out for a beer with Andy, who'd done the big brother thing and checked with Natalie before asking him. The crowd had bothered him a bit. Some people had asked for autographs while others had given him the what-for over retiring. They'd finally retreated to a corner and talked about safe topics: the girl Andy had met at Hairy's with him, Blake's upcoming camp, and Danny, whose antics were always good for a laugh. The only thing Blake had told him about Natalie was that they were hanging out. He hadn't used the word dating, even though that's what they were doing.

When Cormack Daly contacted him on a hazy Wednesday, pushing way too hard for his answer about the high school coaching job, Blake took a deep breath, remembering what Sam had said about not reacting to life. He told Cormack that he wasn't ready to make that kind of commitment yet and suggested they find someone else. At first, Cormack turned on the charm even more.

This job would launch your new career as a coach, the man had said. *Think of all the experience you could pick up. This is the type of position that could take you to the next level. I'm here to work with you every step of the way, Blake.*

This was the kind of guy who'd try to insinuate himself into a position of power within the team. Blake had to bite his tongue to refrain from mentioning the offers he'd received from the next level. He'd simply told him he wasn't interested once again. It had only made the man press harder.

When Cormack finally realized Blake was unmovable, he started sputtering like a prima donna rookie who'd just realized the NFL was a whole heck of a lot harder than college ball. Apparently, the high school's other finalist—the one they'd put on hold for Blake—had taken another job. They didn't have anyone else, the man moaned pitifully. The attempted guilt trip didn't sway Blake. He simply wished the man luck and hung up.

Though he'd essentially just closed the door to a full-time job in Dare Valley, he didn't feel panicked or worried. Sam was right. He had to go with his gut.

He wasn't going to take a full-time position until he was sure his relationship with Natalie was on solid ground...and he wasn't going to accept a coaching gig until he knew he liked coaching. Right now, he was happy with his preparations for camp and the consulting he was doing for Special Olympics. Once camp was over, he could reassess.

Ultimately, he needed to see if Natalie would allow him to venture further into the complicated labyrinth of her heart and the beautiful curves of her body down south. He knew he needed to be patient, though it was getting harder and harder to remind himself of that.

After another solid week of kissing marathons, the kind that left him hard and aching, he invited her over for dinner. It was time to introduce a little more romance to see how she reacted. Since she used to drape their backyard with special party lights—just for them— he ran an extension cord from his house and decorated the bridge with white lights to guide her way to him. If she smiled when she saw them, he'd know it was okay to give her the bouquet he'd bought for her—sunflowers, her favorite.

That night, pink, red, and orange fingers reached across the valley as he waited for her on the edge of the bridge, the better to see her reaction. The first star appeared in the sky, and he made a wish even though it made him feel a bit foolish.

Let her be mine again. All of her.

She emerged from the twilight like a goddess, her curly, brown hair bouncing down her back, her red sleeveless sundress skimming down to her ankles, which were wrapped in gold gladiator sandals. Touchdown, who'd been with her the past few days, reached him first, but for once, he didn't bend to greet him. He zeroed in on her face to see what it would tell him.

Her smile wasn't full as she approached, but the corners of her mouth were curved. "Looks like you had some extra time on your hands."

Even though he wasn't breathing, he made himself smile and gesture to the lights. "I thought you might like it." He gulped.

"I do. It's beautiful."

Fresh mountain air filled his lungs, and this time, it was easier to smile and step forward to kiss her cheek. "Hi."

Okay, her smile seemed fuller now. "Hi."

He held out his hand, and she took it. As he laced their fingers together, he experienced the same euphoric burst he'd always felt after a touchdown. *She's going to allow more romance.*

They started walking down the bridge together. Her skin glowed in the white light, and he wanted so badly to take her in his arms and kiss her. But it was too early in the night for that.

"Come. We'll see if I can impress you with my ribs."

"You cooked ribs?" she asked.

He didn't have to look at her to imagine the shocked expression on her face. "You love them, so I called Jordan's girlfriend and asked her to help me."

You love them, so I made them.

"We Facetimed, and Grace walked me through everything. Hopefully it will be okay." God, he hoped it would be okay. Who knew cooking could be so terrifying?

"Huh. I'm impressed. I never thought about calling up a professional chef like that."

"Probably because you cook like a professional chef. We mere mortals in the kitchen need help from experts like Grace."

The wind rustled the trees, kicking up fallen leaves on the ground as they left the bridge and walked across his backyard.

"How is she? I was so glad Jordan brought me that recipe from her. I've been wanting it forever."

Grace and Jordan had been close friends since

childhood, but they'd only started dating after he moved to Atlanta, where she was a sous chef at one of the hottest restaurants in Buckhead. They were a good match, but Jordan had confided in him that Grace was finding his fame more and more difficult to deal with. Now he was worried about their future together, but that wasn't something he wanted to mention to Natalie right now.

"She's great. Working hard at the restaurant, but still loving it. You know Grace. No one is better named."

"True. Is she planning on coming out here with Jordan for the camp?"

"I doubt it," he replied. "I'm going to keep him busy. I've asked the guys to hang out with the kids in the evening. We have some fun things planned."

Her eyes sparkled. "Sounds like a great time. I'm so happy you're doing this, Blake."

Because he couldn't suppress the urge, he raised their joined hands and kissed the back of hers. "Me too."

His backyard was surrounded with torches that spilled light around them as he led her to the patio table.

"What would you like to drink tonight? I have champagne." Another one of her favorites.

She settled into the chair and pulled Touchdown onto her lap. "Why not?"

"Good. I'll go get it." Another cue. His head was buzzing as he went inside. The sunflowers were tucked away in the one place he didn't think she'd venture into—his office. He brought them out, feeling his palms sweat. He'd already made at least three romantic gestures. Was this too much? Oh, screw it.

He popped the champagne and poured two glasses. Drinking champagne was rare for him, so she'd recognize the gesture. Tucking the flowers into the crook of his arm, he headed back to the patio. She was stroking Touchdown's fur, and the dog was so contented

he looked asleep. Blake hung back for a moment to watch her, and then he set the glasses down and gently arranged
the flowers by the plate he'd set for her.

"Thought you might like a little sunshine," he said. God, he was a total cornball. His cheeks flushed, and he hoped it was too dark for her to see.

She bit her lip, and his whole world stopped. He waited, fighting the urge to snatch them back. What the heck good would that do? He couldn't very well run back into the house with them and pretend he'd never presented them to her.

Her fingers touched the petals. "These are lovely. Thank you, Blake."

His stomach gurgled, and he pressed a hand to it, his cheeks turning even warmer.

"You must be hungry."

No, he thought, I'm stressed out from trying to romance my ex-wife. "I'll...ah...go get the appetizers."

"Appetizers too?" she asked with some surprise in her tone.

"Nothing fancy. Just a simple antipasti tray Grace suggested. Any moron can buy cheese, crackers, and olives."

She was still tracing the sunflowers. "Any moron, huh?"

Rather than answer, he whipped around and headed into the house. Grace had put up with his little freak-out earlier after he realized he'd bought the wrong cheese. She'd suggested blue, so he'd picked up one that *looked* blue to him, only to discover it was called Roquefort. Grace had just laughed and told him it was totally all right. Roquefort *was* a blue cheese.

When he brought out the tray—one he'd bought at the local cheese shop—she made a humming sound in her throat that drove him wild. Her love of food had always been its own aphrodisiac. Watching her enjoy

her meal was like watching porn, and he wasn't
ashamed to admit that.

"I can see Grace's influence here," she said as she
dipped one of the walnuts into the slice of honeycomb
he'd arranged next to the blue cheese. "You're
expanding your horizons."

You expand my horizons.

"Lucky me," he forced out instead and sat down
across from her, feeling sweat gather under his armpits.
Great. He'd need to change shirts before the evening
was over at this rate.

Grabbing his glass of champagne, he raised it for a
toast. "To the most beautiful woman in the world," he
said before he could stop himself.

She flinched, a simple ripple moving across her face.
His gut burned in despair.

"I'm sorry. I shouldn't have said it."

"No...it's...okay."

They missed each other's glasses and had to try
again. They were totally out of sync now. He could feel
their newfound ease drifting away like smoke in the
wind.

"I wanted tonight to be special for you," he decided
to admit. "I might have overdone things. How about we
start again? I can take these flowers inside, and if you
want to take them home later, you can. And I'll put on
some music. How about Imagine Dragons?"

He'd caught her dancing to their music in the
kitchen on their last *Outlander* date. He stood and
reached for the flowers, but before he could pick them
up, she put her hand over his.

"Don't even think about touching my flowers."

His heart drummed under his ribs as their eyes met.
He dropped his hand and went inside. Once the music
was on, the ease came back in stages. He told her his
story about the blue cheese freak-out because he knew it
would make her laugh. And it did. But she also studied

him intently, and he knew it was because she could hear the things he *hadn't* said.

A Super Bowl MVP had freaked out because he was worried about buying the wrong cheese for a date.

When he went to check on the ribs, she came up behind him at the grill. For a man who was known for being good with his hands, he was all thumbs with her beside him. Her perfume tickled his nose. Her body heat was fiercer than the red-hot coals. He dropped the tongs twice before she laid her hand over his and helped.

"Squeeze here," she instructed.

He almost fell to his knees right then and there from the sheer lust that shot through him at those words.

"How about you do it?" he asked, brushing the sweat beading at his temple now.

She rubbed his back, and his hips twitched. God, he hoped she hadn't noticed.

"No. You can do this. I like seeing you cook. It looks good on you."

Sure it did. If looking like a sweat-streaked nervous wreck was considered sexy.

He managed to turn the ribs. Grace had suggested a simple dry rub of brown sugar and chili powder, and it had coated the meat just like she'd promised. He checked the internal temperature with the meat thermometer she'd suggested he purchase, and sure enough, they were finished. After arranging them onto the platter by the grill, he went inside to grab the spinach salad, knowing Natalie wouldn't want too much food for their main course. No, she was a woman who liked to save room for dessert, and tonight he'd planned something special.

Moments later, they were sitting at the table, eating their dinner. "The ribs are excellent," she said as she threw one of the bones into the bowl he'd set in the center of the table. "See. Aren't you proud of yourself?"

He felt like he'd just thrown his first touchdown.

"Sure. Glad you like them."

She'd done most of the cooking in their marriage. He could make simple things like bacon and eggs and grill steaks and cook baked potatoes. He wanted to ask if she'd wished he'd cooked more. Had their division of labor seemed unfair to her? He'd always taken out the garbage, hadn't he? Whenever she cooked, he'd do the cleanup. They'd agreed to let a cleaning lady do the major stuff. It was yet another conversation they couldn't have yet.

"Salad's good too," she added like she was trying to string together a conversation out of torn shoelaces.

"You open a bag. Pour the dressing on. It's not hard."

Her cool blue eyes met his, pleading with him to keep up his part of this delicate conversation.

"Ah...I haven't asked you. Have you met any poker players yet?" It was a dumb question, he realized. The Grand Mountain Hotel was a poker destination, and her boss was a poker player. So was her brother's fiancée.

She brightened and threw another bone into the bowl. "Well, no one makes quite the impression Rhett does. Have you met him yet?"

Since he didn't wander around Dare Valley much because people tended to either ask for an autograph or curse him for retiring, he hadn't. "Not yet."

"Well, I'll have to introduce you." Then she stopped short, and he knew she'd only then realized she was implying they would go out together—in public. Or to a family gathering. Something he knew she wasn't ready for.

His stomach gurgled again. Touchdown even gave a short bark and cocked his head at him. He was now sitting in the chair next to Natalie's so she could eat.

"Goodness, are you still hungry? How many miles did you run today?"

"Ten," he answered, pressing his hand to the center

of his stomach where the pain was most persistent. *Shut up,* he told it.

"Ten? Wow. I guess you go full out when I'm not holding you back."

Because he needed to burn away all his sexual desire somehow. He desperately wanted to reach for her hand. "You've never held me back, Nat." *How many times do I have to tell you that?*

She looked away and continued to eat, no longer attempting to string together a conversation. He did the same, picking at his food. In truth, his body did need fuel after the punishing workouts he'd been putting himself through. When they finished the meal, the flickering torchlights were the only sound between them.

He reached for her plate. "I can clean up."

"But you cooked."

Memories of them kissing as they attempted to load the dishwasher filtered through his mind. Even cleaning up with her had always been filled with laughter and fun. And sometimes, they hadn't finished the dishes. He'd simply pick her up and take her to bed.

He was starting to sweat again. Maybe he could duck in and change. Then he realized she'd notice. Great. He'd have to be more Machiavellian than that. He moved his plate a little to the left so it would knock his champagne over. It fell to the table, the liquid running toward him and soaking the lower part of his shirt and pants.

"Oops," he said. "I'll just take these in and change. You relax. Switch the music if you'd like. I'll get dessert after I'm cleaned up."

He tried to smile to deflect the puzzled expression on her face; then he picked up all the dishes he could carry and headed back inside. He had never been so happy to be soaked with champagne, not even after a championship victory celebration with the guys in the locker room.

He dumped the dishes into the sink as best he could without breaking them and then jogged to the bedroom. Changing and adding some deodorant should take no more than two minutes flat. He sniffed his armpit as he stripped off his shirt and winced. God, he was vile. As a man who expended sweat for a living, he knew there were different kinds. Usually his was a clean sweat from a hard workout, but this...this was the sour odor of fear and nerves.

He whipped off his pants next and dug into his dresser for a new pair. He eyed his favorite pair of well-worn jeans.

He sensed her presence before he heard her clear her throat. His back muscles tensed under the power of her scrutiny, and he was suddenly excruciatingly aware of the fact that he was wearing nothing but black briefs. What was she doing?

Because there was no way she'd gotten lost in his house looking for the bathroom.

Should he turn around? Could he bear it if she looked at him with wariness in her eyes—as he'd seen her do these last weeks—rather than the hunger and frank appreciation he remembered? He couldn't bear to know.

"In case you're looking for the bathroom, it's down the hall." She could take the out if she wanted it.

"I'm not lost," she said, and he clutched the jeans to his stomach.

"What can I do for you then?" he asked, trying to decide if he should put on his jeans or simply wait for her to leave the room.

"You can turn around and tell me why you spilled your drink on purpose."

There was fire in her voice. He turned around, still keeping the jeans against his body. It was almost funny. He'd never been modest before.

"Why are you angry?"

Her brow knit. "Did you do it because you wanted to escape from me? I know tonight has been...strained."

He ran his tongue over his teeth, trying to decide how to answer. "If it's been strained, it's my fault. I was trying to be romantic, and it backfired. Frankly, I've been sweating like a hog all night. I stink, and I didn't want you to end up gagging if we kiss later. The drink was a necessary casualty so I could change clothes without it being weird. But hey? Weird is here."

"You changed because you stink?" she asked, her mouth twitching. "You've been sweating like a hog?" She started laughing.

"It's not funny. I'm trying to be on my best behavior with you. To impress you, but apparently all it does is make me sweat. Are you happy now?" His temper was getting hotter the more she laughed, and he knew he needed to rein it in, but he was so damn tired of glossing over everything. So damn tired of constantly feeling like he was on the chopping block. "So, let me change in peace and put on more deodorant. Then I'll get your dessert."

She pressed her hand to her mouth. "So your whole monster-in-the-stomach sounds weren't from hunger?"

The tips of his ears flushed hot. "Out." He crossed the room toward her, prepared to lift her out of his room and close the door in her face if need be.

"Oh, Blake. What am I going to do with you?" she asked, still giggling. "Here, let me see how bad it is."

He darted back a few steps in horror when she leaned forward to sniff him. "Hey! Cut it out. I'm trying to be nice here."

"Maybe you shouldn't be so nice."

This was not a conversation to be had while he was wearing briefs. He shoved one leg in his jeans. "You're right. Maybe I shouldn't. At the rate we're going, I'm going to end up with IBS."

She made a gurgling noise like his stomach had made, and he was lifting his other leg to pull on his jeans when she reached out a hand and shoved him. He toppled to the floor.

"Hey! What was that for?"

"For trying so hard. For twisting yourself up into knots. Why can't you relax?"

Outrage turned his cheeks red. "Why can't *you?*"

"Because we're trying to date when we've been married. Like Rhett would say, you can't put that horse back into the barn."

"Natalie, you've got to level with me here. I have one leg in my jeans, and I'm sprawled on the floor. I reek of sweat. So don't talk in riddles...what in the hell do you suggest we do?"

She stopped laughing. Her eyes ran up the soles of his bare feet to his thighs, settling on the bulge in his briefs. After an arresting pause, which had his heart pounding, she continued her assessment up his torso. Finally she met his eyes.

"We can't pretend to date, Blake, not when we both remember how it used to be between us."

Then what the hell had they been doing these last weeks? A strangled sound escaped from his throat. He sat up and stared at her. "Tell me what you're trying to say then," he said hoarsely, his skin prickling as he awaited her response.

"Every time we're together, it's like the big elephant in the room, isn't it? That's why it's so hard to find things to talk about when we're together. We're not being normal with each other." She gestured to him. "This is the most normal we've been. This is the first time I've laughed easily with you other than over playing with Touchdown or watching TV."

He snorted. "I do believe you laughed when I wore that Don Johnson 1980s outfit, not to mention when the guys hung all my underwear out in the tree."

Her blue eyes softened. "Yes, I did."

Shaking his head, he tugged his jeans the rest of the way on and lifted his hips to pull them up. "So, basically all I need to do is make a complete ass of myself, and we're normal? Wait. Let me write that one down."

As he pushed off the floor and stood, she took a step closer. Then another, until she could lay her hand against his hard, bare chest. Her touch felt burning hot.

"Not a complete ass. Just...not Super Friend or Pretend Boyfriend or whatever the hell it is you've been playing these last weeks."

If her hand hadn't been on his chest, he would have walked out of the room. "I'm doing the best I can here, Nat. What do you want from me?"

Her eyes narrowed. "I want you to treat me like you used to. I want you to stop treating me like glass, and I need you to tell me when I'm being ridiculous."

"Fine. You're being ridiculous. Are you happy now?"

Her hand lifted and traced his jaw. "I want you to follow me."

"Where?"

In response, she only spun around and left the room. "And don't put on a shirt," she called out over her shoulder.

He gulped, rock hard now as he strode after her. She left the house, then the patio, and headed for the bridge. When she reached it, she fingered the trails of lights as she passed through their soft glow, her sandals echoing on the wooden planks.

When she opened the back door of her house, she turned in the doorway and leaned against it. He could see the unmistakable desire in her eyes. His footsteps ate up the ground between them. When he met her in the doorway, he stared into her brilliant eyes, the blue so dark it was almost indigo now.

"You're going to have to say it." *Please, God, let her say it.*

"I want you," she said and laid her hand on his chest again, right in the center over his thudding heart.

He dipped his head until their mouths were inches apart. Her warm breath rushed over his face when he yanked her body to his rock-hard one.

"And I want you. Only you. Always you."

CHAPTER 23

After weeks of pseudo-dating, Natalie had grown needy and restless. She wanted to be normal with him again and could no longer deny that fact to herself. And so she'd followed him into his bedroom to confront him, worried that he may have simply given up on her, on them, after their awkward conversation had lapsed into silence.

Hearing how nervous and awkward he'd felt—that she'd made him sweat through his shirt... Well, her huge and scary love for him had burst its confines.

She wanted to be herself with him again and laugh, and she wanted to see him let down his guard and relax—and sweat in her presence from a purely different reason.

The only way to do that was for them to be intimate with each other.

If he'd shown her anything over these past weeks, it was that he loved her. He'd do anything for her. Now she needed to see how much she could do for him, with him, once again.

Though he was poised just inches away from her mouth, he still didn't kiss her. She could almost hear him asking her if she was sure. Okay, she wasn't, but the only way she'd know is if she plunged ahead. She rose on her tiptoes and pressed her lips to his, and the groan he released told her everything she needed to know about his state of arousal.

His tongue was like rock striking flint, stirring the smoldering sparks of desire inside her. His lips were the kindling fueling the blaze. Heat spread across her body, and all the years of missing him fanned the flames into an inferno.

She tugged off her sundress in a fit of near madness, desperate for him. "I need you. Right now."

He released her and stepped back a few paces, all the better to see her, she knew. The sight of his muscular, broad chest was enough to make her damp in places that had gone dry since leaving him. Lust swept through her, destroying her fears. She unhooked her bra and let it drop to the floor.

"Touch me," she said, padding forward, lifting his hands to her breasts.

His fingers caressed the undersides first, where he knew she was sensitive. Her head fell back as his touch curved around to the top. God, she had missed his hands on her breasts. It had been torture to keep their contact to kissing and light touching these last few weeks. Suddenly, she realized they were still in the doorway. Touchdown lay on the ground only a few feet away in the kitchen.

"Stop fooling around," she said in a stern voice, pulling him inside and slamming the back door.

"You always were impatient," he answered in a husky voice.

She leaned back against the door, wanting him to take her against it, hard and fast, before she could think of anything else. *"Blake."*

His thumbs rubbed her nipples with agonizing precision, and she cried out. If he would only kiss her there, she would come. She knew it. But he didn't. Blake planned to savor their joining. She could feel it in his every movement, his every gesture. She clenched her eyes shut.

He swept her up into his arms. "Come on. There's no way I'm taking you against the door."

He'd carried her like this so many times before. Good memories flooded back to her as he swept her up the stairs, and she curved a hand around his strong, defined jaw. He'd shaved again for her, she could tell. So thoughtful.

When they reached her bedroom, he closed the door behind them. Touchdown was never allowed in this sanctuary of theirs. He set her down on the bed and looked his fill. She was more than ready, so she laid back and tugged off her underwear. His breath hissed out as she anchored herself with her elbows on the bed.

"You are still so beautiful you steal my breath away."

She let her gaze travel over him—his sculpted chest, the worn jeans that hung loosely on his hips.

"And your body is still the most ridiculous work of art I have ever seen."

His mouth tipped up at the corners. How many times had she called his body ridiculous in that playful tone, making him smile? Not enough and not for what seemed like eons.

When his mouth lowered to kiss her stomach, she opened her legs. One of his hands curved behind her back as he held her to him, taking his sweet time, savoring every inch of skin he touched as he kissed his way up her body.

"I need you," she whispered as her aching breasts rubbed against his bare chest.

His mouth finally found hers, and he took the kiss deeper, wetter, wilder than any they had shared since reuniting. Her belly tightened with the dark strands of desire. She ran her nails gently down his back, knowing how much he loved it.

He groaned, the husky timbre reverberating throughout his chest. "Oh, Nat, Nat...I missed you so much."

He lit a trail of fire across the length of her neck, tracing her sensitive skin with his tongue, his soft lips, and the delicate nip of his teeth. It was enough to warm her skin and make her body clench with need, but there was also a familiar tenderness.

Her skin and bones began to dissolve like a cloud in direct sunlight. With Blake she'd learned the scary truth that bodies weren't boundaries. No, with him, making love had always led to a oneness, a merging undefined by time and space. Her heart was preparing to leave its numb sanctuary, to welcome him again to see the secret, most guarded parts of herself.

A wave of primal terror swept through her chest, and she struggled for air. *Would she have to talk about why she left him? Would she have to talk about Kim after they made love?* Surely he would broach those forbidden subjects.

"Let's move along," she told him, reaching for the waistband of his jeans and unzipping them.

The hard length of him told her he was more than ready, and she had her hand wrapped around him in seconds.

His breath hissed out. "God, your hands are cold." He pressed his forehead to hers as she gave him the long strokes she knew made him wild. "Oh, God, Nat," he whispered, his voice broken now. *"Stop."*

She froze, wondering what she'd done wrong. He'd always liked this before.

He took her hand away and brought it to his mouth for a kiss. "It's not that I don't love it...it's just...been so long."

With that, her heart ventured forth again, edging closer to his warmth. She'd wondered how many other women there had been in their time apart. She hadn't been able to stop the jealousy from creeping into her mind when she couldn't sleep.

"Has it?" she whispered.

His brown eyes burned into hers. "Yes."

It was one simple word, yet it was somehow also an affirmation of his feelings for her. Her lips wobbled with emotion.

"You don't have to wait." She transferred her touch to his chest and kissed him, feeling out of control.

His laugh was more like an agonized sputter as he drew away from her. "If you think I'm going for speed after all this time, you're crazy."

She was afraid *she* was crazy...or that letting herself feel so much again, after spending so long living each day to get through it, would make her that way. "I *want* to touch you."

She pushed him onto his back, or rather he let her, and tugged his jeans and briefs down his legs. Her mouth went dry, seeing all that bare skin, the utterly perfect musculature of a professional athlete. She ran her hands up the hard planes of his calves, the undersides of his knees. He flinched, and she smiled, knowing how ticklish he was there. But she had another target in mind. She curled her hands around his massive thighs, tracing the defined muscles straight to the heart of him.

"No, seriously," he rasped. "I can't take having your hands on me this time even if they aren't freezing cold now."

She leaned over and kissed his belly in response, and his hands jerked her up until she met his mouth. He kissed her again, a sweet slide of his tongue on hers.

Then he rolled her onto her back and proceeded to show her how he put the E into endurance. He kissed her breasts with increasing pressure, going from gentle laves to hard suction. Her back arched against his mouth, but before she could peak, he released her and kissed his way down her stomach.

She wasn't sure she wanted to simply receive pleasure at his hands. To do so would be to make herself too vulnerable. "Don't make me wait."

Intensity flashed through his eyes, but when he lowered his head again, she stopped him with the touch of her hand.

"Not...that way."

His jaw locked, but he nodded, and the shift was so great, she felt the first crack in the earth that had been connecting them. She'd just set a boundary—here—in a space where there never had been any.

"Okay. Are we going to need a condom?" he asked.

There was hesitation in his voice, and she knew why. They both heard the distant cry of an earlier battle. Her demand for a child after Kim's death. His refusal to give in to her. Her horrible excuse for leaving. Oh, how her lies had hurt them both.

"I'm not on anything," she said quietly and gestured to her nightstand. She'd been too afraid to go on the Pill, which would have been akin to making a decision about him, about them before she was ready. It had been easier to buy the condoms—all she'd needed to do was pretend like they were the box of chocolate salted caramels she hid from herself.

After pulling out her drawer, he opened the box. She could practically hear his brain working, trying to figure out when she'd bought it. Buying condoms in Dare Valley would have set the gossips' tongues wagging about her and Blake being back together, so she'd picked them up in Aspen.

Instead of taking out only one of them, Blake shook them all into his hand, like he was counting to see if they matched the product total listed on the box. A noise rose from his throat as he finally grabbed one and shoved the rest back into the drawer, satisfied there were none missing.

She knew he wondered if there had been anyone else. She hoped they'd never talk about that.

His brow was furrowed with tension now, and she realized it wasn't just her arousal which was waning...his was too.

They'd never used a condom. She'd gone on the Pill after deciding she was ready to take that next step with him. It gave her a strange sense of sorrow to think about adding this new barrier between them.

"It's only temporary," he said, reading her mind in that keen way of his.

She glanced up at him. His brown eyes were troubled. It took her a moment to swallow the lump in her throat, but then she grabbed the package from him and tore it open with trembling hands. He reached out and took it from her.

"Here. Let me."

When he was finished, he cupped her face, looking right into her soul. He didn't blink. A pressure rose in her chest, and she clenched her teeth as a wave of powerful grief overwhelmed her.

No, don't say it. Please don't say it now.

"I love you," he whispered. "I've never stopped."

All her defenses came tumbling down. He was forcing her to face it now...the hurt that lay thick between them, the desolation that had bloomed inside her after she left. Squeezing her eyes shut so she couldn't see the longing in his gaze, she pushed away and lay on her back.

"I love you," he repeated, his voice stronger. "Look at me, Nat."

Don't ask me that. Don't make me look.

Her eyelids trembled as she squeezed them shut even tighter. "Make love to me, Blake."

There. I said make love, she wanted to say.

An audible sigh filled the room, and then he was gathering her body up, fitting it over him as he sat in the center of the bed. Her muscles tensed. During their marriage, making love sitting up, wrapped around each other, had been their favorite position.

And it was the most intimate one too.

She couldn't do that with him again. Not this first time.

"I don't want to do it this way," she said, pushing against his strength, her eyes still closed.

His hands caressed her back in comfort. "But it's our favorite, Nat."

"I said *not this way,*" she pleaded, resisting harder now.

The hands holding her left her body. His body shifted, and she fell from his lap in a sprawl. When she opened her eyes, she saw him fling the condom aside.

"You don't want to *make love* with me," he accused with an alarming sheen in his narrowed eyes. "Why did you start this?"

Part of her wanted to cover herself. Without him touching her, she felt too exposed, devoid of all desire. "I want to," she lied. "I just don't want to do it that way."

"Bull." He shook his head. "Why did you even initiate this?"

"Because I want you!" she shouted, the emotional tidal wave too strong to harness now. "It's just...you're making too big a deal of this."

"*I'm* making too big a deal of us making love for the first time in two years?" He stood, all six foot four inches of him towering over her. "I thought you were ready to give us a second chance. And you let me think it. Dammit, Nat."

"You're what...going to leave me now?" she shouted at him as he picked up his clothes and stalked to the door. "You're a tease, Blake."

He swung around, and she wished she could call the words back. His face had turned the dark red of anger.

"So...you just want to get off, huh? Well, that won't

take long."

Before she could blink, he threw his clothes aside and was back beside the bed. His hands tugged her ankles until her bottom was at the edge of the mattress. Then his mouth was on her. He knew exactly where to touch and stroke, and within moments she was helpless to stop the orgasm that exploded through her body, pulsing in waves, making her feel like she was a glacier that had melted too fast and crashed into the ocean, causing endless ripples to radiate out from her.

The hands cupping her hips tightened, and he let his head hang heavy on her stomach. She waited for him to simply take her, to take his pleasure. But he kissed her belly for an achingly long moment, and then she felt him shift away. When she finally opened her eyes, he was gone. His clothes with him.

She rolled onto her side, fighting the pressure in her chest. All pleasure disappeared, replaced by a pain so sharp and bitter it brought tears to her eyes. The cold returned, and with it, an icy sleet to cover her skin.

Stumbling, she ran to the shower. Hot water would bring her back to herself. Stepping under the jets, she dialed up the strongest setting and let the pressure rake over the skin he'd kissed, let it pound away the sweetness of his touch.

But she couldn't erase it. Nothing could.

She pressed her forehead to the tiles and slapped her hand against them, reaching deep for that inner control, that place of numbness where she'd resided for years. She couldn't find it. A wild howl rose up from her belly, echoing up and out of her throat.

"Noooooo," she cried out, her head banging against the wall to stop the pain from hurtling through her like an avalanche.

Sinking to the floor of the shower, she succumbed to the tears she'd been fighting for years, tears finally unleashed by the reality that Blake wasn't coming back.

CHAPTER 24

Blake was halfway to the bridge by the time he realized he was running away. The woods around him swayed under the light of the half moon as he stopped and inhaled the crisp mountain air to calm his raging emotions.

She wasn't ready to let him love her again.

Right now, he wasn't sure that would change, that *she* would change. He hung his head and squeezed his eyes shut to block out the white lights he'd strung on the bridge before their date. An owl hooted off in the distance, and he heard a whine. Felt the soft nudge of Touchdown, who must have followed him out.

He had to go back. He knew it. If he didn't, all would be lost between them. But he dreaded it, dreaded going back in there right now after how close they'd come, how far they'd fallen.

Well, he wasn't a quitter, and he'd promised himself and Natalie he wouldn't give up.

With determined steps, he walked back to the house and let himself in. Heading to the kitchen, he found a plastic bag and filled it with ice. In his line of work, he'd iced just about every part of his body except his dick, but there was a first time for everything.

He turned off all the lights and sat on the couch. In another part of the house, he could hear the shower running. When she finished, he'd...

He didn't know.

His desolation was complete. Usually he had a plan. After the initial shock of her leaving him had worn off, he'd told himself he would win her back. Up until tonight, he'd felt certain, down to his gut, that she'd shut him out because of her inability to face her grief. Perhaps he'd been wrong the whole time. Maybe she just hadn't loved him enough to stay. Tonight, she hadn't even cared about him enough to make love with him in the way that gave them both the most pleasure. She had shut her eyes to block out his professions of love.

Touchdown put his head on his thigh, and Blake stroked it as the dark, piercing thoughts swirled in his mind. He was used to fighting them off, but tonight the demons were too clever, their whispers too real.

He was lost, and he knew it.

The patter of feet sounded behind him, and he tensed. He made himself look over his shoulder, but all he could make out was Natalie's dark shape. Touchdown whined and jumped off the couch. She flicked on a lamp, and her gasp carried across the room.

"I thought you'd left," she whispered, wringing her hands in front of her favorite terry cloth robe riddled with the wear of many years. Her gaze landed on the ice bag on his crotch, and she flinched.

"I almost did," he said softly, "but I swore I wouldn't leave you again. That I'd be here. In good times and in bad." He realized how close those words were to the vows he'd made to her, the vows that were now null and void thanks to a stupid piece of paper.

And he remembered the way she'd smiled as he spoke those vows—a smile so bright it was as if she'd gathered all the light in the universe into herself. This time her face, flushed red from the shower, bunched up in a frown.

"I'm sorry," she whispered in a thready voice.

"You're forgiven," he forced himself to say. If marriage had taught him one thing, it was that carrying a grudge only eroded love.

"Why didn't you...ah...take care of that?" she asked, and she didn't need to point at the object of her speculation.

They both knew he was still rock hard from unfulfilled desire. And perhaps that was where they could start. With the truth.

"The first time I took care of myself after you left me, I thought of you the whole time. When it was over, I didn't feel relief. I felt sick and hurt and...pretty much like shit."

Her eyes narrowed to the point of a squint, but she didn't walk out.

He coughed to clear his voice so he could continue. "The first time I had sex with someone after you left, I felt even sicker. I was in my get-over-you phase, and I hooked up with a groupie for what I thought would be mindless sex. I hadn't done that since my first year in the league, and I wasn't proud of it, but I...I was afraid I'd never get over you. The dreams hadn't stopped, and well...you wouldn't return any of my calls. I was angry, and since I didn't want to drink my way to oblivion— trust me, I tried a few times, and it didn't work—I thought I could find it in sex. I wanted to erase you...even though the very thought of it broke my heart."

Her hands clutched the top of the loveseat, her knuckles white.

"It wasn't fair to her. I thought of you once we got started. But she *wasn't* you. She didn't smell like you or taste like you or even sound like you when I touched her."

"Don't," she entreated in that same harsh whisper.

The tone of her voice gave him the courage to continue. "I waited a while before I tried it again, hoping it would be better. This time, I chose one of my old friends-with-benefits from before I met you. We used to have a good time, and things weren't complicated. She knew the score."

"Blake—"

"She was familiar in her own way," he interrupted, "but she wasn't you either. I had to force myself to hold her and stay over so I wouldn't treat her like a jerk. She didn't deserve that. After that, I stopped trying to move on. So, I took care of myself, telling myself it was only temporary and someday we'd be together again, that I'd make love to you for real, and everything would be okay."

She sunk into the chair perpendicular to the couch, sitting on the edge like she wanted to bolt. But she wasn't leaving, and he took that as a good sign.

"So, now you know the ugly truth," he continued, setting the bag of ice aside. His ardor had disappeared with the revelation of his shame. "Who did you try to move on with? I always thought it would be your friend, Jeremy. You two always had fun together, and he was good looking enough. You would have gone for someone you cared for, someone who'd be safe."

Her eyes flicked down to study the hands clenched in her lap. "Please don't talk about this."

But she didn't try to walk away, so he kept going. "Part of me hoped it would be okay for you when you did." How many times had he imagined her with someone else, every image another slash to the gut? "The rest of me wanted to pull him apart for touching my wife. But the worst part was wondering how you could choose anyone else after saying you loved me."

This time she did dart off the chair. He was sure she was going to run into her room and lock the door, shutting him out yet again. But she shocked him. She sank down beside him and grabbed his hand with all her strength.

"How can you talk about something so painful?" she asked.

He rubbed his brow. "Because it's there, and we've been shoving it into Pandora's box for weeks hoping we could drift along and survive on long runs in the canyon, TV nights, playing with Touchdown, and kissing. It isn't working, and tonight brought that into painful focus. I can't pretend anymore."

She hung her head, the picture of abject misery, but he made no move to comfort her. He didn't dare.

"I might love you and want you back, but there's a whole bunch of hurt and mistrust between us. If we don't talk about it sometime, we'll never come out from under it. And after tonight, I'm all out of charm and guile. My better nature is gone, Nat. This is me, the bruised, hurting guy you left who still loves you. Who only wanted to make love to his wife tonight and then found out she really didn't want him."

Her nails dug into his hand. "I did want you."

The pain in his chest was crushing. "Not enough to let me really love you. When I stood halfway between our houses on the bridge, it finally occurred to me that maybe I've been wrong this whole time—maybe you don't really love me anymore. Maybe I've already lost everything."

She pressed her free hand to her mouth and sniffed. Tears filled her eyes and started to fall down her cheeks. He'd never seen her cry before—*really* cry—so it felt like he was witnessing a miracle. A shaft of hope poured into him.

"I do love you," she whispered.

And with those precious words, he fell through the bottom of his own despair, into a place of new beginnings. Her tears fell on their joined hands, and the warmth of them washed over the hurt in his heart. His throat filled with emotion, but he made himself wait for her to continue.

"I'm scared," she said, dashing at the tears streaming down her face unchecked. "It's like there's this dark room inside me, and it's filled with all the pain of losing Kim—and you. I'm...afraid...that if I go in there I'll never make it out again. I used to think I was...strong, but this pain...Blake, it's too much for me. I don't think I know what true strength is, but I don't think I have it."

He knew that kind of pain, understood the desperate desire to make it stop, to run from it.

"I can't take it," she said, her voice hoarse. "I'm afraid I'll go crazy again, the kind of crazy I was after Kim's funeral, when you found me on my knees in the shower, the cleaning powder dusting my hair, coating my dress. I looked in the mirror and hated myself. And I saw the look on your face. I wasn't...the woman you'd fallen in love with, the woman you'd asked to marry you."

She'd scared him shitless that day, and she wasn't mincing words—she really had looked like a crazy woman. More than anything he'd wanted to take her into his arms and tell her it would be all right, but the words wouldn't have been true, so he hadn't said them. Now, sitting beside her on the couch, he clenched her hand tight in his.

"Before Adam died, I...thought I'd be prepared for it, you know? We had almost a year between that first serious cardiac incident and...his passing. We all knew he was living on borrowed time, and that he wouldn't grow old like the rest of us."

A soft light shone through her eyes as her tears continued to fall. He had to cough to clear his throat.

"When my mom called to tell me...he was gone...I didn't think anything could hurt that bad. Losing you hurt bad. Don't think for a moment I'm saying otherwise. But with Adam...there was no hope of a second chance. He was gone. Just like that. I was never going to see him again or hear him laugh or have him tell one of his silly jokes."

The pain of losing him surfaced anew, and he felt his own eyes fill with tears, his nose start to run.

"I wish...I'd been there for you," Natalie said, pressing closer.

He turned so she could nestle against him and carefully wrapped his arm around her. "Then you would have seen me in my own crazy. I probably threw five hundred passes through my training net in the backyard until I broke down and bawled. It wasn't pretty. I mean I've cried before, but this was..."

"Madness," she finished in a whisper. "When I saw you flinch that day in the bathroom, seeing me like that, I was..."

His gut trembled, afraid of what she was about to confess to him. He knew it was going to be part of the answer to why she'd left. "You were what?" he asked.

"I thought if...I could just stay numb, I wouldn't become that crazy woman I saw in the mirror. I knew you wouldn't let me stay that way. You...loved me too much not to try and comfort me, and I was sure that would only make it worse."

His sixth sense told him there was something more, something a lot scarier hidden in her words. He braced himself to face down the monster. "What else?"

An anguished sound rose from her throat. "I...I thought if I stayed and went crazy, you'd... stop loving me."

Oh shit. He squeezed his eyes shut as the pain flooded him. She hadn't trusted him to love her enough. Somehow that hurt worse than the rest of her fallout from that decision.

"Keep going. Might as well get it all out."

"I...saw your face when you opened the door. Your whole face scrunched up when you looked at me. I felt...like a leper." Her fingernails dug deep grooves into his hands now. "I didn't recognize myself. I hated that crazy woman covered in cleaning powder. How could you love her? I didn't."

The wetness in his eyes welled up, sending tears down his face. So far, they'd been confessing their deepest and darkest secrets without eye contact, but this revelation...she needed to see what was in his eyes. He turned to face her.

"When you looked at Kim at the end, when she weighed less than a hundred pounds, did you love her any less?"

Her lip trembled, and she shook her head fiercely from side to side.

He brought their joined hands to his mouth and kissed hers with all the aching sweetness he felt in his heart. "That's how I felt when I saw you that day. No, you weren't yourself, but I still loved you. Completely. Passionately. I promised to love you, through everything. It...hurt me to see you like that. I wanted to make it all better for you, but I knew I couldn't."

She sniffed loud in the quiet room. "That's how it was when I would visit Kim. I wanted...to make her stop hurting, but I couldn't do a damn thing. I felt so...powerless."

"But you were there for her, and she knew it. Remember how she squeezed your hand after she fell into unconsciousness at the end." Oh, how his throat ached now, remembering that. "She knew you were there, even then. I...wanted to be there for you like that."

"And I picked a fight with you...about having a baby. I thought it was the most unforgiveable thing I could do to you, and that you'd let me go. But you...Blake, your capacity for forgiveness blows me away. I'm so sorry.

For everything." If only she'd told him the truth. How different might things have been?

She pressed her head to his shoulder. "I don't want to keep hurting you. Us."

"I don't want you to keep hurting either, babe."

When she lifted her face, the bleakness in her eyes almost undid him. "Then what are we going to do?"

He brought her hand against his chest. Touchdown crawled onto both of their laps, half on him and half on her, almost like he was joining them together again as a family.

"Let me walk into that dark room with you," he told her. "I won't leave you or think you're crazy. And I won't *ever* stop loving you." He felt like he was renewing his vows to her all over again.

Her face scrunched up. "But it hurts, Blake. It hurts so bad. I cried in the shower tonight, and I never cry. I just couldn't stop it this time."

So the healing was starting. Now he could hold her through it like she'd refused to let him do before.

"I know it hurts," he said gruffly, feeling it between them, the agony of loss. "We'll face it together."

"I don't know how...." Her voice broke, like a pane of glass cracking at the center, the slivers shivering out until they touched everything in their wake.

"I never told you why I'm so...free with my emotions," he said. "Adam used to cry whenever he got upset, but I always tried to be tough. My mom took me aside one day after I fell off my bike and forced myself to shake off the pain. She said I needed to show Adam it was okay for him to cry, or he'd be ashamed of himself."

Everything in her was trembling against him, and he rubbed her arm to warm her. But this cold wasn't the kind that was easily exorcised. No, it was one that dug in with its icy claws.

"At first, I did it for Adam. He always wanted to comfort me when I was hurt, and I did the same for him. Of course, it got harder for me to show my emotions as I got older. Some of the other boys in junior high made fun of me, but then I got ridiculously good at football. People started to say my emotions were what made me a great player. My teammates were willing to follow me because I always put myself out there for them."

"I've...always wondered. Your emotions...sometimes they unhinge me, Blake. Whenever you cried after losing a big game...well, I wouldn't know what to do to help."

He'd realized that, so he'd tried to dial them back around her. What a pair they were. On some level, he hadn't believed she could love him in all his ugliness either.

"You helped just by being there, just by holding me. And that's what we do when the person we love is hurting. Now...tell me what you miss most about Kim," he said and gripped her hand tight, lending strength and comfort to her as she stepped into the abyss.

Tears streamed down her face, but her lips tightened as though she wanted to hold back the words. Refuse to utter them to keep the pain at bay.

"When I first met Kim, I thought she was your sister," he said. "You both had the same brown hair and a laugh that would make any man take a good, long look."

A sob escaped her lips. "She *was*...my sister. Oh, God...I miss her so much."

Her pain was like a bone that needed to be rebroken before it could heal, so he braced himself to finish the task. "She loved you...as much as she loved Andy and Danny."

She started crying, the anguished sounds tearing at his heart. "I know she did...why did it have to happen, Blake? *Why?* She was so young. It's so damn unfair! Sometimes I just want to scream at the sky until I lose my voice."

He understood the whys. With Adam. With Kim. With Natalie. The answers never came.

"Then scream, babe. Scream it out until you're hoarse."

She pushed against his chest with all her might. *"Why?"*

The anguished howl broke her—all the way. Her sobs tore through the last of the walls she'd constructed, and when she punched his chest with her fists, he gathered her into his arms and held her while she cried and cried and cried.

It might have been hours, she cried so long. All he could do was hold her, rub her back, kiss her head, pass her tissues when she couldn't breathe through her sinuses—and swallow the razor blades in his throat because seeing her this broken broke him too.

When Natalie finally fell asleep, he let his own tears come.

CHAPTER 25

When Natalie awoke, dawn's first rays were floating in through the windows in pink and orange ribbons. Her head felt like she'd been beating it against a wall all night. Her face was swollen, her throat scratchy. Beyond her body's distress, the sound of Blake's steady heartbeat echoed in her ears. The warmth from his body felt like a cocoon, as did the arms wrapped around her in a lax embrace.

As she came back to her senses, she could scarcely absorb everything. She hadn't scared him away by letting herself lose control, by letting out some of the crazy grief balled up inside her. How wrong she'd been to leave him. She knew that now, and regret buffeted her like cold hail.

The last words Kim had spoken to her—ones she'd never told another soul—filtered into her mind.

Hold onto Blake, Nat. I swear...that man loves you more than football. I can't wait...to see the family you create together. Laugh a lot for me. I'll find you...when I hear.

She had lost everything, even herself, after Kim's death. But no matter what she had done to drive him away, Blake had held on. And when her efforts to avoid the pain lurking within her had finally crumbled, he'd held her hand and faced it with her. She remembered something else from last night, something that cracked her heart in two. Blake had started softly crying as soon as she drifted off—she'd sensed it from somewhere in the periphery between sleep and wakefulness.

Pain might have separated them from each other, but last night, they'd made each other make-shift bandages.

Touchdown snored softly beside her. Blake's chest had always been massive enough to hold them both. As massive as his heart. She inched her head up slowly so as not to wake him. His sandy brown hair rose in spikes on his head, and his mouth was open slightly, breathing the shallow air of sleep.

The truth stole over her like the stillness after a torrential downpour. She loved him. She really loved him. She'd never stopped. And while she felt hollowed out inside, there was also a peace and a clarity she hadn't possessed yesterday.

The words he'd uttered last night—the ones from their wedding vows—came back to her.

In good times and bad.

They had certainly been dealt more than their share of bad lately, but before that, there had been so many good times. She had abandoned herself and her needs in the bad times, judging them to be madness, judging them to make her unlovable. She'd thought Blake would react the same way. She'd underestimated him.

As she studied the rise of his brow bone, the curve of his jaw, she thought of the vows she'd made to him all those years ago. At that time, she had lived such a life of privilege—the meaning hadn't registered. She'd breezed over the words like the carefree bride she'd been, never doubting their love would be strong enough and steadfast enough for any lean winters ahead.

But all that had changed. The depth of her sadness

over losing Kim had leached her bones with its coldness. And she had closed the door to herself and the one person who could bring spring back to her.

Blake.

Unable to hold back any longer, she inched her hand up and stroked the stubble on his jaw, feeling the bristles against her fingertips. Touchdown snorted loudly and then rose up beside her, his body shaking like he was trying to throw off water instead of sleep. The precious dog lapped at her face like he used to when the three of them awoke together. Then he looked at her with his sweet brown eyes like he was waiting for her to kiss Blake awake—something she'd always loved to do.

Once she did this, she knew there would be no turning back, and she realized she didn't want to. So, like a fairy prince awakening his true love from the troubled sleep of dark dreams, she laid her lips to Blake's and gave him back her full heart, the one covered in scar tissue from her grief, the one that had raised its walls to protect her, the one that was ready to love him enough to allow him into the deepest, most private place inside her: the one that wasn't always pretty or strong or sane.

His body tensed under her as he awakened, as if he were scared of this fragile, numinous connection between them, but he passively allowed her to kiss him. She supped at his lips to feed the starved part of her that had missed him. She traced the bones of his face to imprint into herself that he was still here after seeing her at her lowest last night.

Angling her head to the side, she fitted their mouths together in deeper union, tracing his bottom lip with her tongue. Under her, his heartbeat thundered now in his chest, but still he made no move to touch her other than to maintain the connection of their mouths and lips.

His skin was warm when she traced it, and as she continued to kiss him, she imagined the pink glow surrounding her heart flowing up with her breath and into his mouth, communicating all of the stored up love she'd hidden away in the locked treasure chest of her heart.

She went on kissing him and kissing him. Her body filled with the light of a million sun drops, burning off her grief like it was morning fog. The joy that rose within her breast made her want to cry out in triumph.

I have come home, and here I will stay.

But still he held back, letting her take the lead, and the realization of what he was waiting for finally thundered through her.

"I love you," she said, searching for his eyes at last. "I want to come home. Will you let me?"

He cupped her face with a kind of benediction. "Babe, you can always come home to me."

Their mouths met again, and this time he poured himself into the kiss, nipping at her lips, dueling with her tongue. His arms tightened around her and beckoned her to come closer, to always come closer, as close as she dared.

And she did, laying claim to him again, fitting their mouths together in glorious exploration until she finally had to edge back and give herself life-sustaining breath. His gaze was the loving one she remembered, but it had changed into something even more powerful, like steel forged in fire.

"I love you," she said again, tracing the planes of his face. "Will you make love with me?"

He only nodded, as if he couldn't trust himself to speak. Understanding the fragility of the moment, she shuffled off his body and held out her hand to him. He took it, and together they journeyed back to the room that had held such pain the night before.

She shrugged out of her robe and stood naked before him in the morning sunlight, feeling the warm beams alive on her skin. His gaze burned into hers as he tugged off his jeans and briefs. This time she knew she had to take the next step.

Crossing over to the bed, she climbed into the middle and sat cross-legged in the center. Her body trembled with nerves. A shudder ran through his body as he looked at her, and he swallowed thickly. She held out her hand and waited for him to come to her.

He walked to the side of the bed slowly and opened the drawer to her nightstand, like he was expecting to find a snake. Tension pulled at the skin between her shoulder blades. He drew out a condom with a shuttered breath.

The inside of her cheek hurt where she bit it, seeing the fear and longing play across his face. *Could they do this again and not be destroyed?* She knew he must be thinking that, for she was thinking it too. He rolled the condom onto himself. When their eyes met, she raised the hand she still held out to him. He joined her in the center of the bed, and she rose up over him and wrapped her legs around him like a butterfly closing its wings over a newly emerging blossom.

She caressed his face as she fitted herself over him and took him inside her. Desire wasn't coursing through her yet, but love was. And love was more important than passion right now. His face clenched as her muscles opened to him, and she traced the taut skin of his jaw.

"I love you," she whispered and pressed close until their bellies touched and her breasts teased the hard muscles of his chest.

His hands clutched her waist as he reached her core. Then he pressed his forehead to hers, his sorrow traveling through the ends of her fingers to her aching heart.

"Look at me, Blake," she said softly.

He lifted his head, and in his open gaze, she saw the pain and the love and all the pieces of him she'd missed. Her hips pressed forward, and he met her halfway.

Something ignited inside her belly, and she undulated her hips again, feeling him shift inside her. On the edge of her mind, she heard a cry and strained to listen.

Yes, she heard. *Yes.*

"Oh, God," he rasped, his fingers digging into her hips now. *"Natalie."*

They started to dance, a dance they hadn't forgotten. His eyes met hers and wouldn't let her look away, even when her back arched into him, a ragged moan pouring from her lips.

"Don't close your eyes," he whispered.

"I won't," she promised and knew it was a kind of vow.

They looked into each other's depths as they rocked and rocked and rocked until the passion between them shattered and healed all their remaining wounds in its wake.

Chapter 26

In the weeks that followed, Blake and Natalie renewed their bond. While they didn't officially live together, she would text him when she was on her way home, and he and Touchdown were always waiting for her at the garage door to greet her. It was his favorite moment of the day, another piece weaving the fabric of their life together again.

They took runs together, watched TV together, talked about their days. And they made love, exploring each other's bodies with a renewed joy akin to cherishing.

When her alarm went off, Blake would kiss her good morning so sweetly her eyes sometimes grew moist with unshed tears. Most days she barely made it to the office in time, which they both laughed about. Other times, he would make her coffee and bring it to her while she was putting on her makeup, which was partly an excuse for him to watch as she added to the beauty that took his breath away.

They continued to talk about the last two years and everything that had led to their divorce, but they didn't yet talk about the future. And Blake was okay with that because she was coming back to herself. Sure, there were some extra lines around her eyes from the crying that continued to force its way up and out of her, like an unstoppable geyser that had no choice but to explode, but he was convinced it was healthy. He would hold her when the tears came, and together, they would stand in the midst of the storm until it passed.

They agreed to give their relationship a little more time before he started to accompany her to the family's gatherings. When Blake had asked her if she'd be okay with him asking April to volunteer at the camp as "The Camp Mom," she'd given him her A-OK. April had jumped on his offer with a delighted yes without even asking about his status with her daughter or the high school coaching job she'd mentioned to him weeks ago.

When the week of the camp finally arrived, Blake had mixed feelings. It would be the first week he spent apart from Natalie since their reconciliation. Sure, he could sneak back to see her after lights out, but he would miss spending his evenings with her. He told himself it wouldn't hurt their burgeoning relationship.

Emmits Merriam's practice field had been freshly cut the morning Blake arrived to make sure everything was ready. Touchdown barked as he opened the car door. The kids needed a mascot, Natalie had suggested, which was why they'd decided their dog would be on the sidelines during the day and around after practice to play with the kids. He was more than touched. It was like she had become his help-mate all over again.

His guys were flying in soon and would arrive in Dare Valley by early afternoon. The volunteer coaches from other similar flag football programs would join them at three o'clock. His assistant was staying in Dare Valley the whole week and would lead a short meeting with the rest of the volunteers later on. But no press. His assistant would take pictures and send them to his publicist.

Tomorrow the kids would arrive, kicking off the

advent of camp. He was more than ready. He was stoked. As he tore off a tuft of turf and lifted it to his nose, inhaling the earthy smell, he could feel Adam with him. If his brother had been standing on the field with him, he would have tossed the grass at him, which would have resulted in a silly grass fight.

"Oh, Adam," he whispered as his chest squeezed with grief. "I wish you were here."

He rubbed at the tears in his eyes, and when he removed his hand, his whole body stilled. Natalie was walking across the field toward him, a soft smile on her face. The relief he felt was almost overwhelming.

"Hey," he called out to her, his voice rough from emotion. "I thought you were going to work."

Her hair was a mixture of brown, red, and gold in the morning sun. The Celtic knot tattoo on her ankle spoke of secrets, ones he wanted to know, but was still too afraid to ask.

"I was halfway there, and then I turned around and came this way."

She held out her hands to him, which he took.

"It's a big day for you. I wanted to be here before it gets crazy. I know how you like your pre-game rituals. I hope I'm not interrupting."

"I was...just missing Adam."

She took him in her arms. "I thought you might be."

This time he was the one who cried a bit as she held him tight, bearing his grief. His chest was lighter when he finally settled. "I know he'd be happy I'm doing this. I just miss him, dammit." He wanted his brother to be here. He didn't want to be doing something in his memory.

"He *would* be happy," she said, kissing his jaw. "I brought you something."

When she pressed away to rummage through her tan leather purse, he took some deep cleansing breaths.

"I'm going to miss spending all my evenings with

you," he told her.

Her mouth curved. "I rather like the idea of you breaking curfew to sneak out of camp to make love to me. Makes it feel more forbidden."

He laughed. "I didn't think we needed any help in that department. It's been ridiculously good for me."

"Me too," she said, and then she thrust something into his hands.

Wrapped in burgundy paper with a black string, he knew from the shape it was a picture frame. His heart exploded when he saw what it contained.

The photo, taken by Natalie, was of him and Adam playing catch. She'd shot it in black-and-white, so the green in their Denver backyard didn't dazzle the eyes. What *did* dazzle was the depiction of him playfully extending the football to Adam and his brother grinning from ear to ear as he reached out a hand to take a hold of it. The ball linked them, the perfect sphere of it centered in the photo, showing the passion they shared for the game.

His eyes burned again, and he knuckled away more tears. "Thank you."

She kissed his cheek. "I'm so proud of you, babe. I'll wait up for you tonight."

Even though he knew she would, he still said, "You don't have to. You know the guys."

Everyone was staying in the dorm. He knew darn well knew they would all end up hanging out in the common room reserved for the coaches. It had a pool table, ping pong, darts, and foosball. They were never going to get any sleep.

"If I doze off, you can always kiss me awake." She gave him one last hug, like she too was dreading the time they would have to spend apart this week. "I love you. Remember that."

"I love you too," he said, pressing his face into her hair. His mind flickered back to her tattoo, to the fact he still hadn't asked her about it. "Ah...I've been meaning to ask you about your tattoo."

Her body stilled. "I...ah...got it after...a year or so ago."

He realized she didn't want to say the word divorce any more than he wanted to hear it.

"You don't have to tell me what it means."

She cleared her throat. "Well...I...this is awkward, but the three links were for you, me, and...Kim...and that time in my life." Her face pressed into his neck, her fingers gripped his back. "I wanted to have something to remember it by."

That she would do something so sentimental—and admit to having done it—moved something powerful in his chest. "Thanks for telling me. I...miss you already." He'd always told her that before leaving for a road trip, and the words felt right on his tongue.

"Miss you too," she whispered back.

She stepped away and gave Touchdown a nice rubdown before walking off the field, taking a piece of his heart like she always did. He sat in the center of the field for some time, the sun hot on his ball cap, staring at the picture in his hands.

Jordan was the first to arrive, in a blue convertible Porsche Boxster, no less. His reflective sunglasses and his swagger made him seem more than unusually badass as he approached Blake on the field.

"You're early," he said, rising and giving his buddy a hug.

"Yeah." His shoulder lifted. "Caught an earlier flight."

There was something in his tone. "What's up?"

"Shit." He kicked at the turf, making Touchdown bark. "Sorry. Grace and I had another fight about me getting swept up in all the hype. *People* called. They want to do a feature on me as one of the hottest guys in the NFL. They asked to interview her as part of the piece. She refused."

"Her privacy has always been important to her," Blake said neutrally. Natalie had felt the same way, and he'd respected that.

"I get it, but instead of saying she wouldn't do it, it turned into me becoming someone she sometimes doesn't recognize. She told me I was morphing from the small town boy she knew from Deadwood, South Dakota into someone she didn't even recognize, and it pissed me off."

Blake had been a small town boy from Ohio, so he understood where Jordan was coming from. "Well, you're not a small town boy anymore, are you? The question you have to ask yourself is this: what is more important to you, the hype or football?"

Jordan nudged him like a determined linebacker would. "You know I love football more."

"Then..."

"But I like some of the hype," he said in an exasperated tone. "Why does that make me a bad person?"

"It doesn't. It's just not...what Grace is used to." Or perhaps it wasn't what she wanted. He'd watched a lot of guys split with their girlfriends from high school or college as their careers skyrocketed. Things *did* change. Not everyone was made to be the girlfriend or wife of an NFL quarterback, and Grace was more level-headed than most.

"She says she hates it when people refer to her as 'my piece' or imply she's mooching off me. Hell, sometimes she still fights me over who pays for dinner."

So they were arguing about money too. Not good. "Well, she values her independence." Like someone else he knew whose name started with N.

Jordan leaned down and stroked the field. Touchdown sniffed the grass by his fingers. Blake wasn't the only player who liked to get a sense of the turf.

"Would it upset you if I asked if you and Natalie ever had these kinds of arguments?"

If he and Natalie hadn't been back together, it might have been difficult to discuss it, but now, he could answer his friend without any pain. "We fought about the money more than the hype. She didn't want me to pay for everything either. I hated that at first, but that's what she wanted, so I conceded." He would have conceded pretty much everything to be with her. "She wouldn't accept any money from me when we...divorced."

Okay, it did hurt to say that, more than he'd thought it would. Memories poured back in, ones they hadn't talked about. She hadn't even shown up to sign the divorce papers. He'd scrolled out his name on the legal document ending their marriage with a Mont Blanc pen as a punishing rain streaked the windows of his lawyer's office building.

"Are you two..." Jordan trailed off.

"We're...working through things." He dug out his sunglasses, no longer liking the glare stinging his eyes.

"I'm glad. I hope it sticks." Jordan slapped him on the back. "So, let's do this."

While they waited for the others to arrive, they threw some passes, and then he called in some takeout from Brasserie Dare. Thankfully, no one mobbed him when he went to pick it up. Brian even came out of the kitchen to say hello. Apparently the Hale clan was inclined to keep the peace as he and Natalie worked things out.

They ate lunch in the center of the field, and it felt good to be back on the green grass dotted with white lines every ten yards. Natalie was his home, but this was too. He'd given his whole life to the pursuit of a mere ten yards over and over again.

When the rest of the guys arrived, they hugged and talked trash. Brody challenged Logan to a forty yard dash, causing Zack and Jordan to groan in tandem. They complained they were going to upchuck their lunches, even though that was total bullshit. They just hated to run that fast if there was no need. After all, they were quarterbacks, not wide receivers.

"Are you and Natalie still doing great since our last call?" Sam asked, coming up beside him to clap him on the back.

He and Sam talked every week, and he'd told him where things stood. "Yes." *So far.* He couldn't forget about the things they hadn't discussed—the details of the future and the past—so he still wasn't convinced they were totally out of danger. The pressure grew in his chest.

As Brody and Logan crouched down into their sprint stance, he called out "Wait. I'm joining you guys."

"Your old sack of bones?" Logan taunted. "We are so going to smoke you, Ace."

Yes, they were, no doubt. But at least it would take his mind off the half a dozen doomsday scenarios it was spinning about him and Natalie. His focus needed to be on the camp right now.

"On your mark," Jordan called out, staring down at the stopwatch he'd snagged from the camp's supply table. "Get set. Go."

Blake darted off with the wide receivers, and sure enough, he felt like a sack of old bones as their athletic shorts rippled in the wind a few yards ahead of him. Blake had been considered a passable runner in the NFL. He could run for the first down when necessary. But they smoked him, just as Logan had predicted. If the burn of his muscles and the clearing of his mind hadn't felt so good, he might have been embarrassed.

"All right," he said, sucking in deep breaths and heading over to the coach's table where his clipboard was resting. "Let's run through some last minute details and questions before our coaching partners arrive."

He'd paired all of them up with a coach who had experience running a flag football camp for kids with intellectual disabilities. That way, everyone would be bringing their A game for the kids.

"The other coaches will arrive at three with the rest of the volunteers. Including our camp mom."

"You didn't talk Mrs. Garretty into coming, did you now?" Brody asked, giving Sam a pointed glance.

"Mrs. Garretty has retired." Divorcing Coach had pretty much ended that. "But Natalie's mom volunteered to help, and I can't think of anyone more fun, maternal, or tough. She had five kids, after all."

"Awesome," Hunter said, twirling the whistle hanging from his neck. "She and I did the Electric Slide at your wedding."

The guys laughed, but Blake found it hard to join in. He thought back to opening Natalie's hope chest all those weeks earlier and finding her dress and their favorite wedding picture inside. Those memories were sweet, but now they felt tainted by everything that had followed. Their wedding had become something for them to get beyond. His hands clenched the clipboard.

"Maybe if you get your guys to run the drills right," he said, "you can teach them the Electric Slide after practice."

He'd meant it as a joke, but Hunter grinned. "Cool."

Great. He couldn't wait for that scene to make it onto YouTube.

They ran though the rest of his agenda and took a water break. The other coaches arrived, and he introduced everyone to their partners. Once that was finished, he left them alone to get acquainted. When he saw April cutting across the football field, dressed in his old Raiders jersey, the one he'd signed and given to her at her request, his chest tightened.

She pointed to her shirt. "I hope you don't mind me wearing this. It's one of my favorites, and I so rarely get to wear it."

He kissed her cheek, and she hugged him tight. "It looks good with capri pants. Maybe I should have worn those instead of football pants."

She punched him in the gut, something Natalie would do. "How are you and my daughter doing?" she asked with a knowing gleam in her eye.

Okay, so apparently her earlier silence on that subject was over. "We're talking. Things are...good."

"I'm so happy to hear it. Does this mean you'll be coaching our high school team this fall?"

Lead filled his stomach at the talk of the future. "No. The position didn't feel right for me."

"I see," she said, studying him intently. "Well. Thanks for catching me up. Why don't you show me who I'm supposed to be mothering now?"

He led her around to everyone, grateful for the reprieve from her questions. Some of the guys hammed it up and lifted her off the ground, making her laugh. He let them get all the playful antics out of their systems. When things had finally settled, a hush fell over the field. He headed to the center and turned to face everyone on the sidelines.

"As you all know, this camp means the world to me, so I'll keep this brief. I hereby officially open The Adam Cunningham Flag Football Camp."

Everyone clapped. Tears popped into his eyes.

He wished Natalie had been there to hold his hand.

CHAPTER 27

Blake's opener to the kids and their parents after registration wasn't much more long-winded than the one he'd given to the coaches and volunteers the day before. He introduced Touchdown first, making everyone laugh, then April, and finally all the volunteers and coaches. He told everyone to have fun. And encouraged them to ask questions—nothing was too silly or stupid. After that, he told them the story about how he and his buddies had attended football camp together for years when they were younger, and they were still best friends all these years later. He encouraged the boys to make connections with each other. He didn't talk much about football. They were here to play. Though he mentioned Adam only in passing—to do more would cost him too much—he told them his brother had possessed the heart of a champion.

After the kids had been split up into age groups, he joined his team. He had asked Sam to pair up with him and Frank, a volunteer from Denver, to guide the youngest age group. He'd chosen to work with them because they still crackled with the sheer joy of playing football. Whenever he'd hit a pocket of pressure in his career, Adam had always been there to remind him of why he played. Sure, he didn't need the reminder anymore now that he'd retired, but he rather liked hearing the boys giggle on the field.

They ran the Run and Catch drill first to assess both running and hand-eye-coordination skills. He and Sam took turns in the quarterback box with Frank working the sidelines. The kid they were assessing would line up even with them, and when Blake blew the whistle, the boy would run out to one of the five catching spots marked on the field. If he caught the ball, he would sprint to the finish line. Each kid received a score, and the top three scorers would become the quarterbacks for the next drills on passing accuracy. While Sam passed the football, Blake worked with Frank to help the kids who were receiving the ball refine their catching technique.

There were high-fives, whistles, giggles, cries of frustration, and fists pumps as the morning progressed. At lunch, he, Sam, and Frank huddled to compare notes. They ranked the kids by skill level, something they would continue to do at the various breaks. Blake left Sam and Frank to continue their chat and grabbed a smoked turkey on wheat sandwich from the lunch station. The other guys were huddling as well, so he took a few minutes to check in with them.

He noticed April making her way through the folding tables they'd set up for the kids so they could sit and eat comfortably. She was laughing as she watched one kid throw his arm back like he was about to launch a pass. Blake found himself grinning even though he didn't know the story. After lunch, when they called the kids back to their drill groups, Blake made his way over to April.

"So, what's your take so far?" he asked, pushing up his sunglasses so she could see his eyes. Natalie had always preferred for him to do that when he was talking to her.

"Well, they're still pretty much in the awe mode. All they could talk about was how cool you guys are. You have some big fans here."

Coach Garretty always nipped those sentiments in the bud with his Once Upon A Dare speech. Blake had elected to run on fun and inspiration in this camp, not hard work and fear.

"I'm glad you're here." He leaned down to kiss her cheek. "I need to get back to my team." Man, how he loved that word.

"I'll be here," she said with a wave.

The afternoon continued with more drills, ones they repeated over and over again. He saved the Agility and Speed Handoff drill for last since it required more concentration and teamwork. The kids in his group now knew one another's names, and they easily called them out during the drills when needed. After being in the sun all day, he wished he'd dabbed on more sunscreen, feeling the burn on his nose and cheeks left exposed under the brim of his Raiders ball cap.

When he called it quits, he, Sam, and Frank huddled with the boys to talk about the day and give high-fives. One bold kid asked if he could have his autograph. Blake ruffled the boy's brown hair and said they'd all be giving autographs at the end of camp. Coach Garretty hadn't allowed it. Blake had decided to provide the opportunity, remembering what it had felt like to come to a camp where he was coached by some of the NFL's greatest players.

The camp volunteers escorted the boys back to the dorm. Spirits were mostly high, but he saw one kid moping all by himself, trailing behind the others. Jogging over, he fell into step with the kid. So abject was the boy's misery, he didn't even notice Blake.

"Hey," he said, "what's got you so long in the face?"

The kid's mouth dropped open, and then he grinned,

showing a space where he'd lost his front tooth. "You're Blake Cunningham! I mean Coach Blake."

That was another thing he hadn't wanted to model from Coach Garretty, so all the coaches were being called by their first names.

"What's going on?" he asked. "Did you have a tough day?"

He lifted his shoulder. "I didn't catch most of my passes. I usually do better, but..."

"But you were nervous, right?" The kid slowed down when he did. "Is this your first camp?"

He nodded, kicking at the sidewalk. "Yeah."

"What's your name?"

"Paul."

"Well, Paul, I was nervous the first time I went to camp too, and usually the first day of every camp after that. I *really* wanted to do well."

He remembered those days with fondness. The first camp had been the hardest because he hadn't known anyone. Coach Garretty only took kids who'd been nominated by their school coaches. He'd been nominated for the youngest age group—the ten to twelve year olds—since his arm had shown incredible promise.

"I wanted to prove to everyone I could do well," he told the boy.

This time Paul nodded his head vigorously. "Me too."

"I'll tell you a secret it took me years to learn."

The boy's eyes brightened, and he leaned in when Blake crooked his finger.

"If you have fun and play to make yourself happy, everything else will fall into place." He clapped a hand on the boy's shoulder. "Once you stop worrying about impressing other people, it becomes a lot easier. That other crap...it messes with your head. Now, go on in and have some fun."

"Thanks, Coach Blake."

He held up his hand for a high-five. Their palms connected. The kid gave him one last beaming smile before running inside.

"You're a good coach," Sam said, appearing at his side. "I always thought so. You have the leadership to raise them into good men, not just football players," Sam said, taking off his ball cap and running his fingers through his hair. "We need more coaches like that."

"I appreciate you saying so. We'll have to see how that shapes up, now that I've turned the high school job down," he said, even though he'd told Sam about the rationale for his decision.

"That guy was a pain in the ass. I told you that you don't want to work in that kind of environment."

He didn't. And he had faith he could figure something out.

"Are you thinking about coaching when you retire?"

Sam refitted his Warriors ball cap on his head. "It's a possibility. We'll see when the time comes."

And the time was coming, they both knew. Sam was no spring chicken in the NFL. The early retirement age was something all of them dealt with in their own way.

"Okay, let's go find the guys and play some games of our own before dinner. I'm ready for a little friendly competition."

Sam and Blake found the rest of their buddies in the game room. Logan and Zack were already involved in a heated foosball match, complete with a stack of dollars on the side of the table. He played a few games of foosball when the table came open and lost a round to Jordan, who buffed his nails on his Rebels jersey afterward, like beating him had been a walk in the park. That naturally led to a head-lock and some wrestling— all of which felt good.

After dinner, the kids gathered into the dorm's main lounge with the coaches to hear Sam give a talk on mental conditioning. Blake had asked a few of the guys to talk about the physical and mental aspects of the game, which he believed was as important, if not more so, than the drills and scrimmages.

That night, the guys went back to competing in pool and darts while a baseball game played on ESPN. Blake sat on the couch and watched Brody and Hunter laugh like crazy over Zack's scratch ball at the pool table.

For Blake, being back amid football—even flag football with a bunch of kids—was like walking on a sidewalk riddled with cracks. He wouldn't be returning to *his* team.

Sam sank onto the couch next to him. "You're brooding."

"Yep. Being on the field today...it kinda got to me." He picked up his water bottle and chugged it. They'd all agreed to a no-drinking rule around the kids. Coach Garretty had been right on that score.

"Well, that's perfectly understandable. It's been part of your whole life."

"One of the best parts," he said, making a basket with his bottle in the recycling bin.

But there was another best part, and he could go visit *her*. Being with Natalie reinforced every reason for the sacrifices he'd made. Rising from the sofa, he leaned over so only Sam could hear. "I'm leaving. Don't tell the guys."

He rolled his eyes. "Like they don't know where you're going."

Sure enough, he was halfway to the door with Touchdown when Jordan called out, "Have fun, Ace. Tell Nat baby hi for us."

Spinning around on his heels, he eyed the bunch. "You all look like a bunch of grinning hyenas."

"We're happy for you," Zack said. "But still, it seems like you should have to sneak out or something. Maybe try the window." He tapped the face of his watch. "It *is* past curfew."

"We're on the first floor, you moron." He exited the room, smiling.

Even though he was anxious to leave, he walked to the stairwell to check on the boys. While he was certain the chaperones had everything in hand, he felt a strong investment in these kids, in this camp, and he wanted to make sure everything was all right. When he stopped on the second floor, he heard music, laughter, and raised voices. On the third floor, he was delighted to see a makeshift hacky sack game being played in the hall.

Good, everyone was having fun. That's what camp was all about.

He and Touchdown headed home, or what he now thought of as home. The two-house situation was beginning to seem weirder the closer he and Natalie became. After spending the night with her, he sometimes wanted to destroy the bridge he'd built so he couldn't go back to his own place in the morning.

He wanted to live with her again, full time. Not shuffle back and forth.

He was feeling a little out of sorts by the time he parked in his garage. Touchdown followed him in the house and immediately went for his water bowl. A shower took off the grime from playing, but it didn't restore his mood. He'd spent the day ensuring everyone else was having fun, so maybe now *he* needed to have some fun. He was getting too serious about the camp, his future after it, Natalie. Putting too much pressure on himself.

Zack's joke about climbing out the window to break curfew came back to him, giving him an idea. Natalie's bedroom was on the second floor of her house. He could climb into *hers*. And give her a little fantasy.

He dug out the Fraser kilt and loose white shirt he'd ordered online a week ago. He figured if wrapping a simple plaid throw around his waist like a kilt was enough to turn Natalie on, how might she react to the real thing? The wool itched against his privates because—of course—he had to go bare-ass naked under this getup to complete the fantasy. The green and navy plaid socks looked ridiculous, so he had to dig out some dress shoes to make it more...presentable. When he was finished, he bypassed the mirror. All that mattered was she thought it was smoking hot.

Grabbing an extension ladder from the garage seemed the wisest course. He hauled it across his yard and the bridge, the kilt chafing his balls, as Touchdown ran along behind him. Knowing Natalie was a creature of habit, he wasn't surprised to see a few lights on downstairs and one in her bedroom. She was waiting for him in bed, and the thought of that sent a thrill down his spine. He positioned the ladder as close to the house as he could, pressing against her bushes, and extended it to her window.

As he climbed it, an owl hooted in the darkness, making him start. Now he could understand why kids snuck out of their parents' houses. Of course, this wasn't his parents' house, and he was sneaking in, not out, but that was simply semantics. He felt the allure of the dangerous, the forbidden.

He could already imagine the look on Natalie's face. When he reached her window, he dragged his fingernails against the screen. When she didn't come to the window, he did it louder. The curtains were closed, so he couldn't see her. After a few minutes of nothing, he became irritated. How could she not hear him? He rapped on the window. She still didn't come.

"What in the world are you doing?" he heard a familiar voice ask from below as a flashlight pooled over him.

He turned on the ladder, blinded by the light, as Touchdown gave a happy bark from below. "I'm breaking into your room like a bad kid at camp—or a rogue Highlander. Why aren't you in there?" he asked in what he believed to be a passable Scottish brogue.

He heard her bawdy laughter crest out. She held the flashlight under her chin, giving herself a scary Jack-O-Lantern face. "Why? Because I heard a weird noise outside, you idiot Highlander, so I came out to investigate."

He hadn't thought of that. "Well, go back inside and open your window," he said in the same passable brogue. Jamie Fraser would be proud. "I'm going to ravish you."

Even with the glare of the flashlight, he could still see her eyes roll. "You're *not* serious. Get down from there before you trip on your kilt and fall to the ground."

He shifted on the ladder to better see her and felt it move an inch. Okay, she had a point. "If you'd only cooperate, lass, I wouldn't be hanging onto this ladder trying to have a conversation with you."

"Oh, stop with the Scottish brogue. It's terrible. And don't be a jackass. You aren't going to fit through that window. Your shoulders are too big. Did you even think of that?"

She was dissing her own fantasy? He ground his teeth. "No, I left my tape measure at home," he said in his normal voice. "Natalie, get in the goddamn house and open your window. I'm trying to be romantic here—in case you haven't noticed."

She snorted. "You're trying to get yourself killed, climbing a ladder in the dark in a kilt. Come on, Touchdown. We are not watching this."

When she left, he turned back to face her window, hoping she would head upstairs to open it. He eyed the opening. Okay, so she hadn't been lying. He was going to have a hell of a time getting through her window. The best way would be head first.

So sexy.

This was starting to seem less and less romantic.

And to make it worse, his balls still itched.

The curtains flew back so suddenly, and with such force, he jolted in surprise. The ladder shifted again, and he immediately grabbed the sill to steady himself. She yanked up the window and stood glaring at him through the screen.

"I suppose you want me to remove the screen too?" she asked, her mouth twitching like she was fighting a guffaw.

He reached out to feel for the tabs he remembered as part of window installation. "There should be a thingamabob here to pull."

The lamplight showcased her exasperated face. "These are custom windows designed for security. You can't remove the screens that easily. If you have a knife on you, Jamie, you can cut through it."

Like her voice was cutting through him.

"Then you can call the repair man tomorrow and have him install a new one," she added.

He growled in defeat. "Fine. I'm coming down."

She let out the sputter of a laugh. "Good. My screen thanks you."

"And I'll head home and change," he said with a sulk.

"Oh, no," she said stroking her bottom lip. "You can keep that on."

Now she was excited? Well, he wasn't. She was ruining his attempt to recreate her fantasy. With every rung his feet descended, his cheeks turned redder with embarrassment. He was never going to live this one down. She was waiting for him at the back door, her arms crossed over her chest. The glee on her face was too much.

"Okay, so I totally suck at sneaking out and being Jamie Fraser," he said, pushing up his billowy white sleeves.

Blake Cunningham was wearing sleeves that

billowed. He could hear Jordan say, "Shut the front door."

Natalie's laughter bubbled out as she pointed to his belt buckle. "That's quite a package you have there, lad."

He shook his head, and then the anger slipped away and he was laughing with her.

"Wait until I tell the guys about this," she said between gales. "If only they could see you now. Oh, and your fans. You should have played for the Denver Highlanders."

"Okay, you've made your point. I look ridiculous." He yanked her to him, and he cursed as his sleeves billowed again. "Don't you dare tell anyone! I should get points for trying."

"Maybe. So far your execution has been...less than impressive. "

He smirked and lifted her up and over his shoulder like a sack of flour. She squealed, fighting him for show, and mostly giggling.

"I'm about to show you my skills at execution. Good night, Touchdown."

The dog went to his doggie bed as Blake climbed the stairs with Natalie. After shutting the door to her bedroom, he set her down on the bed.

"I'm still going to ravish you even though this outfit has chafed my balls raw."

"Ah...you poor baby." Chuckling still, she sat on the edge and pointed to the window. "Why don't you close the curtains so you can ravish me without the owls watching?"

"Are you ever going to stop teasing me about this?" he asked.

"No," she said, and since she was tugging off her robe, he didn't care. "You're never going to live this down. What if you had fallen and hurt yourself? Can you imagine the gossip? Former Super Bowl star Blake Cunningham breaks leg executing an *Outlander* fantasy."

She had a point.

She wasn't wearing anything underneath her robe. His mouth pretty much went dry the instant she pulled it off. She stretched out on the bed, his every fantasy, Highlander or no.

"You were worth it, even if I failed."

Her blue eyes darkened. "Take off your clothes. Don't you think you've wasted enough time?"

He eyed the clock. It *was* after midnight, and her alarm would go off at six. "Taking off my clothes now, ma'am."

Stripping before her was exciting and arousing, even if he did want to scratch his privates in relief as the kilt dropped to the floor. Her gaze ran over him.

"Turn around please," she said in a playful tone, and now he could feel the fantasy building between them, hot and consuming.

He complied, his muscles tightening, readying. Before he knew it, she was right behind him, her hands caressing his butt. His skin caught fire as she moved down to stroke his right thigh.

"You still have the best legs on the planet," she told him, leaning down and kissing the length of his hamstring.

"The better to showcase in my kilt," he replied, his voice husky, making her laugh again. But he didn't try to use a Scottish brogue. He'd learned his lesson there.

Her lips continued their trek to the back of his knee and then cruised over to his left leg. Every touch hardened him to the point of pain, and when she kissed his right butt cheek, he hissed out a long breath.

"Are you torturing me for trying to break into your house like a roving Highlander?" he asked.

"You *did* scare me. It's sometimes a little harrowing to be this far out of town."

He didn't want to remind her he was next door if she

needed anything. No, he wanted to be right here, all the time, checking on noises in the house like he used to do when she'd hear something. Or killing bugs for her. She hated to kill her own bugs.

"How about I show you why I donned a scratchy kilt and hauled a clunky extension ladder across about three acres in the middle of the night?"

"Not your best plan," she said, kissing his lower back. "But you did get points for the Highlander costume. You haven't done anything this crazy since you talked me into having sex with you in the laundry room at my mother's house at Christmas."

That *had* been forbidden and more delicious than her mother's honey baked ham. "Thank God she was doing the laundry that day, or I swear they would have heard you."

"Me? You make as much noise as I do."

When her hand slid around to his front and grabbed him, she more than proved her point when he groaned.

"See."

And she just had to rub it in. That's why he loved her.

He slid his hands over hers, caressing her wrists as she continued to stroke his body. When he arched his back, she finally let him go and turned him around to face her. She sat back on her knees at the edge of the bed, a gleam in her eyes.

"Had enough?" she asked.

"Not likely. Lie back."

She did, and he covered her with his body, resting his weight on his elbows.

"You didn't kiss me when I got home," he said, stroking her cheek.

"Oops. Sorry. I was distracted by a clumsy Highlander intruder."

"Smartass," he said before taking her mouth in a deep, wet kiss that had them both breathing hard.

Her breasts were masterpieces, so he touched them next. The long length of her spine arched off the mattress as he kissed them. She rubbed the heel of her leg over his calf, telling him she was more than ready for him. But still he detoured, journeying lower to the very heart of her. He worshipped her there, and she came apart under his mouth.

Before the waves had smoothed out, he rolled on a condom and thrust inside her. She arched into him, her passion taking her higher. Every muscle under him strained again, and he met her tension stroke for stroke until they both flew, letting their releases wash over them.

After he'd cleaned up, he turned out the light and rolled over to face her. His eyes adjusted until he could see the outline of her face on the pillow next to him.

"I love you," he whispered.

"And I love you," she said, but he could tell her tongue was still getting used to rolling those words around again.

She turned onto her side and slung her hand onto his waist. He did the same.

"Tell me about camp."

With that easy connection between them, he outlined his day. She caressed his chest when he told her about his conversation with the young camper, Paul. Laughed when he mentioned Zack suggesting he break curfew.

"I should have known you had help."

When he was finished talking, he traced the curves of her face. He knew she was sleepy, but he was too desperate to hear how she'd passed her time without him not to ask.

"Tell me about your day."

Her response was briefer, less coherent, as she was slipping off into sleep, but it didn't matter—the details of her life were as precious to him as sea glass coughed up on a beach.

And when her breathing was even, he nestled her against his chest, feeling that at least one piece of his life, of his future, was crystal clear.

She was home.

CHAPTER 28

Andy had put off his coffee date with Valerie for as long as he reasonably could. Since he was legitimately busy at the hospital, there were plenty of ready excuses. There had been the emergency appendectomy of the Emmits Merriam sophomore who'd collapsed in her Renaissance History class. The torn bowel of the fifty-six year-old marathon runner. But he eventually decided to make good on his promise to Natalie and go.

The coffee date went okay. Valerie was pretty and sweet, but he still felt unsure of himself...unready. Still, he found himself agreeing to take her out for dinner.

On a Thursday night. Not Friday or Saturday. Way too much pressure there.

Natalie was coming over to babysit since Blake was off doing camp stuff. From what Andy's mother had told him, the camp was going gangbusters. April was beaming from all the fun she was having with the kids. Of course, there had already been mischief. His favorite story was about a prank the kids had pulled on her.

One boy was making a commotion about a fly buzzing around him, and when Andy's mom rushed over to comfort him, the kid next to him slapped a napkin over the bug and killed it. Then he opened up the white paper and picked out the dark bit of fly and put it in his mouth, chewing blissfully. April lurched forward to stop him, horrified by the thought that a kid had just eaten a bug on her watch.

A few of the kids sitting around the area of the "incident" started sputtering. Moments later more of them joined in...until the whole table was laughing. April's mother radar instantly activated, and she asked what prank they were pulling. The fly swatter showed her a handful of raisins and explained the trick. One kid pretends there's a fly, distracting the adult, while the other palms a raisin and slaps it down with the napkin.

Andy thought it was ingenious and had already taught it to Danny so he could pull it on the rest of the family.

He changed into what he hoped would be acceptable second date apparel: tan dress slacks and a black polo shirt. He contemplated adding more aftershave, but decided against it. After all, it wasn't like he was hoping to get lucky. He just...wanted to get through his first dinner date as a widower without feeling like a clown. A second date didn't need to be in the cards. He told himself it was like getting a vaccination. One time would do it. Then he could give himself a lollipop. Kim would be happy in heaven. He would have kept his deal with Natalie. All would be well.

He sat on the bed, his hands on his knees. His shoulders hunched. He knew he had to get moving, but dammit, the truth was he didn't want to go out on a date with anyone other than Kim. It wasn't fair.

"Dad!" Danny shouted. "Aunt Natalie's here."

His pity party was over. He forced himself to go downstairs and found his sister kissing Danny's cheeks like she was the Cookie Monster and he was a plate of cookies.

"Stop kissing me!" Danny cried, wiggling with delight in her arms.

"Okay, but only if you chase me once your dad leaves." She pushed the hair she'd messed up out of his eyes and lowered him to the ground.

"Sure. Dad, are you leaving now?" he asked, pressing back against the doorframe to the dining room like he didn't trust his aunt to leave him alone. He was one smart kid.

He kissed Natalie's cheek in greeting. "Hey. Thanks again for agreeing to watch the munchkin."

"I am *not* a munchkin. I'm a big boy." Danny stood as tall as he could and pointed to himself. "See."

Grabbing his son into his arms, he tapped his nose. "Oh, yes, now I do. How could I have missed it?"

"Because you're blind," his son said.

"Hmm. Well, you must be blind because I thought I asked you to pick up your toys in the den before Aunt Natalie arrived."

He lifted his shoulder. "But we're just going to take them out again."

They'd had this conversation a million times. His son could not understand the logic of picking something up that was going to be disturbed later. "Indulge me. Blind man."

"I want to play Blind Man's Bluff, Aunt Natalie. Can we?" his son asked.

"Sure. Haven't played that in years, but don't you need more people?"

Andy shook his head as Danny ran off, most likely for the handkerchief they used. "Not in Danny's game. He's created his own rules. One person is blind-folded, and the other has to run around the room to avoid being tagged. It can be deadly. Watch out for the cars. He loves to line the floor with them. Hurts like hell if you're barefoot."

She tossed her purse on a chair in the corner. "I'll keep that in mind. So, how nervous are you?"

His belly tossed and turned like he was in a cargo

hold of a ship at sea. "Pretty nervous."

Her eyes darkened. "Don't...force it. Just try and have a good time. Failing that, try and keep yourself entertained. If it sucks, don't be a hero—you don't have to stay for dessert."

Was she thinking of her first few dates after her breakup with Blake? How must those memories seem to her now that they were reconciling? Did she regret dating other people while they were apart? He knew from Moira and Caroline's teasing her that she'd been out with a few guys. Not that they'd ever talked about it. He didn't like to hear *those* kinds of details about his sisters.

"How are things?" he asked, not asking specifically about Blake.

"Great." She pushed him toward the door, apparently not wanting to say more just yet. "Now go. Danny and I have some Blind Man's Bluff to play."

When Danny ran back brandishing a white hanky, Andy swooped him up in his arms. He hadn't told him much about his evening, other than that he was meeting a new friend for dinner.

"Be good for your aunt, and go to bed on time."

He gave his sister a pointed look. None of his family adhered to Danny's bedtime when they babysat. Not even his mother.

"Okay, Dad." Danny gave Andy a smacker on the lips. "Have fun with your friend."

But after thirty minutes at Brasserie Dare with Valerie, Andy concluded fun just wasn't in her vocabulary. She'd fussed about the fifteen minute wait for a table, suggesting he might say he was related to the owner. Andy wasn't the kind of person who would ever do such a thing, but rather than say so, he'd explained that everyone already knew, and besides, it would make no difference. All the tables were occupied.

She must have been nervous too because she kept up

a steady hum of conversation about the recent thriller she'd seen at the movies while he studied the menu. Kim had never bothered him when he was reading something, knowing he liked to give it his full attention.

When she ordered a cosmopolitan, the floor dropped out of his stomach. It was Kim's favorite drink. It wasn't fair she was ordering his wife's favorite drink when Kim couldn't enjoy one anymore. And it certainly wasn't fair he was with a woman who liked cosmopolitans like Kim but was *nothing* like her. This little voice inside his head started listing all of his date's imperfections. Her teeth were too big for her mouth. Her right eyebrow rested a quarter inch higher than the left. And her nose, well, it was too snooty by half.

He could never imagine kissing her, least of all falling in love with her. He'd written her off by the time their appetizers arrived.

Sure, she asked him about his work at the hospital, but there was a certain sheen in her eye—one he'd seen in other women who idolized the idea of dating a doctor. She even asked about his family, knowing he was a Hale. When he brought up Danny, she tensed. Yes, it was only the slightest of reactions, the extra curl of her fingers around the knife as she spread foie gras on a piping hot slice of baguette. That nailed the coffin shut.

A woman who liked cosmos but not his son would never be the right match for him. After their entrees and some more awkward conversation, he told her he needed to get home to his "pride and joy." Her eyes lowered, and he knew she'd received the message. He paid for the check, wished her well, and walked to his car since they'd met at the restaurant.

Inside, he pressed his face to the steering wheel as grief overwhelmed him. *I'm sorry, honey. I didn't want to be there tonight. With her. I want to be with you. I always do. I don't care that you want this. I'd rather be alone. Don't make me get back out there. I can't do it.*

He dashed at the tears that coated the steering wheel and had to dig under the passenger seat for the tissue box he kept in the car for Danny. After blowing his nose, he leaned his head back against the seat and waited until he was settled enough to go home.

When he opened the door at a mere nine o'clock, he heard the pounding of little feet on the stairs. Busted. His sister hadn't enforced the little guy's bedtime. It made him smile.

Natalie appeared in the hall moments later. "How did it go?"

Could one respond *awful?* "Not the greatest show on earth. How was the munchkin?"

He cocked his ear, waiting to see if his son would be upset enough by the nickname that he'd forget he was supposed to be in bed.

"Wonderful, like always."

"How about a glass of wine?" he asked.

"Sure."

They detoured to the kitchen, and he poured them some red from the bottle he'd opened last night. There was something he wanted to ask her, and since it had to be on her mind anyway, he decided to straight out ask.

"So...you've mentioned you and Blake are doing really well," he said, pressing his wine glass to his chest. "Are you planning on bringing him around to any family gatherings in the near future?"

She contemplated her wine like she was looking for bits of cork. "We *are* doing well, but I'm not sure...it's time to bring him back into the fold. Things still need to be...more structured between us."

He read between the lines. What she meant was she had to be sure they were going to get married again, and she wasn't yet. "Okay. I just wanted you to know I'm there for you. For both of you if and when the time comes." He rather hoped it would.

"So tell me more about your date," she said, tracing

the stem of her glass.

She stayed a little longer as he ran through the basics. They weren't compatible. He wasn't that into her. All the excuses.

The real truth he left unsaid. That they both knew acting on a decision was sometimes harder than making one. He'd told himself he could get back out there. Start dating again. After acting on it, he knew he was a liar. He wasn't ready. He wasn't sure he ever would be.

When Natalie left, he journeyed upstairs to his son's bedroom. Danny had chosen seaside blue for his room, and they'd decorated it with a sea theme to match. A lighthouse lamp cast soft muted light on his son's face. There were octopuses, dolphins, and sea horses painted on his walls courtesy of an artist his Aunt Caroline knew from Denver. He sank onto his knees beside his son's bunk bed and looked at him. Simply looked at him.

The shape of his eyes was like Kim's. The curve of his nose like Andy's. Looking at him was like looking at the best blending of two people on the planet. Looking at him reminded Andy of the woman he loved, the one he'd married, thinking they'd share a long and happy life.

But they hadn't.

They'd lived a short and happy life. He was mostly grateful for that. Just not for the way it had ended. Kissing his son, he detoured to his office, unable to seek an empty bed.

His computer purred out of sleep when he jimmied the mouse over the mouse pad. He was checking Facebook when a message box appeared. It was Lucy, and boy, how his heart lightened. Even thousands of miles away, she was a comfort.

Hey! Missed you, he wrote. *How are you doing?*

He never asked if she was safe. It was like a commandment, not to be broken.

Ah...feeling a little sad tonight. There's...a lot to be

sad about here.

He couldn't even imagine. And Lucy wasn't easily daunted—for her, being sad was akin to being devastated.

I had my first date tonight. I'm a little sad too.

He watched the cursor blink on and off as she was typing.

Understandable. Kim would be proud of you, but who cares, right? She doesn't have to do the tough stuff of living, and sometimes living is hard.

Dammit, if tears didn't pop into his eyes as he read that. She was right. Part of him wanted to yell at Kim, to tell her he didn't care that she wanted him to find someone else. That he didn't want to and that was that. Lucy, who worked with the impoverished, with survivors of war, knew better than most how hard living could be.

Thanks for not trying to sugarcoat it.

I'll never do that, Andy Cakes.

A reluctant smile touched his mouth.

You're the best, Luce. Now how can I cheer you up? How about I tell you about a practical joke a kid played on my mom?

He wrote out the story, loving the LOLs and smiley faces she interspersed into their chat. By the time he finished, he knew she was probably laughing in gales halfway around the world.

Andy Cakes. I am so going to try that here. I'm going to have to track down some raisins, but maybe I can find an alternative.

Track down raisins? He couldn't imagine being anywhere that was that difficult. Then he realized she was in the freaking middle of Congo where most people barely had food. A month ago, she'd told him people ate grasshoppers. At first he'd thought it was a joke, but she'd actually tried them. He'd thought he understood poverty. He hadn't understood bupkis.

She was typing. *Listen, I need to catch a few z's since I couldn't sleep. I'll talk to you when I get back from our trip.*

Another trip? How long was she going to stay there? He started to type the questions, but hit the backspace until the line was clear. She didn't need him to heap any more of his worry onto her. A person would have to be stupid not to know the danger involved. Lucy O'Brien was not stupid.

Yeah, I should have asked why you were up.

Nightmare. Couldn't sleep. Shrug. Talk to you later, Andy Cakes. Kiss Danny for me.

You got it. Talk to you later, Luce.

Later, Andy Cakes.

They signed off, and he leaned back in his chair. Nightmares? She'd never mentioned having them before, but it wasn't too surprising when he stopped to think about it. She probably had some form of PTSD after all the places she'd been, things she'd seen.

Even though he was tired, he still couldn't go to bed. He looked online for new lawnmower models, something they didn't even need. After fifty minutes of mindless searching, he told himself to go to sleep. Instead, he went to the den. Toys littered the floor, so he stooped and picked them up.

Unlike Danny, he knew why a person cleaned up only to create a new mess later.

Sometimes there needed to be a break in between bouts of chaos. He decided he needed another break. He didn't care if that meant putting his dating plans on hold.

Nothing good was going to come of it anyway.

CHAPTER 29

Natalie had stayed away from camp for the rest of the week, though Blake had stayed over at her house each night. She still wasn't sure if it had been the right thing to do, but since he hadn't asked her to pop over after work...

He had told her about the camp each night, so she knew that the time after practice was reserved for male bonding, anything from movie night to a dance party hosted by Jordan and Grant. But still... She suspected he understood that if she came, it meant she was willing to publicly declare they were a couple again. It would be the next step in their reconciliation.

She'd struggled all week about making such a declaration. It wouldn't just be to him. It would be to his friends, her family, the town, and the world. They would be back in the public eye, and she wanted to believe she was strong enough to handle the talk about them because sometimes it could be downright intrusive and cruel.

As the week progressed, Natalie also thought more and more about what Blake would do once camp was over. They still hadn't talked about the future. It was an unspoken rule, but the suspense was starting to weigh on her. Surely he'd have to decide about the high school job soon? Not only would it be a big step for their relationship, but it would also be a big step in his new career.

She wasn't ashamed to admit she checked *The Western Independent* every day for information. Surely he would mention his decision to her before any report was published, but she couldn't stop herself from looking. The waiting was slowly becoming agony. He was staying in Dare Valley for her, and he needed to have something to do. There had to be other offers—just not local ones. But she knew he wouldn't want to leave Dare Valley, not when it meant leaving her. The guilt sat in her belly like a bag of marbles.

On Friday, all she could think about was going over to Emmits Merriam. Camp was due to end at four, commemorated by an awards ceremony and then a big party. She realized she wanted to go. She *wanted* to be there for Blake. People could think what they wanted about her public declaration. At lunch, she strolled into High Stakes' kitchen to seek out her boss. Terrance Waters was piping out savory rosemary and goat cheese meringue puffs onto a cookie sheet. They served as the accompaniment to his fabulous veal consommé.

"Hey, Natalie," he said, continuing to dole out rows of the airy white dollops. "What can I do for you?"

She swiped a finger at the batter clinging to the edge of his stainless steel bowl and hummed in appreciation at the taste. Before eating Terrance's confections, she hadn't known savory meringues were possible. "Do you have a problem with me taking off a little before four? I have everything wrapped up for the event this weekend."

He set aside his pastry bag. "No, feel free. I assume you're heading over to Emmits Merriam for the final ceremony of the football camp."

Of course he would know. Everyone in town knew.

Heck, Uncle Arthur had even written an article about it in *The Western Independent* called "The Changing Faces of Sports." Reading it had pinched her heart with pride for what Blake was doing.

"Yes, I thought I might," she answered him.

"Might?" he asked with a raised brow.

"Oh, shut up," she said without heat, "or I'll blow on your meringues and make them collapse."

His smirk was pure mischief. "My meringues are made of stronger stuff than that. And so are you. You know your own mind, all you need to do is trust yourself. And that's the very last thing I'm going to say on the subject."

He turned around with a wink and left the kitchen. She contemplated his meringues. He was right. She was made of stronger stuff, even when she was afraid.

When she stepped onto the football field at Emmits Merriam, as nervous as a virgin bride, the ceremony was starting. Her gaze found Blake in the middle of a group of young boys, standing with Sam and another man who matched his description of Frank. Blake was beaming as he handed out gold medals. Sam and Frank took turns putting them over the boys' heads. The sheer joy on everyone's faces was blinding.

Blake had told her about this—he wasn't giving out special achievement medals to individual players like most camps did. Everyone was going to get a medal. As her gaze scanned the field, she watched as the same process played out in the other teams. Jordan was holding court with a group of high-school-age boys and leading them through a cheer with Zack at his side.

"I wondered if you were going to come today," she heard behind her.

Her mother appeared by her side. She still hadn't confronted her mother about being Cormack Daly's messenger—or pumped her for information—and she didn't plan to. It would only invite more conflict, which she didn't want. She would assume her mother had meant well and leave it at that.

She flushed under her mom's scrutiny. "I wanted to come."

Her mom linked their arms. "I'm glad. I would have wondered if you hadn't...I've heard you and Blake are working things out."

She gave her mom the look.

"Oh, am I blind and deaf now?" she asked. "Blake looks so much happier than when he first arrived in town. It's not just the camp, although he's pretty much glowed all week."

Yes, she'd noticed. Every time he came to her after leaving the guys, he'd practically lit up her bedroom. He *was* happy, and she was so glad to see it again.

Her mom unlinked their arms. "I need to receive my award shortly. You're welcome to join the rest of us."

She'd purposefully chosen a vacant part of the sidelines away from the crowd to give herself time to settle. When she glanced at Blake again, their eyes locked. Had her mother said he glowed? No, he burned.

She found herself smiling back at him, and everything else faded into the background. Her hand ducked up in a girlish wave before she realized it. She almost cursed at her own awkwardness.

Then Jordan saw her and ran across the field. "Hey, Nat baby," he called out, reaching for her arm as he skidded to a halt in front of her. "Come join us. You can help us bestow our medals. I want you to meet my players."

She'd never been so happy to have him pull her onto the field. "Sounds like fun."

"See you later, honey," her mother said, taking off with a ruffle of her fingers.

Plenty of people stared at her as she reached Jordan's team. A few of them even pointed. Her shoulders tightened up so much she wished she'd thought to schedule a sixty-minute Swedish massage at the hotel.

After all the medals had been handed out, she took a place on the sidelines by herself as the boys fanned out on the sidelines, many of them holding hands. Seeing this sweet sign of unity made her heart swell. The sheen of pride she saw in all of the boys' eyes threatened to make it burst.

Adam had told her what it felt like to be different, how hurtful it was to be pointed at and stared at by people. He'd been called names, flat-out ignored, and sometimes even cursed for being too slow. Keeping pride in himself had been an ongoing process, one helped by his loving parents and Blake, who'd never been ashamed of him. No, they'd valued Adam as one of the greatest human beings they'd ever known. Now, Blake was giving that gift to these boys.

Blake stepped into the middle of the field with the other coaches. Dressed simply, in the green T-shirt of his team, navy shorts, and a Raiders ball cap, he looked larger than life.

"I won't say much to all of you," he said in a baritone voice that carried across the field. "I don't need to. What needed to be said has been said on this field, every day of this camp. Every time you caught the ball, you said something. Every time you kept running even when you were exhausted, you said something. Every time you made a new friend, you said something."

He put his hands on his hips and scanned the line of boys watching him.

"You said *you matter,* that you're talented, and that you deserve to play football like anyone else. When you leave this camp, remember that. When someone treats you differently because they *think* you're different, you call one of your teammates so you can remember the truth. What you have done here isn't just a victory. It's a triumph. I'm so proud of all of you, but I mostly want you to be proud of yourselves. As I told one of you boys the first day of camp, your opinion is the *only* one that really matters. Now, let's do some celebrating."

Then Blake stepped forward and held out his arms. The boys from his team rushed him first, followed by the rest of them. Her heart squeezed as she watched him hug the kids, laughing now. The boys converged around the rest of the coaches, and soon the field was filled with the special kind of male bonding Natalie had only seen on the football field, the kind of bonding Blake had always loved.

Until Blake, she'd never known the true power of sports. For her, it had always been about winning and losing and some pretty hot guys wearing tight pants. But football created a bond between the players. It didn't just create winners and losers. It created men. And Blake wasn't simply good at creating men, she realized. He was incredible at it. Coaching looked as natural on him as loving her did.

Love overwhelmed her. Determined to tell him just that, she took one step out onto the field toward him and then another.

Blake had lifted a young boy with red curly hair onto his shoulders and jogged across the field to the end zone with a trail of boys following him. They were all chanting, "Go, go, go."

"Good to see you, Natalie," Sam called out as he hugged a boy to his chest.

She waved to him and kept walking to the end zone. Blake had set the boy down and was demonstrating to his group how to spike the ball in victory. One kid after another tried. It was harder than it looked. Blake laughed as the football ricocheted off his ankle.

That sound of his happiness made her chest feel lighter. She loved him, oh, how she loved him.

One of the kids saw her and pointed. His mouth moved, and Blake spun around.

He missed catching the football a kid passed to him—something he never did—and didn't even lean down to pick it up. His baseball cap was angled low over his forehead, but she could see his eyes. Those beautiful browns were filled with the look of cautious hope she often saw in them when he didn't think she was watching.

When she reached him, the kids fell back, content to spike the ball. He was holding his breath, she could tell, and it reminded her to take a breath herself. She reached out her hands to him. He lifted his slowly and curled his fingers around her moist palms.

Memories of meeting him on the field when he was playing for the Raiders flashed through her mind, filling her with so much love she didn't think her body could hold her heart. Then her mind went blank, and all she could do was feel the power and warmth of the love she had for him.

"You...this..." She couldn't form a sentence.

His mouth shifted a fraction at a time until he was smiling at her, his earlier glow softer now. "I'm glad you're here, babe."

She released his hand and wrapped her arms around him, pulling him close. He squeezed her tight in return. When she saw the camera flashes out of the corner of her eye, she realized the public declaration concerning Blake had been made. They were officially back together.

Truth be told, it was about time.

CHAPTER 30

Few football parties had felt sweeter to Blake—not even the one following the Raiders' Super Bowl win. With Natalie beside him, meeting the boys on his team, his happiness had shot to a whole new level. This, he knew, *this* was contentment.

The tension she'd felt at being back in the public eye with him seemed to have evaporated, though the camera flashes hadn't stopped. She'd made her public declaration, and he knew what a step it had been for her.

He kept his arm wrapped around her as she talked to his team about what they'd learned at camp. A number of the boys told her she was pretty, which only made her laugh. He winked at them.

"Yeah, she is. Make sure and find someone as wonderful as she is when you get old enough."

Sam clapped him on the back at one point, and the other guys gave him knowing looks. Jordan even gave him a thumbs-up. He pretty much grinned like a fool the entire time.

April joined them as they chatted with the kids, and she patted him on the arm. Natalie and her mom still weren't completely easy with each other, but that would smooth out with time. If today was any indication, he would be joining Natalie at family gatherings again soon enough. His whole life stretched out before him, and he liked what he saw. Soon, they'd be getting married again and sharing only one house. They could figure out the details together.

He spotted Emmits Merriam's athletic director talking with Logan, and he leaned down to kiss Natalie on the cheek. "There's someone I need to thank. When you finish talking with the boys, come find me."

Her blue eyes seemed to glow with inner light when he gazed into them, and he allowed himself to become lost in them for a moment. When he walked off, he could hardly even feel the turf under his feet.

"Hey, Tom," he called out to the director and then jogged over to close the gap between them. "I'm so glad you came. I just can't thank you enough for letting us use your facilities. I hope we can arrange it again next year."

While Tom Hudson had played division three football back in the day, he still had a striking physique for a man in his early fifties. "Absolutely, Blake. I was just telling Logan how much this makes me wish Emmits Merriam had a football team. But you know. Funds." The man shrugged. "You can hold your camp here anytime. Maybe you can even do it more than once a year since it's obviously a huge success. Then I can sneak over and watch the drills—which I have to admit I've done a few times this week."

So this man had never been able to get football out of his blood either? Blake felt a new kinship with him. "You should have joined us. It would have been fun to have you involved. How about we throw the ball around a bit later? The guys were talking about playing a pick-up game since some of the kids asked about it."

"We haven't decided who will be the quarterbacks," Logan joked. "We have an abundance of them. What position did you play, Tom?"

"Wide receiver. I still throw the ball around with my sons and grandsons. I probably wouldn't embarrass myself too much."

"Good," Blake said. "We'll find you after we finish up the autograph session." He looked over to the corner of the field where Kelly was setting up the station.

"It's great of you guys to sign autographs," Tom said. "I hate to ask, but do you think I could ask for one for my grandsons? They're five and seven and huge Raiders fans."

"Of course," he said easily. "Anything you need. I owe you and your staff for all the help you've given us. Your facilities were awesome."

"They really were," Logan said. "You have a great school here from what I can tell."

"Thanks," Tom said, puffing out his chest. "We try. I'll let you guys get back to the kids. See you in a bit."

Blake and Logan jogged over to the autograph station to join the others. The boys were already converging on it in droves, jabbering and giggling, high on fruit punch, sliced oranges, and all the other semi-healthy treats set up on the buffet tables on the sidelines.

It felt a little weird for Blake as he scrawled his name on old Raiders merchandise, but he forced himself not to dwell on the past. Natalie was his future. And so was this camp. Everything was finally falling into place.

After they gave autographs to everyone who wanted them, Blake talked to a few parents who had hung around to chat. Then he was surprised to catch sight of Raymond Sandburg, a major player in Special Olympics—a man he'd met at many a fundraiser. He excused himself and walked over to greet him, noting that Natalie was still talking to some of the boys, Jordan by her side like the good friend he was.

"Raymond," he said, shaking the man's hand. "I didn't know you were coming."

"I told Kelly to keep it a secret. All of us at Special Olympics were so excited about this camp. We decided someone needed to visit, and I nominated myself."

"I'm glad," he told him. "I'm really happy to be doing more work with you all now that I have the time."

"Likewise. Your brother would be beyond proud of you, Blake. What you bring to this sport, what you bring to these kids...it's special."

His throat thickened, and he knew a simple cough wouldn't clear it. "Thanks. That means a lot."

"The job offer at headquarters is still open," he said, raising a thick, bushy eyebrow, "but I think I finally understand your hesitation about relocating. You and you ex-wife seem to be on good terms again."

He glanced over at Natalie, who was laughing as Jordan and Grant led a group of the boys in the Electric Slide. "Yes. She has a wonderful job here."

"Let's see what we can do," Raymond said. "We know how important this organization is to you after all your years of support, and your ability to take on a larger role would mean the world to us. Just this week, we've had over a thousand calls at headquarters from parents who have read about your camp in the news. Flag football is just taking off in our organization, and as you've seen, there's a huge need."

"Yes," he answered, feeling a peace settle deep inside him.

"Let's talk next week," Raymond said. "A little bird told me there's going to be a pick-up game between you and the guys and the assistant coaches."

"Feel free to join us. We need more position players. You played tight end, right?"

"Good memory," Raymond said. "I'd love to join."

"I'll gather the guys." He held up his whistle. "Be fun to have them at my beck and call for another little while."

Raymond laughed, and Blake jogged off. Sure enough, it felt fun to blow the whistle one last time.

"All right. Who's ready for some flag football?" he called out in a booming voice across the field.

The boys cheered, and his Once Upon A Dare buddies ran toward him along with the assistant coaches. They broke up into teams, and Tom and Raymond were on his. When it came time to pick a quarterback, Jordan simply handed him the ball.

"Lead us to victory, oh captain, my captain," his friend said.

"I thought we were going to flip for it," he responded, getting all choked up as Zack and Sam shook their heads at him.

"Not this time," Sam said. "Today's your day."

His team huddled around him, and it didn't matter that they weren't wearing helmets, pads, or regular uniforms. This was the sport he loved, with the people he cared about. He told Jordan to run a post play straight out of the gate. The other team wouldn't see it coming.

When they lined up, it felt incredible to stare the opposing team down as he pointed at them, reading their defense. Grant was going to rush him for sure. Then Zack spiked him the ball, and he dropped back in the pocket as Grant darted toward him. He let the ball fly.

Sure enough, no one had picked Jordan up, and the Sunday quarterback was halfway down the field when he caught the ball. He easily ran the rest of the way, yelling like a warrior when he made the touchdown.

Blake ran toward his friend with the rest of his teammates. They engaged in what would have been called excessive celebration, but he didn't care one bit.

He'd found a way to bring football into this new part of his life, post-retirement, and that was something worth celebrating.

CHAPTER 31

Natalie felt a decided pinch in her heart as she watched Blake's victory dance in the end zone with his teammates. Somewhere inside her, she felt a deep sense of sorrow for what she'd cost him. Football was his greatest joy, just like catering was hers, and he'd given it up for her prematurely. All of a sudden, it was too much.

He needed to be on the field. He needed to be with his teammates.

And she'd taken that away from him.

"It's too bad he left the NFL in his prime," a man's voice nasally said from behind her.

When she turned around, she recognized Cormack Daly from Hairy's Irish Pub. Was he here to see Blake's coaching skills on display? Could Blake have invited him here?

"He'll make a wonderful coach," she said, taking the measure of the man. He was wearing a purple polo shirt, tan slacks, and white tennis shoes.

"Yeah, he would have. Too bad he's not interested in coaching."

Her eyes widened at the revelation. "He's—"

"When Blake turned the job down a few weeks ago, I was livid. We had to hustle to find someone for the job.

At first I thought the issue was that he didn't want to commit to being in Dare Valley that long. No one in this town understands your *unusual* relationship."

This guy was a total jerk. She'd sensed it before, but this confirmed it. "No one needs to understand it except for us."

Cormack rolled his eyes at her. "Then I realized what a small pond this is for Blake. He could go anywhere. Based on what I've seen in the media, he's been offered commentator jobs with most of the major networks and head coaching and assistant coaching positions around the country."

While that didn't surprise her, it made her feel even worse.

"I came today because I was hoping he'd suck at coaching." He jingled the change in his pocket. "But he doesn't, dammit." He paused, and then said, "Do you know why I really think he turned us down?"

Blake aired out another pass, which Sam caught beautifully. "Why?"

"Clearly your ex-husband—or whatever he is to you—doesn't have football out of his system. He's not ready to take a step back."

Hadn't she just been thinking that? Part of her felt like she was sinking into a pit of sticky, cloying mud. It would be a crime for Blake to stay here when he was still this happy playing football.

"I'm going to head on home," Cormack said. "You tell Blake we're going to have a great season without him."

The man's bitterness did nothing to alter her inner turmoil. She couldn't tear her eyes away from Blake's face as he and his team continued to score their way to victory.

"It's wonderful to see Blake this happy again," her mom said when she came and joined her.

"Yes," she answered.

She wrapped her arms around herself, fearing she'd have to set him free.

CHAPTER 32

Blake was trying to focus on manning the grill and chatting with Zack, but he couldn't stop watching Natalie as she played queen bee with his friends like old times. Jordan was making her laugh as he gestured widely about something, but there was a tightness to her shoulders now. The rest of her body language seemed off too.

Something had changed. Had the cameras and likely gossip gotten to her? Had it made her regret her decision to declare they were back together?

"I think you have her, Ace," Zack said quietly beside him.

"God, I hope so," he responded and turned back to poke at the steaks.

He overcooked the steaks because he couldn't tear his gaze away from the slight line between Natalie's brows, portending trouble. The baked potatoes he'd stuck on the coals came out charred, but Natalie peeled off the burned skin and whipped them into a delicious makeshift potato salad. Fortunately, he couldn't screw up bagged salad or the fabulous gelato medley his assistant had brought up from Amore Gelato in Denver.

And throughout all of it, Natalie wouldn't sustain eye contact with him. His dread grew.

After dinner, everyone clustered around a Monopoly board. The few who did not play watched, and it came as a surprise to no one when Sam was crowned the victor. When Natalie started to clear the patio tables of the dishes from their meal, clearly in busy mode, Blake stopped her with a gentle touch on her arm.

"You don't have to clean up," he said, rubbing the bare skin of her tense forearm, wanting so badly to snatch her up and haul her off to his bedroom to alleviate this gaping stiffness between them. Whatever the cause.

"I don't mind helping you out," she only answered, stacking the plates, not meeting his eyes again.

Maybe acting like everything was how it used to be— her hanging out with his friends—had made her anxious. Maybe he was over-thinking this.

"Thanks, babe."

She gave him a half smile and wandered inside with a stack of dishes. He felt a hand on his shoulder and looked back to see Sam.

"Breathe," his friend suggested.

"Right." Oxygen. That little thing.

Some of the guys chipped in to help them clean up. When the patio was clear, Jordan wandered inside before coming back out with a bottle of tequila.

"Who wants some?" he said, wiggling the bottle

A couple of the guys groaned and held their heads. Jordan tipped the bottle in Natalie's direction.

She shuddered. "Uh. No."

"I'll have a shot," Blake said.

Everyone's heads swung in his direction.

He shrugged. "It's recently become my favorite drink." He hoped she'd get the message.

Natalie's cheeks only flushed. "Well, I should go if the party is finally getting started. It was great to see all of you. I'm sure..." She paused and wrung her hands. "I'm sure you'll all have great seasons."

She hadn't planned to say that, but she'd obviously bitten back the words. She would only see the guys again if she and Blake permanently reconciled. So, he *wasn't* being paranoid about this new batch of rigidity. What in the hell had happened?

Jordan smoothed over the awkwardness by pulling her into a bear hug and dipping her, a move he'd apparently learned with Grace, who loved to dance. The guys passed her around, giving her sloppy kisses or tickling her, helping to lighten the tension. When Natalie finally reached Sam, she didn't move to hug him, and Blake stilled where he was standing.

Sam cocked a brow and simply opened his arms. "Come here, Hale."

She leaned into him, like she wasn't going to stay long, but Sam tucked her close. Then he bent his head to whisper something in her ear, and she nodded her head twice and stepped back. Her face seemed paler now, but when he gave his friend a look, Sam only smiled.

There were shadows flickering in Natalie's eyes as he walked her to the edge of the porch.

"Well, I'll...see you when you..." She trailed off like the words were too heavy on her tongue.

They hadn't spent a night apart since he'd come back to her bed in *her* house, and the possibility of that happening now yawned between them. He saw her glance at the upper story of the house, as if she too were thinking about the fact that she'd never stayed over.

"I won't be too late," he made himself say, "if you're okay with me coming over, I mean. Or you can take Touchdown."

The dog was snoring on Logan's lap as the man downed a tequila shot with Jordan. He looked tuckered out from a solid week of playing with the kids at camp.

"I'll see you then," she said and took a hesitant step like she was going to lean in and kiss him.

She stopped herself and spun around before he

could grab her to him and plant one on her in front of his friends. Taking off his ball cap, he slapped it against his thigh as he watched her walk back toward the bridge.

When Jordan offered him a tequila shot, he took it without any resistance. Then they all hung out around the fire pit, talking about football. After the earlier elation of playing—even something as simple as a pick-up football game—he was starting to feel a bit like an outsider again, but then Sam cleared his throat, and Jordan immediately launched into how awesome the camp was and how he couldn't wait to do it again next year. Everyone joined in, and while it eased some of Blake's tension, he still had to crack his neck to get it to move right.

When he rose to leave, he put a hand on Hunter's shoulder. "I'm going to turn in."

The guys stopped talking and turned to look at him.

"I...oh crap...I'm going to get emotional here." He rubbed the bridge of his nose with his free hand. "Having you guys here for the camp this week meant the world to me. I'll...never forget it."

Hunter reached out and gripped his hand. "We're here for you, Ace. Any time you need us. That's what our Once Upon A Dare Club is."

"Like I said earlier, camp was awesome, Ace," Grant said. "I feel like Brad Pitt in that movie, you know, the one where he goes to Tibet and comes home inspired."

"Your butt is way too big to be compared to Brad Pitt's," Jordan said with a smirk.

Hunter threw an empty plastic cup at the quarterback, who caught it deftly. "Blake, count me in every year. The kids are awesome, and I learned a whole bunch about what it means to be a true player. I...shit...now I'm getting emotional. I thought I played from my heart, but these kids...they showed me something. Thanks for inviting me, man."

Ah, hell. He knuckled away tears and saw a few of the guys do the same.

"We're having a moment," Zack said with a laugh. "I know we're not supposed to say anything about your future, but you're a damn good coach, Blake. I'd be proud to play on your team."

Shit. Now it was like they were *trying* to make him cry.

"Yeah, if you were like fourteen again, Zack Sprat," Jordan teased to lighten the moment.

Everyone started laughing, and it eased some of the pressure in Blake's chest. Coaching *had* become clearer during camp. He was good at it. Sure, he had a lot to learn, but he loved running drills, helping players, coaching them through scrimmages, watching them grin when something he'd taught them finally clicked. It was another option—one of many he planned to consider now that camp was over.

"I think you might have found your next calling," Sam said quietly when the laughter died down. "Not that I'm surprised. I always knew you were one hell of a leader."

"Then again, I saw that guy from Special Olympics watching you like you were the second coming or something," Logan said. "I have a feeling all you need to do is figure out what you want and ask for it."

"I can't see anyone not giving you exactly what you ask for, Blake," Jordan said.

"Funny. Someone told me the same thing a few weeks ago." He knuckled away more tears as he glanced at Sam. "Hell, I'm going to have to find a box of tissues before I head over to Natalie's," he said as a joke, but it stuck in his throat.

Head over to Natalie's. Tonight that statement seemed like more evidence of their lingering separation. Separate homes. Separate lives.

"Then go find them and head on over," Zack said.

"You don't keep a woman like that waiting."

"Like you'd know, Zack Sprat," Hunter cajoled.

"Up yours, Hunter Punter," Zack shot back.

Blake man-hugged all the guys, promising to catch a few of their games once the season started. It would be hard to sit on the sidelines, but it was something he would have to face. He loved the sport too much to shut it out of his life, and these guys were his best friends. He'd be there to cheer them on like they had always done for him. Unless they were playing the Denver Raiders.

When he walked across the bridge with Touchdown, he stopped and traced one of the infinity circles engraved in the wood, thinking about everything that had brought him to this place, this moment. He crept into the house with Touchdown, who immediately padded over to his doggie bed.

"Night, buddy."

Natalie had left a few lamps on like usual. He turned them off like he always did, shutting the house down. After turning up the air conditioner to the temperature they both preferred at night, he headed into her bedroom.

She was reading on her device in bed, her knees tucked up. "Hey."

"Hey," he said, his mind filled with all the things unsaid between them. "I wanted to thank you...for coming today." He shrugged out of his shirt by his side of the bed. "It meant a lot to me."

She set her device aside after turning it off. "I'm glad I did. You...I wasn't particularly eloquent earlier."

Eloquent? When had she ever used big words with him? He threw his shirt aside, not caring if he was making a mess. "Babe, talk to me."

Her inhale was loud and harsh in the room. "You were incredible. I was...so proud of you. Adam would be too. And your parents."

He had to swallow the lump in his throat. His parents hadn't asked to come, intuiting that he needed to do this on his own. Plus, there had been Natalie to consider. It would have felt awkward for them to stay at his house with her next door. He knew she would have felt obligated to come over, and since she'd wanted to keep her family out of their relationship for the moment, he'd figured it would be best for him to do the same. Maybe next year...

"I sent my folks a lot of texts to keep them updated," he told her, pushing his shorts down his legs and kicking free of them.

Her gaze dropped to her hands, and he could feel it. She wasn't in the mood to make love either. If only he knew why.

"I'm going to shower," he said and fled to the bathroom.

Usually he showered at his place unless they showered together. He used her shampoo and conditioner like usual. Her soap. Even the toothbrush he used from the guest stash she kept under the sink seemed to highlight all the ways in which they were still separate.

His heart was heavy when he climbed into bed beside her. It had elated him to see her stride across the field to him earlier that day. But now he felt as deflated as a leaky party balloon.

Her lamp was already off. Usually they kept the ones by the bed on as they made love. They loved to look at each other, to deepen their connection by staring into each other's eyes while they were joined. He reached over to switch his lamp off too.

All the other nights he'd stayed over, they'd made love, but tension seemed to pour into the room like sand. He didn't take her into his arms, unsure of how she'd react. He could feel how rigid she was on her side of the bed. She didn't cuddle close. They both lay there on their backs, their hands folded over their chests. The two feet between them might have been a thousand miles.

The silence lengthened. He knew every shade of her breath, so he could tell she was as awake as he was. The disquiet in him grew until the pressure in his chest, as powerful as Jordan's boa constrictor, squeezed the words out of him.

"Do you want to tell me what's wrong?" he asked in a level tone that was at odds with the pounding of his heart.

She didn't respond right away. Only pulled the sheet higher over her chest. "You'd be a great coach. I could see that today."

As a response, it was totally unsatisfying, like lukewarm bathwater on a cold day. He turned onto his side to face her.

"*Okay...* Why do I get the sense that's not a good thing?" he asked, his eyes making out the shape of her face in the dark.

She sighed and turned to look at him. "You miss football."

He wanted to inch closer to her or take her hand. "Of course I do."

"Blake, I know the high school offered you a coaching position and you turned it down."

He'd been right to think Cormack wouldn't keep his mouth shut. "It wasn't right for me."

"You can't stay here indefinitely, putting off your life. There's nothing for you here career-wise. Football is your passion. It's what you were meant to do. I can't bear...to be the reason you're not playing ball when you clearly still love it so much. You have a few more years left to give to the sport."

Were they back to this? "Dammit, I left football to prove to you that you were more important."

"And now I know it. But you're too important to me

for me to let you do something that's not satisfying for you."

That eased some of his distress. "Natalie—"

"What's supposed to happen next? You're just supposed to live in this small town with nothing to do?"

"I *have* been doing things. I've been preparing for this camp, and I've been consulting with Special Olympics." Her prickliness grated on his skin. "I plan on fashioning the kind of job I want here once I decide what that is."

"But there's no football here, Blake. Not beyond high school, and you turned that job down. Maybe you really do want to leave, but you haven't been willing to admit that to yourself. Aren't all the offers you've received somewhere else?" she asked, the strain in her voice evident.

His sigh was audible in the dark. "Yes, they are. And I don't have some unconscious agenda here about leaving. Let me say it again. I want to stay with you in Dare Valley, and I will find something I love to do here."

She punched her pillow before lying back down. "So, you're going to what? Commute long-distance?"

"No. I'm going to find a way to be with you and have football somehow. How many times do I have to say it? I just haven't figured that last part out yet. Now that camp is over, it's my number one priority besides you. That means I'm staying here. That this will be my home—of sorts. I...dammit...I don't want to sound all cool and collected about this. I'm not."

Her hand gripped the sheet to her chest. "Maybe you shouldn't insist on the job being in Dare Valley. It only limits you and your career, and I want you to be happy. I saw how you looked out there today. It makes me feel guilty. You can't know how much." Her voice broke on the last word.

"Babe, I love you," he said, his voice harsh with emotion now. "I love you, and I want to be with you. I want to make a home with you again. Don't feel guilty. I don't regret leaving it." And it was mostly true.

"I'm not sure you can have it all here, Blake."

He clenched his hands together at the doubt in her voice. "I know you're scared about the future. I am too. That's why we haven't talked about it before. But we're working through things, aren't we?"

Her whole body was so still next to him, he had the sudden urge to turn on the light.

"Well, say something. *Anything.*"

"Blake," she said finally softly, "when I saw you today, I knew you still loved football like crazy and that you'd be an excellent coach. I've...worried about what you were going to do once the camp ended. You can't stay here in Dare Valley without doing something with it. Not even for me. You'll come to resent me."

"No, I won't," he contradicted. "I told you that I'll find a way to have the career of my dreams and live here with you. Just give me time to make it happen."

She shifted her head on the pillow. "Blake, you don't even go to Denver to see your old friends anymore because I'm here."

Okay, so he'd stayed closer to home. What was wrong with that? "Being here with you was more important. They understand that."

Her hand tentatively reached for him across the dark space between them. She brushed the hair back from his forehead, her fingertips so soft they were only a graze across his skin.

"You can't keep going on like this."

He knew this really wasn't about anything as simple as a job. She didn't think she could be enough for him deep down, and that wouldn't change even if his dream opportunity landed at his feet in Dare Valley. This kind of fear was one he knew he couldn't fight for her. He wanted to pound his chest in frustration. "Babe, do you love me?"

The sound of her head scratching against the pillow as she nodded *yes* eased some of his tension.

"Do you believe I love you?" he asked.

Again, she bobbed her head.

"Then give me time to create the perfect job for myself here so I can be with you." He grabbed the hand lying between them and brought it to his lips for a kiss. "You're going to have to trust me on this." *Make it tonight. Please, babe.*

"Promise me you won't make another huge sacrifice with your career because of me." Her voice was small and afraid, and he didn't know what to say to that.

"I promise you." It was easy to say because he didn't believe it would ever happen.

"Okay," she said, clenching his hand hard. "I'll trust you on this. But I want you to keep me in the loop. I don't want to hear any more important updates for the first time from jerks like Cormack."

"Done." He wanted to celebrate her consent, but he didn't feel like jumping up off the bed and doing a victory dance. "Are you ready to let everyone know we're back together?"

"I thought that's what I did earlier at the field when everyone was taking pictures and whispering about us."

He scooted closer. "I meant, your family."

"Ah...yes, we can tell them."

The deep, dark, burning question he'd tried to stuff away surfaced and could not be silenced. "Do you ever want to be married to me again?"

There was a long silence. "Boy, you're really going for gold tonight. I want to see how your job situation turns out. Blake, I mean it—I won't hold you back. Not again."

He had to bite his tongue to keep from cursing. It didn't escape him that she hadn't answered his question. "Okay. Thanks for telling me that."

She'd been honest with him at least. He might not

have liked all her answers. But at least they were talking about the future. Being together long-term was as much about loving each other and sharing space as it was about making sure each partner felt fulfilled. He would make it work. He'd show her.

He braced himself to touch her, hoping she wouldn't brush him off. Sure, he wasn't in the mood to make love to her, but as he'd discovered in their marriage, sometimes he didn't have to want it to make it the right thing to do. She needed to know she was precious to him right now, that her honesty hadn't widened the gap between them. And he needed to feel the connection between them as she came apart in his arms.

He closed the distance between them and kissed her greedily. Her hand rose to his waist and clutched him, her fingernails digging into his side. So, he thought, as her body pressed closer to his, she knew they were on the edge of another precipice. The precipice of the future. It wasn't going to be easy and gentle tonight. No, their lovemaking was going to have claws, and he welcomed it.

He yanked her to him and took her mouth with greedy possession. She mewed in her throat and raised her leg onto his hip, tunneling close under the covers until they fit skin to skin. There was little foreplay. Their tongues dueled and their hands sought out each other's pleasure centers, raising their arousal to a fevered pitch.

When the pleasure from her touch started to feel too acute, he turned away and grabbed a condom from the drawer. She hadn't gone on the Pill yet, and it felt like another sign of her uncertainty. He hadn't asked about it, and it had taken considerable effort for him to force back the resentment he felt over this additional boundary between them.

After fitting it on, he rolled on top of her, spreading her legs wide. Inch by inch he filled her. Her head was twisting back and forth already, her body straining for release. He knew he would need just a few deep strokes to take her over the edge, but he stopped.

He couldn't take it anymore. It had to be said.

Her hands gripped him, trying to pull him deeper. "Why are you stopping?"

"I want you to go back on the Pill. I don't want there to be anything between us anymore."

"Okay." She dug her nails into his flesh. "Please, Blake."

He thrust in, once, and then stilled again, his heart pounding in his chest. "Tell me you love me."

"I love you," she rasped out.

It should have been enough, but it only made him more desperate. "Tell me you want me."

"I want you. Please don't stop."

Tell me you know you're enough for me, the future be damned. He let his thrusts speak for him. He ground into her, setting off a release that made her whole body shiver.

He primed her again, ignoring his needs, thrusting in shallow bursts and then going deep, right to the heart of her. She arched up against him, crying out another release, but still he kept going.

Believe in yourself. Believe in us. Believe in my love for you. Believe we can make this work.

Even though his body was straining to empty into her, he couldn't seem to stop. Couldn't seem to let go. He continued to thrust into her until he felt her hands on his face, tracing the bones of his cheek and jaw.

"Blake."

She called him back from the verge of desperation, of agony. He pressed his forehead to hers. She lifted to him, open and welcoming now, where before she had been frantic and desperate. He felt her hands stroke his back to help him come.

"Let go, love," she whispered.

He gripped fistfuls of the sheets and lunged into her.

She locked her legs around him, like she was trying to absorb him into her very flesh. With a harsh cry, he finally emptied into her, pouring himself out until he was a hollow shell.

This time it was she who gently pushed him onto his back, cleaned him up, and cuddled him close.

"Go to sleep," she whispered, tracing the space where his heart rested, swollen and unsettled. "Everything will be okay."

He knew she was saying it to reassure both of them.

CHAPTER 33

A few days later, Natalie surrendered to the impulse to stop by her mom's house so she could thank her for all the help she'd given Blake with the camp. Blake was taking another long hike in the mountains to think through his career goals and options, so she had the time.

After their intense talk the other night, he'd told her about the Special Olympics offer, which she knew was right up his alley, but she was worried they wouldn't let him do the job from Dare Valley like he hoped. He'd only kissed her on the cheek and said it was just one of many options.

She had walked around with heartburn since their discussion, wondering if she should offer to relocate, but she'd only just started her job here. And she loved it. Plus, she didn't want to let Terrance and Mac down. She'd forgotten how difficult it could be to manage two people's interests without one of them giving up more than the other.

As soon as her mom opened the door, she noticed April's swollen eyes and ruddy complexion. *"Mom,"* she said, fear lacing her blood. "What's the matter?"

Her mom might cry more than she did, but it still

wasn't often. How many times growing up had she heard that phrase about keeping a stiff upper lip? Too many to remember. Seeing her like this was alarming.

"It's nothing," her mom said, pushing away. "I'm fine. Everything is fine."

Hearing those words, delivered in that tone, was like hearing herself speak. Is this what she had sounded like? Her mom might have told her she was more like her father when it came to handling her emotions, but perhaps it was behavior she'd learned from both her parents.

"Mom, I can tell you're not fine. Tell me what is going on, or I'm going to call Andy and Matt and have them come over right now."

She shook her head violently, her silver earrings brushing her cheeks. "No, you can't! Especially not Andy. Not until I know for sure."

Dread coiled in her gut. "Know what?"

Her mom's lip quivered. "I went in for my annual mammogram."

The buzzing started in her ears, and she felt herself leave her body. "No."

"I went in...and...they found a lump."

Oh, no. Good God, no. Not again.

"They're doing a biopsy." Her mom grabbed one of her hands and clenched it, so hard she came back in focus. "Promise me you won't tell anyone! It will kill Andy if..."

If she ends up having breast cancer like Kim.

Her mom pressed against her then. Hard. They embraced, clutching each other as the reality of what might happen filled the space between them.

"I'm not going to lose you," she told her mom, her eyes burning with tears. "We're not going to lose you."

"Promise me, Natalie. Not a word to anyone."

She nodded against her mom's head. The grip they had on each other was designed to keep the madness at bay. Its cold breath was all around them now, whispering about pain and hurt and death. Of things like needles, tubes, and chemo. Of the erosion of hair and weight, and of the removal of a woman's most beautiful feature, her breasts.

Natalie took her mom's shoulders and looked her straight in the eye. "I'm coming to the biopsy with you."

Her mom's lip wobbled. "Oh, honey. But you have work."

Work? Did she really think that was more important? "I'm coming! And we're going to be together when they give you the results."

Her mom fell against her, trembling. "I'm glad you came. It's been...so hard to keep this to myself. The only other person I told was Ellen. She said she would go with me."

Ellen O'Brien had been April's best friend since kindergarten, and Ellen's daughter had been one of Andy's best friends growing up. "I'm glad you told her."

"She's coming over in a while."

"I'm here for you too, Mom." And suddenly she felt so guilty for holding a grudge against her mom for intruding into her relationship with Blake.

"Shh," her mom said in a soothing tone, smoothing her hands down her hair. "None of that now."

They hugged and swayed back and forth in her mother's small foyer until her mom got a cramp in her foot and broke away to rub it. Natalie made them a pot of tea, and after pouring it, found her mom's playing cards. They played gin rummy and crazy eights to pass the time—just like she and Andy and Blake and the others had done while sitting vigil beside Kim's bed at hospice.

Anything to pass the time. Keep the hands active. Keep the mind from going crazy.

Ellen eventually arrived, and Natalie's mom sent her home. The biopsy was scheduled for two days from today. At the door, Natalie promised to come over the next day. Her mom clutched her hands like she was a life preserver, and though she told her there was no need to come, she didn't fight her when she insisted.

The drive home was done on autopilot, and as soon as Natalie stepped inside, she dropped her purse on the counter. Blake hadn't arrived yet. Touchdown pawed at her legs, wanting to play, so she opened the back door to let him out. She didn't have anything for him right now—the cold phantom was calling her name again. The pain was spreading, so bitter and harsh she wanted to scream.

She didn't want to feel it right now. She didn't want to feel anything ever again.

It was all happening once more. She could feel it. Her mom was going to die, just like Kim, and nothing was going to stop it. She couldn't stop it. She'd have to stand there and watch it unfold.

Blake had been wrong. Learning to express her feelings hadn't changed a damn thing. The pain wasn't less this time. The mad call on the edge of her mind was still there, louder and colder than ever. She wasn't going to let it claim her.

She grabbed the tile powder and a sponge from under the kitchen sink and headed to her bathroom to do the one thing under her control. The tile powder fell down on her like rain as she shook it over the tiles. It burned her skin, and she welcomed the sting. Anything to fight the cold fingers and even colder breath touching her skin. She dug her fingernails into the sponge. Her breathing grew labored as she worked. Her heart raced.

She scrubbed and scrubbed and scrubbed, ignoring cracked nails and bleeding knuckles. *It's not going to happen. Mom's not going to die.*

If she didn't listen to the dark whispers that told her that the worst *could* happen, that she of all people knew it, maybe everything would be all right. Her mind swirled in circles like her hand did as it cleaned the tiles.

"Natalie," Blake called.

Her head came up. She shook herself. He was standing outside the door to the shower. She had to crane her neck to see him. His mouth was parted in shock, his eyes wide and unblinking. She'd seen that look before.

"Babe, what's going on?" he asked, worry woven into his voice.

She couldn't tell him. She'd promised her mother.

Besides, if she spoke the words, they might come true. She shook her head and pressed her lips together tightly.

He crouched down until he was kneeling beside her, outside the shower stall. "Honey."

He only called her honey when she was crazy. She focused back on the tiles, caked over with cleaning powder.

"Leave me alone," she told him with an edge in her voice.

"No. Not until you tell me what happened. Nat, you're scaring me here."

The words were like echoes from their past—the past she'd thought they had moved beyond. It was like her life had turned into a broken record that kept playing the same sorry track again and again. She made herself look at him. "I don't want to talk about it! Go home. I don't want you here."

He flinched. "You don't mean that. What happened? What's wrong?"

"I said I don't want to talk about it!" she yelled, making him rock back on his knees. "Leave. Me. Alone."

"No."

"I can't take this anymore! I don't want to talk about my feelings. I'm tired of bleeding out every time we speak. It doesn't make anything better. Stop hovering over me, dammit! I'm not a child. You're *suffocating* me." *You're making me feel too much.*

His whole face tightened up, and she watched as his hands gripped his thighs. Her head filled again like a mushroom, the cold phantom breathing on her neck.

Your mom is going to die. I'm going to get her. Just like I got Kim.

The darkness started to envelope her. She turned her back on him and dug her hand into the sponge. She started to scrape away the natural brown lines in the grout, but it wouldn't come out.

A deep gust of brutal, punishing cold blew over her, but she kept on cleaning to stay grounded, to stay warm, to stay sane. When she could take it no more, she hurled the sponge against the wall of the shower and screamed until she was hoarse. She grabbed her hair as her sobs poured forth, mad cries, agonized calls for help.

But no one came to help her.

When she finally stopped crying, she curled into a ball on the shower floor, shivering from the cold. No one had come because she'd finally done the worst thing imaginable.

She'd pushed Blake away for the last time.

CHAPTER 34

Blake stumbled across the yard to the bridge. When he reached it, he gripped the wood and bent over at the waist, his breaths heaving out.

It the worst kind of déjà vu he'd ever experienced.

Something had happened, and he couldn't reach her. She wasn't going to let him. The normal, happy person she'd been lately was like the tile powder she'd strewn all around her. Easy to scrub away. As he stared into the dark woods, he realized she was always going to run away when something terrible happened. Rough times would come again, and when they did, she would choose to stay numb. She would shut him out again.

He kicked the bridge, wanting to tear it down with both hands. The infinity symbols mocked him. She didn't love herself enough to let him love her in the worst moments of life, which meant they didn't have the foundation for a happy marriage and never would. Even crafting a dream job in Dare Valley wouldn't change that.

Touchdown barked, and he turned his head, his vision refocusing. Their dog had followed him. His heart broke because he knew he had a decision to make.

He dashed at his tears and picked him up, pressing

him to his chest. She needed their beautiful beagle more than he did. She always had. The dog licked away his tears and nuzzled his face.

"You've been...the best dog ever. I'm..." Oh shit, this hurt. This fucking hurt. "I'm going to miss you, but Mommy needs you more right now."

The pain was spreading, but he kissed the dog and hugged him hard and set him down. "Go."

Touchdown's brown eyes stared at him, then he gave a short bark like he understood. After giving him one last rubdown, Blake forced his hands to his sides. The little dog trotted back to Natalie's.

His next move became clearer. He couldn't stay here.

Not next door to her. Not after what she'd done.

Still, his worry for her couldn't be erased. Whatever had happened to make her backslide like this had to be horrible, and a part of him wanted to call Andy to find out. Surely her brother would know.

But he'd done that before, and going to her family with his concerns wasn't the answer. If she wasn't willing to lean on him in hard times, it was time to face the brutal reality and move on. He was going to return to Denver. Tonight.

It was time to stop holding onto something that would never be.

He turned off the lights on the bridge as he made his way back to the house for the last time.

CHAPTER 35

When Natalie finally pulled herself off the bathroom floor, her head was groggy from crying and her hands burned from the tile powder. Touchdown stirred on the floor outside the shower. He'd come to sit beside her like the loyal dog he was as she surrendered to another batch of horrible, gut wrenching sobs, deep in her belly. She hadn't been able to stop the guttural sounds that had tore from her throat. Touchdown hadn't left her side once, but she'd made him stay outside the shower because she didn't want him to get tile powder on his paws.

She straightened like an old woman who'd sat too long, her bones popping in protest, and looked in the mirror.

There she was again. That crazy woman, maddened by grief, reduced to insanity by the threat of that damn thing called cancer.

Her hair was streaked with powder and in wild disarray like she was the bride of Frankenstein. She brushed the white powder off her shirt, and that's when the full pain of her hands hit her. The blood had coagulated, but they were a fiery red, and they hurt like a million bees had stung them.

Turning on the faucet, she let the water run over them, wincing in the beginning as her hands burned. Everything throbbed. Her knees ached. Her back was tight. Her head was pounding.

She'd succumbed to the cold, to the dark, once more. Looking at herself, she saw the puffy, mascara streaked eyes. The tightness around her mouth from sobbing.

Her eyes gleamed under the lights in the bathroom. *Love me,* she heard a soft voice say, one that had warmth, one that was totally different from the whispers of the cold phantom. *I need you to love me. Even when I'm like this.* It took her a moment to realize the voice was her own.

The faucet continued to run as she braced her hands on the countertop. Tears started to fall as she watched herself start crying again. How was she supposed to love herself like this? How was she supposed to find anything beautiful about this mad woman? How was she supposed to be willing to feel this pain, this agony? Ever since childhood, she'd tried to be strong, to keep a stiff upper lip, to never show weakness. She'd been proud of that.

Then she thought of how she'd found her mother earlier. The woman she admired had been suffering alone with this horrible secret. Would their mother ever have told them if the biopsy turned out to be negative? She doubted it, and while she understood her mother's reasons, she didn't want to be like that.

Her hand lifted to the wild locks of her hair, sticking out like the snakes of Medusa. She gently stroked her hair back from her face. Looked at herself in the mirror again.

Love me, she heard that whisper say again in her mind. *Comfort me. I'm hurting.*

She didn't want to hurt, but it didn't seem like she could escape it as she looked at herself in the mirror.

After Kim's death, she'd stacked brick upon brick around herself to wall off the pain, to keep the cold wasteland away. Many of those bricks had been toppled these last few weeks, toppled from the sheer force of Blake's love for her.

What had he said? *When you looked at Kim at the end, when she weighed less than a hundred pounds, did you love her any less?*

The Kim she'd loved, the woman who'd been her best friend since college, hadn't been recognizable in those final weeks of her life. But Natalie *had* loved her. If Kim had even once called herself ugly and unlovable, she would have told her that it was bullshit. That *she* loved her. That she found her beautiful.

Why couldn't she give herself that same fierce love?

She brushed a tear as it trailed down her face. This woman, this crazy, hurting woman was her too—just like the ravaged body on the hospice bed had still been Kim.

This hurting woman deserved to be loved, not shunned. Not abandoned. She wasn't sure how she was going to do it, but she had to start somehow.

"I...love you," she whispered to the crazy woman in the mirror.

The pain that radiated from her heart was like a supersonic wave, and she started crying harder. But she didn't look away from the woman in the mirror with the wild eyes and hair.

"I love you," she whispered again as the tears streamed. "I'm sorry. *I'm sorry.*"

She wasn't even sure what she was apologizing for as she rocked herself and cried, but she kept saying it until her voice grew even hoarser, looking at that woman in the mirror the whole time, Touchdown nuzzling her legs in comfort.

A new emotion finally flowed in, like a warm breeze after a brutally cold day. The pain started to ebb away, replaced by a feeling so soft and luminous she pressed her hand to her heart. It took her a moment to give it a name.

It was love.

The kind of love she felt when she was with Blake and her family. That simple, beautiful feeling that made her feel whole and complete.

But this time she felt it for herself.

Her hand lifted to her mouth of its own accord, and she blew that woman in the mirror a kiss.

She wasn't crazy. She wasn't mad. She was hurting. And somehow, she now had enough compassion to see that and love that part of herself anyway, the part she'd always judged too ugly for compassion.

Did she like to cry? No. But she sometimes felt better after she did. Maybe it was time to start allowing her emotions to be whatever they were. She loved her mother, but she didn't want to end up like her, concealing a secret and a pain all alone. Or like her father, turning inward whenever he faced a problem. Not when she had so many people who loved her to comfort her through it.

Blake.

Thoughts of him made the cold come back, but this time their whispers rained new ice over her skin.

You said he was suffocating you. You pushed him away. You've lost him for good.

She had pushed him away, trying to scurry back behind the broken wall of numbness he'd been helping her disassemble. She'd wanted to escape the pain of reality. And she'd shoved him away just as she'd shoved that part of herself away.

But she didn't want that anymore, not with this new awareness of herself, not with this soft, sweet feeling of her self-love keeping her warm despite the cold wasteland that surrounded her once again.

She stripped off her clothes and let the water in the

shower clean away the abrasive powder she'd ground into its tiles. Then she washed herself, letting her hands linger over her body in gentle comfort, as if she were bathing Kim, which she'd done several times when her friend was too ill to leave her hospital bed. Her touch was gentle and comforting. Her heart expanded even more in her chest at her ministrations. When she turned off the water and looked at herself in the mirror this time, she saw a new woman standing there. One who'd started to love herself—no matter what.

Touchdown stayed close to her as she dressed in fresh clothes. Her wet hair would have to do. She had one person she needed to see. He wasn't in her house, waiting for her like he had once before. Her belly ached now.

It was after two o'clock in the morning, she realized when she glanced at the clock in the kitchen. It didn't matter. Blake wouldn't be asleep. No, he'd be hurting. But she would make it right. Somehow they'd make it right together. She loved him, and he loved her. She didn't want any more barriers between them. As she made her way across her backyard to the bridge he'd built, the one he'd extended into her frozen wasteland, all her doubts melted away and she knew she wanted to be married to him again.

There was no one for her but Blake.

The stars above seemed so close tonight, as if they were floating around her head. When she reached the bridge, she stuttered to a halt.

For the first time since he'd turned them on, the lights were out on the bridge. Her lips trembled, and her hand felt the wooden beams like she was trying to read Braille until they found the infinity symbol he had carved into the wood there to remind her of the truth.

He was her bridge to a better life.

Gratitude swelled in her heart as she let herself in the back door of his house. There were a few lights on.

"Blake?" she called out.

Then she saw a white piece of paper resting against a water glass on the kitchen island. He had always been an early riser, and back when they first started dating, he used to leave her love notes to read when she came downstairs in the morning. He'd continued it into their marriage, and she'd always found it unbearably sweet.

As she approached the note, her every muscle was rigid with tension. Touchdown barked and headed off, going to the garage door. Alarms immediately starting clanging in her head.

She didn't even need to pick up the note to know what it said, but she did anyway.

Touchdown is yours. You need him more than I do. Be at peace, Nat.

Her arms wrapped around herself as reality filtered in. Even though she knew she wouldn't find his SUV in the garage, she still made herself walk to the door Touchdown was pawing. When she opened it, sure enough, it was empty.

He was gone.

She'd finally pushed him away too much for even his love to bear. Leaning against the doorframe, she didn't fight the tidal wave of grief this time. She went totally and completely to pieces.

After she cried a fresh batch of tears, she shook her head, trying to clear it. Where would he have gone in the dead of night? He had no friends in Dare Valley. Then it hit her. He'd gone back to the home they'd shared, back to the one place he'd always felt the most comfortable. Back to his old life—or what was left of it in the wake of his retirement.

She made her way back to her house with Touchdown. Once inside, she ran upstairs to her bedroom and dug into the bottom of her chest for the item she was seeking. Tucking it into her pocket, she went downstairs and grabbed a bottle of water and her purse.

"Come on Touchdown," she said opening the garage door. "Let's go get Daddy."

CHAPTER 36

Blake's muscles trembled as he lifted the two hundred pound weights over his head for the seventh time in his second rep. After driving to Denver, he hadn't wanted to sleep. Couldn't sleep. Being back in the home he and Natalie had created together was enough to send pain lacing through his system like adrenaline, making him a little crazy, making him way too sensitive.

After changing into workout clothes, he'd gone to his gym and started his burn. Who was he to judge Natalie for the way she dealt with her emotions? She scrubbed the shower. He was fighting his feelings by working out, not eager to drown in their punishing waves just yet. When he succumbed—and he knew he inevitably would—the truth was going to leave him scarred forever.

She was gone from him

He'd run until his legs shook so hard he could barely feel them. Then he'd switched to the rowing machine, pulling until his back muscles twitched under his shirt. Now, he was lifting. His mind wasn't totally focused on what he was doing, but his thoughts quieted occasionally as his whole body strained to surpass its own strength. He lived for those moments.

After his third rep, he set the weights back on the

bar and squeezed his eyes shut. God, he couldn't go through this again. Not this. He'd given her his fucking heart on a platter. He'd even given her his dog. What did he have left? This house they'd created together. He was going to finally have to sell it. He'd only held onto it in the hope she'd come back to him.

His life without her stretched out before him. His whole life had just...died...like it had expired at the end of a game clock. Nothing was clear but the nothingness of it all. He'd never been in this place before, and it shook him to his core. Maybe he should move back to Ohio to be closer to his folks as he sorted things out.

He was preparing himself to lift again when something dropped onto his chest, and he looked down to see a radiant-cut yellow diamond twinkling like sunshine under his overhead lights.

Something exploded in his head, almost like he'd blown a blood vessel. His gaze darted up.

Natalie.

She stood a few feet from his bench press station, her arms wrapped around Touchdown, her hand covering his snout to keep him from barking. Tears were streaming down her face.

"I kept my key. You didn't change the locks."

His heart tore open. "What—"

"I'm sorry, babe," she whispered. *"I'm so sorry."*

He pressed his hand to his face, his eyes, as the pain finally flooded in. She hadn't called him babe once since he'd moved to Dare Valley, and hearing it now took him under. He lay on his back, trembling from fatigue and physical exhaustion as tears leaked onto his temples.

"Oh, God," he rasped out.

She'd driven all the way from Dare Valley in the middle of the night and plopped her engagement ring on his chest after she'd crushed him. *Crushed him.* He didn't know what to say. What to think.

Her hand touched his chest, making him jump, even

though her touch was soft.

"I'm sorry I...retreated again. I...my mom...they found a lump in her breast."

He took his hand from his face and looked at her. He hadn't thought his pain could worsen, but it did, like the mind-numbing razor blade of a torn ligament. "Oh, Nat."

His position was awkward, so he started to sit up. Both their hands moved to protect her engagement ring from falling to the floor. Somehow it created a link between them, and he didn't take his hand away. But he felt the imprint of that band, the press of her diamond in his palm.

She sank to her knees and placed Touchdown on the floor, then rested her hand on his thigh. "I went to her house last night. She'd been crying, which was shocking." She sniffed, a harsh sound. "I knew immediately something was wrong. At first, she didn't want to tell me what, but I wouldn't let up. When she told me...God, it was like Kim all over again."

"Oh, babe. I'm so sorry. For both of you." Scooting off the bench, he fell onto his knees in front of her. Their hands, still linked, still holding her ring, fell onto his lap and stayed there.

"She's having a biopsy...God, I'm so tired I can't remember when...ah...I guess tomorrow because it's already today." She shook her head as if to clear it. "She made me promise not to tell anyone. Especially Andy. You don't know what it did to me."

Having seen her in the shower earlier, he'd had a glimpse. The news would devastate the Hales if it proved to be cancer. There were no two ways about it. Life was so goddamn unfair. No family should have to suffer something like Kim's illness, but if April had the same disease...

"I told Mom I wouldn't tell anyone even though I knew my brothers and sisters would be mad at me for keeping it secret." She lifted a shoulder to wipe her tears with her shirt. "Even though I didn't want to bear the burden alone."

Somehow hearing that helped ease a fraction of the pain in his chest. Natalie never betrayed a confidence.

"I told Mom I was going with her to the biopsy, and that we would hear the news together. Whatever it was."

She started to cry, and he couldn't take it anymore. He laid his free hand against her cheek, hurting for her now in powerful bursts, feeling her every fear, her every ache.

"Oh, honey," he whispered.

She took a deep breath, trying to steady herself. "You only call me honey when I go crazy. Did you know that?"

He shook his head.

"When I left Mom, I *was* going crazy again. She could have cancer. Just like Kim. She could die."

Like his own beloved brother had. Tears streamed down his own face now as all the losses they'd suffered rolled through him like a tidal wave and pounded him into the surf. It was hard to consider the possibility of losing April. She was so dear, so bright. He couldn't tell Natalie that her mom would definitely be okay, just like he hadn't been able to say that about Kim or Adam.

"When I got home," she continued, "I couldn't stand the pain. I know I said I'd face it, but this...this hurt so bad. My mind was screaming horrible thoughts, and the pictures in my head of mom shrinking before my eyes in a hospital bed wouldn't stop. I...had to stop it. Before I knew it, I was grabbing the can of tile powder and the sponge from under the sink and heading to the shower. I wanted to forget everything. I wanted...the pain to go away."

"Then you came in, and I couldn't...snap out of it. I was horrible to you, Blake. And I won't blame you if you say you can't forgive me." Her lips trembled like she was freezing. "Once was...a miracle, but twice?"

When her head dropped forward in defeat, he cupped the back of her neck and lifted her face to his. "I understand why you did it, babe, and I forgive you." If there was one thing he'd learned about love and marriage, it was to never stop forgiving. Ever. Even if she hurt him a thousand times, he wasn't going to deny her absolution.

She inched closer on her knees until their joints touched. Her hand squeezed his, and he felt the press of her ring again against his palm.

"I drove here in the middle of the night because I realized what I'd done to you. What I'd done to myself."

She told him about the revelation she'd experienced when she finally finished crying, how she'd started to see that wild, crazy woman for who she was...herself. When she told him she'd decided to finally love that woman, that human part of her who hurt, he knew she'd turned a corner. More hope flooded his chest.

She turned their hands over until her engagement ring shone in the light again. "I have something to say...please don't interrupt me."

His chest squeezed as she looked straight into his eyes, the full force of her love for him shining in them again. He saw all the parts of her reflected in her gaze, the woman who could tease and joke and laugh, the woman who loved her family, the woman who loved him, and the woman who went crazy when the cold specter of destruction came knocking on her door.

"I, Natalie Hale, offer you, Blake Cunningham, my solemn vow to be your faithful partner in sickness and in health, in good times and in bad..."

Her voice broke.

Tears rained down his face as she renewed the pledge she'd made to him so long ago.

"In joy as well as in sorrow," she continued, inhaling raggedly. "I promise to love you...unconditionally...even though I've failed so many times in the past..."

He pulled her head to his and rubbed their foreheads together in sweet agony.

"I promise...oh what's next...to support you in your new career." She sniffed. " And to...ah...honor and respect you, to laugh with you and cry with you, and to cherish you for as long as we both shall live."

They both started crying then.

"I love you," she whispered fiercely. "And I'm sorry—"

His mouth cut her off from finishing the rest of her declaration, and he traced an infinity symbol into her hand next to where her wedding ring lay.

And set them both free to love each other again for forever at last.

CHAPTER 37

Natalie poured herself into the kiss, imagining her love was as pure and warm and radiant as the yellow diamond Blake had chosen for her engagement ring. She stroked his face to soothe the hurt she'd caused and cried some more when she finally understood he was tracing the infinity symbol over and over again in her palm. She let their breaths merge to communicate how much she wanted to be joined with him again, how much she wanted infinity again.

Touchdown tunneled between them, his face pressing against her stomach. She edged back and looked into Blake's eyes, needing to say the words he'd stopped her from saying moments before. After everything she'd put him through, put *them* through, he deserved them.

"Blake?" she asked, her voice soft.

His head tilted to the side as he gazed at her, simply gazed at her. "Yeah, babe."

"Will you marry me...again?"

The muscles of his face bunched up like he was going to cry, and his jaw locked as he took a moment to answer. "You know I will."

When he picked up her engagement ring, she

extended her left hand to him. His eyes shining, he slid the ring onto her finger and then brought it to his mouth to kiss it. She let out a shaky laugh.

"Now, we need yours," she said.

This time he was the one who let out a shaky laugh. "Shit, you aren't going to believe this. I...ah...left it back at the house in Dare. I thought..."

He didn't need to finish that sentence. She knew what he'd thought.

"Then we can go get it when we head back there," she said, ducking her head. "That is...if you're willing to go. I need to get back so I can go to the doctor with my mom tomorrow. I was hoping...you might come."

He traced infinity over her engagement ring. "You know I will."

She glanced down at their hands. "Blake...I know what you've given up for me, and it...overwhelms me sometimes. In the best way possible." Crap, she was crying again. "I realized tonight that I'll go anywhere with you. I don't want you to have to make something work in Dare Valley. I want you to have your dream job. I can find another dream job or open another business. I can help Mac and Terrance find a replacement."

It would be hard to leave Dare Valley again, but she wanted to support him after everything he'd done for her. She wanted him to understand that she would do for him the things he had already done for her, that she wasn't going to step back from him like she had earlier tonight.

"And what about your family?" he asked.

Her shoulder lifted, in contrast to the hurt his question caused. "I can visit them, just like you visit yours."

"That's not the kind of life I want for our kids," he said, his voice like sandpaper now. "They should have cousins to play with...and aunts and uncles to dote on them."

She jolted in surprise at his words, and their gazes locked. Kids. Hearing him share his vision after she'd used children as a sword to sever their remaining bonds of matrimony reduced her to tears. God, she couldn't seem to stop crying now that she'd started.

"And let's not forget about your mom. She'll be a great grandma."

That did it. Hearing him talk about her mom and the future broke her, it simply broke her. He brought her to his chest, her sobs a renewed torrent from deep inside her.

"I'm so scared for her," she whispered against his hard frame.

"I am too," he said against her ear. "Whatever happens, we'll face it together. And we'll be there for her."

She nodded. "On the way here I realized I have more...healing to do. About Kim. About this thing with my mom. About running from my emotions. I'm going to see a grief counselor. I don't want to do that to myself—or you—ever again."

"How about we both go? God knows, I have grief too, and that's what partners do. They share their pain."

She raised her head to look at him. His eyes were as puffy as hers had to be. He wasn't having the best hair day either. But he was so beautiful. She didn't ever want to look away again, push him away ever again. Her fingertips traced his face.

"I love you. Do you have any idea how much?"

His throat moved. "I love you too, and God, after all this, I hope you know how much."

They'd reached the moment where words faded, where the mind stopped. She stood on shaky legs and extended her left hand to him, the diamond shining like a yellow star in the night sky.

He clasped their hands together, and she led him out of the gym. Together, they traveled through this house they'd shared. Her eyes latched onto the familiar surroundings. The bold art they'd chosen from Denver's galleries still hung on the walls. As they crested the top of the stairs, her heart simply cried out, unable to help itself. The same wedding picture she'd stowed in her hope chest was displayed on the mahogany wall curio.

She tried to imagine the fortitude he possessed to keep that picture there, to see it day after day. Biting her lip did no good. Fresh tears streamed down her face. They continued to flow as she stepped into their bedroom with him. He hadn't changed a thing. Her lavender lotion was still on her bedside stand along with the sticky notes she kept next to the bed for when she had an idea about a catering job.

Her breath simply evaporated in her lungs, and she wheezed. "You kept...everything?"

"I took everything out of storage and put it back when...I decided to go to Dare Valley and get you back." He lifted his hand to rub away the tears falling from his face. "How could I get rid of everything? It would be like...getting rid of you."

Oh, my. She hadn't truly understood until this moment how much she loved him, how much he loved her. Like a man tending to a special storehouse, he'd kept their marital treasures in one place, waiting for her to come home.

She unlinked their hands so she could remove her clothes. No barriers could be between them. Not anymore. His gaze held hers as he did the same. When they stood before each other, it was as if their Eden had been renewed, their garden of paradise rediscovered after being lost. They reached for each other at the same time.

When their mouths met, she surrendered to the sense of wonder, the sacredness of touching him, and allowed him to touch her without holding anything back. She didn't stop the moans from spilling from her mouth as she raised his hands to her breasts, giving him back the full and complete promise of her love.

He stroked her with a gentleness that brought back all the warmth inside her. She cuddled closer as she caressed his body, the ridges and edges of his muscles, with something akin to cherishing. Told him with her touch that she'd never again take for granted what they had together.

His body flowed with hers onto the bed. Their mouths joined in a deep, heated kiss. Passion carried her to a new shore, and she guided him on top of her as the force of their love washed over her. And when they could no longer wait to join together, she looked into his eyes and slowly took him inside her without any barriers between them.

There was only a slight change in the shape of his eyes as he met her gaze with something akin to wonder, but she knew he understood what she was saying. She said it aloud anyway.

"Make a baby with me," she whispered.

He clutched her hands as he slid deep into her, and she gave herself up to the new bridge between their bodies and souls.

CHAPTER 38

Blake sat in the waiting room of the doctor's office, ignoring the curious glances of the people around him. No one had asked for his autograph, thank God. He'd never snapped at a fan, but today his nerves were stretched to the max as he thought of what was going on in one of the examining rooms.

The most recent copy of *Sports Illustrated* lay idle in his hands, open to an article on the upcoming NFL season. He used his thumb to rub the wedding band on his ring finger. As soon as he and Natalie had arrived back in Dare Valley, she'd insisted they immediately retrieve it. But she hadn't simply let him put it on. No, she'd dragged him out to the bridge he'd built to their better life and put it on his finger there, tracing infinity symbols all over his hand.

The door opened, and he straightened in his seat. Natalie had her arms around April, who gave him a brave smile as he rose and walked over to them.

"The doctor said they should have the results in a day or so," Natalie said as they all left the building.

He knew how long a day or so could feel under these circumstances. A fucking eternity.

"It wasn't that bad," April added.

Since Natalie's free hand was fisted by her side, he knew it hadn't been easy for April. Everything Natalie had learned about being a tough guy had come from her parents. He hoped her mom could learn to be a little kinder to the part of herself that must be scared and hurting—just like her daughter had.

He drove them back to April's house, where Natalie had to press her mom to let them come inside. She helped her get settled on the couch and then made her some tea. After one cup, April told them they could go home. Ellen O'Brien was going to come over later. Natalie ignored her and opened the refrigerator to look for fixings for dinner.

Together he and Natalie peeled potatoes, and standing next to her, he could feel it—they were a unit once more, just like the figure eights engraved into their bands, only this time they were stronger than they'd been, like metal re-shaped by fire.

No one ate much of the mashed potatoes, pork chops, and roasted beet chips Natalie had served. But that hadn't been the point. When April finally said she wanted to go to bed, she refused to let Natalie stay and turned to Blake.

"Please take my daughter home now," she said. "I want...to be alone for a while."

He and Natalie shared a look before his soon-to-be-wife for the second time nodded in defeat. After they both kissed April goodnight, he took Natalie's hand and led her toward the car. He opened her door, and when he came around and got in himself, she had her hand pressed to her mouth, tears streaming down her face. She hadn't cried in front of her mom.

His heart twisted in his chest.

"I hate seeing her like this." Then she turned her head. "Was I like this?"

They'd promised to always be honest with each other now. "Yes."

"I'm sorry," she said and wrapped her arms around herself.

When they returned to her house, she let him comfort her again, let him see the part of her that was wild and scared and hurting. He held her, rocked her—feeling that familiar helplessness of knowing he couldn't fix her pain.

She didn't go to work the next day in case the doctor called. Natalie had made his nurse promise to alert her when he had the results so she could drive to April's house and join her for the call.

To pass the time, Blake and Natalie sat together in the sunlight and talked about their living arrangements. They agreed to keep the house in Denver for when Blake wanted to head back for a Raiders game or for them to visit friends and family. And they decided to build a new house together in Dare Valley, one they both loved. In the meantime, they would live in the one she'd bought from her brother. The other one—the one he'd bought—could be resold. He still insisted on fashioning his new career in Dare Valley, and Natalie had finally agreed to trust him all the way. He'd meant every word he'd said about raising their children in Dare Valley around family.

The call from the nurse came the next morning, and he drove them to April's house with icy dread lining his belly, praying the whole way. *Please let her be okay. Please let the test be negative.*

April opened the door like a brave soldier and barely allowed either one of them to hug her. The doctor's call came shortly after they arrived, and Natalie put it on speaker for everyone to hear.

"Mrs. Hale," the doctor said in a serious voice, one that gave nothing away.

"Yes, I'm here," she responded in a stiff tone.

"I'm happy to report your biopsy came back negative. The cyst is benign. You don't have cancer."

Blake let out his breath and pulled them both into his arms.

"Oh, thank God," April said.

"Yes!" Natalie yelled. "Yes!"

After a perfunctory signoff with the doctor, Blake lifted them up and spun them around. When he put them down, they fell onto each other, their arms gripping each other tightly.

And while April didn't cry as much as Natalie, she cried too. He watched them both with a sheen of tears in his eyes.

When everyone was calmer, he extended his arms to them. "Okay, this calls for a celebration." Life deserved to be celebrated—especially after a close call to the abyss. "What should we do? Go out for champagne and dinner at High Stakes?"

"How about we invite my sons and grandson over for dinner?" April suggested, picking up her phone.

"Are you going to tell them what happened?" Natalie asked.

"Don't you want me to?" April responded, tucking a strand of hair behind her ear.

"Yes, I want you to. I don't want to keep this from them. And I want you to call Moira and Caroline too."

Her mom nodded. "I can call the girls when the boys arrive so they can all hear the news together. Blake, would you be able to take Danny outside and keep him occupied? I don't want to upset him."

No, the five-year-old didn't need to know about this. "Of course, April."

April's boys showed up with searching glances. They must have sensed something was wrong over the phone because their eyes were wide with worry. Jane gripped Matt's hand in comfort. They were expecting bad news to come from this last-minute dinner invitation.

"Uncle Blake," Danny said, tugging on his pant leg. "Are you living with Aunt Natalie again?"

He looked over at Natalie to confirm his answer. "Yes, we're going to renew our vows pretty soon. Wanna come?"

He'd insisted they refer to their ceremony as renewing their vows. She'd played along.

"Of course," Danny said as Blake lifted him into his arms. "But what's 'vows?'"

He laughed. "How about I tell you in the backyard? We can grab a football from the garage, and you can show me how far you can throw it."

Andy's shoulders were rigid with tension, but he managed a smile. "I'm glad to hear you're renewing your vows. We'll be there."

"With bells on," Matt added, his mouth grim.

"Good." Blake nodded at Natalie. "Danny and I will go find the football and play some catch."

Once they were outside, Danny chattered away, asking him question after question as he attempted to divide his attention between the boy and the scene inside. The windows revealed the group to him, the bowed heads and then the lingering embraces.

When Andy finally stepped outside and walked over to him, Blake's gut clenched at the grief ravaging the man's face. Like he would have done with one of his guys, he stepped forward and gave Andy a hug. The man gripped him and then pounded him on the back.

When they broke apart, Andy knuckled away the tears in his eyes. "Thanks."

"You looked like you needed it."

"You have no idea."

"Dad. Why are you hugging Uncle Blake and crying?"

Andy took off in a perfect thirty degree angle, and Blake threw him the pass. He caught it perfectly over his shoulder and turned around. "I was telling him I missed him and welcoming him back to the family."

Blake understood brotherly love. He'd felt it for his

Once Upon A Dare guys and his teammates. He'd felt it for Adam. And he'd felt it from the first moment he'd met the Hale boys.

"I missed you guys too." There was a catch in his voice.

Andy nodded. "Danny! Watch Daddy catch this one."

This time he ran a slant route, and Blake hit him on the fly so he could snag it before he ended up in April's bushes.

Matt came out with Jane and joined in. His fiancée didn't know how to catch a football, least of all throw one, so they clustered around her, insisting she had to learn. When Natalie emerged with April, she gave him a brave smile.

He tipped up his chin in greeting, feeling the love between them grow, the one made stronger by her family—and possibly the baby they'd made already growing cell by cell in her belly.

Time would tell.

But he finally knew what the future held, and he savored it. They would have a baby soon, and someday not too far off, he'd be playing in the backyard with their own kids as the Hale clan surrounded them.

"Blake," Natalie called out. "Hit me."

And he threw the ball as she ran a beautiful post pattern like he'd taught her, with her brothers on her heels, eager to bat the ball down. When she spiked the ball and did a victory dance, he spun her around and kissed her smack on the lips.

The Hale family clustered around them, and they all did a victory dance together this time, pumping their fists at the sky, knowing every victory was to be savored in this game called life.

CHAPTER 39

When Andy carried a sleeping Danny into their house, he took every step with care, feeling the fragility of life all over again. He treasured getting his son ready for bed, watching him rub his eyes and roll over and curl up like a baby porcupine under the covers.

Then he sat there and watched him sleep.

Everything was precious. Every moment was precious.

His mother's close call had reminded him of it once again, and as he kissed his son's forehead, he vowed not to take her for granted. They would have dinner with her at least once a week. He and Matt had shaken on it, both trembling with the knowledge of what might have been.

He bypassed his bedroom, not wanting to go to bed yet. His body was too wired from adrenaline, the kind that came when bad news was expected and good news was received instead. The relief was like parachuting off a cliff. He was still screaming on the inside.

His mom should have told him. He could have talked to her doctor. *Something.* The knowledge that she'd only told Natalie, and only then because Nat had stumbled along at a weak moment, angered him. Both his parents were too damn tough if you asked him. He wasn't going to raise Danny that way.

He was glad Blake and Natalie were back together, and he planned to invite Blake on the runs he and Matt regularly took, although he expected his past and future brother-in-law would smoke them both. But still...it was a gesture.

Blake was part of the Hale clan again.

After popping open a beer in the kitchen, he headed to his office. With a touch of the mouse, his computer purred to life. He clicked open his email and was relieved to see a message from Lucy. She hadn't touched base since their last chat, and while he knew her trips in the bush could be protracted, something hadn't felt right.

He clicked on it.

Hey Andy,

Wanted to let you know I'm heading your way. Decided to take a trip home. Decompress a while. See you soon.

Luce

He stared at the message. She was flying home? From the Congo? He clicked Google open to find out how many miles separated them. *Eight thousand four hundred and fifty?* He tried to wrap his head around that. She'd been home a subtotal of twice in the last couple of years, and now she was flying over eight thousand miles to get to Dare Valley, without a specific holiday or event to bring her there.

Something was wrong. He could feel it. First, she hadn't called him Andy Cakes—which he pretended annoyed him, but he actually kind of liked—and second, she hadn't told him a joke or sent him a picture of her trip like she usually did.

He glanced at the clock, wishing he could call Mrs. O'Brien to ask her what she knew, but it was after eleven, and he didn't want to alarm her. She was probably as shaken as the rest of them after his mother's scare. And maybe he was reading too much into Lucy's email.

He settled back into his chair, his skin crawling with the same fear he'd felt with Kim's illness. God.

He scrubbed his eyes and reached for the picture of them sitting in the corner of his desk. Kim was already glowing in the photo. He'd dragged her to the nearest photographer the day they'd found out she was pregnant to capture the newness of the miracle growing inside her. His hands were caressing her belly, like he was the only other person in the universe who knew the secret. He'd never imagined he could love her more, but he'd felt his heart grow bigger that day, like a kid growing out of a shirt size.

Pressing the photo to his chest, he closed his eyes.

Oh, babe. God, babe. It was so close with Mom.

He wasn't sure he could have taken it, and from the look in her eyes, he could tell his mother had thought it too.

Now he was worried about Lucy, and he slumped in his seat.

Would he ever stop fearing he was going to lose someone else he loved?

CHAPTER 40

The party Natalie had thrown for Blake's new career was going strong—even if Blake hadn't made the announcement yet. As she wound around clusters of the Hale clan, the old and the adopted, she spotted her sisters talking to Uncle Arthur.

Slipping her hands around their waists, she nudged her way between them. "Hey, there. You girls need a refill?"

The rims of their margaritas were mostly devoid of salt now.

"Yes, please. These margaritas are incredible." Moira thrust out her glass, signaling she was already a bit tipsy. "I don't think I've ever had a better one."

"Me either," Caroline said, extending her glass too. "What's the secret?"

Blake appeared next to Uncle Arthur and put his arm around the old man, who elbowed him.

"Don't put your giant mitts around me, you big lug," he told Blake. "You might crush my bones. I have osteoporosis."

She and her sisters snickered at his indignant tone.

"Big lug?" Natalie said. "Oh, Uncle Arthur, you have such a way with words. I'll have to remember that one."

"When are you planning on making your announcement?" Uncle Arthur asked, tapping his cane on the floor. "I go to bed early since I'm an old man."

She kissed him on the cheek and gave Blake a wink. "He's probably hoping he can get the story in before the Sunday paper is printed."

Her uncle winked at her. "Are you sure you don't have black ink in your veins, my dear? That's a canny reporter talking."

"I'm pretty sure I'm doing what I love, Uncle Arthur, but I'll let you know if that ever changes."

Blake whistled shrilly beside her. "Everyone. Can I have your attention for a moment? Uncle Arthur needs to get to bed early, so I'm going to share my big news now."

"You didn't have to pierce an old man's ear drum," her uncle muttered. "I'm charging you if my doctor prescribes me a new hearing aid on my next visit."

The crowd laughed. Blake reached for her hand, rubbing her wedding ring.

"As you probably know, Natalie and I will be renewing our vows soon, so this isn't the end of the partying. However, the love of my life has insisted that we celebrate my new career. And yes, Uncle Arthur, you can consider this an exclusive story since you're family."

"Take heed, Meredith and Tanner," her uncle boomed out. "You'll be coming back to the office with me tonight."

They both gave him a thumbs up.

"When I came back to Dare Valley after retiring, I knew only two things for certain: I wanted Natalie back, and I wanted to run a football camp for kids with intellectual disabilities as a tribute to my brother, who—as all of you know—passed away recently."

She clenched his hand and scooted closer to his side as the emotion welled up in his eyes.

"A good friend told me never to settle when it came

to my next career, and after some serious scheming, I'm happy to report that I'll be serving as a special football coach for kids with intellectual disabilities who want to compete in Special Olympics at the Adam Cunningham Training Center at Emmits Merriam. Some of you know the athletic director, Tom Hudson, and he agreed to match my contribution to make such a center possible. According to Special Olympics, who will also be a contributor, this is the first center of its kind. The kids will have the option to stay in our assigned university dorm for anywhere from a few weeks to a month to train with me and our staff during the year."

Natalie knew she was beaming. It had been one of the greatest joys of her life to watch Blake's dream come together.

"I've been beyond lucky to have my long-time football friends also donate to this center. Right now, they have contributed financially, but they will also be contributing their time. I expect other players from the league will do the same."

Sure enough, all of his Once Upon A Dare friends had given sizeable contributions, but so had his former teammates and assistant coaches. Everyone had been waiting for Blake's announcement tonight so they could broadcast their affiliation with the new center on social media.

"The president and board of trustees for Emmits Merriam met this morning and approved our interim plans. We're going to break ground on this new facility next spring, and I couldn't be happier."

Someone whistled, and she looked over to see Andy grinning from ear to ear.

"The best news about this center is that I won't have to travel for games and I won't have to stay up late watching game film when I could be spending it with my loving wife and the family we plan to have. So...expect more parties like tonight, and thanks again for coming to share our good news."

She wrapped her arms around him just as he reached for her, and she simply basked in his new radiance. He planned to change the world with his center, and she had no doubt that he would.

Everyone finally clustered around them to give them their best wishes.

Uncle Arthur shook Blake's hand first. "Heck of an announcement, son. I wish you all the best. I feel a moving Sunday editorial coming on. You'll have to excuse me."

Her family kissed Blake and hugged him, and it was chaotic and wonderful in all the best of ways. This was something to celebrate. In two weeks, he'd be flying to Atlanta for a guys' weekend to celebrate the news with his Once Upon A Dare guys, and part of her wished she could come along. But it was boys only. They'd just have to host another weekend soon so she could thank the guys herself for everything they'd done for Blake.

When everything finally settled back down, she realized she and Blake hadn't moved from their spot for the last hour.

"We were talking about getting more margaritas earlier," she told him with a playful nudge to his ribs.

"Right. Your uncle is one demanding guy."

"That's why we love him."

They found her sisters in the corner, giggling like crazy, more than a little tipsy.

"I believe we were going to get you ladies a drink before your uncle asked for his exclusive," Blake said. "Do you still want one?"

Moira and Caroline shared a conspiratorial look.

"We...ah...finished off the margaritas during the well wishes," Moira confessed, which explained the red flush on her cheeks.

"I'm glad you didn't wait. Natalie, do you think you can help me in the kitchen? I need to make another batch."

That was probably code for a little necking in their food pantry, which they'd always done when hosting parties. "Sure thing, babe."

"Blake," Moira said. "You didn't tell us your secret to the margaritas?"

His mouth twitched. "It's a new brand of tequila. You can thank my friend, Jordan. It's very...intoxicating."

Natalie waggled her brows at him. "Har-de-har-har." The next time she saw Jordan, she planned to give him a big kiss for pushing that tequila on her, which Blake had confessed his friend had done on purpose.

"And we added blue Curacao," Blake shared.

"Oh! Is that why Caroline's tongue is blue?"

"Yours is too, moron," her sister said.

"We'll have your drinks in a jiffy," Blake said, rolling his eyes at them.

Natalie linked her arm through his and leaned in to whisper. "Are we really going to make them drinks right now?"

"Of course not." He bumped her with his hip. "I thought we could take a little time for ourselves and then make some more margaritas. In say...ten or fifteen minutes."

"I thought so," she purred. Her body was already revving with desire. Maybe they could have more than a necking session in the pantry.

She was already imagining a quickie when they entered the kitchen. Jane and Matt caught sight of them first and grinned.

"Three cheers to your new career," Matt called out.

They were standing at the counter with Terrance and Elizabeth, who also added another round of congratulations. So much for sneaking into the pantry.

Blake gave her a frown. "Later, babe," he whispered.

"Definitely."

There were two blindfolds on the counter and five bottles of wine wrapped in brown paper. Terrance gave Natalie a nudge when she joined them at the kitchen island, and she nudged him right back.

"Jane was just demonstrating her wine superiority again," Elizabeth told them.

Blake settled beside Natalie and slid an arm around her waist and gave it a squeeze. "Who won?" he asked.

Everyone knew Jane kept besting Terrance head-to-head.

"Who do you think?" her boss said in an aggrieved tone. "She's got a perfect record."

Blake put his other arm around Jane's shoulder, and the two of them shared a conspiratorial wink. "I know exactly how that feels, sweetheart."

Jane laughed and reached for Natalie's left hand. "I still can't get over how beautiful your ring is."

"It really is," Elizabeth said, touching it as well from across the counter. "So, have you set a date yet for your renewal ceremony?"

Natalie had been insistent they see to Blake's career first. She'd wanted to put him first since he'd done that so many times for her. Fortunately, he'd let her.

"As soon as possible," she said.

After all, they were doing their best to get pregnant. Neither of them wanted a big ceremony this time around. Only family and close friends. Then they planned to have another party—a big, loud, raucous party with lots and lots of champagne.

"That soon?" Elizabeth asked. "Most of the venues around here get booked up pretty fast. Trust me. Terrance and I know about this. Don't we?"

Natalie felt her mouth curve. "Actually it won't be a problem."

Blake gave her an answering grin. "We've already picked out a place."

Which was another reason he'd agreed to wait until

his career was settled. It wasn't like they would have to do any crazy planning in advance. And the hotel could easily cater the ceremony for them.

"You have?" Jane asked. "Oh, I didn't know. Have you found some super wedding planner with connections? If so, Elizabeth and I *have* to hire her."

Natalie fingered her ring. "No. We actually own the place. We're going to get married on the bridge Blake built. It's out back."

"Oh," Jane said, not understanding the significance. "I haven't seen it. After all, it didn't exist when Matt lived here."

Natalie walked to the back door. "Here, I'll show you."

She led them all outside and pointed to one of her favorite sights on earth. She'd already told Blake they were going to bring that bridge with them to their new house. She was not leaving it behind. No way. They were going to tell their kids about that bridge and stroll across it at night after they'd tucked them in for the night.

"It's the bridge to a better life," she told the group, her eyes holding Blake's the whole time. "Right, babe?"

He swallowed thickly and nodded. "Right, babe."

Then she rushed him like a linebacker, knowing she didn't need the bridge anymore to find her way back to a better life.

She was holding that life and all it promised to be. She was holding *him*.

Dear Reader,

This story affected me like no other. I had already fallen in love with Blake, but Natalie was the one I was learning to love while I wrote this. Her transformation in this book has been my own, and ultimately is every person's journey of self-love and the openness to the complete love of another. Many of you write and tell me you have found this. Others write and say you are still looking. Wherever you are, simply know you are right on track.

If you enjoyed this book, I would love for you to post a review since it helps more readers want to read my story. You can write a review at any online retailer or on Goodreads. When you post one, kindly let me know at readavamiles@gmail.com so I can personally thank you. To keep up with all my new releases, please sign up for my newsletter, and connect with me on Facebook. I continue to post about food and other fun stuff, so come and join our Dare family party.

There's so much coming up for you Dare Valley fans. Soon I will be releasing a novella called DARING BRIDES filled with the weddings of Meredith and Tanner, Jill and Brian, Peggy and Mac, and Abbie and Rhett. So many of you have wanted to know more about your favorite couples, so this was my way of sharing the love we all have for these special people. You even get to meet Rhett's mama, and boy is she a trip. Then there's the special new mini-series. It involves a billionaire inventor, Evan Michaels, who can't *live* like he's a billionaire in Dare Valley after losing to Jane in a poker game. Part of the story is set in Paris, which is why it's a mini-series. I adore Paris and have been trying to figure out a way to have Dare Valley connect with all the city's awesome food and romantic vistas. And it involves Don't Soy With Me's manager, Margie Waters, who plans to open her own bakery called Hot Cross Buns. I can't wait to share it with you. And of course, Andy and Lucy will have their day in the sun too in THE CALENDAR OF NEW BEGINNINGS. I'll also be releasing a new series called Once Upon a Dare with all of the football stars you met in this book. Jordan and Grace are up first in THE GATE TO EVERYTHING. Stay tuned.

Thank you so much for loving Dare Valley as much as I do.

Lots of light and joy,
Ava

Sign up for Ava's newsletter so you don't miss any news.

About the Author

USA Today Bestselling Author Ava Miles burst onto the contemporary romance scene after receiving Nora Roberts' blessing for her use of Ms. Roberts' name in her debut novel, the #1 National Bestseller NORA ROBERTS LAND, which kicked off her small town series, Dare Valley. Ava's books have reached the #1 spot at Barnes & Noble and ranked in Amazon and iBooks' Top 10. Both NORA ROBERTS LAND and COUNTRY HEAVEN have been chosen as Best Books of the Year. Ava has also released a connected series called Dare River about the power of love and family. She's fast becoming a favorite author in light contemporary romance (Tome Tender) and is known for funny, sweet, emotional stories, sometimes with a touch of mystery and magic. Ava's background is as diverse as her characters. She's a former chef, worked as a long-time conflict expert rebuilding warzones, and now writes full-time from her own small town community. Ava is a big believer in living happily ever after and writes about her own journey on The Happiness Corner blog every Friday on her website.

If you'd like to connect with Ava Miles or hear more about her upcoming books, visit www.avamiles.com or find Ava on Facebook, Twitter, or Pinterest.

Made in the USA
Columbia, SC
22 September 2020